THE
ROMANCE
OF
KING ARTHUR

THE ROMANCE OF KING ARTHUR

ILLUSTRATED BY
ARTHUR RACKHAM

STUDIO
EDITIONS

The Romance of King Arthur

First published in 1920 by Macmillan, New York.

This edition published in 1994 by Studio Editions Ltd, Princess House, 50 Eastcastle Street, London W1N 7AP, England

ISBN 1 85891 112 5

Printed at Thomson Press (India) Ltd.

AND·THERE·OPENLY·SIR·MADOR·APPEALED·THE·QUEEN·OF·THE DEATH·OF·HIS·COUSIN·SIR·PATRISE

PREFACE

THE story of King Arthur and his Knights is one of the greatest that men have ever made, greater by far than that of Charlemagne, which had come into fashion a little earlier, greater perhaps even than the Tale of Troy, already some two thousand years old, which for some centuries it eclipsed. It is through the fifteenth-century prose of Sir Thomas Malory, in which homeliness and nobility go hand-in-hand, that it holds its place in our hearts, but the story itself was the outcome of the second half of the twelfth century and the beginning of the thirteenth, the days in England of Henry II. and his three turbulent sons, Geoffrey, Richard Cœur de Lion, and John, the days in France of trouvère and troubadour, the days in Italy of S. Francis of Assisi and the worldliness against which he strove. Something of the spirit of all these entered into the story, together with some contemporary theology, while the stuff of which it was woven was largely derived from the Celtic borderland with which the Norman rulers of England had come in contact in Wales and Brittany.

In the days when the Arthurian romances were coming into existence, violence, cruelty, and luxury were rampant, and the story bears many traces of them; but the greatness of these evils called forth some great virtues to counter them, and the story bears traces of these also and strives gallantly to be true to its ideals, though when primitive notions, more especially the old belief in magic, crop up in it, it sometimes stumbles. Despite such stumblings, it is penetrated to its very core by the special virtues of days in which men were content to live dangerously (dangerously for themselves, not merely dangerously as against others), carrying their lives in their hands and willing to lay them down lightly rather than break the rules of the game or be faithless to word or friend.

A wandering knight challenges a great lord in a trial of skill, to be fought out to death or exhaustion, beneath the walls of the lord's castle. The wandering knight wins the day, and the lord becomes his vassal, takes him into his castle, feasts him, appoints a guard for his protection, and, when the victor bids him report himself at Arthur's court, comes on the appointed day attended by all his retinue. That the lord's men should interfere in the fight, or the lord himself break his promise, was unthinkable to these romancers; and on this simple basis of gallantry and good faith there was built up a code full of fine courtesies, such as those which forbade a great jouster to interfere with a lesser one on a day when he was outdoing himself, or a fresh knight to challenge one already tired with many victories.

The determination to live dangerously brought a strange and evil convention into the relations between knights and their ladies. A good knight held himself at the service of every woman who asked his help — to rescue a woman he must needs leave even his own brother in jeopardy — but he also owed a special service to the lady whose badge, if she so graced him, he wore, whose presence spurred him to excel himself, and whose pre-eminence over the ladies of other knights he maintained at the risk of his life. This lady might not be his own wife, if he had one, and she might quite properly be some one else's wife, her knight's homage be approved by her husband as a tribute to her worth, and the whole relation be treated as part of the great game of chivalry. But if it passed beyond a game and the husband hated to see his wife caring more for another man than for himself, then it became dangerous, and because it was dangerous, although every one knew it was wrong, it made a story more exciting, and all the writers of these Arthurian romances chose this exciting subject as a literary fashion. In the story of Tristram and Isoud, which forms one section of this book, we see clearly how overmastering the fashion had become. Tristram had taken Isoud as his lady, while she was still unmarried; Isoud was (openly and humbly) in love with him; her father, the King of Ireland, was eager for the match; but the romancer thought that their marriage would spoil the story, so he made Tristram, after he had gained Isoud's love, woo her, not for himself, but for his uncle, King Mark of Cornwall, and then made Tristram and Isoud drink, by mischance, a magic love-potion, to excuse them for loving each other ever after.

The literary fashion or convention which imposed itself in this way on the romancers was thoroughly bad; but the saving merit in this respect of the Arthurian romances is that, though they insist on this situation in order to show the hero daring all sorts of dangers, they make it perfectly clear that the situation was wrong and could not go unpunished. With one exception every knight who yielded to this sin is shown as paying for it with his life. The one exception is Sir Launcelot, and him we see maimed and marred by thus setting his love where he should not, and atoning for it, as much as a man may atone for wrecking the lives of others, by bitter repentance.

The story of the Arthurian romances is a great story, because it shows us the effect on many different characters of this obligation to live dangerously. The men and women who fill its pages are not just names or figures to which adventures are tacked on. They are men and women of real flesh and blood, no two of them alike (save when the writer of one section deliberately copied another), each with his own virtues and failings. King Arthur himself is, as we say nowadays, a typical sportsman. He loves jousting — to take part in it, to see it, and to talk about it — more than anything else, as some men now love less dangerous games. He cares for the men with whom he shares his sport, but he cares for them as his fellow-jousters, and he never gets much further. He falls below lesser knights who had borne imprisonment rather than fight in a bad cause, for which he cheerfully does battle; he is so keen on his own side winning that he overrides the etiquette that forbade a strong knight to attack a good fighter tired by his own successes; he is weak in his own life and weak in suffering the outrages of his nephews. His great merit is that, though a king, he never spared to take his risks, and by that courage he held men's hearts, so that "all men of worship said it was merry to be under such a chieftain, that would put his person in adventure as other poor knights did." Also, to the very last, he could be trusted to keep his word.

Sir Launcelot is made of much finer stuff than Arthur. He is perhaps the most splendid study of a great gentleman in all our literature, generous to friend and foe, courteous to every one, eager to set himself ever harder adventures, unwilling to be praised above his fellows, always bearing himself with an easy dignity which lets him use very straight speech and yet is no whit impaired. He is more than a great gentleman; he is a very subtle study of a soul in which spirit and flesh, aspiration and evil habit, strive for the mastery, and now and again he is pourtrayed with a rare knowledge of the human heart. More wonderful even than the closing scenes with Guenevere seems to me the story of the coming of Sir Urre to have his wounds healed by "the best knight of the world," and how when all others in Arthur's court had failed Launcelot touched the wounds in all humility, and when his touch brought healing, while King Arthur and all the kings and knights gave thanks, "ever Sir Launcelot wept as he had been a child that had been beaten."

Sir Tristram is a curiously different study. Perhaps because of the love-potion, his fault sits lightly upon him; he has a most detailed memory for the services he renders, and is quite unconscious of there being any set off. But he is delightfully easy-tempered and forgiving, joyous and humorous, and deserves kindly remembrance for much else than his harping and his nicety of skill in ordering the technical terms of the chase, which so impressed his chroniclers. But he never touches greatness.

Tristram's assiduous opponent, Sir Palomides, the Saracen, is a rather laboured but quite successful portrait. Probably because he was a Saracen he is represented as not quite a gentleman, but pathetically anxious to become one. He is constantly doing things which Sir Launcelot, or even Sir Tristram, would have died sooner than do, and then he pulls himself together and apologises and tries manfully to play the game. His final appearance, when he is badly mauled by Sir Tristram as a preliminary to being christened, is singularly successful, none the less so for its touches of humour.

To attempt to study here others of the men and women who live in Malory's story would give to this preface too great a resemblance to the page in school magazines headed

"Characters of the Team." It remains to say a brief word as to what has been done in this abridgment. There is good reason to believe that Sir Thomas Malory was a Lancastrian knight who himself knew the pains of sickness and imprisonment, as to which he wrote so feelingly. He had to make his compilation from such books as he could get (he apparently never obtained the last volume of the romance of Sir Tristram), and it is probable that when his version was made his life was drawing to a close, and that, even if he had the wish, he had not time or strength to revise it. That version is so great a book, written, as I have said, in a style in which homely charm and nobility are so closely interlinked, that to tamper with it may seem a crime. But during the last few years there have been many complete texts of the *Morte d'Arthur* — I have passed one through the press myself — and an invitation to act as Malory's abridger, even as Malory had abridged the romances themselves, found me daring enough to think that such a further abridgment would be a very interesting experiment. There is much repetition in the *Morte d'Arthur*, as Malory left it. How often Sir Breuse sans Pitié played his ugly tricks, or Tristram rescued Palomides, or minor knights met at adventure and emulated their betters, it is not easy to count. I have tried to clear away some of the underwoods that the great trees may be better seen, and though I know that I have cleared away some small timber that is fine stuff in itself, if the great trees stand out the better, the experiment may be forgiven. In attempting it I have introduced, I think, not more than a hundred words of my own, but in certain places I have taken over the readings devised half a century ago for the well-known Globe edition by Sir Edward Strachey, which has justified itself by passing through some twenty editions, and has probably brought Malory more readers than all other texts put together.

ALFRED W. POLLARD.

CONTENTS

Of King Arthur

Of Sir Launcelot

Of Sir Gareth

Of Sir Tristram

Of Sir Launcelot and Dame Elaine

Of Sir Galahad and the Quest of the Holy Grail

Of Launcelot, Guenever, and King Arthur

OF KING ARTHUR

OF THE BIRTH OF KING ARTHUR AND OF HIS NURTURE. It befell in the days of Uther Pendragon, when he was king of all England, and so reigned, that there was a mighty duke in Cornwall that held war against him long time. And the duke was called the Duke of Tintagil. And so by means King Uther sent for this duke, charging him to bring his wife with him, for she was called a fair lady, and a passing wise, and her name was called Igraine.

So when the duke and his wife were come unto the king, by the means of great lords they were accorded both. The king liked and loved this lady well, and he made them great cheer out of measure, and desired to have had her love. But she was a passing good woman, and would not assent unto the king. And then she told the duke her husband, and said, I suppose that we were sent for that I should be dishonoured; wherefore, husband, I counsel you, that we depart from hence suddenly, that we may ride all night unto our own castle. And in like wise as she said so they departed, that neither the king nor none of his council were ware of their departing. All so soon as King Uther knew of their departing so suddenly, he was wonderly wroth. Then he called to him his privy council, and told them of the sudden departing of the duke and his wife.

Then they advised the king to send for the duke and his wife by a great charge; and if he will not come at your summons, then may ye do your best, then have ye cause to make mighty war upon him. So that was done, and the messengers had their answers; and that was this shortly, that neither he nor his wife would not come at him.

Then was the king wonderly wroth. And then the king sent him plain word again, and bade him be ready and stuff him and garnish him, for within forty days he would fetch him out of the biggest castle that he hath.

When the duke had this warning, anon he went and furnished and garnished two strong castles of his, of the which the one hight Tintagil, and the other castle hight Terrabil. So his wife Dame Igraine he put in the castle of Tintagil, and himself he put in the castle of Terrabil, the which had many issues and posterns out. Then in all haste came Uther with a great host, and laid a siege about the castle of Terrabil. Then for pure anger and for great love of fair Igraine the king Uther fell sick. So came to the king Uther Sir Ulfius, a noble knight, and asked the king why he was sick. I shall tell thee, said the king, I am sick for anger and for love of fair Igraine, that I may not be whole. Well, my lord, said Sir Ulfius, I shall seek

Merlin, and he shall do you remedy, that your heart shall be pleased. So Ulfius departed, and by adventure he met Merlin in a beggar's array, and there Merlin asked Ulfius whom he sought. And he said he had little ado to tell him. Well, said Merlin, I know whom thou seekest, for thou seekest Merlin; therefore seek no farther, for I am he; and if King Uther will well reward me, and be sworn unto me to fulfil my desire, that shall be his honour and profit more than mine; for I shall cause him to have all his desire. All this will I undertake, said Ulfius, that there shall be nothing reasonable but thou shalt have thy desire. Well, said Merlin, he shall have his intent and desire. And therefore, said Merlin, ride on your way, for I will not be long behind.

Then Ulfius was glad, and rode on more than a pace till that he came to King Uther Pendragon, and told him he had met with Merlin. Where is he? said the king. Sir, said Ulfius, he will not dwell long. Therewithal Ulfius was ware where Merlin stood at the porch of the pavilion's door. And then Merlin was bound to come to the king. When King Uther saw him, he said he was welcome. Sir, said Merlin, I know all your heart every deal; so ye will be sworn unto me, as ye be a true king anointed, to fulfil my desire, ye shall have your desire. Then the king was sworn upon the Four Evangelists. Sir, said Merlin, this is my desire: after that ye shall win Igraine ye shall have a child by her, and when that is born, that it shall be delivered to me for to nourish there as I will have it; for it shall be your worship, and the child's avail, as mickle as the child is worth. I will well, said the king, as thou wilt have it. Now make you ready, said Merlin, this night ye shall be with Igraine in the castle of Tintagil;

and ye shall be like the duke her husband, Ulfius shall be like Sir Brastias, a knight of the duke's, and I will be like a knight that hight Sir Jordanus, a knight of the duke's. But wait ye make not many questions with her nor her men, but say ye are diseased, and so hie you to bed, and rise not on the morn till I come to you, for the castle of Tintagil is but ten miles hence; so this was done as they devised. But the duke of Tintagil espied how the king rode from the siege of Terrabil, and therefore that night he issued out of the castle at a postern, for to have distressed the king's host. And so, through his own issue, the duke himself was slain or ever the king came at the castle of Tintagil.

So after the death of the duke, King Uther came to the castle more than three hours after his death, and there he found Igraine, and before day came Merlin to the king, and bade him make him ready, and so he kissed the lady Igraine and departed in all haste. But when the lady heard tell of the duke her husband, and by all record he was dead or ever King Uther came to her, then she marvelled who that might be that came to her in likeness of her lord; so she mourned privily and held her peace. Then all the barons by one assent prayed the king of accord betwixt the lady Igraine and him; the king gave them leave, for fain would he have been accorded with her. So the king put all the trust in Ulfius to entreat between them, so by the entreaty at the last the king and she met together. Now will we do well, said Ulfius, our king is a lusty knight and wifeless, and my lady Igraine is a passing fair lady; it were great joy unto us all, an it might please the king to make her his queen. Unto that they all well accorded and moved it to the king. And anon, like a lusty knight, he assented thereto with good will, and so in all haste they were married in a morning with great mirth and joy.

And King Lot of Lothian and of Orkney then wedded Margawse that was Gawaine's mother, and King Nentres of the land of Garlot wedded Elaine. All this was done at the request of King Uther. And the third sister Morgan le Fay was put to school in a nunnery, and there she learned so much that she was a great clerk of necromancy. And after she was wedded to King Uriens of the land of Gore.

Then the time came that Queen Igraine should bear a child. So it befell after within half a year, as King Uther was with his queen, he asked her, by the faith she owed to him, whose was the child that should be born; then was she sore abashed to give answer. Dismay you not, said the king, but tell me the truth, and I shall love you the better, by the faith of my body. Sir, said she, I shall tell you the truth. The same night that my lord was dead, the hour of his death, as his knights record, there came into my castle of Tintagil a man like my lord in speech and in countenance, and two knights with him in likeness of his two knights Brastias and Jordanus, and so I welcomed him as I ought to welcome my lord, and the same night, as I shall answer unto God, this child was begotten. That is truth, said the king, as ye say; for it was I myself that came in the likeness, and therefore dismay you not, for I am father of the child; and there he told her all the cause, how it was by Merlin's counsel. Then the queen made great joy when she knew who was the father of her child.

Soon came Merlin unto the king, and said, Sir, ye must purvey you for the nourishing of your child. As thou wilt, said the king, be it. Well, said Merlin, I know a lord of yours in this land, that is a passing true man and a faithful, and he shall have the nourishing of your child, and his name is Sir Ector, and he is a lord of fair livelihood in many parts in England and Wales; and this lord, Sir Ector, let him be sent for, for to come and speak with you, and desire him yourself, as he loveth you, that he will put his own child to nourishing to another woman, and that his wife nourish yours. And when the child is born let it be delivered to me at yonder privy postern unchristened. So like as Merlin devised it was done. And when Sir Ector was come he made fiaunce to the king for to nourish the child like as the king desired; and there the king granted Sir Ector great rewards. Then when the lady was delivered, the king commanded two knights and two ladies to take the child, bound in a cloth of gold, and that ye deliver him to what poor man ye meet at the postern gate of the castle. So the child was delivered unto Merlin, and so he bare it forth unto Sir Ector, and made an holy man to christen him, and named him Arthur; and so Sir Ector's wife nourished him with her own breast.

OF THE DEATH OF KING UTHER PENDRAGON, AND HOW ARTHUR WAS CHOSEN KING. Then within two years King Uther fell sick of a great malady. And in the meanwhile his enemies usurped upon him, and did a great battle upon his men, and slew many of his people. Sir, said Merlin, ye may not lie so as ye do, for ye must to the field though ye ride on an horse-litter: for ye

SO·THE·CHILD·WAS·DELIVERED·UNTO·MERLIN

shall never have the better of your enemies but if your person be there, and then shall ye have the victory. So it was done as Merlin had devised, and they carried the king forth in an horse-litter with a great host towards his enemies. And at St. Albans there met with the king a great host of the North. And that day Sir Ulfius and Sir Brastias did great deeds of arms, and King Uther's men overcame the Northern battle and slew many people, and put the remnant to flight. And then the king returned unto London, and made great joy of his victory. And then he fell passing sore sick, so that three days and three nights he was speechless: wherefore all the barons made great sorrow, and asked Merlin what counsel were best. There is none other remedy, said Merlin, but God will have his will. But look ye all barons be before King Uther to-morn, and God and I shall make him to speak. So on the morn all the barons with Merlin came to-fore the king; then Merlin said aloud unto King Uther, Sir, shall your son Arthur be king after your days, of this realm with all the appurtenance? Then Uther Pendragon turned him, and said in hearing of them all, I give him God's blessing and mine, and bid him pray for my soul, and righteously and worshipfully that he claim the crown, upon forfeiture of my blessing; and therewith he yielded up the ghost, and then was he interred as longed to a king. Wherefore the queen, fair Igraine, made great sorrow, and all the barons.

Then stood the realm in great jeopardy long while, for every lord that was mighty of men made him strong, and many weened to have been king. Then Merlin went to the Archbishop of Canterbury, and counselled him for to send for all the lords of the realm, and all the gentlemen of arms, that they should to London come by Christmas, upon pain of cursing; and for this cause, that Jesus, that was born on that night, that he would of his great mercy, as he was come to be king of mankind, show some miracle who should be rightwise king of this realm. So the Archbishop, by the advice of Merlin, sent for all the Lords and gentlemen of arms that they should come by Christmas even unto London. And many of them made them clean of their life, that their prayer might be the more acceptable unto God. So in the greatest church of London, whether it were Paul's or not the French book maketh no mention, all the estates were long ere day in the church for to pray. And when matins and the first mass was done, there was seen in the churchyard, against the high altar, a great stone four square, like unto a marble stone; and in midst thereof was like an anvil of steel a foot on high, and therein stuck a fair sword naked by the point, and letters there were written in gold about the sword that said thus:—Whoso pulleth out this sword of this stone and anvil, is rightwise king born of all England. Then the people marvelled, and told it to the Archbishop. I command, said the Archbishop, that ye keep you within your church and pray unto God still, that no man touch the sword till the high mass be all done. So when all masses were done all the lords went to behold the stone and the sword. And when they saw the scripture some assayed, such as would have been king. But none might stir the sword nor move it. He is not here, said the Archbishop, that shall achieve the sword, but doubt not God will make him known. But this is my counsel, said the Archbishop, that we let purvey ten knights, men of good fame, and they to keep this sword.

So it was ordained, and then there was made a cry, that every man should assay that would, for to win the sword. And upon New Year's Day the barons let make a jousts and a tournament, that all knights that would joust or tourney there might play, and all this was ordained for to keep the lords together and the commons, for the Archbishop trusted that God would make him known that should win the sword.

So upon New Year's Day, when the service was done, the barons rode unto the field, some to joust and some to tourney, and so it happed that Sir Ector, that had great livelihood about London, rode unto the jousts, and with him rode Sir Kay his son, and young Arthur that was his nourished brother; and Sir Kay was made knight at All Hallowmas afore. So as they rode to the jousts-ward, Sir Kay lost his sword, for he had left it at his father's lodging, and so he prayed young Arthur for to ride for his sword. I will well, said Arthur, and rode fast after the sword, and when he came home, the lady and all were out to see the jousting. Then was Arthur wroth, and said to himself, I will ride to the churchyard, and take the sword with me that sticketh in the stone, for my brother Sir Kay shall not be without a sword this day. So when he came to the churchyard, Sir Arthur alighted and tied his horse to the stile, and so he went to the tent, and found no knights there, for they were at the jousting. And so he handled the sword by the handles, and lightly and fiercely pulled it out of the stone, and took his horse and rode his way until he came to his brother Sir Kay, and delivered him the sword. And as soon as Sir Kay saw the sword, he wist well it was the sword of the stone, and so he rode to his father Sir Ector, and said: Sir, lo here is the sword of the stone, wherefore I must be king of this land. When Sir Ector beheld the sword, he returned again and came to the church, and there they alighted all three, and went into the church. And anon he made Sir Kay swear upon a book how he came to that sword. Sir, said Sir Kay, by my brother Arthur, for he brought it to me. How gat ye this sword? said Sir Ector to Arthur. Sir, I will tell you. When I came home for my brother's sword, I found nobody at home to deliver me his sword; and so I thought my brother Sir Kay should not be swordless, and so I came hither eagerly and pulled it out of the stone without any pain. Found ye any knights about this sword? said Sir Ector. Nay, said Arthur. Now, said Sir Ector to Arthur, I understand ye must be king of this land. Wherefore I, said Arthur, and for what cause? Sir, said Ector, for God will have it so; for there should never man have drawn out this sword, but he that shall be rightwise king of this land. Now let me see whether ye can put the sword there as it was, and pull it out again. That is no mastery, said Arthur, and so he put it in the stone; wherewithal Sir Ector assayed to pull out the sword and failed.

Now assay, said Sir Ector unto Sir Kay. And anon he pulled at the sword with all his might; but it would not be. Now shall ye assay, said Sir Ector to Arthur. I will well, said Arthur, and pulled it out easily. And therewithal Sir Ector knelt down to the earth, and Sir Kay. Alas, said Arthur, my own dear father and brother, why kneel ye to me? Nay, nay, my lord Arthur, it is not so; I was never your father nor of your blood, but I wot well ye are of an higher blood than I weened ye were. And then Sir Ector told him all, how he was betaken him for to nourish him, and by whose commandment, and by Merlin's deliverance.

Then Arthur made great dole when he understood that Sir Ector was not his father. Therewithal they went unto the Archbishop, and told him how the sword was achieved, and by whom; and on Twelfth-day all the barons came thither, and to assay to take the sword, who that would assay. But there afore them all, there might none take it out but Arthur; wherefore there were many lords wroth, and said it was great shame unto them all and the realm, to be over governed with a boy of no high blood born. And so they fell out at that time that it was put off till Candlemas, and then all the barons should meet there again; but always the ten knights were ordained to watch the sword day and night, and so they set a pavilion over the stone and the sword, and five always watched. So at Candlemas many more great lords came thither for to have won the sword, but there might none prevail. And right as Arthur did at Christmas, he did at Candlemas, and pulled out the sword easily, whereof the barons were sore aggrieved and put it off in delay till the high feast of Easter. And as Arthur sped before, so did he at Easter; yet there were some of the great lords had indignation that Arthur should be king, and put it off in a delay till the feast of Pentecost.

HOW KING ARTHUR WAS CROWNED, AND HOW HE MADE OFFICERS AND HELD A GREAT FEAST, & OF THE WAR THAT HE HAD, AND HOW HE HELD THE FIELD. And at the feast of Pentecost all manner of men assayed to pull at the sword that would assay; but none might prevail but Arthur, and pulled it out afore all the lords and commons that were there, wherefore all the commons cried at once, We will have Arthur unto our king, we will put him no more in delay, for we all see that it is God's will that he shall be our king, and who that holdeth against it, we will slay him. And therewithal they kneeled at once, both rich and poor, and cried Arthur mercy because they had delayed him so long, and Arthur forgave them, and took the sword between both his hands, and offered it upon the altar where the Archbishop was, and so was he made knight of the best man that was there. And so anon was the coronation made. And there was he sworn unto his lords and the commons for to be a true king, to stand with true justice from thenceforth the days of this life.

When this was done, that the king had stablished all the countries about London, then he let make Sir Kay seneschal of England; and Sir Baudwin of Britain was made constable; and Sir Ulfius was made chamberlain; and Sir Brastias was made warden to wait upon the north from Trent forwards, for it was that time the most party the king's enemies. But within few years after Arthur won all the north, Scotland, and all that were under their obeissance. Also Wales, a part of it, held against Arthur, but he overcame them all, as he did the remnant, through the noble prowess of himself and his knights of the Round Table.

Then the king removed into Wales, and let cry a great feast that it should be holden at Pentecost after the incoronation of him at the city of Carlion. Unto the feast came King Lot of Lothian and of Orkney, with five hundred knights with him. Also there came to the feast King Uriens of Gore with four hundred knights with him. Also there came to that feast King Nentres of Garlot, with seven hundred knights with him. Also there came to the feast the king of Scotland with six hundred knights with him, and he was but a young man. Also there came to the feast a king that was called the King with the Hundred Knights, but he and his men were passing well beseen at all points. Also there came the king of Carados with five hundred knights. And King Arthur was glad of their coming, for he weened that all the kings and knights had come for great love, and to have done him worship at his feast; wherefore the king made great joy, and sent the kings and knights great presents. But the kings would none receive, but rebuked the messengers shamefully, and said they had no joy to receive no gifts of a beardless boy that was come of low blood, and sent him word they would none of his gifts, but that they were come to give him gifts with hard swords betwixt the neck and the shoulders: and therefore they came thither, so they told to the messengers plainly, for it was great shame to all them to see such a boy to have a rule of so noble a realm as this land was. With this answer the messengers departed and told to King Arthur this answer.

Wherefore, by the advice of his barons, he took him to a strong tower with five hundred good men with him. And all the kings aforesaid in a manner laid a siege to-fore him, but King Arthur was well victualed. And within fifteen days there came Merlin among them into the city of Carlion. Then all the kings were passing glad of Merlin, and asked him, For what cause is that boy Arthur made your king? Sirs, said Merlin, I shall tell you the cause, for he is King Uther Pendragon's son, born in wedlock of Igraine, the duke's wife of Tintagil. After the death of the duke, thirteen days, King Uther wedded Igraine. And who saith nay, he shall be king and overcome all his enemies. Some of the kings had marvel of Merlin's words, and deemed well that it should be as he said; and some of them laughed him to scorn, as King Lot; and more other called him a witch. But then were they accorded with Merlin, that King Arthur should come out and speak with the kings, and to come safe and to go safe, such surance there was made.

Then King Arthur came out of his tower, and had under his gown a jesseraunt of double mail, and there went with him the Archbishop of Canterbury, and Sir Baudwin of Britain, and Sir Kay, and Sir Brastias: these were the men of most worship that were with him. And when they were met there was no meekness, but stout words on both sides; but always King Arthur answered them, and said he would make them to bow an he lived. Wherefore they departed with wrath, and King Arthur bade keep them well, and they bade the king keep him well. So the king returned him to the tower again and armed him and all his knights. With that Merlin came to King Arthur, and bade him set on them fiercely; and in the meanwhile there were three hundred good men, of the best that were with the kings, that went straight unto King Arthur, and that comforted him greatly. Sir, said Merlin to Arthur, fight not with the sword that ye had by miracle, till that ye see ye go unto the worse, then draw it out and do your best. So forthwithal King Arthur set upon them in their lodging. And Sir Baudwin, Sir Kay, and Sir Brastias slew on the right hand and on the left hand that it was marvel; and always King Arthur on horseback laid on with a sword, and did marvellous deeds of arms, that many of the kings had great joy of his deeds and hardiness.

Then King Lot brake out on the back side, and the King with the Hundred Knights, and King Carados, and set on Arthur fiercely behind him. With that Sir Arthur turned with his knights, and smote behind and before, and ever Sir Arthur was in the foremost press till his horse was slain underneath him. And therewith King Lot smote down King Arthur. With that his four knights received him and set him on horseback. Then he drew his sword Excalibur, but it was so bright in his enemies' eyes, that it gave light like thirty torches. And therewith he put them a-back, and slew much people. And then the commons of Carlion arose with clubs and staves and slew many knights; but all the kings held them together with their knights that were left alive, and so fled and departed. And Merlin came unto Arthur and counselled him to follow them no further.

OF KING ARTHUR AND KING PELLINORE AND HOW ARTHUR SENT FOR HIS MOTHER. Then came to King Arthur, King Lot's wife, of Orkney, in manner of a message, but she was sent thither to espy the court of King Arthur; and she came richly beseen, with her four sons, Gawaine, Gaheris, Agravine, and Gareth, with many other knights and ladies, and she was a passing fair lady, wherefore the king cast great love unto her, and so was Mordred born, and she was his sister, on his mother's side, Igraine. So there she rested her a month, and at the last departed. Then the king dreamed a marvellous dream whereof he was sore adread. But all this time King Arthur knew not that King Lot's wife was his sister. Thus was the dream of Arthur: Him thought there was come into this land griffins and serpents, and him thought they burnt and slew all the people in the land, and then him thought he fought with them, and they did him passing great harm, and wounded him full sore, but at the last he slew them. When the king awaked, he was passing heavy of his dream, and so to put it out of thoughts, he made him ready with many knights to ride a-hunting. As soon as he was in the forest the king saw a great hart afore him. This hart will I chase, said King Arthur, and so he spurred the horse, and rode after long, and so by fine force oft he was like to have smitten the hart; whereas the king had chased the hart so long, that his horse lost his breath, and fell down dead. Then a yeoman fetched the king another horse.

So the king saw the hart embushed, and his horse dead, he set him down by a fountain, and there he fell in great thoughts. And as he sat so, him thought he heard a noise of hounds, to the sum of thirty. And with that the king saw coming toward him the strangest beast that ever he saw or heard of; so the beast went to the well and drank, and the noise was in the beast's belly like unto the questing of thirty couple hounds; but all the while the beast drank there was no noise in the beast's belly: and therewith the beast departed with a great noise, whereof the king had great marvel. And so he was in a great thought, and therewith he fell asleep. Right so there came a knight afoot unto Arthur and said, Knight full of thought and sleepy, tell me if thou sawest a strange beast pass this way. Such one saw I, said King Arthur, that is past two mile; what would ye with the beast? said Arthur. Sir, I have followed that beast long time, and killed mine horse, so would I had another to follow my quest. Right so came one with the king's horse, and when the knight saw the horse, he prayed the king to give him the horse: for I have followed this quest this twelvemonth, and either I shall achieve him, or bleed of the best blood of my body. Pellinore, that time king, followed the Questing Beast, and after his death Sir Palamides followed it.

Sir knight, said the king, leave that quest, and suffer me to have it, and I will follow it another twelvemonth. Ah, fool, said the knight unto Arthur, it is in vain thy desire, for it shall never be achieved but by me, or my next kin. Therewith he started unto the king's horse and mounted into the saddle, and said, Gramercy, this horse is my own. Well, said the king, thou mayst take my horse by force, but an I might prove thee whether thou were better on horseback or I. — Well, said the knight, seek me here when thou wilt, and here nigh this well thou shalt find me, and so passed on his way. Then the king sat in a study, and bade his men fetch his horse as fast as ever they might. Right so came by him Merlin like a child of fourteen year of age, and saluted the king, and asked him why he was so pensive. I may well be pensive, said the king, for I have seen the marvellest sight that ever I saw. That know I well, said Merlin, as well as thyself, and of all thy thoughts, but thou art but a fool to take thought, for it will not amend thee. Also I know what thou art, and who was thy father, and of whom thou wert born; King Uther Pendragon was thy father, and had thee of Igraine. That is false, said King Arthur, how shouldest thou know it, for thou art not so old of years to know my father? Yes, said Merlin, I know it better than ye or any man living. I will not believe thee, said Arthur, and was wroth with the child. So departed Merlin, and came again in the likeness of an old man of fourscore year of age, whereof the king was right glad, for he seemed to be right wise.

Then said the old man, Why are ye so sad? I may well be heavy, said Arthur, for many things. Also here was a child, and told me many things that meseemeth he should not know, for he was not of age to know my father. Yes, said the old man, the child told you truth, and more would he have told you an ye would have suffered him. But ye have done a thing late that God is displeased with you, and your sister shall have a child that shall destroy you and all the knights of your realm. What are ye, said Arthur, that tell me these tidings ? I am Merlin, and I was he in the child's likeness. Ah, said King Arthur, ye are a marvellous man, but I marvel much of thy words that I must die in battle. Marvel not, said Merlin, for it is God's will your body to be punished for your foul deeds ; but I may well be sorry, said Merlin, for I shall die a shameful death, to be put in the earth quick, and ye shall die a worshipful death. And as they talked thus, came one with the king's horse, and so the king mounted on his horse, and Merlin on another, and so rode unto Carlion. And anon the king asked Ector and Ulfius how he was begotten, and they told him Uther Pendragon was his father and Queen Igraine his mother. Then he said to Merlin, I will that my mother be sent for, that I may speak with her. Then in all haste, the queen was sent for, and she came and brought with her Morgan le Fay, her daughter, that was as fair a lady as any might be, and the king welcomed Igraine in the best manner.

Then Merlin took the king by the hand, saying, This is your mother. And therewith Sir Ector bare witness how he nourished him by Uther's commandment. And therewith King Arthur took his mother, Queen Igraine, in his arms and kissed her, and either wept upon other. And then the king let make a feast that lasted eight days.

HOW ARTHUR FOUGHT WITH KING PELLINORE AND HOW MERLIN SAVED ARTHUR'S LIFE, AND ARTHUR BY THE MEAN OF MERLIN GAT HIS SWORD EXCALIBUR. Then on a day there came in the court a squire on horseback, leading a knight before him wounded to the death, and told him how there was a knight in the forest had reared up a pavilion by a well, and hath slain my master, a good knight, his name was Miles; wherefore I beseech you that my master may be buried, and that some knight may revenge my master's death. Then the noise was great of that knight's death in the court, and every man said his advice. Then came Griflet that was but a squire, and he was but young, of the age of the king Arthur, so he besought the king for all his service that he had done him to give the order of knighthood.

Thou art full young and tender of age, said Arthur, for to take so high an order on thee. Sir, said Griflet, I beseech you make me knight. Sir, said Merlin, it were great pity to lose Griflet, for he will be a passing good man when he is of age, abiding with you the term of his life. And if he adventure his body with yonder knight at the fountain, it is in great peril if ever he come again, for he is one of the best knights of the world, and the strongest man of arms. Well, said Arthur. So at the desire of Griflet the king made him knight. Now, said Arthur unto Sir Griflet, sith I have made you knight thou must give me a gift. What ye will, said Griflet. Thou shalt promise me by the faith of thy body, when thou hast jousted with the knight at the fountain, whether it fall ye be on foot or on horseback, that right so ye shall come again unto me without making any more debate. I will promise you, said Griflet, as you desire. Then took Griflet his horse in great haste, and dressed his shield and took a spear in his hand, and so he rode a great wallop till he came to the fountain, and thereby he saw a rich pavilion, and thereby under a cloth stood a fair horse well saddled and bridled, and on a tree a shield of divers colours and a great spear. Then Griflet smote on the shield with the butt of his spear, that the shield fell down to the ground. With that the knight came out of the pavilion, and said, Fair knight, why smote ye down my shield? For I will joust with you, said Griflet. It is better ye do not, said the knight, for ye are but young, and late made knight, and your might is nothing to mine. As for that, said Griflet, I will joust with you. That is me loath, said the knight, but sith I must needs, I will dress me thereto. Of whence be ye? said the knight. Sir, I am of Arthur's court. So the two knights ran together that Griflet's spear all to-shivered; and therewithal he smote Griflet through the shield and the left side, and brake the spear that the truncheon stuck in his body, that horse and knight fell down.

When the knight saw him lie so on the ground, he alighted, and was passing heavy, for he weened he had slain him, and then he unlaced his helm and gat him wind, and so with the truncheon he set him on his horse, and so betook him to God, and said he had a mighty heart, and if he might live he would prove a passing good knight. And so Sir Griflet rode to the court, where great dole was made for him. But through good leeches he was healed and saved. Then King Arthur was passingly wroth for the hurt of Sir Griflet. And so he commanded a privy man of his chamber that ere it be day his best horse and armour, with all that longeth unto his person, be without the city or to-morrow day. Right so or to-morrow day he met with his man and his horse, and so mounted up and dressed his shield and took his spear, and bade his chamberlain tarry there till he came again. And so Arthur rode a soft pace till it was day, and then was he ware of three churls chasing Merlin, and would have slain him. Then the king rode unto them, and bade them: Flee, churls! then were they afeard when they saw a knight, and fled. O Merlin, said Arthur, here hadst thou been slain for all thy crafts had I not been. Nay, said Merlin, not so, for I could save myself an I would; and thou art more near thy death than I am, for thou goest to the deathward, an God be not thy friend.

So as they went thus talking they came to the fountain, and the rich pavilion there by it. Then King Arthur was ware where sat a knight armed in a chair. Sir knight, said Arthur, for what cause abidest thou here, that there may no knight ride this way but if he joust with thee? said the king. I rede thee leave that custom, said Arthur. This custom, said the knight, have I used and will use maugre who saith nay, and who is grieved with my custom let him amend it that will. I will amend it, said Arthur. I shall defend thee, said the knight. Anon he took his horse and dressed his shield and took a spear, and they met so hard either in other's shields, that all to-shivered their spears. Therewith anon Arthur pulled out his sword. Nay, not so, said the knight; it is fairer, said the knight, that we twain run more together with sharp spears. I will well, said Arthur, an I had any more spears. I have enow, said the knight; so there came a squire and brought two good spears, and Arthur chose one and he another; so they spurred their horses and came together with all their mights, that either brake their spears to their hands. Then Arthur set hand on his sword. Nay, said the knight, ye shall do better, ye are a passing good jouster as ever I met withal, and for the love of the high order of knighthood let us joust once again. I assent me, said Arthur. Anon there were brought two great spears, and every knight gat a spear, and therewith they ran together that Arthur's spear all to-shivered. But the other knight hit him so hard in midst of the shield, that horse and man fell to the earth, and therewith Arthur was eager, and pulled out his sword, and said, I will assay thee, sir knight, on foot, for I have lost the honour on horseback. Then the knight alighted and dressed his shield unto Arthur. And there began a strong battle with many great strokes, and so hewed with their swords that the cantels flew in the fields. So at the last they smote together that both their swords met even together. But the sword of the knight smote King Arthur's sword in two pieces, wherefore he was heavy. Then said the knight unto Arthur, Thou art in my danger whether me list to save thee or slay thee, and but thou yield thee as overcome and recreant, thou shalt die. As for death, said King Arthur, welcome be it when it cometh, but to yield me unto thee as recreant I had liefer die than to be so shamed. And therewithal the king leapt unto Pellinore, and took him by the middle and threw him down, and raced off his helm. When the knight felt that he was adread, and anon he brought Arthur under him, for he was a passing big man of might, and raced off his helm and would have smitten off his head.

Therewithal came Merlin and said, Knight, hold thy hand, for an thou slay that knight thou puttest this realm in the greatest damage that ever was realm: for this knight is a man of more worship than thou wotest of. Why, who is he? said the knight. It is King Arthur. Then would he have slain him for dread of his wrath, and heaved up his sword, and therewith Merlin cast an enchantment to the knight, that he fell to the earth in a great sleep. Then Merlin took up King Arthur, and rode forth on the knight's horse. Alas! said Arthur, what hast thou done, Merlin? hast thou slain this good knight by thy crafts? There liveth not so worshipful a knight as he was; I had liefer than the stint of my land a year that he were alive. Care ye not, said Merlin, for he is wholer than ye; for he is but asleep, and will awake within three hours. I told you, said Merlin, what a knight he was; here had ye been slain had I not been.

Right so the king and he departed, and went unto an hermit that was a good man and a great leech. So the hermit searched all his wounds and gave him good salves; so the king was there three days, and then were his wounds well amended that he might ride and go, and so departed. And as they rode, Arthur said, I have no sword. No force, said Merlin, hereby is a sword that shall be yours, an I may. So they rode till they came to a lake, the which was a fair water and broad, and in the midst of the lake Arthur was ware of an arm clothed in white samite, that held a fair sword in that hand. Lo! said Merlin, yonder is that sword that I spake of. With that they saw a damosel going upon the lake. What damosel is that? said Arthur. That is the Lady of the Lake, said Merlin; and within that lake is a rock, and therein is as fair a place as any on earth, and richly beseen; and this damosel will come to you anon, and then speak ye fair to her that she will give you that sword. Anon withal came the damosel unto Arthur, and saluted him, and he her again. Damosel, said Arthur, what sword is that, that yonder the arm holdeth above the water? I would it were mine, for I have no sword. Sir Arthur, king, said the damosel, that sword is mine, and if ye will give me a gift when I ask it you, ye shall have it. By my faith, said Arthur, I will give you what gift ye will ask. Well! said the damosel, go ye into yonder barge, and row yourself to the sword, and take it and the scabbard with you, and I will ask my gift when I see my time. So Sir Arthur and Merlin alighted and tied their horses to two trees, and so they went into the ship, and when they came to the sword that the hand held, Sir Arthur took it up by the handles, and took it with him, and the arm and the hand went under the water. And so they came unto the land and rode forth.

Then Sir Arthur looked on the sword, and liked it passing well. Whether liketh you better, said Merlin, the sword or the scabbard? Me liketh better the sword, said Arthur. Ye are more unwise, said Merlin, for the scabbard is worth ten of the swords, for whiles ye have the scabbard upon you, ye shall never lose no blood, be ye never so sore wounded; therefore keep well the scabbard always with you. So they came unto Carlion, whereof his knights were passing glad. And when they heard of his adventures, they marvelled that he would jeopard his person so, alone. But all men of worship said it was merry to be under such a chieftain, that would put his person in adventure as other poor knights did.

HOW KING ARTHUR WEDDED GUENEVER, DAUGHTER TO LEODEGRANCE, KING OF THE LAND OF CAMELIARD, WITH WHOM HE HAD THE ROUND TABLE, AND HOW TOR AND GAWAINE WERE MADE KNIGHTS. So it fell on a time King Arthur said unto Merlin, My barons will let me have no rest, but needs I must take a wife, and I will none take but by thy counsel and by thine advice. It is well done, said Merlin, that ye take a wife, for a man of your bounty and noblesse should not be without a wife. Now is there any that ye love more than another? Yea, said King Arthur, I love Guenever the king's daughter, Leodegrance of the land of Cameliard, the which holdeth in his house the Table Round that ye told he had of my father Uther. And this damosel is the most valiant and fairest lady that I know living, or yet that ever I could find. Sir, said Merlin, as of her beauty and fairness she is one of the fairest alive, but, an ye loved her not so well as ye do, I should find you a damosel of beauty and of goodness that should like you and please you, an your heart were not set; but there as a man's heart is set, he will be loath to return. That is truth, said King Arthur.

Then Merlin went forth unto King Leodegrance of Cameliard, and told him of the desire of the king that he would have unto his wife Guenever his daughter. That is to me, said King Leodegrance, the best tidings that ever I heard, that so worthy a king of prowess and noblesse will wed my daughter. And as for my lands, I will give him, wist I it might please him, but he hath lands enow, him needeth none; but I shall send him a gift shall please him much more, for I shall give him the Table Round, the which

Uther Pendragon gave me, and when it is full complete, there is an hundred knights and fifty. And as for an hundred good knights I have myself, but I faute fifty, for so many have been slain in my days. And so Leodegrance delivered his daughter Guenever unto Merlin, and the Table Round with the hundred knights, and so they rode freshly, with great royalty, what by water and what by land, till that they came nigh unto London.

When King Arthur heard of the coming of Guenever and the hundred knights with the Table Round, then King Arthur made great joy for her coming, and that rich present, and said openly, This fair lady is passing welcome unto me, for I have loved her long, and therefore there is nothing so lief to me. And these knights with the Round Table please me more than right great riches. And in all haste the king let ordain for the marriage and the coronation in the most honourable wise that could be devised. Now, Merlin, said King Arthur, go thou and espy me in all this land fifty knights which be of most prowess and worship. Within short time Merlin had found such knights that should fulfil twenty and eight knights, but no more he could find. Then the Bishop of Canterbury was fetched, and he blessed the sieges with great royalty and devotion, and there set the eight and twenty knights in their sieges. And when this was done Merlin said, Fair sirs, ye must all arise and come to King Arthur for to do him homage; he will have the better will to maintain you. And so they arose and did their homage, and when they were gone Merlin found in every sieges letters of gold that told the knights' names that had sitten therein. But two sieges were void. And so anon came young Gawaine and asked the king a gift. Ask, said the king, and I shall grant it you. Sir, I ask that ye will make me knight that same day ye shall wed fair Guenever. I will do it with a good will, said King Arthur, and do unto you all the worship that I may, for I must by reason ye are my nephew, my sister's son.

Forthwithal there came a poor man into the court, and brought with him a fair young man of eighteen years of age riding upon a lean mare; and the poor man asked all men that he met, Where shall I find King Arthur? Yonder he is, said the knights, wilt thou anything with him? Yea, said the poor man, therefore I came hither. Anon as he came before the king, he saluted him and said: O King Arthur, the flower of all knights and kings, I beseech Jesu save thee. Sir, it was told me that at this time of your marriage ye would give any man the gift that he would ask, out except that were unreasonable. That is truth, said the king, such cries I let make, and that will I hold, so it apair not my realm nor mine estate. Ye say well and graciously, said the poor man; Sir, I ask nothing else but that ye will make my son here a knight. It is a great thing thou askest of me, said the king. What is thy name? said the king to the poor man. Sir, my name is Aries the cowherd. Whether cometh this of thee or of thy son? said the king. Nay, sir, said Aries, this desire cometh of my son and not of me, for I shall tell you I have thirteen sons, and all they will fall to what labour I put them, and will be right glad to do labour, but this child will not labour for me, for anything that my wife or I may do, but always he will be shooting or casting darts, and glad for to see battles and to behold knights, and always day and night he desireth of me to be made a knight. What is thy name?

said the king unto the young man. Sir, my name is Tor. The king beheld him fast, and saw he was passingly well-visaged and passingly well made of his years. Well, said King Arthur unto Aries the cowherd, fetch all thy sons afore me that I may see them. And so the poor man did, and all were shaped much like the poor man. But Tor was not like none of them all in shape nor in countenance, for he was much more than any of them. Now, said King Arthur unto the cowherd, where is the sword he shall be made knight withal? It is here, said Tor. Take it out of the sheath, said the king, and require me to make you a knight.

Then Tor alighted off his mare and pulled out his sword, kneeling, and requiring the king that he would make him knight, and that he might be a knight of the Table Round. As for a knight I will make you, and therewith smote him in the neck with the sword, saying, Be ye a good knight, and so I pray to God so ye may be, and if ye be of prowess and of worthiness ye shall be a knight of the Table Round. Now Merlin, said Arthur, say whether this Tor shall be a good knight or no. Yea, sir, he ought to be a good knight, for he is come of as good a man as any is alive, and of kings' blood. How so, sir? said the king. I shall tell you, said Merlin: This poor man, Aries the cowherd, is not his father; he is nothing sib to him, for King Pellinore is his father. I suppose nay, said the cowherd. Fetch thy wife afore me, said Merlin, and she shall not say nay. Anon the wife was fetched, which was a fair housewife, and there she answered Merlin full womanly, and there she told the king and Merlin that when she was a maid, and went to milk kine, there met with her a stern knight, and half by force he held me, and after that time was born my son Tor, and the knight took away from me my greyhound that I had that time with me, and said that he would keep the greyhound for my love. Ah, said the cowherd, I weened not this, but I may believe it well, for he had never no tatches of me. Sir, said Tor unto Merlin, dishonour not my mother. Sir, said Merlin, it is more for your worship than hurt, for your father is a good man and a king, and he may right well advance you and your mother, for ye were begotten or ever she was wedded. That is truth, said the wife. It is the less grief unto me, said the cowherd.

So on the morn King Pellinore came to the court of King Arthur, which had great joy of him, and told him of Tor, how he was his son, and how he had made him knight at the request of the cowherd. When Pellinore beheld Tor, he pleased him much. So the king made Gawaine knight, but Tor was the first he made at the feast. What is the cause, said King Arthur, that there be two places void in the sieges? Sir, said Merlin, there shall no man sit in those places but they that shall be of most worship. But in the Siege Perilous there shall no man sit therein but one, and if there be any so hardy to do it he shall be destroyed, and he that shall sit there shall have no fellow. And therewith Merlin took King Pellinore by the hand, and in the one next the two sieges and the Siege Perilous he said, in open audience, This is your place and best ye are worthy to sit therein of any that is here. Thereat sat Sir Gawaine in great envy and told Gaheris his brother, yonder knight is put to great worship, the which grieveth me sore, for he slew our father King Lot, therefore I will slay him, said Gawaine, with a sword that was sent me that is passing trenchant. Ye shall not so, said Gaheris, at this time, for at this time I am but a squire, and when I am made knight I will be avenged on him, and therefore, brother, it is best ye suffer till another time, that we may have him out of the court, for an we did so we should trouble this high feast. I will well, said Gawaine, as ye will.

Then was the high feast made ready, and the king was wedded at Camelot unto Dame Guenever in the church of Saint Stephen's, with great solemnity.

HOW MERLIN WAS ASSOTTED AND DOTED ON ONE OF THE LADIES OF THE LAKE, AND HOW HE WAS SHUT IN A ROCK UNDER A STONE AND THERE DIED. So after this Merlin fell in a dotage on one of the damosels of the lake, that hight Nimue. But Merlin would let her have no rest, but always he would be with her. And ever she made Merlin good cheer till she had learned of him all manner thing that she desired; and he was assotted upon her, that he might not be from her. So on a time he told King Arthur that he should not dure long, but for all his crafts he should be put in the earth quick. And so he told the king many things that should befall, but always he warned the king to keep well his sword and the scabbard, for he told him how the sword and the scabbard should be stolen by a woman from him that he most trusted. Also he told King Arthur that he should miss him, — Yet, had ye liefer than all your lands to have me again. Ah, said the king, since ye know of your adventure, purvey for it, and put away by your crafts that misadventure. Nay, said Merlin, it will not be; so he departed from the king. And within a while the Damosel of the Lake departed, and Merlin went with her ever more wheresomever she went. And ofttimes Merlin would have had her privily away by his subtle crafts; then she made him to swear that he should never do none enchantment upon her if he would have his will. And so he sware; so she and Merlin went over the sea unto the land of Benwick, whereas King Ban was king that had great war against King Claudas, and there Merlin spake with King Ban's wife, a fair lady and a good, and her name was Elaine, and there he saw young Launcelot. There the queen made great sorrow for the mortal war that King Claudas made on her lord and on her lands. Take none heaviness, said Merlin, for this same child within this twenty year shall revenge you on King Claudas, that all Christendom shall speak of it; and this same child shall be the most man of worship of the world, and his first name is Galahad, that know I well, said Merlin, and since ye have confirmed him Launcelot. That is truth, said the queen, his first name was Galahad. O Merlin, said the queen, shall I live to see my son such a man of prowess? Yea, lady, on my peril ye shall see it, and live many winters after.

And so, soon after, the lady and Merlin departed, and by the way Merlin showed her many wonders, and came into Cornwall. And always Merlin lay about the lady to have her love, and she was ever passing weary of him, and fain would have been delivered of him, for she was afeard of him because he was a devil's son, and she could not put him away by no means. And so on a time it happed that Merlin showed to her in a rock whereas was a great wonder, and wrought by enchantment, that went under a great stone. So by her subtle working she made Merlin to go under that stone to let her wit of the marvels there; but she wrought so there for him that he came never out for all the craft he could do. And so she departed and left Merlin.

HOW KING ARTHUR, KING URIENS, AND SIR ACCOLON OF GAUL, CHASED AN HART, AND OF THEIR MARVELLOUS ADVENTURES, AND HOW KING ARTHUR AND ACCOLON TOOK UPON THEM TO DO BATTLE.

Then it befell that Arthur and many of his knights rode a-hunting into a great forest, and it happed King Arthur, King Uriens, and Sir Accolon of Gaul, followed a great hart, for they three were well horsed, and so they chased so fast that within a while they three were then ten mile from their fellowship. And at the last they chased so sore that they slew their horses underneath them. Then were they all three on foot, and ever they saw the hart afore them passing weary and embushed. What will we do? said King Arthur, we are hard bestead. Let us go on foot, said King Uriens, till we may meet with some lodging. Then were they ware of the hart that lay on a great water bank, and a brachet biting on his throat, and more other hounds came after. Then King Arthur blew the prise and dight the hart.

Then the king looked about the world, and saw afore

him in a great water a little ship, all apparelled with silk down to the water, and the ship came right unto them and landed on the sands. Then Arthur went to the bank and looked in, and saw none earthly creature therein. Sirs, said the king, come thence, and let us see what is in this ship. So they went in all three, and found it richly behanged with cloth of silk. By then it was dark night, and there suddenly were about them an hundred torches set upon all the sides of the ship boards, and it gave great light; and therewithal there came out twelve fair damosels and saluted King Arthur on their knees, and called him by his name, and said he was right welcome, and such cheer as they had he should have of the best. The king thanked them fair. Therewithal they led the king and his two fellows into a fair chamber, and there was a cloth laid, richly beseen of all that longed unto a table, and there were they served of all wines and meats that they could think; of that the king had great marvel, for he fared never better in his life as for one supper. And so when they had supped at their leisure, King Arthur was led into a chamber, a richer beseen chamber saw he never none, and so was King Uriens served, and led into such another chamber, and Sir Accolon was led into the third chamber passing richly and well beseen; and so they were laid in their beds easily. And anon they fell asleep, and slept marvellously sore all the night. And on the morrow King Uriens was in Camelot with his wife, Morgan le Fay. And when he awoke he had great marvel, how he came there, for on the even afore he was two days' journey from Camelot. And when King Arthur awoke he found himself in a dark prison, hearing about him many complaints of woful knights.

What are ye that so complain? said King Arthur. We be here twenty knights, prisoners, said they, and some of us have lain here seven year, and some more and some less. For what cause? said Arthur. We shall tell you, said the knights; this lord of this castle, his name is Sir Damas, and he is the falsest knight that liveth, and full of treason, and a very coward as any liveth, and he hath a younger brother, a good knight of prowess, his name is Sir Ontzlake; and this traitor Damas, the elder brother will give him no part of his livelihood, but as Sir Ontzlake keepeth thorough prowess of his hands, and so he keepeth from him a full fair manor and a rich, and therein Sir Ontzlake dwelleth worshipfully, and is well beloved of all people. And this Sir Damas, our master, is as evil beloved, for he is without mercy, and he is a coward, and great war hath been betwixt them both, but Ontzlake hath ever the better, and ever he proffereth Sir Damas to fight for the livelihood, body for body, but he will not do; other-else to find a knight to fight for him. Unto that Sir Damas hath granted to find a knight, but he is so evil beloved and hated, that there is never a knight will fight for him. And when Damas saw this, that there was never a knight would fight for him, he hath daily lain await with many knights with him, and taken all the knights in this country to see and espy their adventures, he hath taken them by force and brought them to his prison. And so he took us severally as we rode on our adventures, and many good knights have died in this prison for hunger, to the number of eighteen knights; and if any of us all that here is, or hath been, would have foughten with his brother Ontzlake, he would have delivered us, but for because this Damas is so false and so full of treason we would never fight for him to die for it. And we be so lean for hunger that unnethe we may stand on our feet. God deliver you, for his mercy, said Arthur.

Anon, therewithal there came a damosel unto Arthur, and asked him, What cheer? I cannot say, said he. Sir, said she, an ye will fight for my lord, ye shall be delivered out of prison, and else ye escape never the life. Now, said Arthur, that is hard, yet had I liefer to fight with a knight than to die in prison; with this, said Arthur, I may be delivered and all these prisoners, I will do the battle. Yes, said the damosel. I am ready, said Arthur, an I had horse and armour. Ye shall lack none, said the damosel. Meseemeth, damosel, I should have seen you in the court of Arthur. Nay, said the damosel, I came never there, I am the lord's daughter of this castle. Yet was she false, for she was one of the damosels of Morgan le Fay.

Anon she went unto Sir Damas, and told him how he would do battle for him, and so he sent for Arthur. And when he came he was well coloured, and well made of his limbs, that all knights that saw him said it were pity that such a knight should die in prison. So Sir Damas and he were agreed that he should fight for him upon this covenant, that all other knights should be delivered; and unto that was Sir Damas sworn unto Arthur, and also to do the battle to the uttermost. And with that all the twenty knights were brought out of the dark prison into the hall, and delivered, and so they all abode to see the battle.

Now turn we unto Accolon of Gaul, that when he awoke he found himself by a deep well-side, within half a foot, in great peril of death. And there came out of that fountain a pipe of silver, and out of that pipe ran water all on high in a stone of marble. When Sir Accolon saw this, he blessed him and said, Jesus save my lord King Arthur, and King Uriens, for these damosels in this ship have betrayed us, they were devils and no women; and if I may escape this misadventure, I shall destroy all where I may find these false damosels that use enchantments. Right with that there came a dwarf with a great mouth and a flat nose, and saluted Sir Accolon, and said how he came from Queen Morgan le Fay, and she greeteth you well, and biddeth you be of strong heart, for ye shall fight to-morrow with a knight at the hour of prime, and therefore she hath sent you here Excalibur, Arthur's sword, and the scabbard, and she biddeth you as ye love her, that ye do the battle to the uttermost, without any mercy, like as ye had promised her when ye spake together in privity; and what damosel that bringeth her the knight's head, which ye shall fight withal, she will make her a queen. Now I understand you well, said Accolon, I shall hold that I have promised her now I have the sword: when saw ye my Lady Queen Morgan le Fay? Right late, said the dwarf. Then Accolon took him in his arms and said, Recommend me unto my lady queen, and tell her all shall be done that I have promised her, and else I will die for it. Now I suppose, said Accolon, she hath made all these crafts and enchantments for this battle. Ye may well believe it, said the dwarf. Right so there came a knight and a lady with six squires, and saluted Accolon, and prayed him for to arise, and come and rest him at his manor. And so Accolon mounted upon a void horse, and went with the knight unto a fair manor by a priory, and there he had passing good cheer.

Then Sir Damas sent unto his brother Sir Ontzlake,

and bade make him ready by to-morn at the hour of prime, and to be in the field to fight with a good knight, for he had found a good knight that was ready to do battle at all points. When this word came unto Sir Ontzlake he was passing heavy, for he was wounded a little to-fore through both his thighs with a spear, and made great dole; but as he was wounded, he would have taken the battle on hand. So it happed at that time, by the means of Morgan le Fay, Accolon was with Sir Ontzlake lodged; and when he heard of that battle, and how Ontzlake was wounded, he said that he would fight for him. Because Morgan le Fay had sent him Excalibur and the sheath for to fight with the knight on the morn: this was the cause Sir Accolon took the battle on hand. Then Sir Ontzlake was passing glad, and thanked Sir Accolon with all his heart that he would do so much for him. And therewithal Sir Ontzlake sent word unto his brother Sir Damas, that he had a knight that for him should be ready in the field by the hour of prime.

So on the morn Sir Arthur was armed and well horsed, and asked Sir Damas, When shall we to the field? Sir, said Sir Damas, ye shall hear mass. And so Arthur heard a mass, and when mass was done there came a squire on a great horse, and asked Sir Damas if his knight were ready, for our knight is ready in the field. Then Sir Arthur mounted upon horseback, and there were all the knights and commons of that country; and so by all advices there were chosen twelve good men of the country for to wait upon the two knights. And right as Arthur was on horseback there came a damosel from Morgan le Fay, and brought unto Sir Arthur a sword like unto Excalibur, and the scabbard, and said unto Arthur, Morgan le Fay sendeth here your sword for great love. And he thanked her, and weened it had been so; but she was false, for the sword and the scabbard was counterfeit, and brittle, and false.

OF THE BATTLE BETWEEN KING ARTHUR AND ACCOLON, AND HOW ACCOLON CONFESSED THE TREASON OF MORGAN LE FAY. And then they dressed them on both parties of the field, and let their horses run so fast that either smote other in the midst of the shield with their spear-heads, that both horse and man went to the earth; and then they started up both, and pulled out their swords. The meanwhile that they were thus at the battle, came the Damosel of the Lake into the field, that put Merlin under the stone; and she came thither for love of King Arthur, for she knew how Morgan le Fay had so ordained that King Arthur should have been slain that day, and therefore she came to save his life. And so they went eagerly to the battle, and gave many great strokes, but always Arthur's sword bit not like Accolon's sword; but for the most part, every stroke that Accolon gave he wounded sore Arthur, that it was marvel he stood, and always his blood fell from him fast.

When Arthur beheld the ground so sore be-bled he was dismayed, and then he deemed treason that his sword was changed; for his sword bit not steel as it was wont to do, therefore he dreaded him sore to be dead, for ever him seemed that the sword in Accolon's hand was Excalibur, for at every stroke that Accolon struck he drew blood on Arthur. Now, knight, said Accolon unto Arthur, keep thee well from me; but Arthur answered not again, and gave him such a buffet on the helm that it made him to stoop, nigh falling down to the earth. Then Sir Accolon withdrew him a little, and came on with Excalibur on high, and smote Sir Arthur such a buffet that he fell nigh to the earth. Then were they wroth both, and gave each other many sore strokes, but always Sir Arthur lost so much blood that it was marvel he stood on his feet, but he was so full of knighthood that knightly he endured the pain. Then always they fought together as fierce knights, and Sir Arthur withdrew him a little for to rest him, and Sir Accolon called him to battle and said, It is no time for me to suffer thee to rest. And therewith he came fiercely upon Arthur, and Sir Arthur was wroth for the blood that he had lost, and smote Accolon on high upon the helm, so mightily, that he made him nigh to fall to the earth; and therewith Arthur's sword brast at the cross, and fell in the grass among the blood, and the pommel and the sure handles he held in his hands. When Sir Arthur saw that, he was in great fear to die, but always he held up his shield and lost no ground, nor bated no cheer.

Then Sir Accolon began with words of treason, and said, Knight, thou art overcome, and mayst not endure, and also thou art weaponless, and thou hast lost much of thy blood, and I am full loath to slay thee, therefore yield thee to me as recreant. Nay, said Sir Arthur, I may not so, for I have promised to do the battle to the uttermost, by the faith of my body, while me lasteth the life, and therefore I had liefer to die with honour than to live with shame; and if it were possible for me to die an hundred times, I had liefer to die so oft than yield me to thee; for though I lack weapon, I shall lack no worship, and if thou slay me weaponless that shall be thy shame. Well, said Accolon, as for the shame I will not spare: now keep thee from me, for thou art but a dead man. And therewith Accolon gave him such a stroke that he fell nigh to the earth, and would have had Arthur to have cried him mercy. But Sir Arthur pressed unto Accolon with his shield, and gave him with the pommel in his hand such a buffet that he went three strides aback.

When the Damosel of the Lake beheld Arthur, how full of prowess his body was, and the false treason that was wrought for him to have had him slain, she had great pity that so good a knight and such a man of worship should so be destroyed. And at the next stroke Sir Accolon struck him such a stroke that by the damosel's enchantment the sword Excalibur fell out of Accolon's hand to the earth. And therewithal Sir Arthur lightly leapt to it, and gat it in his hand, and forthwithal he knew that it was his sword Excalibur, and said, Thou hast been from me all too long, and much damage hast thou done me; and therewith he espied the scabbard hanging by his side, and suddenly he sterte to him and pulled the scabbard from him, and threw it from him as far as he might throw it. O knight, said Arthur, this day hast thou done me great damage with this sword; now are ye come unto your death, for I shall not warrant you but ye shall as well be rewarded with this sword, or ever we depart, as thou hast rewarded me; for much pain have ye made me to endure, and much blood have I lost. And therewith Sir Arthur rushed on him with all his might and pulled him to the earth, and then rushed off his helm, and gave him such a buffet on the head that the blood came out at his ears, his nose, and his mouth. Now will I slay thee, said Arthur. Slay me ye may well, said

Accolon, an it please you, for ye are the best knight that ever I found, and I see well that God is with you. But for I promised to do this battle, said Accolon, to the uttermost, and never to be recreant while I lived, therefore shall I never yield me with my mouth, but God do with my body what he will. Then Sir Arthur remembered him, and thought he should have seen this knight. Now tell me, said Arthur, or I will slay thee, of what country art thou, and of what court? Sir Knight, said Sir Accolon, I am of the court of King Arthur, and my name is Accolon of Gaul. Then was Arthur more dismayed than he was beforehand; for then he remembered him of his sister Morgan le Fay, and of the enchantment of the ship. O sir knight, said he, I pray you tell me who gave you this sword, and by whom ye had it.

Then Sir Accolon bethought him, and said, Woe worth this sword, for by it have I got my death. It may well be, said the king. Now, sir, said Accolon, I will tell you; this sword hath been in my keeping the most part of this twelvemonth; and Morgan le Fay, King Uriens' wife, sent it me yesterday by a dwarf, to this intent, that I should slay King Arthur, her brother. For ye shall understand King Arthur is the man in the world that she most hateth, because he is most of worship and of prowess of any of her blood; also she loveth me out of measure as paramour, and I her again; and if she might bring about to slay Arthur by her crafts, she would slay her husband King Uriens lightly, and then had she me devised to be king in this land, and so to reign, and she to be my queen; but that is now done, said Accolon, for I am sure of my death. Well, said Sir Arthur, I feel by you ye would have been king in this land. It had been great damage to have destroyed your lord, said Arthur. It is truth, said Accolon, but now I have told you truth, wherefore I pray you tell me of whence ye are, and of what court? O Accolon, said King Arthur, now I let thee wit that I am King Arthur, to whom thou hast done great damage. When Accolon heard that he cried aloud, Fair, sweet lord, have mercy on me, for I knew not you. O Sir Accolon, said King Arthur, mercy shalt thou have, because I feel by thy words at this time thou knewest not my person; but I understand well by thy words that thou hast agreed to the death of my person, and therefore thou art a traitor; but I wite thee the less, for my sister Morgan le Fay by her false crafts made thee to agree and consent to her false lusts, but I shall be sore avenged upon her an I live, that all Christendom shall speak of it; God knoweth I have honoured her and worshipped her more than all my kin, and more have I trusted her than mine own wife and all my kin after.

Then Sir Arthur called the keepers of the field, and said, Sirs, come hither, for here are we two knights that have fought unto a great damage unto us both, and like each one of us to have slain other, if it had happed so; and had any of us known other, here had been no battle, nor stroke stricken. Then all aloud cried Accolon unto all the knights and men that were then there gathered together, and said to them in this manner, O lords, this noble knight that I have fought withal, the which me sore repenteth, is the most man of prowess, of manhood, and of worship in the world, for it is himself King Arthur, our alther liege lord, and with mishap and with misadventure have I done this battle with the king and lord that I am holden withal.

Then all the people fell down on their knees and cried

King Arthur mercy. Mercy shall ye have, said Arthur: here may ye see what adventures befall ofttime of errant knights, how that I have fought with a knight of mine own unto my great damage and his both. But, sirs, because I am sore hurt, and he both, and I had great need of a little rest, ye shall understand the opinion betwixt you two brethren: As to thee, Sir Damas, for whom I have been champion and won the field of this knight, yet will I judge, because ye, Sir Damas, are called an orgulous knight, and full of villainy and not worth of prowess of your deeds, therefore I will that ye give unto your brother all the whole manor with the appurtenance, under this form, that Sir Ontzlake hold the manor of you, and yearly to give you a palfrey to ride upon, for that will become you better to ride on than upon a courser. Also I charge thee, Sir Damas, upon pain of death, that thou never distress no knights errant that ride on their adventure. And also that thou restore these twenty knights that thou hast long kept prisoners, of all their harness, that they be content for; and if any of them come to my court and complain of thee, by my head thou shalt die therefore. Also, Sir Ontzlake, as to you, because ye are named a good knight, and full of prowess, and true and gentle in all your deeds, this shall be your charge I will give you, that in all goodly haste ye come unto me and my court, and ye shall be a knight of mine, and if your deeds be thereafter I shall so prefer you, by the grace of God, that ye shall in short time be in ease for to live as worshipfully as your brother Sir Damas. God thank your largeness of your goodness and of your bounty, I shall be from henceforward at all times at your commandment, said Sir Ontzlake. Now, tell me, said Arthur, how far

am I from Camelot? Sir, ye are two days' journey therefrom. I would fain be at some place of worship, said Sir Arthur, that I might rest me. Sir, said Sir Ontzlake, hereby is a rich abbey of your elders' foundation, of nuns, but three miles hence. So the king took his leave of all the people, and mounted upon horseback, and Sir Accolon with him. And when they were come to the abbey, he let fetch leeches and search his wounds and Accolon's both; but Sir Accolon died within four days, for he had bled so much blood that he might not live, but King Arthur was well recovered. So when Accolon was dead he let send him on an horse-bier with six knights unto Camelot, and said: Bear him to my sister Morgan le Fay, and say that I send her him to a present, and tell her I have my sword Excalibur and the scabbard; so they departed with the body.

HOW QUEEN MORGAN LE FAY MADE GREAT SORROW FOR THE DEATH OF ACCOLON, AND HOW SHE STOLE AWAY THE SCABBARD FROM ARTHUR, AND OF THE MANTLE SHE SENT TO HIM. Then came tidings unto Morgan le Fay that Accolon was dead, and his body brought unto the church, and how King Arthur had his sword again. But when Queen Morgan wist that Accolon was dead, she was so sorrowful that near her heart to-brast. But because she would not it were known, outward she kept her countenance, and made no semblant of sorrow. But well she wist an she abode till her brother Arthur came thither, there should no gold go for her life.

So early on the morn, or it was day, she took her horse and rode all that day and most part of the night, and on the morn by noon she came to the same abbey of nuns whereas lay King Arthur; and she knowing he was there, asked where he was. And they answered how he had laid him in his bed to sleep, for he had had but little rest these three nights. Well, said she, I charge you that none of you awake him till I do, and then she alighted off her horse, and thought for to steal away Excalibur his sword, and so she went straight unto his chamber, and no man durst disobey her commandment, and there she found Arthur asleep in his bed, and Excalibur in his right hand naked. When she saw that she was passing heavy that she might not come by the sword without she had awaked him, and then she wist well she had been dead. Then she took the scabbard and went her way on horseback. When the king awoke and missed his scabbard, he was wroth, and he asked who had been there, and they said his sister, Queen Morgan, had been there, and had put the scabbard under her mantle and was gone. Alas, said Arthur, falsely ye have watched me. Sir, said they all, we durst not disobey your sister's commandment. Ah, said the king, let fetch the best horse may be found, and bid Sir Ontzlake arm him in all haste, and take another good horse and ride with me. So anon the king and Ontzlake were well armed, and rode after this lady, and so they came by a cross and found a cowherd, and they asked the poor man if there came any lady riding that way. Sir, said this poor man, right late came a lady riding with a forty horses, and to yonder forest she rode. Then they spurred their horses, and followed fast, and within a while Arthur had a sight of Morgan le Fay; then

WHEN·SHE·SAW·SHE·MUST·BE·OVERTAKEN·SHE·SHAPED HERSELF·HORSE·AND·MAN·BY·ENCHANTMENT·UNTO·A·GREAT MARBLE·STONE

he chased as fast as he might. When she espied him following her, she rode a greater pace through the forest till she came to a plain, and when she saw she might not escape, she rode unto a lake thereby, and said, Whatsoever come of me, my brother shall not have this scabbard. And then she let throw the scabbard in the deepest of the water so it sank, for it was heavy of gold and precious stones.

Then she rode into a valley where many great stones were, and when she saw she must be overtaken, she shaped herself, horse and man, by enchantment unto a great marble stone. Anon withal came Sir Arthur and Sir Ontzlake whereas the king might know his sister and her men, and one knight from another. Ah, said the king, here may ye see the vengeance of God, and now am I sorry that this misadventure is befallen. And then he looked for the scabbard, but it would not be found, so he returned to the abbey where he came from. So when Arthur was gone she turned all into the likeliness as she and they were before, and said, Sirs, now may we go where we will. And so she departed into the country of Gore, and there was she richly received, and made her castles and towns passing strong, for always she dreaded much King Arthur.

When the king had well rested him at the abbey, he rode unto Camelot, and found his queen and his barons right glad of his coming. And when they heard of his strange adventures as is afore rehearsed, then all had marvel of the falsehood of Morgan le Fay; many knights wished her burnt. So on the morn there came a damosel from Morgan to the king, and she brought with her the richest mantle that ever was seen in that court, for it was set as full of precious stones as one might stand by another, and there were the richest stones that ever the king saw. And the damosel said, Your sister sendeth you this mantle, and desireth that ye should take this gift of her; and in what thing she hath offended you, she will amend it at your own pleasure. When the king beheld this mantle it pleased him much, but he said but little.

With that came the Damosel of the Lake unto the king, and said, Sir, I must speak with you in privity. Say on, said the king, what ye will. Sir, said the damosel, put not on you this mantle till ye have seen more, and in no wise let it not come on you, nor on no knight of yours, till ye command the bringer thereof to put it upon her. Well, said King Arthur, it shall be done as ye counsel me. And then he said unto the damosel that came from his sister, Damosel, this mantle that ye have brought me, I will see it upon you. Sir, she said, It will not beseem me to wear a king's garment. By my head, said Arthur, ye shall wear it ere it come on my back, or any man's that here is. And so the king made it to be put upon her, and forthwithal she fell down dead, and never more spake word after and burnt to coals. Then was the king wonderly wroth, more than he was to-forehand, and said unto King Uriens, My sister, your wife, is alway about to betray me, and well I wot either ye, or my nephew, your son, is of counsel with her to have me destroyed; but as for you, said the king to King Uriens, I deem not greatly that ye be of her counsel, for Accolon confessed to me by his own mouth, that she would have destroyed you as well as me, therefore I hold you excused; but as for your son, Sir Uwaine, I hold him suspect, therefore I charge you put him out of my court.

So Sir Uwaine was discharged. And when Sir Gawaine wist that, he made him ready to go with him; and said, Whoso banisheth my cousin-germain shall banish me. So they two departed.

OF SIR LAUNCELOT

HOW SIR LAUNCELOT AND SIR LIONEL DEPARTED FROM THE COURT, AND HOW SIR LIONEL WAS TAKEN, AND HOW FOUR QUEENS FOUND SIR LAUNCELOT SLEEPING AND LED HIM TO A CASTLE. Then all the knights of the Table Round resorted unto the king, and made many jousts and tournaments, and some there were that were but knights, which increased so in arms and worship that they passed all their fellows in prowess and noble deeds, and that was well proved on many; but in especial it was proved on Sir Launcelot du Lake, for in all tournaments and jousts and deeds of arms, both for life and death, he passed all other knights, and at no time he was never overcome but if it were by treason or enchantment. Wherefore Queen Guenever had him in great favour above all other knights, and in certain he loved the queen again above all other ladies and damosels of his life.

Thus Sir Launcelot rested him long with play and game. And then he thought himself to prove himself in strange adventures; then he bade his nephew, Sir Lionel, for to make him ready, for we two will seek adventures.

So they mounted on their horses, armed at all rights, and rode into a deep forest and so into a deep plain. And then the weather was hot about noon, and Sir Launcelot had great lust to sleep. Then Sir Lionel espied a great apple-tree that stood by an hedge, and said, Brother, yonder is a fair shadow, there may we rest us and our horses. It is well said, fair brother, said Sir Launcelot, for this eight year I was not so sleepy as I am now; and so they there alighted and tied their horses unto sundry trees, and so Sir Launcelot laid him down under an apple-tree, and his helm he laid under his head. And Sir Lionel waked while he slept. So Sir Launcelot was asleep passing fast.

And in the meanwhile there came three knights riding, as fast fleeing as ever they might ride. And there followed them three but one knight. And when Sir Lionel saw him, him thought he saw never so great a knight, nor so well faring a man, neither so well apparelled unto all rights. So within a while this strong knight had overtaken one of these knights, and there he smote him to the cold earth that he lay still. And then he rode unto the second knight, and smote him so that man and horse fell down. And then straight to the third knight he rode, and smote him behind his horse's arse a spear length. And then he alighted down and reined his horse on the bridle, and bound all the three knights fast with the reins of their own bridles. When Sir Lionel saw him do thus, he thought to assay him, and made him ready, and stilly and privily he took his horse, and thought not for to awake Sir Launcelot. And when he was mounted upon his horse, he overtook this strong knight, and bade him turn, and the other smote Sir Lionel so hard that horse and man he bare to the earth, and so he alighted down and bound him fast, and threw him overthwart his own horse, and so he served them all four, and rode with them away to his own castle. And when he came there he gart unarm them, and beat them with thorns all naked, and after put them in a deep prison where were many more knights, that made great dolour.

Now leave we these knights prisoners, and speak we of Sir Launcelot du Lake that lieth under the apple-tree sleeping. Even about the noon there came by him four queens of great estate; and, for the heat should not annoy them, there rode four knights about them, and bare a cloth of green silk on four spears, betwixt them and the sun, and the queens rode on four white mules. Thus as they rode they heard by them a great horse grimly neigh; then were they ware of a sleeping knight, that lay all armed under an apple-tree; anon as these queens looked on his face, they knew it was Sir Launcelot. Then they began for to strive for that knight, everych one said they would have him to her love. We shall not strive, said Morgan le Fay, that was King Arthur's sister, I shall put an enchantment upon him that he shall not awake in six hours, and then I will lead him away unto my castle, and when he is surely within my hold, I shall take the enchantment from him, and then let him choose which of us he will have for his love.

So this enchantment was cast upon Sir Launcelot, and then they laid him upon his shield, and bare him so on horseback betwixt two knights, and brought him unto the castle Chariot, and there they laid him in a chamber cold, and at night they sent unto him a fair damosel with his supper ready dight. By that the enchantment was past, and when she came she saluted him, and asked him what cheer.

I cannot say, fair damosel, said Sir Launcelot, for I wot not how I came into this castle but it be by an enchantment. Sir, said she, ye must make good cheer, and if ye be such a knight as it is said ye be, I shall tell you more to-morn by prime of the day. Gramercy, fair damosel, said Sir Launcelot, of your good will I require you. And so she departed. And there he lay all that night without comfort of anybody. And on the morn early came these four queens, passingly well beseen, all they bidding him good morn, and he them again.

Sir knight, the four queens said, thou must understand thou art our prisoner, and we here know thee well that thou art Sir Launcelot du Lake, King Ban's son, and because we understand your worthiness, that thou art the noblest knight living, and as we know well there can no lady have thy love but one, and that is Queen Guenever, and now thou shalt lose her for ever, and she thee, and therefore thee behoveth now to choose one of us four. I am the Queen Morgan le Fay, queen of the land of Gore, and here is the queen of Northgalis, and the queen of Eastland, and the queen of the Out Isles; now choose one of us which thou wilt have to thy love, or else in this prison to die. This is an hard case, said Sir Launcelot, that either I must die or else choose one of you, yet I had liefer to die in this prison with worship, than to have one of you to my love maugre my head. And therefore ye be answered, I will none of you, for ye be false enchantresses, and as for my lady, Dame Guenever, were I at my liberty as I was, I would prove it on you or on yours, that she is the truest lady unto her lord living. Well, said the queens, is this your answer, that ye will refuse us? Yea, on my life, said Sir Launcelot, refused ye be of me. So they departed and left him there alone that made great sorrow.

HOW SIR LAUNCELOT WAS DELIVERED BY THE MEAN OF A DAMOSEL, AND FOUGHT FOR HER FATHER, KING BAGDEMAGUS, IN A TOURNAMENT. Right so at the noon came the damosel unto him with his dinner, and asked him what cheer. Truly, fair damosel, said Sir Launcelot, in my life days never so ill. Sir, she said, that me repenteth, but an ye will be ruled by me, I shall help you out of this distress, and ye shall have no shame nor villainy, so that ye hold me a promise. Fair damosel, I will grant you, and sore I am of these queen-sorceresses afeard, for they have destroyed many a good knight. Sir, said she, that is sooth, and for the renown and bounty that they hear of you they would have your love, and Sir, they say, your name is Sir Launcelot du Lake, the flower of knights, and they be passing wroth with you that ye have refused them. But Sir, an ye would promise me to help my father on Tuesday next coming, that hath made a tournament betwixt him and the King of Northgalis — for the last Tuesday past my father lost the field through three knights of Arthur's court — an ye will be there on Tuesday next coming, and help my father, to-morn ere prime, by the grace of God, I shall deliver you clean. Fair maiden, said Sir Launcelot, tell me what is your father's name, and then shall I give you an answer. Sir knight, she said, my father is King Bagdemagus, that was foul rebuked at the last tournament. I know your father well, said Sir Launcelot, for a noble king and a good knight, and by the faith of my body, ye shall have my body ready to do your father and you service at that day. Sir, she said, gramercy, and to-morn await ye be ready betimes, and I shall be she that shall deliver you and take you your armour and your horse, shield and spear, and hereby, within this ten mile, is an abbey of white monks, there I pray you that ye me abide, and thither shall I bring my father unto you. All this shall be done, said Sir Launcelot, as I am true knight.

And so she departed, and came on the morn early, and found him ready; then she brought him out of twelve locks, and brought him unto his armour, and when he was clean armed, she brought him until his own horse, and lightly he saddled him and took a great spear in his hand, and so rode forth, and said, Fair damosel, I shall not fail you, by the grace of God. And so he rode in a great forest all that day and never could find no highway, but the next day he came to the abbey.

And soon as Sir Launcelot came within the abbey yard, the daughter of King Bagdemagus heard a great horse go on the pavement. And she then arose and went unto a window, and there she saw Sir Launcelot, and anon she made men fast to take his horse from him and let lead him into a stable, and himself was led into a fair chamber, and unarmed him, and the lady sent him a long gown, and anon she came herself. And then she made Launcelot passing good cheer, and she said he was the knight in the world was most welcome to her. Then in all haste she sent for her father Bagdemagus that was within twelve mile of that Abbey, and afore even he came, with a fair fellowship of knights with him. And when the king was alighted off his horse he went straight unto Sir Launcelot's chamber and there he found his daughter, and then the king embraced Sir Launcelot in his arms, and either made other good cheer.

Anon Sir Launcelot made his complaint unto the king how he was betrayed, and how his brother Sir Lionel was departed from him he wist not where, and how his daughter had delivered him out of prison; Therefore while I live I shall do her service and all her kindred. Then am I sure of your help, said the king, on Tuesday next coming. Yea, sir, said Sir Launcelot, I shall not fail you, for so I have promised my lady your daughter. But, sir, what knights be they of my lord Arthur's that were with the King of Northgalis? And the king said it was Sir Mador de la Porte, and Sir Mordred and Sir Gahalantine that all forfared my knights, for against them three I nor my knights might bear no strength. Sir, said Sir Launcelot, as I hear say that the tournament shall be here within this three mile of this abbey, ye shall send unto me three knights of yours, such as ye trust, and look that the three knights have all white shields, and I also, and no painture on the shields, and we four will come out of a little wood in midst of both parties, and we shall fall in the front of our enemies and grieve them that we may; and thus shall I not be known what knight I am.

So they took their rest that night, and this was on the Sunday, and so the king departed, and sent unto Sir Launcelot three knights with the four white shields. And on the Tuesday they lodged them in a little leaved wood beside there the tournament should be. And there were scaffolds and holes that lords and ladies might behold and to give the prize. Then came into the field the King of Northgalis with eight score helms. And then the three knights of Arthur's stood by themselves. Then came into the field King Bagdemagus with four score of helms. And then they feutred their spears, and came together with a great dash, and there were slain of knights at the first recounter twelve of King Bagdemagus' party, and six of the King of Northgalis' party, and King Bagdemagus' party was far set aback.

With that came Sir Launcelot du Lake, and he thrust in with his spear in the thickest of the press, and there he smote down with one spear five knights, and of four of them he brake their backs. And in that throng he smote down the king of Northgalis, and brake his thigh in that fall. All this doing of Sir Launcelot saw the three knights of Arthur's. Yonder is a shrewd guest, said Sir Mador de la Porte, therefore have here once at him. So they encountered, and Sir Launcelot bare him down horse and man, so that his shoulder went out of lith. Now befalleth it to me to joust, said Mordred, for Sir Mador hath a sore fall. Sir Launcelot was ware of him, and gat a great spear in his hand, and met him, and Sir Mordred brake a spear upon him, and Sir Launcelot gave him such a buffet that the arson of his saddle brake, and so he flew over his horse's tail, that his helm butted into the earth a foot and more, that nigh his neck was broken, and there he lay long in a swoon.

Then came in Sir Gahalantine with a great spear and Launcelot against him, with all their strength that they might drive, that both their spears to-brast even to their hands, and then they flang out with their swords and gave many a grim stroke. Then was Sir Launcelot wroth out of measure, and then he smote Sir Gahalantine on the helm that his nose brast out on blood, and ears and mouth both, and therewith his head hung low. And therewith his horse ran away with him, and he fell down to the earth. Anon therewithal Sir Launcelot gat a great spear in his hand, and or ever that great spear brake, he bare down to the earth sixteen knights, some horse and man, and some the man and not the horse, and there was none but that he hit surely, he bare none arms that day. And then he gat another great spear, and smote down twelve knights, and the most part of them never throve after. And then the knights of the King of Northgalis would joust no more. And there the gree was given to King Bagdemagus.

HOW SIR LAUNCELOT FOUGHT WITH SIR TURQUINE AND SLEW HIM, AND SENT SIR GAHERIS TO DELIVER ALL SIR TURQUINE'S PRISONERS. So either party departed unto his own place, and Sir Launcelot rode forth with King Bagdemagus unto his castle, and there he had passing good cheer both with the king and with his daughter, and they proffered him great gifts. And on the morn he took his leave, and told the king that he would go and seek his brother Sir Lionel, that went from him when that he slept; so he took his horse, and betaught them all to God. And there he said unto the king's daughter, If ye have need any time of my service I pray you let me have knowledge, and I shall not fail you as I am true knight. And so Sir Launcelot departed, and by adventure he came into the same forest there he was taken sleeping. And in the midst of a highway he met a damosel riding on a white palfrey, and there either saluted other. Fair damosel, said Sir Launcelot, know ye in this country any adventures?

Sir knight, said that damosel, here are adventures near hand, an thou durst prove them. Why should I not prove adventures? said Sir Launcelot, for that cause come I hither. Well, said she, thou seemest well to be a good knight, and if thou dare meet with a good knight, I shall bring thee where is the best knight, and the mightiest that ever thou found, so thou wilt tell me what is thy name, and what knight thou art. Damosel, as for to tell thee my name I take no great force; truly my name is Sir Launcelot du Lake. Sir, thou beseemest well, here be adventures by that fall for thee, for hereby dwelleth a knight that will not be overmatched for no man I know but ye overmatch him, and his name is Sir Turquine. And, as I understand, he hath in his prison, of Arthur's court, good knights three score and four, that he hath won with his own hands. But when ye have done that journey ye shall promise me as ye are a true knight for to go with me, and to help me and other damosels that are distressed daily with a false knight. All your intent, damosel, and desire I will fulfil, so ye will bring me unto this knight. Now, fair knight, come on your way; and so she brought him unto the ford and the tree where hung the basin.

So Sir Launcelot let his horse drink, and then he beat on the basin with the butt of his spear so hard with all his might till the bottom fell out, and long he did so, but he saw nothing. Then he rode endlong the gates of that manor nigh half-an-hour. And then was he ware of a great knight that drove an horse afore him, and overthwart the horse there lay an armed knight bound. And ever as they came near and near, Sir Launcelot thought he should know him. Then Sir Launcelot was ware that it was Sir Gaheris, Gawaine's brother, a knight of the Table Round.

Now, fair damosel, said Sir Launcelot, I see yonder cometh a knight fast bounden that is a fellow of mine, and brother he is unto Sir Gawaine. And at the first beginning I promise you, by the leave of God, to rescue that knight; but if his master sit better in the saddle I shall deliver all the prisoners that he hath out of danger, for I am sure he hath two brethren of mine prisoners with him. By that time that either had seen other, they gripped their spears unto them. Now, fair knight, said Sir Launcelot, put that wounded knight off the horse, and let him rest awhile, and let us two prove our strengths; for as it is informed me, thou doest and hast done great despite and shame unto knights of the Round Table, and therefore now defend thee. An thou be of the Table Round, said Turquine, I defy thee and all thy fellowship. That is overmuch said, said Sir Launcelot.

And then they put their spears in the rests, and came together with their horses as fast as they might run, and either smote other in midst of their shields, that both their horses' backs brast under them, and the knights were both astonied. And as soon as they might avoid their horses, they took their shields afore them, and drew out their swords, and came together eagerly, and either gave other many strong strokes, for there might neither shields nor harness hold their strokes. And so within a while they had both grimly wounds, and bled passing grievously. Thus they fared two hours or more trasing and rasing either other, where they might hit any bare place.

Then at the last they were breathless both, and stood leaning on their swords. Now, fellow, said Sir Turquine, hold thy hand a while, and tell me what I shall ask thee. Say on. Then Turquine said, Thou art the biggest man that ever I met withal, and the best breathed, and like one knight that I hate above all other knights; so be it that thou be not he I will lightly accord with thee, and for thy love I will deliver all the prisoners that I have, that is three score and four, so thou wilt tell me thy name. And thou and I we will be fellows together, and never to fail thee while that I live. It is well said, said Sir Launcelot, but sithen it is so that I may have thy friendship, what knight is he that thou so hatest above all other? Faithfully, said Sir Turquine, his name is Sir Launcelot du Lake, for he slew my brother, Sir Carados, at the dolorous tower, that was one of the best knights alive; and therefore him I except of all knights, for may I once meet with him, the one of us shall make an end of other, I make mine avow. And for Sir Launcelot's sake I have slain an hundred good knights, and as many I have maimed all utterly that they might never after help themselves, and many have died in prison, and yet have I three score and four, and all shall be delivered so thou wilt tell me thy name, so be it that thou be not Sir Launcelot.

Now see I well, said Sir Launcelot, that such a man I might be, I might have peace, and such a man I might be, that there should be war mortal betwixt us. And now, sir knight, at thy request I will that thou wit and know that I am Launcelot du Lake, King Ban's son of Benwick, and very knight of the Table Round. And now I defy thee, and do thy best. Ah, said Turquine, Launcelot, thou art unto me most welcome that ever was knight, for we shall never depart till the one of us be dead. Then they hurtled together as two wild bulls, rashing and lashing with their shields and swords, that sometime they fell both over their noses. Thus they fought still two hours and more, and never would have rest, and Sir Turquine gave Sir Launcelot many wounds that all the ground thereas they fought was all bespeckled with blood.

Then at the last Sir Turquine waxed faint, and gave somewhat aback, and bare his shield low for weariness. That espied Sir Launcelot, and leapt upon him fiercely and gat him by the beaver of his helmet, and plucked him down on his knees, and anon he raced off his helm, and smote his neck in sunder. And when Sir Launcelot had done this, he went unto the damosel and said, Damosel, I am ready to go with you where ye will have me, but I have no horse. Fair sir, said she, take this wounded knight's horse and send him into this manor, and command him to deliver all the prisoners. So Sir Launcelot went unto Gaheris, and prayed him not to be aggrieved for to lend him his horse. Nay, fair lord, said Gaheris, I will that ye take my horse at your own commandment, for ye have both saved me and my horse, and this day I say ye are the best knight in the world, for ye have slain this day in my sight the mightiest man and the best knight except you that ever I saw, and, fair sir, said Gaheris, I pray you tell me your name. Sir, my name is Sir Launcelot du Lake, that ought to help you of right for King Arthur's sake, and in especial for my lord Sir Gawaine's sake, your own dear brother; and when that ye come within yonder manor, I am sure ye shall find there many knights of the Round Table, for I have seen many of their shields that I know on yonder tree. Wherefore I pray you greet them all from me, and say that I bid them take such stuff there as they find, and that in any wise my brethren go unto the court and abide me there till that I come, for by the feast of Pentecost I cast me to be there, for as at this time I must ride with this damosel for to save my promise.

And so he departed from Gaheris, and Gaheris went into the manor, and there he found a yeoman porter keeping there many keys. Anon withal Sir Gaheris threw the porter unto the ground and took the keys from him, and hastily he opened the prison door, and there he let out all the prisoners, and every man loosed other of their bonds. And when they saw Sir Gaheris, all they thanked him, for they weened that he was wounded. Not so, said Gaheris, it was Launcelot that slew him worshipfully with his own hands. I saw it with mine own eyes. And he greeteth you all well, and prayeth you to haste you to the court.

Then all those knights sought the house thereas the armour was, and then they armed them, and every knight found his own horse, and all that ever longed unto him. And when this was done, there came a forester with four horses laden with fat venison. Anon, Sir Kay said, Here is good meat for us for one meal, for we had not many a day no good repast. And so that venison was roasted, baken, and sodden, and so after supper some abode there all night, but Sir Lionel and Ector de Maris and Sir Kay rode after Sir Launcelot to find him if they might.

HOW SIR LAUNCELOT RODE WITH A DAMOSEL AND SLEW A KNIGHT THAT DISTRESSED ALL LADIES AND HOW HE DELIVERED SIR KAY. Now turn we unto Sir Launcelot, that rode with the damosel in a fair highway. Sir, said the damosel, here by this way haunteth a knight that distresseth all ladies and gentlewomen, and at the least he robbeth them or lieth by them. What, said Sir Launcelot, is he a thief and a knight and a ravisher of women? he doth shame unto the order of knighthood, and contrary unto his oath; it is pity that he liveth. But, fair damosel, ye shall ride on afore, yourself, and I will keep myself in covert, and if that he trouble you or distress you I shall be your rescue and learn him to be ruled as a knight.

So the maid rode on by the way a soft ambling pace, and within a while came out that knight on horseback out of the wood, and his page with him, and there he put the damosel from her horse, and then she cried. With that came Launcelot as fast as he might till he came to that knight, saying, O thou false knight and traitor unto knighthood, who did learn thee to distress ladies and gentlewomen? When the knight saw Sir Launcelot thus rebuking him he answered not, but drew his sword and rode unto Sir Launcelot, and Sir Launcelot threw his spear from him, and drew out his sword, and struck him such a buffet on the helmet that he clave his head and neck unto the throat. Now hast thou thy payment that long thou hast deserved! That is truth, said the damosel, for like as Sir Turquine watched to destroy knights, so did this knight attend to destroy and distress ladies, damosels, and gentlewomen, and his name was Sir Peris de Forest Savage. Now, damosel, said Sir Launcelot, will ye any more service of me? Nay, sir, she said, at this time, but almighty Jesu preserve you wheresomever ye ride or go, for the curteist knight thou art, and meekest unto all ladies and gentlewomen, that now liveth.

Then Sir Launcelot mounted upon his horse, and rode into many strange and wild countries, and through many waters and valleys, and evil was he lodged. And at the last by fortune him happened, against a night, to come to a fair courtelage, and therein he found an old gentlewoman that lodged him with good will, and there he had good cheer for him and his horse. And when time was, his host brought him into a fair garret, over the gate, to his bed. There Sir Launcelot unarmed him, and set his harness by him, and went to bed, and anon he fell asleep. So, soon after, there came one on horseback, and knocked at the gate in great haste, and when Sir Launcelot heard this, he arose up and looked out at the window, and saw by the moonlight three knights came riding after that one man, and all three lashed on him at once with swords, and that one knight turned on them knightly again, and defended him. Truly, said Sir Launcelot, yonder one knight shall I help, for it were shame for me to see three knights on one, and if he be slain I am partner of his death; and therewith he took his harness, and went out at a window by a sheet down to the four knights, and then Sir Launcelot said on high, Turn you knights unto me, and leave your fighting with that knight. And then they all three left Sir Kay, and turned unto Sir Launcelot, and there began great battle, for they alighted all three, and struck many great strokes at Sir Launcelot, and assailed him on every side. Then Sir Kay dressed him for to have holpen Sir Launcelot. Nay, sir, said he, I will none of your help; therefore as ye will have my help, let me alone with them. Sir Kay, for the pleasure of the knight, suffered him for to do his will, and so stood aside. And then anon within six strokes, Sir Launcelot had stricken them to the earth.

And then they all three cried: Sir knight, we yield us

unto you as a man of might makeless. As to that, said Sir Launcelot, I will not take your yielding unto me. But so that ye will yield you unto Sir Kay the Seneschal, on that covenant I will save your lives, and else not. Fair knight, said they, that were we loath to do; for as for Sir Kay, we chased him hither, and had overcome him had not ye been, therefore to yield us unto him it were no reason. Well, as to that, said Launcelot, advise you well, for ye may choose whether ye will die or live, for an ye be yolden it shall be unto Sir Kay. Fair knight, then they said, in saving of our lives we will do as thou commandest us. Then shall ye, said Sir Launcelot, on Whitsunday next coming, go unto the court of King Arthur, and there shall ye yield you unto Queen Guenever, and put you all three in her grace and mercy, and say that Sir Kay sent you thither to be her prisoners. Sir, they said, it shall be done by the faith of our bodies, an we be living, and there they swore every knight upon his sword. And so Sir Launcelot suffered them so to depart. And then Sir Launcelot knocked at the gate with the pommel of his sword, and with that came his host, and in they entered Sir Kay and he. Sir, said his host, I weened ye had been in your bed. So I was, said Sir Launcelot, but I rose and leapt out at my window for to help an old fellow of mine. And so when they came nigh the light, Sir Kay knew well that it was Sir Launcelot, and therewith he kneeled down and thanked him of all his kindness that he had holpen him twice from the death. Sir, he said, I have nothing done but that I ought to do, and ye are welcome, and here shall ye repose you and take your rest.

So when Sir Kay was unarmed, he asked after meat; so there was meat fetched him, and he ate strongly. And when he had supped they went to their beds and were lodged together in one bed. On the morn Sir Launcelot arose early, and left Sir Kay sleeping, and Sir Launcelot took Sir Kay's armour and his shield, and armed him, and so he went to the stable, and took his horse, and took his leave of his host, and so he departed. Then soon after arose Sir Kay and missed Sir Launcelot. And then he espied that he had his armour and his horse. Now by my faith I know well that he will grieve some of the court of King Arthur; for on him knights will be bold, and deem that it is I, and that will beguile them. And because of his armour and shield I am sure I shall ride in peace. And then soon after departed Sir Kay and thanked his host.

HOW SIR LAUNCELOT RODE DISGUISED IN SIR KAY'S HARNESS AND OVERTHREW FOUR KNIGHTS OF THE ROUND TABLE, AND HOW HE WAS REQUIRED OF A DAMOSEL TO HEAL HER BROTHER. Now turn we unto Sir Launcelot that rode into a deep forest, and thereby in a slade he saw four knights hoving under an oak, and they were of Arthur's court, one was Sir Sagramour le Desirous, and Ector de Maris, and Sir Gawaine, and Sir Uwaine. Anon as these four knights had espied Sir Launcelot they weened by his arms it had been Sir Kay. Now by my faith, said Sir Sagramour, I will prove Sir Kay's might, and gat his spear in his hand, and came toward Sir Launcelot. Therewith Sir Launcelot was ware and knew him well, and feutred his spear against him, and smote Sir Sagramour so sore that horse and man fell both to the earth. Lo, my fellows, said Sir Ector, yonder ye may see what a buffet he hath; that knight is much bigger than ever was Sir Kay. Now shall ye see what I may do to him. So Sir Ector gat his spear in his hand and galloped toward Sir Launcelot, and Sir Launcelot smote him through the shield and shoulder that man and horse went to the earth, and ever his spear held.

By my faith, said Sir Uwaine, yonder is a strong knight, and I am sure he hath slain Sir Kay; and I see by his great strength it will be hard to match him. And therewithal, Sir Uwaine gat his spear in his hand and rode toward Sir Launcelot, and Sir Launcelot knew him well, and so he met him on the plain, and gave him such a buffet that he was astonied, that long he wist not where he was. Now see I well, said Sir Gawaine, I must encounter with that knight. Then he dressed his shield and gat a good spear in his hand, and Sir Launcelot knew him well; and then they let run their horses with all their mights, and either knight smote other in midst of the shield. But Sir Gawaine's spear to-brast, and Sir Launcelot charged so sore upon him that his horse reversed up-so-down. And much sorrow had Sir Gawaine to avoid his horse, and so Sir Launcelot passed on a pace and smiled, and said, God give him joy that this spear made, for there came never a better in my hand.

Then the four knights went each one to other and comforted each other. What say ye by this guest? said Sir Gawaine, that one spear hath felled us all four. We commend him unto the devil, they said all, for he is a man of great might. Ye may well say it, said Sir Gawaine, that he is a man of might, for I dare lay my head it is Sir Launcelot, I know it by his riding. Let him go, said Sir Gawaine, for when we come to the court then shall we wit; and then had they much sorrow to get their horses again.

Now leave we there and speak of Sir Launcelot that rode a great while in a deep forest, where he saw a black brachet, seeking in manner as it had been in the feute of an hurt deer. And therewith he rode after the brachet, and he saw lie on the ground a large feute of blood. And then Sir Launcelot rode after. And ever the brachet looked behind her, and so she went through a great marsh, and ever Sir Launcelot followed. And then was he ware of an old manor, and thither ran the brachet, and so over the bridge. So Sir Launcelot rode over that bridge that was old and feeble; and when he came in midst of a great hall, there he saw lie a dead knight that was a seemly man, and that brachet licked his wounds. And therewithal came out a lady weeping and wringing her hands; and then she said, O knight, to much sorrow hast thou brought me. Why say ye so? said Sir Launcelot, I did never this knight no harm, for hither by feute of blood this brachet brought me; and therefore, fair lady, be not displeased with me, for I am full sore aggrieved of your grievance. Truly, sir, she said, I trow it be not ye that hath slain my husband, for he that did that deed is sore wounded, and he is never likely to recover, that shall I ensure him. What was your husband's name? said Sir Launcelot. Sir, said she, his name was called Sir Gilbert the Bastard, one of the best knights of the world, and he that hath slain him I know not his name. Now God send you better comfort, said Sir Launcelot; and so he departed and went into the forest again, and there he met with a damosel, the which knew him well, and she said aloud, Well be ye found, my lord; and now

I require thee, on thy knighthood, help my brother that is sore wounded, and never stinteth bleeding; for this day he fought with Sir Gilbert the Bastard and slew him in plain battle, and there was my brother sore wounded, and there is a lady, a sorceress, that dwelleth in a castle here beside, and this day she told me my brother's wounds should never be whole till I could find a knight that would go into the Chapel Perilous, and there he should find a sword and a bloody cloth that the wounded knight was lapped in, and a piece of that cloth and sword should heal my brother's wounds, so that his wounds were searched with the sword and the cloth. This is a marvellous thing, said Sir Launcelot, but what is your brother's name? Sir, she said, his name was Sir Meliot de Logres. That me repenteth, said Sir Launcelot, for he is a fellow of the Table Round, and to his help I will do my power. Then, sir, said she, follow even this highway, and it will bring you into the Chapel Perilous; and here I shall abide till God send you here again, and, but you speed, I know no knight living that may achieve that adventure.

HOW SIR LAUNCELOT CAME INTO THE CHAPEL PERILOUS AND HOW HE HEALED THE DAMOSEL'S BROTHER AND RETURNED TO KING ARTHUR'S COURT. Right so Sir Launcelot departed, and when he came unto the Chapel Perilous he alighted down, and tied his horse unto a little gate. And as soon as he was within the churchyard he saw on the front of the chapel many fair rich shields turned up-so-down, and many of the shields Sir Launcelot had seen knights bear beforehand. With that he saw by him there stand a thirty great knights, more by a yard than any man that ever he had seen, and all those grinned and gnashed at Sir Launcelot. And when he saw their countenance he dreaded him sore, and so put his shield afore him, and took his sword ready in his hand, ready unto battle, and they were all armed in black harness ready with their shields and their swords drawn. And when Sir Launcelot would have gone throughout them, they scattered on every side of him, and gave him the way, and therewith he waxed all bold, and entered into the chapel, and then he saw no light but a dim lamp burning, and then was he ware of a corpse covered with a cloth of silk. Then Sir Launcelot stooped down, and cut a piece away of that cloth, and then it fared under him as the earth had quaked a little; therewithal he feared. And then he saw a fair sword lie by the dead knight, and that he gat in his hand and hied him out of the chapel.

Anon as ever he was in the chapel yard all the knights spake to him with a grimly voice, and said, Knight, Sir Launcelot, lay that sword from thee or else thou shalt die. Whether that I live or die, said Sir Launcelot, with no great word get ye it again, therefore fight for it an ye list. Then right so he passed throughout them, and beyond the chapel yard there met him a fair damosel, and said, Sir Launcelot, leave that sword behind thee, or thou wilt die for it. I leave it not, said Sir Launcelot, for no treaties. No, said she, an thou didst leave that sword, Queen Guenever should thou never see. Then were I a fool an I would leave this sword, said Launcelot. Now, gentle knight, said the damosel, I require thee to kiss me but once. Nay, said Sir Launcelot, that God me forbid. Well, sir, said she, an thou hadst kissed me thy life days had been done, but now, alas, she said, I have lost all my labour, for I ordained this chapel for thy sake, and for Sir Gawaine. And once I had Sir Gawaine within me, and at that time he fought with that knight that lieth there dead in yonder chapel, Sir Gilbert the Bastard; and at that time he smote the left hand off of Sir Gilbert the Bastard. And, Sir Launcelot, now I tell thee, I have loved thee this seven year, but there may no woman have thy love but Queen Guenever. But sithen I may not rejoice thee to have thy body alive, I had kept no more joy in this world but to have thy body dead. Then would I have balmed it and preserved it, and so have kept it my life days, and daily I should have clipped thee, and kissed thee, in despite of Queen Guenever. Ye say well, said Sir Launcelot, Jesu preserve me from your subtle crafts. And therewithal he took his horse and so departed from her. And as the book saith, when Sir Launcelot was departed she took such sorrow that she died within a fourteen night, and her name was Hellawes the sorceress, Lady of the Castle Nigramous.

Anon Sir Launcelot met with the damosel, Sir Meliot's sister. And when she saw him she clapped her hands, and wept for joy. And then they rode unto a castle thereby where lay Sir Meliot. And anon as Sir Launcelot saw him he knew him, but he was passing pale, as the earth, for bleeding. When Sir Meliot saw Sir Launcelot he kneeled upon his knees and cried on high: O lord Sir Launcelot, help me! Anon Sir Launcelot leapt unto him and touched his wounds with Sir Gilbert's sword. And then he wiped his wounds with a part of the bloody cloth that Sir Gilbert was wrapped in, and anon an wholer man in his life was he never. And then there was great joy between them, and they made Sir Launcelot all the cheer that they might, and so on the morn Sir Launcelot took his leave, and bade Sir Meliot hie him to the court of my lord Arthur, and there by the grace of God ye shall find me. And therewith they departed.

Then Sir Launcelot du Lake came home two days afore the Feast of Pentecost; and the king and all the court were passing fain of his coming. And when Sir Gawaine, Sir Uwaine, Sir Sagramore, Sir Ector de Maris, saw Sir Launcelot in Kay's armour, then they wist well it was he that smote them down all with one spear. Then there was laughing and smiling among them. And ever now and now came all the knights home that Sir Turquine had prisoners, and they all honoured and worshipped Sir Launcelot.

Then Sir Kay told the king how Sir Launcelot had rescued him when he should have been slain, and how he made the knights yield them to me, and not to him. And there they were all three, and bare record. And in truth, said Sir Kay, because Sir Launcelot took my harness and left me his I rode in good peace, and no man would have ado with me.

And then Sir Meliot de Logres came home, and told the king how Sir Launcelot had saved him from the death. And so at that time Sir Launcelot had the greatest name of any knight of the world, and most he was honoured of high and low.

OF SIR GARETH

HOW BEAUMAINS CAME TO KING ARTHUR'S COURT AND ASKED THREE GIFTS OF KING ARTHUR, AND OF A DAMOSEL THAT DESIRED A KNIGHT TO FIGHT FOR A LADY, AND HOW BEAUMAINS DESIRED THE BATTLE. When Arthur held his Round Table most plenour, it fortuned that he commanded that the high feast of Pentecost should be holden at a city and a castle, the which in those days was called Kynke Kenadonne, upon the sands that marched nigh Wales. So ever the king had a custom that at the feast of Pentecost in especial, afore other feasts in the year, he would not go that day to meat until he had heard or seen of a great marvel. And for that custom all manner of strange adventures came before Arthur as at that feast before all other feasts. And so Sir Gawaine, a little to-fore noon of the day of Pentecost, espied at a window three men upon horseback, and a dwarf on foot, and so the three men alighted, and the dwarf kept their horses, and one of the three men was higher than the other twain by a foot and an half. Then Sir Gawaine went unto the king and said, Sir, go to your meat, for here at the hand come strange adventures. So Arthur went unto his meat with many other kings.

Right so came into the hall two men well beseen and richly, and upon their shoulders there leaned the goodliest young man and the fairest that ever they all saw, and he was large and long, and broad in the shoulders, and well visaged, and the fairest and the largest handed that ever man saw, but he fared as though he might not go nor bear himself but if he leaned upon their shoulders. Anon as Arthur saw him there was made peace and room, and right so they went with him unto the high dais, without saying of any words. Then this much young man pulled him aback, and easily stretched up straight, saying, King Arthur, God you bless and all your fair fellowship, and in especial the fellowship of the Table Round. And for this cause I am come hither, to pray you and require you to give me three gifts, and they shall not be unreasonably asked, but that ye may worshipfully and honourably grant them me, and to you no great hurt nor loss. And the first don and gift I will ask now, and the other two gifts I will ask this day twelvemonth, wheresomever ye hold your high feast. Now ask, said Arthur, and ye shall have your asking.

Now, sir, this is my petition for this feast, that ye will give me meat and drink sufficiently for this twelvemonth, and at that day I will ask mine other two gifts.

My fair son, said Arthur, ask better, I counsel thee, for this is but a simple asking; for my heart giveth me to thee greatly, that thou art come of men of worship, and greatly my conceit faileth me but thou shalt prove a man of right great worship. Sir, he said, thereof be as it be may, I have asked that I will ask. Well, said the king, ye shall have meat and drink enough; I never defended that none, neither my friend nor my foe. But what is thy name I would wit? I cannot tell you, said he. That is marvel, said the king, that thou knowest not thy name, and thou art the goodliest young man that ever I saw. Then the king betook him to Sir Kay the steward, and charged him that he should give him of all manner of meats and drinks of the best, and also that he had all manner of finding as though he were a lord's son. That shall little need, said Sir Kay, to do such cost upon him; for I dare undertake he is a villain born, and never will make man, for an he had come of gentlemen he would have asked of you horse and armour, but such as he is, so he asketh. And sithen he hath no name, I shall give him a name that shall be Beaumains, that is Fair-hands, and into the kitchen I shall bring him, and there he shall have fat brose every day, that he shall be as fat by the twelve-months' end as a pork hog. Right so the two men departed and beleft him to Sir Kay, that scorned him and mocked him.

Thereat was Sir Gawaine wroth, and in especial Sir Launcelot bade Sir Kay leave his mocking, for I dare lay my head he shall prove a man of great worship. Let be, said Sir Kay, it may not be by no reason, for as he is, so he hath asked.

And so Sir Kay bade get him a place, and sit down to meat; so Beaumains went to the hall door, and set him down among boys and lads, and there he ate sadly. And then Sir Launcelot after meat bade him come to his chamber, and there he should have meat and drink enough. And so did Sir Gawaine: but he refused them all; he would do none other but as Sir Kay commanded him, for no proffer.

But as touching Sir Gawaine, he had reason to proffer him lodging, meat, and drink, for that proffer came of his blood, for he was nearer kin to him than he wist. But that as Sir Launcelot did was of his great gentleness and courtesy.

So thus he was put into the kitchen, and lay nightly as the boys of the kitchen did. And so he endured all that twelvemonth, and never displeased man nor child, but always he was meek and mild. But ever when that he saw any jousting of knights, that would he see an he might. And ever Sir Launcelot would give him gold to spend, and clothes, and so did Sir Gawaine, and where there were any masteries done, thereat would he be, and there might none cast bar nor stone to him by two yards. Then would Sir Kay say, How liketh you my boy of the kitchen? So it passed on till the feast of Whitsuntide. And at that time the king held it at Carlion in the most royallest wise that might be, like as he did yearly. But the king would no meat eat upon the Whitsunday, until he heard some adventures. Then came there a squire to the king and said, Sir, ye may go to your meat, for here cometh a damosel with some strange adventures. Then was the king glad and sat him down.

Right so there came a damosel into the hall and saluted the king, and prayed him of succour. For whom? said the king, what is the adventure?

Sir, she said, I have a lady of great worship and renown, and she is besieged with a tyrant, so that she may not out of her castle; and because here are called the noblest knights of the world, I come to you to pray you of succour. What hight your lady, and where dwelleth she, and who is she, and what is his name that hath besieged her? Sir king, she said, as for my lady's name that shall not ye know for me as at this time, but I let you wit she is a lady of great worship and of great lands; and as for the tyrant that besiegeth her and destroyeth her lands, he is called the Red Knight of the Red Launds. I know him not, said the king. Sir, said Sir Gawaine, I know him well, for he is one of the periloust knights of the world; men say that he hath seven men's strength, and from him I escaped once full hard with my life. Fair damosel, said the king, there be knights here would do their power for to rescue your lady, but because you will not tell her name, nor where she dwelleth, therefore none of my knights that here be now shall go with you by my will. Then must I speak further, said the damosel.

With these words came before the king Beaumains, while the damosel was there, and thus he said, Sir king, God thank you, I have been this twelvemonth in your kitchen, and have had my full sustenance, and now I will ask my two gifts that be behind. Ask, upon my peril, said the king. Sir, this shall be my two gifts, first that ye will grant me to have this adventure of the damosel, for it belongeth unto me. Thou shalt have it, said the king, I grant it thee. Then, sir, this is the other gift, that ye shall bid Launcelot du Lake to make me knight, for of him I will be made knight and else of none. And when I am passed I pray you let him ride after me, and make me knight when I require him. All this shall be done, said the king. Fie on thee, said the damosel, shall I have none but one that is your kitchen page? Then was she wroth, and took her horse and departed. And with that there came one to Beaumains and told him his horse and armour was come for him; and there was the dwarf come with all thing that him needed, in the richest manner; thereat all the court had much marvel from whence came all that gear. So when he was armed there was none but few so goodly a man as he was; and right so he came into the hall and took his leave of King Arthur, and Sir Gawaine, and Sir Launcelot, and prayed that he would hie after him, and so departed and rode after the damosel.

HOW BEAUMAINS DEPARTED, AND HOW HE GAT OF SIR KAY A SPEAR AND A SHIELD, AND HOW HE JOUSTED WITH SIR LAUNCELOT, AND OF HIM WAS DUBBED KNIGHT. But there went many after to behold how well he was horsed and trapped in cloth of gold, but he had neither shield nor spear. Then Sir Kay said all open in the hall, I will ride after my boy in the kitchen, to wit whether he will know me for his better. Said Sir Launcelot and Sir Gawaine, Yet abide at home. So Sir Kay made him ready and took his horse and his spear, and rode after him. And right as Beaumains overtook the damosel, right so came Sir Kay and said, Beaumains, what, sir, know ye not me? Then he turned his horse, and knew it was Sir Kay, that had done him all the despite as ye have heard afore. Yea, said Beaumains, I know you for an ungentle knight of the court, and therefore beware of me. Therewith Sir Kay put his spear in the rest, and ran straight upon him; and Beaumains came as fast upon him with his sword in his hand, and so he put away his spear with his sword, and with a foin thrust him through the side, that Sir Kay fell down as he had been dead; and he alighted down and took Sir Kay's shield and his spear, and stert upon his own horse and rode his way.

All that saw Sir Launcelot, and so did the damosel. And then he bade his dwarf stert upon Sir Kay's horse, and so he did. By that Sir Launcelot was come, then he proffered Sir Launcelot to joust; and either made them ready, and they came together so fiercely that either bare down other to the earth, and sore were they bruised. Then Sir Launcelot arose and helped him from his horse. And then Beaumains threw his shield from him, and proffered to fight with Sir Launcelot on foot; and so they rashed together like boars, tracing, racing, and foining to the mountenance of an hour; and Sir Launcelot felt him so big that he marvelled of his strength, for he fought more liker a giant than a knight, and that his fighting was durable and passing perilous. For Sir Launcelot had so much ado with him that he dreaded himself to be shamed, and said, Beaumains, fight not so sore, your quarrel and mine is not so great but we may leave off. Truly that is truth, said Beaumains, but it doth me good to feel your might, and yet, my lord, I showed not the utterance.

In God's name, said Sir Launcelot, for I promise you, by the faith of my body, I had as much to do as I might to save myself from you unshamed, and therefore have ye no doubt of none earthly knight. Hope ye so that I may any while stand a proved knight? said Beaumains. Yea, said Launcelot, do as ye have done, and I shall be your warrant. Then, I pray you, said Beaumains, give me the order of knighthood. Then must ye tell me your name, said Launcelot, and of what kin ye be born. Sir, so that ye will not discover me I shall, said Beaumains. Nay, said Sir Launcelot, and that I promise you by the faith of my body, until it be openly known. Then, sir, he said, my name is Gareth, and brother unto Sir Gawaine of father and mother. Ah, sir, said Sir Launcelot, I am more gladder of you than I was; for ever me thought ye should be of a great blood, and that ye came not to the court neither for meat nor for drink. And then Sir Launcelot gave him the order of knighthood, and then Sir Gareth prayed him for to depart and let him go.

So Sir Launcelot departed from him and came to Sir Kay, and made him to be borne home upon his shield, and so he was healed hard with the life; and all men scorned Sir Kay, and in especial Sir Gawaine and Sir Launcelot; and so we leave Sir Kay and turn we unto Beaumains.

When he had overtaken the damosel, anon she said, What dost thou here? thou stinkest all of the kitchen, thy clothes be bawdy of the grease and tallow that thou gainest in King Arthur's kitchen; weenest thou, said she, that I allow thee, for yonder knight that thou killest. Nay truly, for thou slewest him unhappily and cowardly; therefore turn again, bawdy kitchen page, I know thee well, for Sir Kay named thee Beaumains. What art thou but a lusk and a turner of broaches and a ladle-washer? Damosel, said Beaumains, say to me what ye will, I will not go from you whatsomever ye say, for I have undertaken to King Arthur for to achieve your adventure, and so shall I finish it to the end, either I shall die therefore.

So thus as they rode in the wood, there came a man flying all that ever he might. Whither wilt thou? said Beaumains. O lord, he said, help me, for here by in a slade are six thieves that have taken my lord and bound him, so I am afeard lest they will slay him. Bring me thither, said Beaumains. And so they rode together until they came there as was the knight bounden; and then he rode unto them, and struck one unto the death, and then another, and at the third stroke he slew the third thief, and then the other three fled. And he rode after them, and he overtook them; and then those three thieves turned again and assailed Beaumains hard, but at the last he slew them, and returned and unbound the knight. And the knight thanked him, and prayed him to ride with him to his castle there a little beside, and he should worshipfully reward him for his good deeds. Sir, said Beaumains, I will no reward have: I was this day made knight of noble Sir Launcelot, and therefore I will no reward have, but God reward me. And also I must follow this damosel.

And when he came nigh her she bade him ride from her, For thou smellest all of the kitchen: weenest thou that I have joy of thee, for all this deed that thou hast done is but mishapped thee: but thou shalt see a sight shall make thee turn again, and that lightly. Then the same knight which was rescued of the thieves rode after that damosel, and prayed her to lodge with him all that night. And because it was near night the damosel rode with him to his castle, and there they had great cheer, and at supper the knight sat Sir Beaumains afore the damosel. Fie, fie, said she, Sir knight, ye are uncourteous to set a kitchen page afore me; him beseemeth better to stick a swine than to sit afore a damosel of high parage. Then the knight was ashamed at her words, and took him up, and set him at a sideboard, and set himself afore him, and so all that night they had good cheer and merry rest.

HOW BEAUMAINS FOUGHT AND SLEW TWO KNIGHTS AT A PASSAGE, AND HOW HE SLEW ALSO THE KNIGHT OF THE BLACK LAUNDS. And on the morn the damosel and he took their leave and thanked the knight, and so departed, and rode on their way until they came to a great forest. And there was a great river and but one passage, and there were ready two knights on the farther side to let them the passage. What sayest thou, said the damosel, wilt thou match yonder knights or turn again? Nay, said Sir Beaumains, I will not turn again an they were six more. And therewithal he rushed into the water, and in midst of the water either brake their spears upon other to their hands, and then they drew their swords, and smote eagerly at other. And at the last Sir Beaumains smote the other upon the helm that his head stonied, and therewithal he fell down in the water, and there was he drowned. And then Sir Beaumains spurred his horse upon the land, where the other knight fell upon him, and brake his spear, and so they drew their swords and fought long together. At the last Sir Beaumains clave his helm and his head down to the shoulders; and so he rode unto the damosel and bade her ride forth on her way.

Alas, she said, that ever a kitchen page should have that fortune to destroy such two doughty knights: thou weenest thou hast done doughtily, that is not so; for the first knight his horse stumbled, and there he was drowned in the water, and never it was by thy force, nor by thy might. And the last knight by mishap thou camest behind him and mishappily thou slew him.

Damosel, said Beaumains, ye may say what ye will, but with whomsomever I have ado withal, I trust to God to serve him or he depart. And therefore I reck not what ye say, so that I may win your lady. Fie, fie, foul kitchen knave, thou shalt see knights that shall abate thy boast. Fair damosel, give me goodly language, and then my care is past, for what knights somever they be, I care not, nor

I doubt them not. Also, said she, I say it for thine avail, yet mayest thou turn again with thy worship; for an thou follow me, thou art but slain, for I see all that ever thou dost is but by misadventure, and not by prowess of thy hands. Well, damosel, ye may say what ye will, but where-somever ye go I will follow you. So this Beaumains rode with that lady till evensong time, and ever she chid him, and would not rest. And they came to a black laund; and there was a black hawthorn, and thereon hung a black banner, and on the other side there hung a black shield, and by it stood a black spear great and long, and a great black horse covered with silk, and a black stone fast by.

There sat a knight all armed in black harness, and his name was the Knight of the Black Laund. Then the damosel, when she saw that knight, she bade Beaumains flee down that valley, for the knight's horse was not saddled. Gramercy, said Beaumains, for always ye would have me a coward. With that the Black Knight, when she came nigh him, spake and said, Damosel, have ye brought this knight of King Arthur to be your champion? Nay, fair knight, said she, this is but a kitchen knave that was fed in King Arthur's kitchen for alms. Why cometh he, said the knight, in such array? it is shame that he beareth you company. Sir, I cannot be delivered of him, said she, for with me he rideth maugre mine head: would that ye should put him from me, other to slay him an ye may, for he is an unhappy knave, and unhappily he hath done this day: through mishap I saw him slay two knights at the passage of the water; and other deeds he did before right marvellous and through un-happiness. That marvelleth me, said the Black Knight, that any man that is of worship will have ado with him.

They know him not, said the damosel, and for because he rideth with me, they ween that he be some man of worship born. That may be, said the Black Knight; howbeit as ye say that he be no man of worship, he is a full likely person, and full like to be a strong man: but thus much shall I grant you, said the Black Knight; I shall put him down upon one foot, and his horse and his harness he shall leave with me, for it were shame to me to do him any more harm.

When Sir Beaumains heard him say thus, he said, Sir knight, thou art full large of my horse and my harness; I let thee wit it cost thee nought, and whether it liketh thee or not, this laund will I pass maugre thine head. And horse nor harness gettest thou none of mine, but if thou win them with thy hands; and therefore let see what thou canst do. Sayest thou that? said the Black Knight, now yield thy lady from thee, for it beseemeth never a kitchen page to ride with such a lady. Thou liest, said Beaumains, I am a gentleman born, and of more high lineage than thou, and that will I prove on thy body.

Then in great wrath they departed with their horses, and came together as it had been the thunder, and the Black Knight's spear brake, and Beaumains thrust him through both his sides, and therewith his spear brake, and the truncheon left still in his side. But nevertheless the Black Knight drew his sword, and smote many eager strokes, and of great might, and hurt Beaumains full sore. But at the last the Black Knight, within an hour and an half, he fell down off his horse in swoon, and there he died. And when Beaumains saw him so well horsed and armed, then he alighted down and armed him in his armour, and so took his horse and rode after the damosel.

When she saw him come nigh, she said, Away, kitchen knave, out of the wind, for the smell of thy bawdy clothes grieveth me. Alas, she said, that ever such a knave should by mishap slay so good a knight as thou hast done, but all this is thine unhappiness. But here by is one shall pay thee all thy payment, and therefore yet I counsel thee, flee. It may happen me, said Beaumains, to be beaten or slain, but I warn you, fair damosel, I will not flee away, nor leave your company, for all that ye can say; for ever ye say that they will kill me or beat me, but howsomever it happeneth I escape, and they lie on the ground.

HOW TWO BROTHERS OF THE BLACK KNIGHT MET WITH BEAUMAINS, AND FOUGHT WITH BEAUMAINS TILL THEY WERE YIELDEN, AND HOW THE DAMOSEL STILL REBUKED HIM. Thus as they rode together, they saw a knight come driving by them all in green, both his horse and his harness; and when he came nigh the damosel, he asked her, Is that my brother the Black Knight that ye have brought with you? Nay, nay, she said, this unhappy kitchen knave hath slain your brother through unhappiness. Alas, said the Green Knight, that is great pity, that so noble a knight as he was should so unhappily be slain, and namely of a knave's hand, as ye say that he is. Ah! traitor, said the Green Knight, thou shalt die for slaying of my brother; he was a full noble knight, and his name was Sir Pereard. I defy thee, said Beaumains, for I let thee wit I slew him knightly and not shamefully.

Therewithal the Green Knight rode unto an horn that was green, and it hung upon a thorn, and there he blew three deadly motes, and there came two damosels and armed him lightly. And then he took a great horse, and a green shield and a green spear. And then they ran together with all their mights, and brake their spears unto their hands. And then they drew their swords, and gave many sad strokes, and either of them wounded other full ill. And at the last, at an overthwart, Beaumains with his horse struck the Green Knight's horse upon the side, that he fell to the earth. And then the Green Knight avoided his horse lightly, and dressed him upon foot. That saw Beaumains, and therewithal he alighted, and they rushed together like two mighty kemps a long while, and sore they bled both. With that came the damosel, and said, My lord the Green Knight, why for shame stand ye so long fighting with the kitchen knave? Alas, it is shame that ever ye were made knight, to see such a lad to match such a knight, as the weed overgrew the corn. Therewith the Green Knight was ashamed, and therewithal he gave a great stroke of might, and clave his shield through. When Beaumains saw his shield cloven asunder he was a little ashamed of that stroke and of her language; and then he gave him such a buffet upon the helm that he fell on his knees. And so suddenly Beaumains pulled him upon the ground grovelling. And then the Green Knight cried him mercy, and yielded him unto Sir Beaumains, and prayed him to slay him not. All is in vain, said Beaumains, for thou shalt die but if this damosel that came with me pray me to save thy life. And therewithal he unlaced his helm like as he would slay him. Fie upon thee, false kitchen page, I will never pray thee to save his life, for I will never be so much in thy danger. Then shall he die, said Beaumains. Not so hardy, thou bawdy knave, said the damosel, that thou slay him. Alas, said the Green knight, suffer me not to die for a fair word may save me. Fair Knight, said the Green Knight, save my life, and I will forgive thee the death of my brother, and for ever to become thy man, and thirty knights that hold of me for ever shall do you service. In the devil's name, said the damosel, that such a bawdy kitchen knave should have thee and thirty knights' service.

Sir knight, said Beaumains, all this availeth thee not, but if my damosel speak with me for thy life. And therewithal he made a semblant to slay him. Let be, said the damosel, thou bawdy knave; slay him not, for an thou do thou shalt repent it. Damosel, said Beaumains, your charge is to me a pleasure, and at your commandment his life shall be saved, and else not. Then he said, Sir knight with the green arms, I release thee quit at this damosel's request, for I will not make her wroth, I will fulfil all that she chargeth me. And then the Green Knight kneeled down, and did him homage with his sword. Then said the damosel, Me repenteth, Green Knight, of your damage, and of your brother's death, the Black Knight, for of your help I had great need, for I dread me sore to pass this forest. Nay, dread you not, said the Green Knight, for ye shall lodge with me this night, and to-morn I shall help you through this forest. So they took their horses and rode to his manor, which was fast there beside.

And ever she rebuked Beaumains, and would not suffer him to sit at her table, but as the Green Knight took him and sat him at a side table. Marvel methinketh, said the Green Knight to the damosel, why ye rebuke this noble knight as ye do, for I warn you, damosel, he is a full noble knight, and I know no knight is able to match him; therefore ye do great wrong to rebuke him, for he shall do you right good service, for whatsomever he maketh himself, ye shall prove at the end that he is come of a noble blood and of king's lineage. Fie, fie, said the damosel, it is shame for you to say of him such worship.

And so on the morn they all arose, and heard their mass and brake their fast; and then they took their horses and rode on their way, and the Green Knight conveyed them through the forest; and there the Green Knight said, My lord Beaumains, I and these thirty knights shall be always at your summons, both early and late, at your calling and whither that ever ye will send us. It is well said, said Beaumains; when that I call upon you ye must yield you unto King Arthur, and all your knights. If that ye so command us, we shall be ready at all times, said the Green Knight. Fie, fie upon thee, in the devil's name, said the damosel, that any good knights should be obedient unto a kitchen knave. So then departed the Green Knight and the damosel. And then she said unto Beaumains, Why followest thou me, thou kitchen boy? Cast away thy shield and thy spear, and flee away, yet I counsel thee, betimes, or thou shalt say right soon, alas; for wert thou as wight as ever was Wade or Launcelot, Tristram, or the good knight Sir Lamorak, thou shalt not pass a pass here that is called the Pass Perilous. Damosel, said Beaumains, who is afeard let him flee, for it were shame to turn again sithen I have ridden so long with you. Well, said the damosel, ye shall soon, whether ye will or not.

So within a while they saw a tower as white as any snow, well matchecold all about, and double dyked. And over the tower gate there hung a fifty shields of divers colours, and under that tower there was a fair meadow. And therein were many knights and squires to behold, scaffolds and pavilions; for there upon the morn should be a great tournament: and the lord of the tower was in his castle and looked out at a window, and saw a damosel, a dwarf, and a knight armed at all points. With that knight will I joust, said the lord, for I see that he is a knight-errant. And so he armed him and horsed him hastily. And when he was on horseback with his shield and his spear, it was all red, both his horse and his harness, and all that to him longeth. And when that he came nigh him he weened it had been his brother the Black Knight; and then he cried aloud, Brother, what do ye in these marches? Nay, nay, said the damosel, it is not he; this is but a kitchen knave that was brought up for alms in King Arthur's court. Nevertheless, said the Red Knight, I will speak with him or he depart. Ah, said the damosel, this knave hath killed thy brother, and Sir Kay named him Beaumains, and this horse and this harness was thy brother's, the Black Knight. Also I saw thy brother the Green Knight overcome of his hands. Now may ye be revenged upon him, for I may never be quit of him.

With this either knights departed in sunder, and they came together with all their might, and either of their horses fell to the earth, and they avoided their horses, and put their shields afore them and drew their swords, and either gave other sad strokes, now here, now there, racing, tracing, foining, and hurling like two boars, the space of two hours. And then she cried on high to the Red Knight, Alas, thou noble Red Knight, think what worship hath followed thee, let never a kitchen knave endure thee so long as he doth. Then the Red Knight waxed wroth and doubled his strokes, and hurt Beaumains wonderly sore, that the blood ran down to the ground, that it was wonder to see that strong battle. Yet at the last Sir Beaumains struck him to the earth, and as he would have slain the Red Knight, he cried mercy, saying, Noble knight, slay me not, and I shall yield me to thee with fifty knights with me that be at my commandment. And I forgive thee all the despite that thou hast done to me, and the death of my brother the Black Knight. All this availeth not, said Beaumains, but if my damosel pray me to save thy life. And therewith he made semblant to strike off his head. Let be, thou Beaumains, slay him not, for he is a noble knight, and not so hardy, upon thine head, but thou save him.

Then Beaumains bade the Red Knight, Stand up, and thank the damosel now of thy life. Then the Red Knight prayed him to see his castle, and to be there all night. So the damosel then granted him, and there they had merry cheer. But always the damosel spake many foul words unto Beaumains, whereof the Red Knight had great marvel; and all that night the Red Knight made three score knights to watch Beaumains, that he should have no shame nor villainy. And upon the morn they heard mass and dined, and the Red Knight came before Beaumains with his three score knights, and there he proffered him his homage and fealty at all times, he and his knights to do him service. I thank you, said Beaumains, but this ye shall grant me: when I call upon you, to come afore my lord King Arthur, and yield you unto him to be his knights. Sir, said the Red Knight, I will be ready, and my fellowship, at your summons. So Sir Beaumains departed and the damosel, and ever she rode chiding him in the foulest manner.

HOW SIR BEAUMAINS ANSWERED THE DAMOSEL PATIENTLY, AND HOW HE FOUGHT WITH THE FOURTH BROTHER, SIR PERSANT OF INDE, AND MADE HIM TO BE YOLDEN. Damosel, said Beaumains, ye are uncourteous so to rebuke me as ye do, for meseemeth I have done you good service, and ever ye threaten me I shall be beaten with knights that we meet, but ever for all your boast they lie in the dust or in the mire, and therefore I pray you rebuke me no more; and when ye see me beaten or yolden as recreant, then may ye bid me go from you shamefully; but first I let you wit I will not depart from you, for I were worse than a fool an I would depart from you all the while that I win worship. Well, said she, right soon there shall meet a knight shall pay thee all thy wages, for he is the most man of worship of the world, except King Arthur. I will well, said Beaumains, the more he is of worship, the more shall be my worship to have ado with him.

Then anon they were ware where was afore them a city rich and fair. And betwixt them and the city a mile and an half there was a fair meadow that seemed new mown, and therein were many pavilions fair to behold. Lo, said the damosel, yonder is a lord that owneth yonder city, and his custom is, when the weather is fair, to lie in this meadow to joust and tourney. And ever there be about him an hundred knights and gentlemen of arms, and there be all manner of games that any gentleman can devise. That goodly lord, said Beaumains, would I fain see. Thou shalt see him time enough, said the damosel, and so as she rode near she espied the pavilion where he was. Lo, said she, seest thou yonder pavilion that is all of the colour of Inde, and all manner of thing that there is about men and women, and horses trapped, shields and spears were all of the colour of Inde, and his name is Sir Persant of Inde, the most lordliest knight that ever thou lookedst on. It may well be, said Beaumains, but be he never so stout a knight, in this field I shall abide till that I see him under his shield. Ah, fool, said she, thou wert better flee betimes. Why, said Beaumains, an he be such a knight as ye make him, he will not set upon me with all his men, or with his hundred knights. For an there come no more but one at once, I shall him not fail whilst my life lasteth. Fie, fie, said the damosel, that ever such a stinking knave should blow such a boast. Damosel, he said, ye are to blame so to rebuke me, for I had liefer do five battles than so to be rebuked; let him come and then let him do his worst.

Sir, she said, I marvel what thou art and of what kin thou art come; boldly thou speakest, and boldly thou hast done, that have I seen; therefore I pray thee save thyself an thou mayest, for thy horse and thou have had great travail, and I dread we dwell over long from the siege, for it is but hence seven mile, and all perilous passages we are passed save all only this passage, and there I dread me sore lest ye shall catch some hurt; therefore I would ye were hence, that ye were not bruised nor hurt with this strong knight. But I let you wit this Sir Persant of Inde is nothing of might nor strength unto the knight that laid the siege about my lady. As for that, said Sir Beaumains, be it as it be may. For sithen I am come so nigh this knight I will prove his might or I depart from him, and else I shall be shamed an I now withdraw me from him. And therefore, damosel, have ye no doubt by the grace of God I shall so deal with this knight that within two hours after noon I shall deliver him. And then shall we come to the siege by daylight. O Jesu, marvel have I, said the damosel, what manner a man ye be, for it may never be otherwise but that ye be come of a noble blood, for so foul nor shamefully did never woman rule a knight as I have done you, and ever courteously ye have suffered me, and that came never but of a gentle blood.

Damosel, said Beaumains, a knight may little do that may not suffer a damosel, for whatsomever ye said unto me I took none heed to your words, for the more ye said the more ye angered me, and my wrath I wreaked upon them that I had ado withal. And therefore all the missaying that ye missaid me furthered me in my battle, and caused me to think to show and prove myself at the end what I was; for peradventure though I had meat in King Arthur's kitchen, yet I might have had meat enough in other places, but all that I did it for to prove and assay my friends, and that shall be known another day; and whether that I be a gentleman born or none, I let you wit, fair damosel, I have done you gentleman's service, and peradventure better service yet will I do or I depart from you. Alas, she said, fair Beaumains, forgive me all that I have missaid or done against thee. With all my heart, said he, I forgive it you, for ye did nothing but as ye should do, for all your evil words pleased me; and damosel, said Beaumains, since it liketh you to say thus fair unto me, wit ye well it gladdeth my heart greatly, and now meseemeth there is no knight living but I am able enough for him.

With this Sir Persant of Inde had espied them as they

hoved in the field, and knightly he sent to them whether he came in war or in peace. Say to thy lord, said Beaumains, I take no force, but whether as him list himself. So the messenger went again unto Sir Persant and told him all his answer. Well then will I have ado with him to the utterance, and so he purveyed him and rode against him. And Beaumains saw him and made him ready, and there they met with all that ever their horses might run, and brast their spears either in three pieces, and their horses rushed so together that both their horses fell dead to the earth ; and lightly they avoided their horses and put their shields afore them, and drew their swords, and gave many great strokes that sometime they hurtled together that they fell grovelling on the ground. And at the last Beaumains smote Sir Persant above upon the helm, that he fell grovelling to the earth ; and then he leapt upon him overthwart and unlaced his helm to have slain him.

Then Sir Persant yielded him and asked him mercy. With that came the damosel and prayed to save his life. I will well, for it were pity this noble knight should die. Gramercy, said Persant, gentle knight and damosel. For certainly now I wot well it was ye that slew my brother the Black Knight at the black thorn ; he was a full noble knight, his name was Sir Pereard. Also I am sure that ye are he that won mine other brother the Green Knight, his name was Sir Pertolepe. Also ye won my brother the Red Knight, Sir Perimones. And now since ye have won these, this shall I do for to please you : ye shall have homage and fealty of me, and an hundred knights to be always at your commandment, to go and ride where ye will command us. And so they went unto Sir Persant's pavilion and drank the wine, and ate spices, and afterward Sir Persant made him to rest upon a bed until supper time, and after supper to bed again.

OF THE GOODLY COMMUNICATION BETWEEN SIR PERSANT AND BEAUMAINS, AND HOW THE LADY THAT WAS BESIEGED HAD WORD FROM HER SISTER THAT SHE HAD BROUGHT A KNIGHT TO FIGHT FOR HER. And so on the morn the damosel and Sir Beaumains heard mass and brake their fast, and so took their leave. Fair damosel, said Persant, whitherward are ye way-leading this knight? Sir, she said, this knight is going to the siege that besiegeth my sister in the Castle Dangerous. Ah, ah, said Persant, that is the Knight of the Red Laund, the which is the most perilous knight that I know now living, and a man that is without mercy, and men say that he hath seven men's strength. God save you, said he to Beaumains, from that knight, for he doth great wrong to that lady, and that is great pity, for she is one of the fairest ladies of the world, and meseemeth that your damosel is her sister: is not your name Linet? said he. Yea, sir, said she, and my lady my sister's name is Dame Lionesse. Now shall I tell you, said Sir Persant, this Red Knight of the Red Laund hath lain long at the siege, well-nigh this two years, and many times he might have had her an he had would, but he prolongeth the time to this intent, for to have Sir Launcelot du Lake to do battle with him, or Sir Tristram, or Sir Lamorak de Galis, or Sir Gawaine, and this is his tarrying so long at the siege.

Now my lord Sir Persant of Inde, said the damosel Linet, I require you that ye will make this gentleman knight or ever he fight with the Red Knight. I will with all my heart, said Sir Persant, an it please him to take the order of knighthood of so simple a man as I am. Sir, said Beaumains, I thank you for your good will, for I am better sped, for certainly the noble knight Sir Launcelot made me knight. Ah, said Sir Persant, of a more renowned knight might ye not be made knight; for of all knights he may be called chief of knighthood; and so all the world saith, that betwixt three knights is departed clearly knighthood, that is Launcelot du Lake, Sir Tristram de Liones, and Sir Lamorak de Galis: these bear now the renown. Therefore God speed you well, said Sir Persant, for an ye may match the Red Knight ye shall be called the fourth of the world.

Sir, said Beaumains, I would fain be of good fame and of knighthood. And I let you wit I came of good men, for I dare say my father was a noble man, and so that ye will keep it in close, and this damosel, I will tell you of what kin I am. We will not discover you, said they both, till ye command us, by the faith we owe unto God. Truly then, said he, my name is Gareth of Orkney, and King Lot was my father, and my mother is King Arthur's sister, her name is Dame Morgawse, and Sir Gawaine is my brother, and Sir Agravaine and Sir Gaheris, and I am the youngest of them all. And yet wot not King Arthur nor Sir Gawaine what I am.

So the book saith that the lady that was besieged had word of her sister's coming by the dwarf, and a knight with her, and how he had passed all the perilous passages. What manner a man is he? said the lady. He is a noble knight, truly, madam, said the dwarf, and but a young man, but he is as likely a man as ever ye saw any. What is he? said the damosel, and of what kin is he come, and of whom was he made knight? Madam, said the dwarf, he is the king's son of Orkney, but his name I will not tell you as at this time; but wit ye well, of Sir Launcelot was he made knight.

Dwarf, said the lady, I am glad of these tidings, therefore go thou in an hermitage of mine hereby, and there shalt thou bear with thee of my wine in two flagons of silver, they are of two gallons, and also two cast of bread with fat venison baked, and dainty fowls; and a cup of gold here I deliver thee, that is rich and precious; and bear all this to mine hermitage, and put it in the hermit's hands. And sithen go thou unto my sister and greet her well, and commend me unto that gentle knight, and pray him to eat and to drink and make him strong, and say ye him I thank him of his courtesy and goodness, that he would take upon him such labour for me that never did him bounty nor courtesy. Also pray him that he be of good heart and courage, for he shall meet with a full noble knight, but he is neither of bounty, courtesy, nor gentleness; for he attendeth unto nothing but to murder, and that is the cause I cannot praise him nor love him.

So this dwarf departed, and came to Sir Persant, where he found the damosel Linet and Sir Beaumains, and there he told them all as ye have heard; and then they took their leave, but Sir Persant took an ambling hackney and conveyed them on their ways, and then beleft them to God; and so within a little while they came to that hermitage, and there they drank the wine, and ate the venison and the fowls baken.

HOW BEAUMAINS BLEW A HORN, AND THEN THE KNIGHT OF THE RED LAUNDS CAME TO FIGHT WITH HIM, AND HOW BEAUMAINS MADE HIM YIELD TO THE LADY AND GO UNTO KING ARTHUR'S COURT AND CRY SIR LAUNCELOT MERCY, AND OF THE TROTH PLIGHT OF BEAUMAINS AND THE LADY. Upon the morn Beaumains and the damosel Linet heard their mass and brake their fast. And then they took their horses and came to a plain, and saw where were many pavilions and tents, and a fair castle, and there was much smoke and great noise; and when they came near the siege Sir Beaumains espied upon great trees, as he rode, how there hung full goodly armed knights by the neck, and their shields about their necks with their swords, and gilt spurs upon their heels, and so there hung nigh a forty knights shamefully with full rich arms.

Then Sir Beaumains abated his countenance and said, What meaneth this? Fair sir, said the damosel, abate not your cheer for all this sight, for ye must courage yourself, or else ye be all shent, for all these knights came hither to this siege to rescue my sister Dame Lionesse, and when the Red Knight of the Red Launds had overcome them, he put them to this shameful death without mercy and pity. And in the same wise he will serve you, but if you quit you the better.

Now Jesu defend me, said Beaumains, from such a villainous death and shenship of arms. For rather than I should so be faren withal, I would be slain manly in plain battle. So were ye better, said the damosel; for trust not, in him is no courtesy, but all goeth to the death or shameful murder, and that is pity, for he is a full noble knight of prowess.

And then they rode to the dykes, and saw them double dyked with full warlike walls; and there were lodged many great lords nigh the walls; and there was great noise of minstrelsy; and the sea beat upon the one side of the walls, where were many ships and mariners' noise with "hale and how." And also there was fast by a sycamore tree, and there hung an horn, the greatest that ever they saw, of an elephant's bone; and this Knight of the Red Launds had hanged it up there, that if there came any errant-knight, he must blow that horn, and then will he make him ready and come to him to do battle. But, sir, I pray you, said the damosel Linet, blow ye not the horn till it be high noon, for now it is about prime, and now increaseth his might, that as men say he hath seven men's strength. Ah, fie for shame, fair damosel, say ye never so more to me; for, an he were as good a knight as ever was, I shall never fail him in his most might, for either I will win worship worshipfully, or die knightly in the field. And therewith he spurred his horse straight to the sycamore tree, and blew so the horn eagerly that all the siege and the castle rang thereof. And then there leapt out knights out of their tents and pavilions, and they within the castle looked over the walls and out at windows.

Then the Red Knight of the Red Launds armed him hastily, and two barons set on his spurs upon his heels, and all was blood red, his armour, spear and shield. And an earl buckled his helm upon his head, and then they brought him a red spear and a red steed, and so he rode into a little vale under the castle, that all that were in the castle and at the siege might behold the battle.

Sir, said the damosel Linet unto Sir Beaumains, look ye be glad and light, for yonder is your deadly enemy, and at yonder window is my lady sister, Dame Lionesse. Where? said Beaumains. Yonder, said the damosel, and pointed with her finger. That is truth, said Beaumains. She beseemeth afar the fairest lady that ever I looked upon; and truly, he said, I ask no better quarrel than now for to do battle, for truly she shall be my lady, and for her I will fight. And ever he looked up to the window with glad countenance, and the Lady Lionesse made curtsey to him down to the earth, with holding up both their hands.

With that the Red Knight of the Red Launds called to Sir Beaumains, Leave, sir knight, thy looking, and behold me, I counsel thee; for I warn thee well she is my lady, and for her I have done many strong battles. If thou have so done, said Beaumains, meseemeth it was but waste labour, for she loveth none of thy fellowship, and thou to love that loveth not thee is but great folly. For an I understood that she were not glad of my coming, I would be advised or I did battle for her. But I understand by the besieging of this castle she may forbear thy fellowship. And therefore wit thou well, thou Red Knight of the Red Launds, I love her, and will rescue her, or else to die. Sayst thou that? said the Red Knight, meseemeth thou ought of reason to be ware by yonder knights that thou sawest hang upon yonder trees. Fie for shame, said Beaumains, that ever thou shouldest say or do so evil, for in that thou shamest thyself and knighthood, and thou mayst be sure there will no lady love thee that knoweth thy wicked customs. And now thou weenest that the sight of these hanged knights should fear me. Nay truly, not so; that shameful sight causeth me to have courage and hardiness against thee, more than I would have had against thee an thou wert a well-ruled knight. Make thee ready, said the Red Knight of the Red Launds, and talk no longer with me.

Then Sir Beaumains bade the damosel go from him; and then they put their spears in their rests, and came together with all their might that they had both, and either smote other in midst of their shields that the paitrelles, surcingles, and cruppers brast, and fell to the earth both, and the reins of their bridles in their hands; and so they lay a great while sore astonied. Then they avoided their horses and put their shields afore them, and drew their swords and ran together like two fierce lions.

Thus they fought till it was past noon, and never would stint, till at the last they lacked wind both; and when they had rested them a while they went to battle again, tracing, racing, foining as two boars. And thus they endured till evensong time, that there was none that beheld them might know whether was like to win the battle; and their armour was so far hewn that men might see their naked sides; and in other places they were naked, but ever the naked places they did defend. And the Red Knight was a wily knight of war, and his wily fighting taught Sir Beaumains to be wise; but he abought it full sore ere he did espy his fighting.

And thus by assent of them both they granted either other to rest; and so they set them down upon two mole-hills there beside the fighting place, and either of them unlaced his helm, and took the cold wind. And then when Sir Beaumains' helm was off, he looked up to the window, and there he saw the fair lady Dame Lionesse, and she made him such countenance that his heart waxed light and jolly; and therewith he bade the Red Knight of the Red Launds make him ready, and let us do the battle to the utterance.

I will well, said the knight, and then they laced up their helms and fought freshly; but the Red Knight of the Red Launds awaited him, and at an overthwart smote him within the hand, that his sword fell out of his hand; and yet he gave him another buffet upon the helm that he fell grovelling to the earth, and the Red Knight fell over him, for to hold him down.

Then cried the maiden Linet on high: O Sir Beaumains, where is thy courage become? Alas, my lady my sister beholdeth thee, and she sobbeth and weepeth, that maketh mine heart heavy. When Sir Beaumains heard her say so, he abraid up with a great might and gat him upon his feet, and lightly he leapt to his sword and gripped it in his hand, and doubled his pace unto the Red Knight, and there they fought a new battle together. But Sir Beaumains then doubled his strokes, and smote so thick that he smote the sword out of his hand, and then he smote him upon the helm that he fell to the earth, and Sir Beaumains fell upon him, and unlaced his helm to have slain him; and then he yielded him and asked mercy, and said with a loud voice: O noble knight, I yield me to thy mercy.

Then Sir Beaumains bethought him upon the knights that the Red Knight had made to be hanged shamefully, and then he said: I may not with my worship save thy life, for the shameful deaths that thou hast caused many full good knights to die. Sir, said the Red Knight of the Red Launds, hold your hand and ye shall know the causes why I put them to so shameful a death. Say on, said Sir Beaumains. Sir, I loved once a lady, a fair damosel, and she had her brother slain; and she said it was Sir Launcelot du Lake, or else Sir Gawaine; and she prayed me as that I loved her heartily, that I would make her a promise by the faith of my knighthood, for to labour daily in arms until I met with one of them; and all that I might overcome I should put them unto a villainous death; and this is the cause that I have put all these knights to death, and so I ensured her to do all the villainy unto King Arthur's knights, and that I should take vengeance upon all these knights

Then came there many earls, and barons, and noble knights, and prayed that knight to save his life, and take him to your prisoner. Fair lords, said Beaumains, wit you well I am full loath to slay this knight, nevertheless he hath done passing ill and shamefully; but insomuch all that he did was at a lady's request I blame him the less; and so for your sake I will release him that he shall have his life upon this covenant, that he go within the castle, and yield him there to the lady, and if she will forgive and quit him, I will well; with this he make her amends of all the trespass he hath done against her and her lands. And also, when that is done, that ye go unto the court of King Arthur, and there that ye ask Sir Launcelot mercy, and Sir Gawaine, for the evil will ye have had against them. Sir, said the Red Knight of the Red Launds, all this will I do as ye command, and siker assurance and borrows ye shall have. And so then when the assurance was made, he made his homage and fealty, and all those earls and barons with him.

And then the maiden Linet came to Sir Beaumains, and unarmed him and searched his wounds, and stinted his blood, and in like wise she did to the Red Knight of the Red Launds. And there they sojourned ten days in their tents; and the Red Knight made his lords and servants to do all the pleasure that they might unto Sir Beaumains.

And so within a while the Red Knight of the Red Launds went unto the castle, and put him in her grace. And so she received him upon sufficient surety, so all her hurts were well restored of all that she could complain. And then came forth Dame Lionesse arrayed like a princess, and there she made Sir Gareth passing good cheer, and he her again; and they had goodly language and lovely countenance together. And then she let fetch to-fore him Linet, the damosel that had ridden with him many wildsome ways. Then was Sir Gareth more gladder than he was to-fore. And then they troth-plight each other to love and never to fail whiles their life lasteth.

HOW THE QUEEN OF ORKNEY CAME TO KING ARTHUR'S COURT, AND HOW KING ARTHUR SENT FOR DAME LIONESSE AND OF THE TOURNEY HELD AT HER CASTLE. So turn we unto King Arthur, that at the next feast of Pentecost held his feast. And there came the Green Knight with thirty knights and yielded them all unto King Arthur. And so there came the Red Knight, his brother, and yielded him to King Arthur and threescore knights with him. Also there came the Blue Knight, brother to them, with an hundred knights. These three brethren told King Arthur how they were overcome by a knight that a damosel had with her, and called him Beaumains. I marvel, said the King, what knight he is and of what lineage he is come. He was with me a twelvemonth and poorly and shamefully he was fostered, and Sir Kay in scorn named him Beaumains. So right as the king stood so talking with these three brethren there came Sir Launcelot du Lake and told the king there was come a goodly lord with five hundred knights with him. Then the king went out of Carlion, for there was the feast, and there came to him this lord, and saluted the king in the most goodly manner. Sir, he said, my name is the Red Knight of the Red Launds, and I am sent to you of a knight that is called Beaumains, for he won me in pleyn battle, and both I and these five hundred knights shall always be at your summons to do you service as may lie in our powers. Well, my fair lords, said King Arthur, wit you well I shall do you honour for the love of Sir Beaumains. So then the king and they went to meat, and were served in the best manner. And as they sat at the meat, there came in the Queen of Orkney, with ladies and knights a great number. And then Sir Gawaine, Sir Agravaine, and Gaheris arose, and went to her and saluted her upon their knees, and asked her blessing; for in fifteen year they had not seen her. Then she spake on high to her brother King Arthur: Where have ye done my young son Sir Gareth? He was here amongst you a twelvemonth, and ye made a kitchen knave of him, the which is shame to you all. Alas, where have ye done my dear son that was my joy and bliss? O dear mother, said Sir Gawaine, I knew him not. Nor I, said the king, that now me repenteth, but thanked be God he is proved a worshipful knight as any is now living of his years, and I shall never be glad till I may find him.

Ah, brother, said the Queen unto King Arthur, and unto Sir Gawaine, and to all her sons, ye did yourself great shame when ye amongst you kept my son in the kitchen and fed him like a poor hog. Fair sister, said King Arthur, ye shall right well wit I knew him not, nor no more did Sir Gawaine, nor his brethren; but sithen it is so, said the king, that he is thus gone from us all, we must shape a remedy to find him.

So then goodly letters were made, and a messenger sent forth, that night and day he went till he came unto the Castle Perilous. And then the lady Dame Lionesse was sent for. And when she understood this message, she bade him ride on his way unto King Arthur, and she would come after in all goodly haste.

So Dame Lionesse departed and came to King Arthur, where she was nobly received, and there she was sore questioned of the king and of the Queen of Orkney. And she answered, where Sir Gareth was she could not tell. But thus much she said unto Arthur: Sir, I will let cry a tournament that shall be done before my castle at the Assumption of our Lady, and the cry shall be this: that you, my lord Arthur, shall be there, and your knights, and I will purvey that my knights shall be against yours; and then I am sure ye shall hear of Sir Gareth. This is well advised, said King Arthur; and so she departed. And the king and she made great provision to that tournament.

And so the cry was made in England, Wales, and Scotland, Ireland, Cornwall, and in all the Out Isles, and in Brittany and in many countries; that at the feast of our Lady the Assumption next coming, men should come to the Castle Perilous beside the Isle of Avilion; and there all the knights that there came should have the choice whether them list to be on the one party with the knights of the castle, or on the other party with King Arthur. And two months was to the day that the tournament should be. And so there came many good knights that were at their large, and held them for the most part against King Arthur and his knights of the Round Table and came on the side of them of the castle.

And then Sir Gareth prayed Dame Lionesse and the Red

Knight of the Red Launds, and Sir Persant and his brother, and Sir Gringamore, that in no wise there should none of them tell not his name, and make no more of him than of the least knight that there was, For, he said, I will not be known of neither more nor less, neither at the beginning neither at the ending. Then Dame Lionesse said unto Sir Gareth: Sir, I will lend you a ring, but I would pray you as you love me heartily let me have it again when the tournament is done, for that ring increaseth my beauty much more than it is of itself. And the virtue of my ring is that that is green it will turn to red, and that is red it will turn in likeness to green, and that is blue it will turn to likeness of white, and that is white it will turn in likeness to blue, and so it will do of all manner of colours. Also who that beareth my ring shall lose no blood, and for great love I will give you this ring. Gramercy, said Sir Gareth, mine own lady, for this ring is passing meet for me, for it will turn all manner of likeness that I am in, and that shall cause me that I shall not be known.

And upon the Assumption Day, when mass and matins were done, there were heralds with trumpets commanded to blow to the field. And so there came out Sir Tristram, Sir Sadok, and Sir Dinas, knights of the castle, and there encountered Sir Tristram with Sir Bedivere, and there Sir Bedivere was smitten to the earth both horse and man. And Sir Sadok encountered with Sir Petipase, and there Sir Sadok was overthrown. And there Uwaine les Avoutres smote down Sir Dinas, the Seneschal. Then came in Sir Persant of Inde, a knight of the castle, and there encountered with him Sir Launcelot du Lake, and there he smote Sir Persant, horse and man, to the earth. Then came Sir Pertolepe, the Green Knight, and smote down Sir Lionel, brother to Sir Launcelot. All this was marked by noble heralds, who bare him best, and their names.

And then came into the field Sir Perimones, the Red Knight, Sir Persant's brother, that was a knight of the castle, and he encountered with Sir Ector de Maris, and either smote other so hard that both their horses and they fell to the earth. And then came in the Red Knight of the Red Launds, and Sir Gareth, from the castle, and there encountered with them Sir Bors de Ganis and Sir Bleoberis, and there the Red Knight and Sir Bors either smote other so hard that their spears brast, and their horses fell grovelling to the earth. Then Sir Bleoberis brake his spear upon Sir Gareth, but of that stroke Sir Bleoberis fell to the earth. When Sir Galihodin saw that he bade Sir Gareth keep him, and Sir Gareth smote him to the earth. Then Sir Galihud gat a spear to avenge his brother, and in the same wise Sir Gareth served him, and Sir Dinadan and his brother, La Cote Male Taile, and Sir Sagramore le Desirous, and Sir Dodinas le Savage. All these he bare down with one spear.

When King Agwisance of Ireland saw Sir Gareth fare so, he marvelled what he might be that one time seemed green, and another time, at his again coming, he seemed blue. And thus at every course that he rode to and fro he changed his colour, so that there might neither king nor knight have ready cognisance of him. Then Sir Agwisance, the King of Ireland, encountered with Sir Gareth, and there Sir Gareth smote him from his horse, saddle and all. And then came King Carados of Scotland, and Sir Gareth smote him down horse and man. And in the same wise he served King Uriens of the land of Gore. And then Sir Galahault, the noble prince, cried on high: Knight with the many colours, well hast thou jousted; now make thee ready that I may joust with thee. Sir Gareth heard him, and he gat a great spear, and so they encountered together, and there the prince brake his spear; but Sir Gareth smote him upon the left side of the helm that he reeled here and there, and he had fallen down had not his men recovered him.

That same knight with the many colours is a good knight, said King Arthur. Wherefore the king called unto him Sir Launcelot, and prayed him to encounter with that knight. Sir, said Launcelot, I may well find in my heart for to forbear him as at this time, for he hath had travail enough this day; and when a good knight doth so well upon some day, it is no good knight's part to let him of his worship, and namely, when he seeth a knight hath done so great labour; for peradventure, said Sir Launcelot, his quarrel is here this day, and peradventure he is best beloved with this lady of all that be here; for I see well he paineth him and enforceth him to do great deeds, and therefore, said Sir Launcelot, as for me, this day he shall have the honour; though it lay in my power to put him from it I would not.

Then Sir Gareth rode out on the one side to amend his helm; and then said his dwarf: Give me your ring, that ye lose it not while that ye drink. And so when he had drunk he gat on his helm, and eagerly took his horse and rode into the field, and left his ring with his dwarf; and the dwarf was glad the ring was from him, for then he wist well he should be known. And then when Sir Gareth was in the field all folks saw him well and plainly that he was in yellow colours; and there he rased off helms and pulled down knights, that King Arthur had marvel what knight he was, for the king saw by his hair that it was the same knight. But before he was in so many colours, and now he is but in one colour; that is yellow. Now go, said King Arthur unto divers heralds, and ride about him, and espy what manner knight he is, for I have spered of many knights this day that be upon his party, and all say they know him not. And so an herald rode nigh Gareth as he could; and there he saw written about his helm in gold, This helm is Sir Gareth of Orkney. Then the herald cried as he were wood, and many heralds with him:—This is Sir Gareth of Orkney in the yellow arms; wherby all kings and knights of Arthur's beheld him and awaited; and then they pressed all to behold him, and ever the heralds cried: This is Sir Gareth of Orkney, King Lot's son. And when Sir Gareth espied that he was discovered, then he doubled his strokes, and smote down Sir Sagramore, and his brother Sir Gawaine. O brother, said Sir Gawaine, I weened ye would not have stricken me.

So when he heard him say so he thrang here and there, and so with great pain he gat out of the press, and there he met with his dwarf. O boy, said Sir Gareth, thou hast beguiled me foul this day that thou kept my ring; give it me anon again, that I may hide my body withal; and so he took it him. And then they all wist not where he was become; and Sir Gawaine had in manner espied where Sir Gareth rode, and then he rode after with all his might. That espied Sir Gareth, and rode lightly into the forest, that Sir Gawaine wist not where he was become. And then fell there a thunder and a rain, as heaven and earth should go together. And Sir Gareth was not a little weary, for of all that day he had but little rest, neither his horse nor he. So this Sir Gareth rode so long in that forest until the night came. And ever it lightened and thundered, as it had been wood. At the last by fortune he came to a castle, and there he heard the waits upon the walls.

HOW SIR GARETH CAME TO A CASTLE WHERE HE WAS WELL LODGED, AND HOW HE JOUSTED WITH THE LORD OF THE CASTLE, AND HOW SIR GARETH AND SIR GAWAINE FOUGHT EACH AGAINST OTHER AND KNEW EACH OTHER BY THE DAMOSEL LINET. Then Sir Gareth rode unto the barbican, and prayed the porter fair to let him into the castle. The porter answered ungoodly again, and said, Thou gettest no lodging here. Fair sir, say not so, for I am a knight of King Arthur's, and pray the lord or the lady of this castle to give me harbour for the love of King Arthur. Then the porter went unto the duchess, and told her how there was a knight of King Arthur's would have harbour. Let him in, said the duchess, for I will see that knight, and for King Arthur's sake he shall not be harbourless. Then she went up into a tower over the gate, with great torch-light.

When Sir Gareth saw that torch-light he cried on high: Whether thou be lord or lady, giant or champion, I take no force so that I may have harbour this night; and if it so be that I must needs fight, spare me not to-morn when I have rested me, for both I and mine horse be weary. Sir knight, said the lady, thou speakest knightly and boldly; but wit thou well the lord of this castle loveth not King Arthur, nor none of his court, for my lord hath ever been against him; and therefore thou were better not to come within this castle; for an thou come in this night, thou must come in under such form, that wheresomever thou meet my lord, by stigh or by street, thou must yield thee to him as prisoner. Madam, said Sir Gareth, what is your lord, and what is his name? Sir, my lord's name is the Duke de la Rowse. Well madam, said Sir Gareth, I shall promise you in what place I meet your lord I shall yield me unto him and to his good grace; with that I understand he will do me no harm: and if I understand that he will, I will release myself, an I can, with my spear and my sword. Ye say well, said the duchess; and then she let the drawbridge down, and so he rode into the hall, and there he alighted, and his horse was led into a stable; and in the hall he unarmed him and said, Madam, I will not out of this hall this night; and when it is daylight, let see who will have ado with me, he shall find me ready. Then was he set unto supper, and had many good dishes. Then Sir Gareth list well to eat, and knightly he ate his meat, and eagerly; there was many a fair lady by him, and some said they never saw a goodlier man nor so well of eating. Then they made him passing good cheer, and shortly when he had supped his bed was made there; so he rested him all night.

And on the morn he heard mass, and brake his fast and took his leave at the duchess, and at them all; and thanked her goodly of her lodging, and of his good cheer. So Sir Gareth departed and rode up into a mountain, and there he found a goodly knight that bade him, Abide sir knight, and joust with me. What are ye? said Sir Gareth. My name is, said he, the Duke de la Rowse. Ah sir, ye are the same knight that I lodged in your castle; and there I made promise unto your lady that I should yield me unto you. Make thee ready, said the duke, for I will have ado with you. So they let their horses run, and there Sir Gareth smote the duke down from his horse. But the duke lightly avoided his horse, and dressed his shield and drew his sword, and bade Sir Gareth alight and fight with him. So he did alight, and they did great battle together more than an hour, and either hurt other full sore. At the last Sir Gareth gat the duke to the earth, and then he yield him to him. Then must ye go, said Sir Gareth, unto Sir Arthur my lord at the next feast, and say that I, Sir Gareth of Orkney, sent you unto him. It shall be done, said the duke, and I will do to you homage and fealty with an hundred knights with me; and all the days of my life to do you service where ye will command me.

So the duke departed, and Sir Gareth stood there alone; and there he saw an armed knight coming toward him. Then Sir Gareth took the duke's shield, and mounted upon horseback, and so without biding they ran together as it had been the thunder. And there that knight hurt Sir Gareth under the side with his spear. And then they alighted and drew their swords, and gave great strokes that the blood trailed to the ground. And so they fought two hours.

At the last there came the damosel Linet, that some men called the damosel Savage, riding upon an ambling mule; and there she cried all on high, Sir Gawaine, Sir Gawaine, leave thy fighting with thy brother Sir Gareth. And when he heard her say so he threw away his shield and his sword, and ran to Sir Gareth, and took him in his arms, and sithen kneeled down and asked him mercy. What are ye, said Sir Gareth, that right now were so strong and so mighty, and now so suddenly yield you to me? O Gareth, I am your brother Sir Gawaine, that for your sake have had great sorrow and labour. Then Sir Gareth unlaced his helm, and kneeled down to him, and asked him mercy. Then they rose both, and embraced either other in their arms, and wept a great while ere they might speak, and either of them gave other the prize of the battle. And there were many kind words between them.

Alas, my fair brother, said Sir Gawaine, perdy I owe of right to worship you an ye were not my brother, for ye have worshipped King Arthur and all his court, for ye have sent him more worshipful knights this twelvemonth than six the best of the Round Table have done, except Sir Launcelot.

Then came the damosel Savage that was the Lady Linet, that rode with Sir Gareth so long, and there she did staunch Sir Gareth's wounds and Sir Gawaine's. Now what will ye do? said the damosel Savage; meseemeth that it were well done that Arthur had witting of you both, for your horses are so brised that they may not bear. Now, fair damosel, said Sir Gawaine, I pray you ride unto my lord mine uncle, King Arthur, and tell him what adventure is to me betid here, and I suppose he will not tarry long. Then she took her mule, and lightly she came to King Arthur that was but two mile thence. And when she had told him tidings the king bade get him a palfrey. And when he was upon his back he bade the lords and ladies come after, who that would; and there was saddling and bridling of queens' horses and princes' horses, and well was him that soonest might be ready.

So when the king came thereas they were, he saw Sir Gawaine and Sir Gareth sit upon a little hill-side, and then the king avoided his horse. Wit ye well the king made great joy, and many a piteous complaint he made to Sir Gareth, and ever he wept as he had been a child. With that came his mother, the Queen of Orkney, Dame Morgawse, and when she saw Sir Gareth readily in the visage she might not weep, but suddenly fell down in a swoon, and lay there a great while like as she had been dead. And then Sir Gareth recomforted his mother in such wise that she recovered and made good cheer.

OF THE WEDDING OF SIR GARETH AND DAME LIONESSE AND OF THE OFFICERS MADE AT THE FEAST. Then said King Arthur unto the damosel Savage: I marvel that your sister, Dame Lionesse, cometh not to visit her knight, my nephew Sir Gareth, that hath had so much travail for her love. My lord, said the damosel Linet, ye must of your good grace hold her excused, for she knoweth not that my lord, Sir Gareth, is here. Go then for her, said King Arthur, that we may be appointed what is best to be done, according to the pleasure of my nephew. Sir, said the damosel, that shall be done, and so she rode unto her sister. And as lightly as she might she made her ready; and she came on the morn with her brother Sir Gringamore, and with her forty knights. And so when she was come she had all the cheer that might be done, both of the king, and of many other kings and queens.

And among all these ladies she was named the fairest, and peerless. Then the king asked his nephew, Sir Gareth, whether he would have that lady to his wife. My lord, wit you well that I love her above all ladies living. Now, fair lady, said King Arthur, what say ye? Most noble King, said Dame Lionesse, wit you well that my lord, Sir Gareth, is to me more liefer to have and wield as my husband, than any king or prince that is christened; and if I may not have him I promise you I will never have none. For, my lord Arthur, said Dame Lionesse, wit ye well he is my first love, and he shall be the last; and if ye will suffer him to have his will and free choice I dare say he will have me. That is truth, said Sir Gareth; an I have not you and wield not you as my wife, there shall never lady nor gentlewoman rejoice me. What, nephew, said the king, is the wind in that door? for wit ye well I would not for the stint of my crown to be causer to withdraw your hearts; and wit ye well ye cannot love so well but I shall rather increase it than distress it. And also ye shall have my love and my lordship in the uttermost wise that may lie in my power. And in the same wise said Sir Gareth's mother.

Then there was made a provision for the day of marriage; and by the king's advice it was provided that it should be at Michaelmas following, at Kink Kenadon by the seaside, for there is a plentiful country. And so it was cried in all the places through the realm. And then Sir Gareth sent his summons to all these knights and ladies that he had won in battle to-fore, that they should be at his day of marriage at Kink Kenadon by the sands. And then Dame Lionesse, and the damosel Linet with Sir Gringamore, rode to their castle; and a goodly and a rich ring she gave to Sir Gareth, and he gave her another. And King Arthur gave her a rich pair of beads of gold; and so she departed; and King Arthur and his fellowship rode toward Kink Kenadon, and Sir Gareth brought his lady on the way, and so came to the king again and rode with him. Lord! the great cheer that Sir Launcelot made of Sir Gareth and he of him, for there was never no knight that Sir Gareth loved so well as he did Sir Launcelot; and ever for the most part he would be in Sir Launcelot's company; for after Sir Gareth had espied Sir Gawaine's conditions, he withdrew himself from his brother, Sir Gawaine's, fellowship, for he was vengeable, and where he hated he would be avenged with murder, and that hated Sir Gareth.

So it drew fast to Michaelmas; and thither came Dame Lionesse, the lady of the Castle Perilous, and her sister,

Dame Linet, with Sir Gringamore, her brother, with them, for he had the conduct of these ladies. And there they were lodged at the device of King Arthur. And upon Michaelmas Day the Bishop of Canterbury made the wedding betwixt Sir Gareth and the Lady Lionesse with great solemnity. And King Arthur made Gaheris to wed the Damosel Savage, that was Dame Linet; and King Arthur made Sir Agravaine to wed Dame Lionesse's niece, a fair lady, her name was Dame Laurel.

And so when this solemnization was done, then came in the Green Knight, Sir Pertolepe, with thirty knights, and there he did homage and fealty to Sir Gareth, and these knights to hold of him for evermore. Also Sir Pertolepe said: I pray you that at this feast I may be your chamberlain. With a good will, said Sir Gareth, sith it liketh you to take so simple an office. Then came in the Red Knight, with three score knights with him, and did to Sir Gareth homage and fealty, and all those knights to hold of him for evermore. And then this Sir Perimones prayed Sir Gareth to grant him to be his chief butler at that high feast. I will well, said Sir Gareth, that ye have this office, and it were better. Then came in Sir Persant of Inde, with an hundred knights with him, and there he did homage and fealty, and all his knights should do him service, and hold their lands of him for ever; and there he prayed Sir Gareth to make him his sewer-chief at the feast. I will well, said Sir Gareth, that ye have it, and it were better. Then came the Duke de la Rowse, with an hundred knights with him, and there he did homage and fealty to Sir Gareth, and so to hold their lands of him for ever. And he required Sir Gareth that he might serve him of the wine that day of that feast. I will well, said Sir Gareth, and it were better.

Then came in the Red Knight of the Red Launds, that was Sir Ironside, and he brought with him five hundred knights, and there he did homage and fealty, and all these knights to hold their lands of him for ever. And then he asked Sir Gareth to be his carver. I will well, said Sir Gareth, an it please you.

So then the kings and queens, princes and earls, barons and many bold knights, went unto meat; and well may ye wit there were all manner of meat plenteously, all manner revels and games, with all manner of minstrelsy that was used in those days. Also there was great jousts three days. But the king would not suffer Sir Gareth to joust, because of his new bride; for, as the French book saith, that Dame Lionesse desired of the king that none that were wedded should joust at that feast.

OF SIR TRISTRAM

HOW SIR TRISTRAM DE LIONES WAS BORN, AND HOW HIS MOTHER DIED AT HIS BIRTH, WHEREFORE SHE NAMED HIM TRISTRAM, AND HOW HIS STEPMOTHER WOULD HAVE POISONED HIM AND HOW HE WAS SENT INTO FRANCE. It was a king that hight Meliodas, and he was lord and king of the country of Liones, and this Meliodas was a likely knight as any was that time living. And by fortune he wedded King Mark's sister of Cornwall, and she was called Elizabeth, that was called both good and fair.

So the time came when she should bear a child, and she was a full meek lady, and well she loved her lord, and he her again, so there was great joy betwixt them. Then there was a lady in that country that had loved King Meliodas long, and by no mean she never could get his love; therefore she let ordain upon a day, as King Meliodas rode a-hunting, for he was a great chaser, and there by an enchantment she made him chase an hart by himself alone till that he came to an old castle and there anon he was taken prisoner by the lady that him loved. When Elizabeth, King Meliodas' wife, missed her lord, she was nigh out of her wit, and she took a gentlewoman with her, and ran into the forest to seek her lord. And when she was far in the forest she might no farther, for she began to travail fast of her child; and so by miracle of Our Lady of Heaven she was delivered with great pains. But she had taken such cold for the default of help that deep draughts of death took her, that needs she must die and depart out of this world; there was none other bote.

And when this Queen Elizabeth saw that there was none other bote, then she made great dole, and said unto her gentlewoman: When ye see my lord, King Meliodas, recommend me unto him, and tell him what pains I endure here for his love, and how I must die here for his sake for default of good help; and let him wit that I am full sorry to depart out of this world from him, therefore pray him to be friend to my soul. Now let me see my little child, for whom I have had all this sorrow. And when she saw him she said thus: Ah, my little son, thou hast murdered thy mother, and therefore I suppose, thou that art a murderer so young, thou art full likely to be a manly man in thine age. And because I shall die of the birth of thee, I charge thee, gentlewoman, that thou pray my lord, King Meliodas, that when he is christened let call him Tristram, that is as much to say as a sorrowful birth. And therewith this queen gave up the ghost and died. Then the gentlewoman laid her under an umbre of a great tree, and then she lapped the child as well as she might for cold. Right so there came the barons, following after the queen, and when they saw that she was dead, then they let carry home the dead queen, and much dole was made for her.

Then this meanwhile Merlin delivered King Meliodas out of prison on the morn after his queen was dead. But the sorrow that the king made for his queen that might no tongue tell. So then the king let inter her richly, and after he let christen his child as his wife had commanded afore her death. And then he let call him Tristram, the sorrowful born child. Then the King Meliodas endured seven years without a wife, and all this time Tristram was nourished well. Then it befell that King Meliodas wedded King Howell's daughter of Brittany, and anon she had children of King Meliodas: then was she heavy and wroth that her children should not rejoice the country of Liones, wherefore this queen ordained for to poison young Tristram. So she let poison be put in a piece of silver in the chamber whereas Tristram and her children were together, unto that intent that when Tristram was thirsty he should drink that drink. And so it fell upon a day, the queen's son, as he was in that chamber, espied the piece with poison, and he weened it had been good drink, and because the child was thirsty he took the piece with poison and drank freely; and therewithal suddenly the child brast and was dead.

When the queen of Meliodas wist of the death of her son, wit ye well that she was heavy. But yet the king understood nothing of her treason. Notwithstanding the queen would not leave this, but eft she let ordain more poison, and put it in a piece. And by fortune King Meliodas, her husband, found the piece with wine where was the poison, and he that was much thirsty took the piece for to drink thereout. And as he would have drunken thereof the queen espied him, and then she ran unto him, and pulled the piece from him suddenly. The king marvelled why she did so, and remembered him how her son was suddenly slain with poison. And then he took her by the hand, and said: Thou false traitress, thou shalt tell me what manner of drink this is, or else I shall slay thee. And therewith he pulled out his sword, and sware a great oath that he should slay her but if she told him truth. Ah! mercy, my lord, said she, and I shall tell you all. And then she told him why she would have slain Tristram, because her children should rejoice his land. Well, said King Meliodas, and therefore shall ye have the law. And so she was condemned by the assent of the barons to be burnt; and then was there made a great fire, and right as she was at the fire to take her execution, young Tristram kneeled afore King Meliodas, and besought him to give him a boon. I will well, said the king again. Then said young Tristram, Give me the life of thy queen, my stepmother. That is unrightfully asked, said King Meliodas, for thou ought of right to hate her, for she would have slain thee with that poison an she might have had her will; and for thy sake most is my cause that she should die.

Sir, said Tristram, as for that, I beseech you of your mercy that you will forgive it her, and as for my part, God forgive it her, and I do; and so much it liked your highness to grant me my boon, for God's love I require you hold your promise. Sithen it is so, said the king, I will that ye have her life. Then, said the king, I give her to you, and go ye to the fire and take her, and do with her what ye will. So Sir Tristram went to the fire, and by the commandment of the king delivered her from the death. But after that King Meliodas would not suffer young Tristram to abide no longer in his court.

And then he let ordain a gentleman that was well learned and taught, his name was Gouvernail; and then he sent young Tristram with Gouvernail into France to learn the language, and nurture, and deeds of arms. And there was Tristram more than seven years. And then when he well could speak the language, and had learned all that he might learn in that country, then he came home to his father, King Meliodas, again. And so Tristram learned to be an harper passing all other, that there was none such called in no country, and so on harping and in instruments of music he applied him in his youth for to learn.

And after, as he grew in might and strength, he laboured ever in hunting and in hawking, so that never gentleman more, that ever we heard read of. And as the book saith, he began good measures of blowing of beasts of venery, and beasts of chase, and all manner of vermin, and all these terms we have yet of hawking and hunting. And therefore the book of venery, of hawking, and hunting, is called the book of Sir Tristram. Wherefore, as meseemeth, all gentlemen that bear old arms ought of right to honour Sir Tristram for the goodly terms that gentlemen have and use, and shall to the day of doom, that thereby in a manner all men of worship may dissever a gentleman from a yeoman, and from a yeoman a villain. For he that gentle is will draw him unto gentle tatches, and to follow the customs of noble gentlemen.

Thus Sir Tristram endured in Cornwall until he was big and strong, of the age of eighteen years. And then the King Meliodas had great joy of Sir Tristram, and so had the queen, his wife. For ever after in her life, because Sir Tristram saved her from the fire, she did never hate him more after, but loved him ever after, and gave Tristram many great gifts; for every estate loved him, where that he went.

HOW SIR MARHAUS CAME OUT OF IRELAND FOR TO ASK TRUAGE OF CORNWALL, AND HOW SIR TRISTRAM ENTERPRIZED TO FIGHT WITH HIM. Then it befell that King Anguish of Ireland sent unto King Mark of Cornwall for his truage, that Cornwall had paid many winters. And all that time King Mark was behind of the truage for seven years. And King Mark and his barons gave unto the messenger of Ireland these words and answer, that they would none pay; and bade the messenger go unto his King Anguish, and tell him we will pay him no truage, but tell your lord, an he will always have truage of us of Cornwall, bid him send a trusty knight of his land, that will fight for his right, and we shall find another for to defend our right. With this answer the messengers departed into Ireland. And when King Anguish understood the answer of the messengers he was wonderly wroth. And then he called unto him Sir Marhaus, the good knight, that was nobly proved, and a Knight of the Table Round. And this Marhaus was brother unto the queen of Ireland. Then the king said thus: Fair brother, Sir Marhaus, I pray you go into Cornwall for my sake, and do battle for our truage that of right we ought to have; and whatsomever ye spend ye shall have sufficiently, more than ye shall need. Sir, said Marhaus, wit ye well that I shall not be loath to do battle in the right of you and your land with the best knight of the Table Round; for I know them, for the most part, what be their deeds; and for to advance my deeds and to increase my worship I will right gladly go unto this journey for our right.

So in all haste there was made purveyance for Sir Marhaus, and he had all things that to him needed; and so he departed out of Ireland, and arrived up in Cornwall even fast by the Castle of Tintagil. And when King Mark understood that he was there arrived to fight for Ireland, then made King Mark great sorrow when he understood that the good and noble knight Sir Marhaus was come. For they knew no knight that durst have ado with him. For at that time Sir Marhaus was called one of the famousest and renowned knights of the world. And thus Sir Marhaus abode in the sea, and every day he sent unto King Mark for to pay the truage that was behind of seven year, other else to find a knight to fight with him for the truage. This manner of message Sir Marhaus sent daily unto King Mark.

When young Tristram heard of this he was wroth, and sore ashamed that there durst no knight in Cornwall have ado with Sir Marhaus of Ireland. As for that, said King Meliodas, wit you well, son Tristram, that Sir Marhaus is called one of the best knights of the world, and Knight of the Table Round; and therefore I know no knight in this country that is able to match with him. Alas, said Sir Tristram, that I am not made knight; and if Sir Marhaus should thus depart into Ireland, God let me never have worship: an I were made knight I should match him. And sir, said Tristram, I pray you give me leave to ride to King Mark; and, so ye be not displeased, of King Mark will I be made knight. I will well, said King Meliodas, that ye be ruled as your courage will rule you. Then Sir Tristram thanked his father much. And then he made him ready to ride into Cornwall.

In the meanwhile there came a messenger with letters of love from King Faramon of France's daughter unto Sir Tristram, that were full piteous letters, and in them were written many complaints of love; but Sir Tristram had no joy of her letters nor regard unto her. Also she sent him a little brachet that was passing fair. But when the king's daughter understood that Sir Tristram would not love her, as the book saith she died for sorrow. And then the same squire that brought the letter and the brachet came again unto Sir Tristram, as after ye shall hear in the tale.

So this young Sir Tristram rode unto his eme, King Mark of Cornwall, and said: Sir, if ye will give me the order of knighthood, I will do battle with Sir Marhaus. What are ye, said the king, and from whence be ye come? Sir, said Tristram, I come from King Meliodas that wedded your sister, and a gentleman wit ye well I am. King Mark beheld Sir Tristram and saw that he was but a young man of age, but he was passingly well made and big. Fair sir, said the king, what is your name, and where were ye born? Sir, said he again, my name is Tristram, and in the country of Liones was I born. Ye say well, said the king; and if ye will do this battle I shall make you knight. Therefore I come to you, said Sir Tristram, and for none other cause. But then King Mark made him knight. And therewithal, anon as he had made him knight, he sent a messenger unto Sir Marhaus with letters that said that he had found a young knight ready for to take the battle to the uttermost. It may well be, said Sir Marhaus; but tell King Mark I will not fight with no knight but he be of blood royal, that is to say, other king's son, other queen's son, born of a prince or princess.

When King Mark understood that, he sent for Sir Tristram de Liones and told him what was the answer of Sir Marhaus. Then said Sir Tristram: Sithen that he saith so, let him wit that I am come of father side and mother side of as noble blood as he is: for, sir, now shall ye know that I am King Meliodas' son, born of your own sister, Dame Elizabeth, that died in the forest in the birth of me. Fair nephew, said King Mark, ye are welcome to me. Then in all the haste the king let horse Sir Tristram, and armed him in the best manner that might be had or gotten for gold or silver. And then King Mark sent unto Sir Marhaus, and did him to wit that a better born man than he was himself should fight with him, and his name is Sir Tristram de Liones, gotten of King Meliodas, and born of King Mark's sister. Then was Sir Marhaus glad and blithe that he should fight with such a gentleman. And so by the assent of King Mark and of Sir Marhaus they let ordain that they should fight within an island nigh Sir Marhaus' ships; and so was Sir Tristram put into a vessel, both his horse and he, and all that to him longed both for his body and for his horse. And when King Mark and his barons of Cornwall beheld how young Sir Tristram departed with such a carriage to fight for the right of Cornwall, there was neither man nor woman of worship but they wept to see and understand so young a knight to jeopardy himself for their right.

HOW SIR TRISTRAM FOUGHT AGAINST SIR MARHAUS AND ACHIEVED HIS BATTLE, AND HOW SIR MARHAUS FLED TO HIS SHIP. So when Sir Tristram was arrived within the island he looked to the farther side, and there he saw at an anchor six ships nigh to the land; and under the shadow of the ships upon the land, there hoved the noble knight, Sir Marhaus of Ireland. Then Sir Tristram commanded his servant Gouvernail to bring his horse to the land, and dress his harness at all manner of rights. And then when he had so done he mounted upon his horse; and when he was in his saddle well apparelled, and his shield dressed upon his shoulder, Tristram asked Gouvernail, Where is this knight that I shall have ado withal? Sir, said Gouvernail, see ye him not? I weened ye had seen him; yonder he hoveth under the shadow of his ships on horseback, with his spear in his hand and his shield upon his shoulder. That is truth, said the noble knight, Sir Tristram, now I see him well enough.

Then he commanded his servant Gouvernail to go to his vessel again: And commend me unto mine eme King Mark, and pray him, if that I be slain in this battle, for to inter my body as him seemeth best; and as for me, let him wit that I will never yield me for cowardice; and if I be slain and flee not, then they have lost no truage for me; and if so be that I flee or yield me as recreant, bid mine eme never bury me in Christian burials. And upon thy life, said Sir Tristram to Gouvernail, come thou not nigh this island till that thou see me overcome or slain, or else that I win yonder knight. So either departed from other sore weeping.

And then Sir Marhaus avised Sir Tristram, and said thus: Young knight, Sir Tristram, what dost thou here? me sore repenteth of thy courage, for wit thou well I have matched with the best knights of the world, and therefore by my counsel return again unto thy vessel. And fair knight, and well-proved knight, said Sir Tristram, thou shalt well wit I may not forsake thee in this quarrel, for I am for thy sake made knight. And now wit thou well, Sir Marhaus, that I cast me to get worship on thy body; and if that I be not proved, I trust to God that I shall be worshipfully proved upon thy body, and to deliver the country of Cornwall for ever from all manner of truage from Ireland for ever.

When Sir Marhaus had heard him say what he would, he said then thus again: Fair knight, sithen it is so that thou castest to win worship of me, I let thee wit worship may thou none lose by me if thou mayest stand me three strokes; for I let thee wit for my noble deeds, proved and seen, King Arthur made me Knight of the Table Round.

Then they began to feutre their spears, and they met so fiercely together that they smote either other down, both horse and all. But Sir Marhaus smote Sir Tristram a great wound in the side with his spear, and then they avoided their horses, and pulled out their swords, and threw their shields afore them. And then they lashed together as men that were wild and courageous. Thus they fought still more than half a day, and either were wounded passing sore. By then Sir Tristram waxed more fresher than Sir Marhaus, and better winded and bigger; and with a mighty stroke he smote Sir Marhaus upon the helm such a buffet that it went through his helm, and through the coif of steel, and through the brain-pan, and the sword stuck so fast in the helm and in his brain-pan that Sir Tristram pulled thrice at his sword or ever he might pull it out from his head; and there Marhaus fell down on his knees, the edge of Tristram's sword left in his brain-pan. And suddenly Sir Marhaus rose grovelling, and threw his sword and his shield from him, and so ran to his ships and fled his way, and Sir Tristram had ever his shield and his sword.

And when Sir Tristram saw Sir Marhaus withdraw him, he said: Ah! Sir Knight of the Round Table, why withdrawest thou thee? thou dost thyself and thy kin great shame, for I am but a young knight, or now I was never proved, and rather than I should withdraw me from thee, I had rather be hewn in an hundred pieces. Sir Marhaus answered no word, but went his way sore groaning, and anon he and his fellowship departed into Ireland. And as soon as he came to the king, his brother, he let search his wounds. And when his head was searched a piece of Sir Tristram's sword was found therein, and might never be had out of his head for no surgeons, and so he died of Sir Tristram's sword; and that piece of the sword the queen, his sister, kept it for ever with her, for she thought to be revenged an she might.

HOW SIR TRISTRAM WENT TO IRELAND TO BE HEALED OF THE POISON OF HIS WOUND AND THERE WAS PUT TO THE KEEPING OF LA BEALE ISOUD, AND HOW HE WON THE DEGREE AT A TOURNAMENT AND MADE SIR PALAMIDES BEAR NO HARNESS OF WAR FOR A YEAR. Now turn we again unto Sir Tristram, that was sore wounded. Then anon came Gouvernail, his man, with his vessel. And when Sir Tristram was come unto the land, King Mark took him in his arms, and the king and Sir Dinas, the seneschal, led him into the castle of Tintagil. And then was he searched in the best manner, and laid in his bed. And when King Mark saw his wounds he wept heartily, and so did all his lords. So God me help, said King Mark, I would not for all my lands that my nephew died. So Sir Tristram lay there a month and more, and ever he was like to die of that stroke that Sir Marhaus smote him first with the spear. For, as the French book saith, the spear's head was envenomed, that Sir Tristram might not be whole.

Then came there a lady that was a right wise lady, and she said plainly that Sir Tristram should never be whole but if he went in the same country that the venom came from, and in that country should he be holpen or else never.

When King Mark understood that, he let purvey for Sir Tristram a fair vessel, well victualled, and therein was put Sir Tristram, and Gouvernail with him, and Sir Tristram took his harp with him, and so he was put into the sea to sail into Ireland; and so by good fortune he arrived up in Ireland, even fast by a castle where the king and the queen was; and at his arrival he sat and harped in his bed a merry lay, such one heard they never none in Ireland before that time.

And when it was told the king and the queen of such a knight that was such an harper, anon the king sent for him, and let search his wounds, and then asked him his name. Then he answered, I am of the country of Liones, and my name is Tramtrist, that thus was wounded in a battle as I fought for a lady's right. So God me help, said King Anguish, ye shall have all the help in this land that ye may have here; but I let you wit, in Cornwall I had a great loss as ever had king, for there I lost the best knight of the world; his name was Marhaus, a full noble knight, and Knight of the Table Round; and there he told Sir Tristram wherefore Sir Marhaus was slain. Sir Tristram made semblant as he had been sorry, and better knew he how it was than the king.

Then the king for great favour made Tramtrist to be put in his daughter's ward and keeping, because she was a noble surgeon. And when she had searched him she found in the bottom of his wound that therein was poison, and so she healed him within a while; and therefore Tramtrist cast great love to La Beale Isoud, for she was at that time the fairest maid and lady of the world. And there Tramtrist learned her to harp, and she began to have a great fantasy unto him. And at that time Sir Palamides, the Saracen, was in that country, and well cherished with the king and the queen. And every day Sir Palamides drew unto La Beale Isoud and proffered her many gifts, for he loved her passingly well. All that espied Tramtrist, and full well knew he Sir Palamides for a noble knight and a mighty man. And wit you well Sir Tramtrist had great despite at Sir Palamides, for La Beale Isoud told Tramtrist that Palamides was in will to be christened for her sake. Thus was there great envy betwixt Tramtrist and Sir Palamides.

Then it befell that King Anguish let cry a great jousts and a great tournament for a lady that was called the Lady of the Launds, and she was nigh cousin unto the king. And what man won her, three days after he should wed her and have all her lands. This cry was made in England, Wales, Scotland, and also in France and in Brittany. It befell upon a day La Beale Isoud came unto Sir Tramtrist, and told him of this tournament. He answered and said: Fair lady, I am but a feeble knight, and but late I had been dead had not your good ladyship been. Now, fair lady, what would ye I should do in this matter? well ye wot, my lady, that I may not joust. Ah, Tramtrist, said La Beale Isoud, why will ye not have ado at that tournament? well I wot Sir Palamides shall be there, and to do what he may; and therefore Tramtrist, I pray you for to be there, for else Sir Palamides is like to win the degree. Madam, said Tramtrist, as for that, it may be so, for he is a proved knight, and I am but a young knight and late made; and the first battle that I did it mishapped me to be sore wounded as ye see. But an I wist ye would be my better lady, at that tournament I will be, so that ye will keep my counsel and let no creature have knowledge that I shall joust but yourself, and such as ye will to keep your counsel. My poor person shall I jeopard there for your sake, that, peradventure, Sir Palamides shall know when that I come. Thereto, said La Beale Isoud, do your best, and as I can, said La Beale Isoud, I shall purvey horse and armour for you at my device. As ye will so be it, said Sir Tramtrist, I will be at your commandment.

So at the day of jousts there came Sir Palamides with a black shield, and he overthrew many knights, that all the people had marvel of him. For he put to the worse Sir Gawaine, Gaheris, Agravaine, Bagdemagus, Kay, Dodinas le Savage, Sagramore le Desirous, Gumret le Petit, and Griflet le Fise de Dieu. All these the first day Sir Palamides struck down to the earth. And then all manner of knights were adread of Sir Palamides, and many called him the Knight with the Black Shield. So that day Sir Palamides had great worship.

Then came there the same squire that was sent from the king's daughter to France unto Sir Tristram. And when he had espied Sir Tristram he fell flat to his feet. All that espied La Beale Isoud, what courtesy the squire made unto Sir Tristram. And therewithal suddenly Sir Tristram ran unto his squire, whose name was Hebes le Renoumes, and prayed him heartily in no wise to tell his name. Sir, said Hebes, I will not discover your name but if ye command me.

And on the morn Sir Palamides made him ready to come into the field as he did the first day. And there he smote down the King with the Hundred Knights, and the King of Scots. Then had La Beale Isoud ordained and well arrayed Sir Tristram in white horse and harness. And right so she let put him out at a privy postern, and so he came into the field as it had been a bright angel. And anon Sir Palamides espied him, and therewith he feutred a spear unto Sir Tramtrist, and he again unto him. And there Sir Tristram smote down Sir Palamides unto the earth. And then there was a great noise of people: and wit you well La Beale Isoud was passing glad.

And when Sir Palamides had received this fall, he was sore ashamed, and as privily as he might he withdrew him out of the field. All that espied Sir Tristram, and lightly he rode after Sir Palamides and overtook him, and bade him turn, for better he would assay him or ever he departed. Then Sir Palamides turned him, and either lashed at other with their swords. But at the first stroke Sir Tristram smote down Palamides, and gave him such a stroke upon the head that he fell to the earth. So then Tristram bade yield him, and do his commandment, or else he would slay him. When Sir Palamides beheld his countenance, he dread his buffets so, that he granted all his askings. Well said, said Sir Tristram, this shall be your charge. First, upon pain of your life that ye forsake my lady La Beale Isoud, and in no manner wise that ye draw not to her. Also this twelvemonth and a day that ye bear none armour nor none harness of war. Now promise me this, or here shalt thou die. Alas, said Palamides, for ever am I ashamed. Then he sware as Sir Tristram had commanded him. Then for despite and anger Sir Palamides cut off his harness, and threw them away.

And so Sir Tristram turned again to the castle and rode privily unto the postern, where kept him La Beale Isoud, and there she made him good cheer, and thanked God of his good speed. So anon, within a while, the king and the queen understood that it was Tramtrist that smote down Sir Palamides; then was he much made of, more than he was before.

HOW THE QUEEN ESPIED THAT SIR TRISTRAM HAD SLAIN HER BROTHER SIR MARHAUS BY HIS SWORD, AND IN WHAT JEOPARDY HE WAS, AND HOW THE KING SUFFERED HIM TO RETURN TO CORNWALL. Thus was Sir Tramtrist long there well cherished with the king and the queen, and namely with La Beale Isoud. So upon a day the queen and La Beale Isoud made a bath for Sir Tramtrist. And when he was in his bath the queen and Isoud, her daughter, roamed up and down in the chamber; and therewhiles Gouvernail and Hebes attended upon Tramtrist, and the queen beheld his sword thereas it lay upon his bed. And then by unhap the queen drew out his sword and beheld it a long while, and both they thought it a passing fair sword; but within a foot and an half of the point there was a great piece thereof out-broken of the edge. And when the queen espied that gap in the sword, she remembered her of a piece of a sword that was found in the brain-pan of Sir Marhaus, the good knight that was her brother. Alas then, said she unto her daughter, La Beale Isoud, this is the same traitor knight that slew my brother, thine eme. When Isoud heard her say so she was passing sore abashed, for passing well she loved Tramtrist, and full well she knew the cruelness of her mother the queen.

Anon therewithal the queen went unto her own chamber, and sought her coffer, and there she took out the piece of the sword that was pulled out of Sir Marhaus' head after that he was dead. And then she ran with that piece of iron to the sword that lay upon the bed. And when she put that piece of steel and iron unto the sword, it was as meet as it might be when it was new broken. And then the queen gripped that sword in her hand fiercely, and with all her might she ran straight upon Tramtrist where he sat in his bath, and there she had rived him through had not Sir Hebes gotten her in his arms, and pulled the sword from her, and else she had thrust him through.

Then when she was let of her evil will she ran to the King Anguish, her husband, and said on her knees: O my lord, here have ye in your house that traitor knight that slew my brother and your servant, that noble knight, Sir Marhaus. Who is that, said King Anguish, and where is he? Sir, she said, it is Sir Tramtrist, the same knight that my daughter healed. Alas, said the king, therefore am I right heavy, for he is a full noble knight as ever I saw in field. But I charge you, said the king to the queen, that ye have not ado with that knight, but let me deal with him.

Then the king went into the chamber unto Sir Tramtrist, and then was he gone unto his chamber, and the king found him all ready armed to mount upon his horse. When the king saw him all ready armed to go unto horseback, the king said: Nay, Tramtrist, it will not avail to compare thee against me; but thus much I shall do for my worship and for thy love; in so much as thou art within my court it were no worship for me to slay thee: therefore upon this condition I will give thee leave for to depart from this court in safety, so thou wilt tell me who was thy father, and what is thy name, and if thou slew Sir Marhaus, my brother.

Sir, said Tristram, now I shall tell you all the truth: my father's name is Sir Meliodas, King of Liones, and my mother hight Elizabeth, that was sister unto King Mark of Cornwall; and my mother died of me in the forest, and because thereof she commanded, or she died, that when I were christened they should christen me Tristram; and because I would not be known in this country I turned my name and let me call Tramtrist; and for the truage of Cornwall I fought for my eme's sake, and for the right of Cornwall that ye had posseded many years. And wit ye well, said Tristram unto the king, I did the battle for the love of mine uncle, King Mark, and for the love of the country of Cornwall, and for to increase mine honour; for that same day that I fought with Sir Marhaus I was made knight, and never or then did I battle with no knight, and from me he went alive, and left his shield and his sword behind.

Truly, said the king, I may not say but ye did as a knight should, and it was your part to do for your quarrel, and to increase your worship as a knight should; howbeit I may not maintain you in this country with my worship, unless that I should displease my barons, and my wife and her kin. Sir, said Tristram, I thank you of your good lordship that I have had with you here, and the great goodness my lady, your daughter, hath shewed me, and therefore, said Sir Tristram, it may so happen that ye shall win more by my life than by my death, for in the parts of England it may happen I may do you service at some season, that ye shall be glad that ever ye shewed me your good lordship.

Then Sir Tristram went unto La Beale Isoud and took his leave of her. And then he told her all, what he was, and how he had changed his name because he would not be known, and how a lady told him that he should never be whole till he came into this country where the poison was made, wherethrough I was near my death had not your ladyship been. O gentle knight, said La Beale Isoud, full woe am I of thy departing, for I saw never man that I owed so good will to. And therewithal she wept heartily. Madam, said Sir Tristram, ye shall understand that my name is Sir Tristram de Liones, son of King Meliodas and of his queen. And I promise you faithfully that I shall be all the days of my life your knight. Gramercy, said La Beale Isoud, and I promise you there-against that I shall not be married this seven years but by your assent; and to whom that ye will I shall be married him will I have, and he will have me if ye will consent.

And then Sir Tristram gave her a ring, and she gave him another; and therewith he departed from her, leaving her making great dole and lamentation.

So Sir Tristram departed, and took the sea, and with good wind he arrived up at Tintagil in Cornwall; and when there came tidings that Sir Tristram was arrived, and whole of his wounds, thereof was King Mark passing glad, and so were all the barons; and when Sir Tristram saw his time he rode unto his father, King Meliodas, and there he had all the cheer that the king and the queen could make him. And then largely King Meliodas and his queen departed of their lands and goods to Sir Tristram.

HOW KING MARK SENT SIR TRISTRAM FOR LA BEALE ISOUD TOWARD IRELAND, AND HOW BY FORTUNE HE ARRIVED INTO ENGLAND AND FOUGHT FOR KING AN-

GUISH AGAINST SIR BLAMORE. Then King Mark imagined in himself to send Sir Tristram into Ireland for La Beale Isoud. For Sir Tristram had so praised her beauty and her goodness that King Mark said that he would wed her, whereupon he prayed Sir Tristram to take his way into Ireland for him on message. So Sir Tristram departed and took the sea with all his fellowship. And anon, as he was in the broad sea a tempest took him and his fellowship, and drove them back into the coast of England; and there they arrived fast by Camelot, and when they were landed Sir Tristram set up his pavilion.

Then it fell that Sir Bleoberis and Sir Blamore de Ganis, that were brethren, they had summoned the King Anguish of Ireland for to come to Arthur's court upon pain of forfeiture of King Arthur's good grace. And if the King of Ireland came not in, at the day assigned and set, the king should lose his lands. So it happened that at the day assigned, King Arthur neither Sir Launcelot might not be there for to give the judgment, for King Arthur was with Sir Launcelot at the Castle Joyous Garde. And so King Arthur assigned King Carados and the King of Scots to be there that day as judges. So when the kings were at Camelot King Anguish of Ireland was come to know his accusers. Then was there Sir Blamore de Ganis, and appealed the King of Ireland of treason, that he had slain a cousin of his in his court in Ireland by treason. The king was sore abashed of his accusation, forwhy he was come at the summons of King Arthur, and ere that he came at Camelot he wist not wherefore he was sent after. And when the king heard Sir Blamore say his will, he understood well there was none other remedy but to answer him knightly; for the custom was such in those days, that an any man were appealed of any treason or murder he should fight body for body, or else to find another knight for him. And all manner of murders in those days were called treason.

So when King Anguish understood his accusing he was passing heavy, for he knew Sir Blamore de Ganis that he was a noble knight, and of noble knights come. Then the King of Ireland was simply purveyed of his answer; therefore the judges gave him respite by the third day to give his answer. So the king departed unto his lodging.

Then when Sir Tristram was in his pavilion Gouvernail, his man, came and told him how that King Anguish of Ireland was come thither, and was summoned and appealed of murder. These be the best tidings, said Sir Tristram, that ever came to me this seven years, for now shall the King of Ireland have need of my help; for I daresay there is no knight in this country that is not of Arthur's court dare do battle with Sir Blamore de Ganis; and for to win the love of the King of Ireland I will take the battle upon me; and therefore Gouvernail bring me, I charge thee, to the king.

Then Gouvernail went unto King Anguish of Ireland, and saluted him fair. The king welcomed him and asked him what he would. Sir, said Gouvernail, here is a knight near hand that desireth to speak with you: he bade me say he would do you service. What knight is he? said the king. Sir, said he, it is Sir Tristram de Liones, that for your good grace that ye showed him in your lands will reward you in this country. Come on, fellow, said the king, with me anon and show me unto Sir Tristram. So the king took a little hackney and but few fellowship with him, until he came unto Sir Tristram's pavilion. And when Sir Tristram saw the king he ran unto him and would have holden his stirrup. But the king leapt from his horse lightly, and either halsed other in arms. My gracious lord, said Sir Tristram, gramercy of your great goodnesses showed unto me in your marches and lands: and at that time I promised you to do my service an ever it lay in my power. And, gentle knight, said the king unto Sir Tristram, now have I great need of you, never had I so great need of no knight's help. How so, my good lord? said Sir Tristram. I shall tell you, said the king: I am assummoned and appealed from my country for the death of a knight that was kin unto the good knight Sir Launcelot; wherefore Sir Blamore de Ganis, brother to Sir Bleoberis, hath appealed me to fight with him, outher to find a knight in my stead. And well I wot, said the king, these that are come of King Ban's blood, as Sir Launcelot and these other, are passing good knights, and hard men for to win in battle as any that I know now living. Sir, said Sir Tristram, for the good lordship ye showed me in Ireland, and for my lady your daughter's sake, La Beale Isoud, I will take the battle for you upon this condition that ye shall grant me two things: that one is that ye shall swear to me that ye are in the right, that ye were never consenting to the knight's death; then, when that I have done this battle, if God give me grace that I speed, that ye shall give me a reward, what thing reasonable that I will ask of you. So God me help, said the king, ye shall have whatsomever ye will ask. It is well said, said Sir Tristram. Now make your answer that your champion is ready, for I shall die in your quarrel rather than to be recreant.

So King Anguish departed unto King Carados and the kings that were that time as judges, and told them that he had found his champion ready. Then by the commandment of the kings Sir Blamore de Ganis and Sir Tristram were sent for to hear the charge. And when they were come before the judges there were many kings and knights beheld Sir Tristram, and much speech they had of him because that he slew Sir Marhaus, the good knight, and because he forjousted Sir Palamides the good knight. So when they had taken their charge they withdrew them to make them ready to do battle.

Then said Sir Bleoberis unto his brother, Sir Blamore: Fair dear brother, remember of what kin we be come of, and what a man is Sir Launcelot du Lake, neither farther nor nearer but brother's children, and there was never none of our kin that ever was shamed in battle; and rather suffer death, brother, than to be shamed. Brother, said Blamore, have ye no doubt of me, for I shall never shame none of my blood; howbeit I am sure that yonder knight is called a passing good knight, as of his time one of the world, yet shall I never yield me, nor say the loath word: well may he happen to smite me down with his great might of chivalry, but rather shall he slay me than I shall yield me as recreant. God speed you well, said Sir Bleoberis, for ye shall find him the mightiest knight that ever ye had ado withal, for I know him, for I have had ado with him. God me speed, said Sir Blamore de Ganis; and therewith he took his horse at the one end of the lists, and Sir Tristram at the other end of the lists, and so they feutred their spears and came together as it had been thunder; and there Sir Tristram through great might smote down Sir Blamore and his horse to the earth. Then anon Sir Blamore avoided his horse and pulled out his sword and threw his shield afore him, and bade Sir Tristram alight: For though an horse hath failed me, I trust to God the earth will not fail me. And then Sir Tristram alighted, and dressed him unto battle; and there they lashed together strongly as racing and tracing, foining and dashing, many sad strokes, and at the last, Sir Tristram smote Sir Blamore such a buffet upon the helm that he there fell down upon his side, and Sir Tristram stood and beheld him.

Then when Sir Blamore might speak, he said thus: Sir Tristram de Liones, I require thee, as thou art a noble knight, and the best knight that ever I found, that thou wilt slay me out, for I would not live to be made lord of all the earth, for I have liefer die with worship than live with shame; and needs, Sir Tristram, thou must slay me, or else thou shalt never win the field, for I will never say the loath word. And therefore if thou dare slay me, slay me, I require thee. When Sir Tristram heard him say so knightly, he wist not what to do with him; he remembering him of both parties, of what blood he was come, and for Sir Launcelot's sake he would be loath to slay him; and in the other party in no wise he might not choose, but that he must make him to say the loath word, or else to slay him.

Then Sir Tristram stert aback, and went to the kings that were judges, and there he kneeled down to-fore them, and besought them for their worships, and for King Arthur's and Sir Launcelot's sake, that they would take this matter in their hands. For, my fair lords, said Sir Tristram, it were shame and pity that this noble knight that yonder lieth should be slain; for ye hear well, shamed will he not be, and I pray to God that he never be slain nor shamed for me. And as for the king for whom I fight for, I shall require him, as I am his true champion and true knight in this field, that he will have mercy upon this good knight. So God me help, said King Anguish, I will for your sake, Sir Tristram, be ruled as ye will have me, for I know you for my true knight; and therefore I will heartily pray the kings that be here as judges to take it in their hands. And the kings that were judges called Sir Bleoberis to them, and asked him his advice. My lords, said Bleoberis, though my brother be beaten, and hath the worse through might of arms, I dare say, though Sir Tristram hath beaten his body he hath not beaten his heart, and I thank God he is not shamed this day; and rather than he should be shamed I require you, said Bleoberis, let Sir Tristram slay him out. It shall not be so, said the kings, for his part adversary, both the king and the champion, have pity of Sir Blamore's knighthood. My lords, said Bleoberis, I will right well as ye will.

Then the kings called the King of Ireland, and found him goodly and treatable. And then, by all their advices, Sir Tristram and Sir Bleoberis took up Sir Blamore, and the two brethren were accorded with King Anguish, and kissed and made friends for ever. And then Sir Blamore and Sir Tristram kissed together, and there they made their oaths that they would never none of them two brethren fight with Sir Tristram, and Sir Tristram made the same oath. And for that gentle battle all the blood of Sir Launcelot loved Sir Tristram for ever.

Then King Anguish and Sir Tristram took their leave, and sailed into Ireland with great noblesse and joy. So when they were in Ireland the king let make it known throughout all the land how and in what manner Sir Tristram had done for him. Then the queen and all that there were made the most of him that they might. But the joy that La Beale

Isoud made of Sir Tristram there might no tongue tell, for of all men earthly she loved him most.

HOW SIR TRISTRAM DEMANDED LA BEALE ISOUD FOR KING MARK, AND HOW SIR TRISTRAM AND ISOUD DRANK THE LOVE DRINK, AND HOW SIR TRISTRAM RESCUED ISOUD FROM SIR PALAMIDES. Then upon a day King Anguish asked Sir Tristram why he asked not his boon, for whatsomever he had promised him he should have it without fail. Sir, said Sir Tristram, now is it time; this is all that I will desire, that ye will give me La Beale Isoud, your daughter, not for myself, but for mine uncle, King Mark, that shall have her to wife, for so have I promised him. Alas, said the king, I had liefer than all the land that I have ye would wed her yourself. Sir, an I did, then I were shamed for ever in this world, and false of my promise. Therefore, said Sir Tristram, I pray you hold your promise that ye promised me; for this is my desire, that ye will give me La Beale Isoud to go with me into Cornwall for to be wedded to King Mark, mine uncle. As for that, said King Anguish, ye shall have her with you to do with her what it please you; that is for to say if that ye list to wed her yourself, that is me liefest, and if ye will give her unto King Mark, your uncle, that is in your choice. So, to make short conclusion, La Beale Isoud was made ready to go with Sir Tristram, and Dame Bragwaine went with her for her chief gentlewoman, with many other.

Then the queen, Isoud's mother, gave to her and Dame Bragwaine, her daughter's gentlewoman, and unto Gouvernail, a drink, and charged them that what day King Mark should wed, that same day they should give him that drink, so that King Mark should drink to La Beale Isoud, and then, said the queen, I undertake either shall love other the days of their life. So this drink was given unto Dame Bragwaine, and unto Gouvernail. And then anon Sir Tristram took the sea, and La Beale Isoud; and when they were in their cabin, it happed so that they were thirsty, and they saw a little flasket of gold stand by them, and it seemed by the colour and the taste that it was noble wine. Then Sir Tristram took the flasket in his hand, and said, Madam Isoud, here is the best drink that ever ye drank, that Dame Bragwaine, your maiden, and Gouvernail, my servant, have kept for themselves. Then they laughed and made good cheer, and either drank to other freely, and they thought never drink that ever they drank to other was so sweet nor so good. But by that their drink was in their bodies, they loved either other so well that never their love departed for weal neither for woe.

Then Sir Tristram and La Beale Isoud came into Cornwall, and there all the barons met them. And anon King Mark and La Beale Isoud were richly wedded with great noblesse. Then was there great jousts and great tourneying, and many lords and ladies were at that feast, and Sir Tristram was most praised of all other.

Thus dured the feast long, and after the feast was done, within a little while after, by the assent of two ladies that were with Queen Isoud, they ordained for hate and envy for to destroy Dame Bragwaine, that was maiden and lady unto La Beale Isoud; and she was sent into the forest for to fetch herbs, and there she was met, and bound feet and hand to a tree, and so she was bounden three days. And by fortune,

Sir Palamides found Dame Bragwaine, and there he delivered her from the death, and brought her to a nunnery there beside, for to be recovered. When Isoud the queen missed her maiden, wit ye well she was right heavy as ever was any queen, for of all earthly women she loved her best: the cause was for she came with her out of her country. And so upon a day Queen Isoud walked into the forest to put away her thoughts, and there she went herself unto a well and made great moan. And suddenly there came Palamides to her, and had heard all her complaint, and said: Madam Isoud, an ye will grant me my boon, I shall bring to you Dame Bragwaine safe and sound. And the queen was so glad of his proffer that suddenly unadvised she granted all his asking. Well, Madam, said Palamides, I trust to your promise, and if ye will abide here half an hour I shall bring her to you. I shall abide you, said La Beale Isoud. And Sir Palamides rode forth his way to that nunnery, and lightly he came again with Dame Bragwaine; but by her good will she would not have come again, because for love of the queen she stood in adventure of her life. Notwithstanding, half against her will, she went with Sir Palamides unto the queen. And when the queen saw her she was passing glad. Now, Madam, said Palamides, remember upon your promise, for I have fulfilled my promise. Sir Palamides, said the queen, I wot not what is your desire, but I will that ye wit, howbeit I promised you largely, I thought none evil, nor I warn you none evil will I do. Madam, said Sir Palamides, as at this time, ye shall not know my desire, but before my lord your husband there shall ye know that I will have my desire that ye have promised me. And therewith the queen departed, and rode home to the king, and Sir Palamides rode after her.

And when Sir Palamides came before the king, he said: Sir King, I require you, as ye be a righteous king, that ye will judge me the right. Tell me your cause, said the king, and ye shall have right. Sir, said Palamides, I promised your Queen Isoud to bring again Dame Bragwaine that she had lost, upon this covenant, that she should grant me a boon that I would ask, and without grudging, outher advisement, she granted me. What say ye, my lady? said the king. It is as he saith, said the queen; to say thee sooth I promised him his asking for love and joy that I had to see her. Well, Madam, said the king, and if ye were hasty to grant him what boon he would ask, I will well that ye perform your promise. Then, said Palamides, I will that ye wit that I will have your queen to lead her and govern her whereas me list. Therewith the king stood still, and bethought him of Sir Tristram, and deemed that he would rescue her. And then hastily the king answered: Take her with the adventures that shall fall of it, for as I suppose thou wilt not enjoy her no while. As for that, said Palamides, I dare right well abide the adventure. And so, to make short tale, Sir Palamides took her by the hand and said: Madam, grudge not to go with me, for I desire nothing but your own promise. As for that, said the queen, I fear not greatly to go with thee, howbeit thou hast me at advantage upon my promise, for I doubt not I shall be worshipfully rescued from thee. As for that, said Sir Palamides, be it as it be may. So Queen Isoud was set behind Palamides, and rode his way.

Anon the king sent after Sir Tristram, but in no wise he could be found, for he was in the forest a-hunting; for that was always his custom, but if he used arms, to chase and to hunt in the forests. Alas, said the king, now I am shamed for ever, that by mine own assent my lady and my queen shall be devoured. Then came forth a knight, his name was Lambegus, and he was a knight of Sir Tristram. My lord, said this knight, sith ye have trust in my lord, Sir Tristram, wit ye well for his sake I will ride after your queen and rescue her, or else I shall be beaten. Gramercy, said the king, as I live, Sir Lambegus, I shall deserve it. And then Sir Lambegus armed him, and rode after as fast as he might. And then within a while he overtook Sir Palamides. And then Sir Palamides left the queen. What art thou, said Palamides, art thou Tristram? Nay, he said, I am his servant, and my name is Sir Lambegus. That me repenteth, said Palamides. I had liefer thou hadst been Sir Tristram. I believe you well, said Lambegus, but when thou meetest with Sir Tristram thou shalt have thy hands full. And then they hurtled together and all to-brast their spears, and then they pulled out their swords, and hewed on helms and hauberks. At the last Sir Palamides gave Sir Lambegus such a wound that he fell down like a dead knight to the earth.

Then he looked after La Beale Isoud, and then she was gone he nist where. Wit ye well Sir Palamides was never so heavy. So the queen ran into the forest, and there she found a well, and therein she had thought to have drowned herself. And as good fortune would, there came a knight to her that had a castle thereby, his name was Sir Adtherp. And when he found the queen in that mischief he rescued her, and brought her to his castle. And when he wist what she was he armed him, and took his horse, and said he would be avenged upon Palamides; and so he rode on till he met with him, and there Sir Palamides wounded him sore, and by force he made him to tell him the cause why he did battle with him, and how he had led the queen unto his castle. Now bring me there, said Palamides, or thou shalt die of my hands. Sir, said Sir Adtherp, I am so wounded I may not follow, but ride you this way and it shall bring you into my castle, and there within is the queen. Then Sir Palamides rode still till he came to the castle. And at a window La Beale Isoud saw Sir Palamides; then she made the gates to be shut strongly. And when he saw he might not come within the castle, he put off his bridle and his saddle, and put his horse to pasture, and set himself down at the gate like a man that was out of his wit that recked not of himself.

Now turn we unto Sir Tristram, that when he was come home and wist La Beale Isoud was gone with Sir Palamides, wit ye well he was wroth out of measure. Alas, said Sir Tristram, I am this day shamed. Then he cried to Gouvernail his man: Haste thee that I were armed and on horseback, for well I wot Lambegus hath no might nor strength to withstand Sir Palamides: alas that I have not been in his stead! So anon as he was armed and horsed Sir Tristram and Gouvernail rode after into the forest, and within a while he found his knight Lambegus almost wounded to the death; and Sir Tristram bare him to a forester, and charged him to keep him well. And then he rode forth, and there he found Sir Adtherp sore wounded, and he told him how the queen would have drowned herself had he not been, and how for her sake and love he had taken upon him to do battle with Sir Palamides. Where is my lady? said Sir Tristram. Sir, said the knight, she is sure enough within my castle, an she can hold her within it. Gramercy, said Sir Tristram, of thy great goodness. And so he rode till he came nigh to that castle; and then Sir Tristram saw where Sir Palamides sat at the gate sleeping, and his horse pastured fast afore him. Now go thou, Gouvernail, said Sir Tristram, and bid him awake, and make him ready. So Gouvernail rode unto him and said: Sir Palamides, arise, and take to thee thine harness. But he was in such a study he heard not what Gouvernail said. So Gouvernail came again and told Sir Tristram he slept, or else he was mad. Go thou again, said Sir Tristram, and bid him arise, and tell him that I am here, his mortal foe. So Gouvernail rode again and put upon him the butt of his spear, and said: Sir Palamides, make thee ready, for wit ye well Sir Tristram hoveth yonder, and sendeth thee word he is thy mortal foe.

And therewithal Sir Palamides arose stilly, without words, and gat his horse, and saddled him and bridled him, and lightly he leapt upon, and gat his spear in his hand, and either feutred their spears and hurtled fast together; and there Tristram smote down Sir Palamides over his horse's tail. Then lightly Sir Palamides put his shield afore him and drew his sword. And there began strong battle on both parts, for both they fought for the love of one lady, and ever she lay on the walls and beheld them how they fought out of measure, and either were wounded passing sore, but Palamides was much sorer wounded. Thus they fought tracing and traversing more than two hours, that well-nigh for dole and sorrow La Beale Isoud swooned. Alas, she said, that one I loved and yet do, and the other I love not, yet it were great pity that I should see Sir Palamides slain; for well I know by that time the end be done Sir Palamides is but a dead knight: because he is not christened I would be loath that he should die a Saracen. And therewithal she came down and besought Sir Tristram to fight no more. Ah, madam, said he, what mean you, will ye have me shamed? Well ye know I will be ruled by you. I will not your dishonour, said La Beale Isoud, but I would that ye would for my sake spare this unhappy Saracen Palamides. Madam, said Sir Tristram, I will leave fighting at this time for your sake. Then she said to Sir Palamides: This shall be your charge, that thou shalt go out of this country while I am therein. I will obey your commandment, said Sir Palamides, the which is sore against my will. Then take thy way, said La Beale Isoud, unto the court of King Arthur, and there recommend me unto Queen Guenever, and tell her that I send her word that there be within this land but four lovers, that is, Sir Launcelot du Lake and Queen Guenever, and Sir Tristram de Liones and Queen Isoud.

OF THE DEBATE OF KING MARK AND SIR TRISTRAM, AND HOW SIR TRISTRAM SMOTE DOWN SIR LAMORAK, AND IN DESPITE OF SIR TRISTRAM SIR LAMORAK SENT AN HORN TO KING MARK. And so Sir Palamides departed with great heaviness. And Sir Tristram took the queen and brought her again to King Mark, and then was there made great joy of her home-coming. Who was cherished but Sir Tristram! But ever Sir Andred, that was nigh cousin to Sir Tristram, lay in a watch to wait betwixt Sir Tristram and La Beale Isoud, for to take them and slander them. So upon a day Sir Tristram talked with La Beale Isoud in a window, and that espied Sir Andred, and told it to the King. Then King Mark took a sword in his hand and came to Sir Tristram, and called him false traitor, and would have stricken him.

But Sir Tristram was nigh him, and ran under his sword, and took it out of his hand. And then the King cried: Where are my knights and my men? I charge you slay this traitor. But at that time there was not one would move for his words. When Sir Tristram saw.that there was not one would be against him, he shook the sword to the king, and made countenance as though he would have stricken him. And then King Mark fled, and Sir Tristram followed him, and smote upon him five or six strokes flatling on the neck, that he made him to fall upon the nose. And then Sir Tristram went his way and armed him, and took his horse and his man, and so he rode into that forest.

Then King Mark called his council unto him, and asked advice of his barons what was best to do with Sir Tristram. Sir, said the barons, in especial Sir Dinas, the Seneschal, Sir, we will give you counsel for to send for Sir Tristram, for we will that ye wit many men will hold with Sir Tristram an he were hard bestead. And sir, said Sir Dinas, ye shall understand that Sir Tristram is called peerless and makeless of any Christian knight, and of his might and hardiness we knew none so good a knight, but if it be Sir Launcelot du Lake. And if he depart from your court and go to King Arthur's court, wit ye well he will get him such friends there that he will not set by your malice. And therefore, sir, I counsel you to take him to your grace. I will well, said the king, that he be sent for, that we may be friends. Then the barons sent for Sir Tristram under a safe conduct. And so when Sir Tristram came to the king he was welcome, and no rehearsal was made, and there was game and play. And then the king and the queen went a-hunting, and Sir Tristram.

The king and the queen made their pavilions and their tents in that forest beside a river, and there was daily hunting and jousting, for there were ever thirty knights ready to joust unto all them that came in at that time. And there by fortune came Sir Lamorak de Galis and Sir Driant; and there Sir Driant jousted right well, but at the last he had a fall. Then Sir Lamorak proffered to joust. And when he began he fared so with the thirty knights that there was not one of them but that he gave him a fall, and some of them were sore hurt. I marvel, said King Mark, what knight he is that doth such deeds of arms. Sir, said Sir Tristram, I know him well for a noble knight as few now be living, and his name is Sir Lamorak de Galis. It were great shame, said the king, that he should go thus away, unless that some of you meet with him better. Sir, said Sir Tristram, meseemeth it were no worship for a noble man to have ado with him, insomuch as he and his horse are weary both; for the deeds of arms that he hath done this day, and they be well considered, it were enough for Sir Launcelot du Lake. As for that, said King Mark, I require you, as ye love me and my lady the queen, La Beale Isoud, take your arms and joust with Sir Lamorak de Galis. Sir, said Sir Tristram, ye bid me do a thing that is against knighthood; but because I will not displease you, as ye require me so will I do, and obey your commandment.

And so Sir Tristram armed him and took his horse, and put him forth, and there Sir Lamorak met him mightily, and what with the might of his own spear, and of Sir Tristram's spear, Sir Lamorak's horse fell to the earth, and he sitting in the saddle. Then anon as lightly as he might he avoided the saddle and his horse, and put his shield afore him and drew his sword. And then he bade Sir Tristram: Alight, thou knight, an thou durst. Nay, said Sir Tristram, I will no more have ado with thee, for I have done to thee over much unto my dishonour and to thy worship. As for that, said Sir Lamorak, I can thee no thank; since thou hast for-jousted me on horseback I require thee and I beseech thee, an thou be Sir Tristram, fight with me on foot. I will not so, said Sir Tristram; and wit ye well my name is Sir Tristram de Liones, and well I know ye be Sir Lamorak de Galis, and this that I have done to you was against my will, but I was required thereto; but to say that I will do at your request as at this time, I will have no more ado with you, for me shameth of that I have done. As for the shame, said Sir Lamorak, on thy part or on mine, bear thou it an thou wilt, for though a mare's son hath failed me, now a queen's son shall not fail thee; and therefore, an thou be such a knight as men call thee, I require thee, alight, and fight with me. Sir Lamorak, said Sir Tristram, I understand your heart is great, and cause why ye have, to say thee sooth; for it would grieve me an any knight should keep him fresh and then to strike down a weary knight, for that knight nor horse was never formed that alway might stand or endure. And therefore, said Sir Tristram, I will not have ado with you, for me forthinketh of that I have done. As for that, said Sir Lamorak, I shall quit you, an ever I see my time. So he departed from him with Sir Driant, and by the way they met with a knight that was sent from Morgan le Fay unto King Arthur; and this knight had a fair horn harnessed with gold, and the horn had such a virtue that there might no lady nor gentlewoman drink of that horn but if she were true to her husband, and if she were false she should spill all the drink, and if she were true to her lord she might drink peaceable. And because of the Queen Guenever, and in the despite of Sir Launcelot, this horn was sent unto King Arthur; and by force Sir Lamorak made that knight to tell all the cause why he bare that horn. Now shalt thou bear this horn, said Lamorak, unto King Mark, or else choose thou to die for it; for I tell thee plainly, in despite and reproof of Sir Tristram thou shalt bear that horn unto King Mark, his uncle, and say thou to him that I sent it him for to assay his lady, and if she be true to him he shall prove her. So the knight went his way unto King Mark, and brought him that rich horn, and said that Sir Lamorak sent it him, and thereto he told him the virtue of that horn. Then the king made Queen Isoud to drink thereof, and an hundred ladies, and there were but four ladies of all those that drank clean. Alas, said King Mark, this is a great despite, and sware a great oath that she should be burnt and the other ladies.

Then the barons gathered them together, and said plainly they would not have those ladies burnt for an horn made by sorcery, that came from as false a sorceress and witch as then was living. For that horn did never good, but caused strife and debate, and always in her days she had been an enemy to all true lovers. So there were many knights made their avow, an ever they met with Morgan le Fay, that they would show her short courtesy. Also Sir Tristram was passing wroth that Sir Lamorak sent that horn unto King Mark, for well he knew that it was done in the despite of him. And therefore he thought to quite Sir Lamorak.

HOW SIR TRISTRAM WAS TAKEN WITH LA BEALE ISOUD, AND HOW HE ESCAPED TO BRITTANY AND SERVED IN WAR KING HOWEL. Then, always, Sir Tristram used to go to Queen Isoud when he might, and ever Sir Andred his cousin watched him night and day for to take him with La Beale Isoud. And so upon a day Sir Andred espied the hour and the time when Sir Tristram went to his lady. Then Sir Andred gat unto him twelve knights, and he set upon Sir Tristram secretly and suddenly, and there Sir Tristram was taken with La Beale Isoud, and then was he bound hand and foot, and so was he kept until the next day. And then by the assent of King Mark, and of Sir Andred, and of some of the barons, Sir Tristram was led unto a chapel that stood upon the sea rocks, there for to take his judgment: and so he was led bounden with forty knights. And when Sir Tristram saw that there was none other remedy but needs that he must die, then said he: Fair lords, remember what I have done for the country of Cornwall, and in what jeopardy I have been in for the weal of you all. Fie upon thee, said Sir Andred, false traitor that thou art, with thine avaunting; for all thy boast thou shalt die this day; and therewith he drew his sword, and would have slain him.

When Sir Tristram saw him make such countenance he looked upon both his hands that were fast bounden unto two knights, and suddenly he pulled them both to him, and unwrast his hands, and then he leapt unto his cousin, Sir Andred, and writhed his sword out of his hands; then he smote Sir Andred that he fell to the earth, and so Sir Tristram fought till that he had killed ten knights. So then Sir Tristram gat the chapel and kept it mightily. Then the cry was great, and the people drew fast unto Sir Andred, mo than an hundred. When Sir Tristram saw the people draw unto him, he brake the bars of a window, and so he leapt out and fell upon the crags in the sea. And so at that time Sir Andred nor none of his fellows might get to him, at that time.

So when Gouvernail, and Sir Lambegus, and Sir Sentraille de Lushon, that were Sir Tristram's men, heard he was escaped then they were passing glad; and on the rocks they found him, and with towels they pulled him up. And then Sir Tristram asked them where was La Beale Isoud, for he weened she had been had away of Andred's people. Sir, said Gouvernail, she is put in a lazar-cote. Alas, said Sir Tristram, this is a full ungoodly place for such a fair lady, and if I may she shall not be long there. And so he took his men and went thereas was La Beale Isoud, and fetched her away, and brought her into a forest to a fair manor, and Sir Tristram there abode with her. So the good knight bade his men go from him: For at this time I may not help you. So they departed all save Gouvernail. And so upon a day Sir Tristram went into the forest for to disport him, and then it happened that there he fell asleep; and there came a man that Sir Tristram aforehand had slain his brother, and when this man had found him he shot him through the shoulder with an arrow, and Sir Tristram leapt up and killed that man. And in the meantime it was told King Mark how Sir Tristram and La Beale Isoud were in that same manor, and as soon as ever he might thither he came with many knights to slay Sir Tristram. And when he came there he found him gone; and there he took La Beale Isoud home with him, and kept her strait that by no means never she might wit nor send unto Tristram, nor he unto her. And then when Sir Tristram came toward the old manor he found the track of many horses, and thereby he wist his lady was gone. And then Sir Tristram took great sorrow, and endured with great pain long time, for the arrow that he was hurt withal was envenomed.

Then by the mean of La Beale Isoud a lady that was cousin unto Dame Bragwaine, came to Sir Tristram, and told him that he might not be whole by no means. For thy lady, La Beale Isoud, may not help thee, therefore she biddeth you haste into Brittany to King Howel, and there ye shall find his daughter, Isoud la Blanche Mains, and she shall help thee. Then Sir Tristram and Gouvernail gat them shipping, and so sailed into Brittany. And when King Howel wist that it was Sir Tristram he was full glad of him. Sir, he said, I am come into this country to have help of your daughter, for it is told me that there is none other may heal me but she; and so within a while she healed him.

There was an earl that hight Grip, and this earl made great war upon the king, and put the king to the worse, and besieged him. And on a time Sir Kehydius, that was son to King Howel, as he issued out he was sore wounded, nigh to the death. Then the king went unto Sir Tristram, and prayed him in his wars to help him: For my son, Kehydius, may not go into the field. Sir, said Sir Tristram, I will go to the field and do what I may. Then Sir Tristram issued out of the town, and by great might and force slew the Earl Grip with his own hands, and more than an hundred knights he slew that day. Then King Howel embraced him in his arms, and said: Sir Tristram, all my kingdom I will resign to thee. God defend, said Sir Tristram, for I am beholden unto you for your daughter's sake to do for you.

HOW SIR TRISTRAM WAS MARRIED TO KING HOWEL'S DAUGHTER, ISOUD LA BLANCHE MAINS, AND HOW HE RETURNED TO CORNWALL AND OF THE LOVE OF SIR KEHYDIUS FOR LA BEALE ISOUD. Then by the means of King Howel and Kehydius his son, there grew great love betwixt Isoud and Sir Tristram, for that lady was both good and fair, and a woman of noble blood and fame. And for because Sir Tristram had such cheer and riches, and all other pleasaunce that he had, almost he had forsaken La Beale Isoud. And so upon a time Sir Tristram agreed to wed Isoud la Blanche Mains. And at the last they were wedded, and solemnly held their marriage.

But when La Beale Isoud understood that he was wedded she sent to him by her maiden Bragwaine as piteous letters as could be thought and made, and her conclusion was that, an it pleased Sir Tristram, that he would come to her court, and bring with him Isoud la Blanche Mains, and they should be kept as well as she herself. Then Sir Tristram called unto him Sir Kehydius, and asked him whether he would go with him into Cornwall secretly. He answered him that he was ready at all times. And then he let ordain privily a little vessel, and therein they went, Sir Tristram, Kehydius, Dame Bragwaine, and Gouvernail, Sir Tristram's squire, and so they sailed into Cornwall. And by assent and information of Dame Bragwaine when they were landed they rode unto Sir Dinas, the Seneschal, a trusty friend of Sir Tristram's. And so Dame Bragwaine and Sir Dinas rode to the court of King Mark, and told the queen, La Beale Isoud, that Sir

Tristram was nigh her in that country. Then for very pure joy La Beale Isoud swooned; and when she might speak she said: Gentle knight Seneschal, help that I might speak with him, outher my heart will brast. Then Sir Dinas and Dame Bragwaine brought Sir Tristram and Kehydius privily unto the court, unto a chamber whereas La Beale Isoud had assigned it; and to tell the joy that was betwixt La Beale Isoud and Sir Tristram, there is no tongue can tell it, nor heart think it, nor pen write it. And as the French book maketh mention, at the first time that ever Sir Kehydius saw La Beale Isoud he was so enamoured upon her that for very pure love he might never withdraw it. And then privily he wrote unto her letters and ballads of the most goodliest that were used in those days. And when La Beale Isoud understood his letters she had pity of his complaint, and unavised she wrote another letter to comfort him withal.

And Sir Tristram was all this while in a turret at the commandment of La Beale Isoud, and when she might she came unto Sir Tristram. So on a day King Mark played at the chess under a chamber window; and at that time Sir Tristram and Sir Kehydius were within the chamber over King Mark, and as it mishapped Sir Tristram found the letter that Kehydius sent unto La Beale Isoud, also he had found the letter that she wrote unto Kehydius, and at that same time La Beale Isoud was in the same chamber. Then Sir Tristram came unto La Beale Isoud and said: Madam, here is a letter that was sent unto you, and here is the letter that ye sent unto him that sent you that letter. Alas, Madam, the good love that I have loved you; and many lands and riches have I forsaken for your love, and now ye are a traitress to me, the which doth me great pain. But as for thee, Sir

How Dame Lionesse came forth arrayed like a princess.

How Tristram and Isoud drank the love drink.

How Tristram was known by the little brachet in the garden of King Mark's castle.

The Questing Beast.

Merlin and Nimue

How by her subtle working she made Merlin to go under the stone to let her wit of the marvels there: and she wrought so there for him that he came never out for all the craft he could do.

How Sir Launcelot slew the knight Sir Peris de Forest Savage that did distress ladies, damosels, and gentlewomen.

How Beaumains defeated the Red Knight, and always the damosel spake many foul words unto him.

How Arthur drew his sword Excalibur for the first time.

Kehydius, I brought thee out of Brittany into this country, and thy father, King Howel, I won his lands, howbeit I wedded thy sister Isoud la Blanche Mains for the goodness she did unto me; but wit thou well, Sir Kehydius, for this falsehood and treason thou hast done me, I will revenge it upon thee. And therewithal Sir Tristram drew out his sword and said: Sir Kehydius, keep thee, and then La Beale Isoud swooned to the earth. And when Sir Kehydius saw Sir Tristram come upon him he saw none other remedy, but leapt out at a bay-window even over the head where sat King Mark playing at the chess. And when the king saw one come hurling over his head he said: Fellow, what art thou, and what is the cause thou leapest out at that window? My lord the king, said Kehydius, it fortuned me that I was asleep in the window above your head, and as I slept I slumbered, and so I fell down. And thus Sir Kehydius excused him.

HOW SIR TRISTRAM DEPARTED FROM TINTAGIL, AND HOW HE SORROWED AND WAS SO LONG IN A FOREST TILL HE WAS OUT OF HIS MIND, AND IT WAS NOISED THAT HE WAS DEAD, AND HOW LA BEALE ISOUD WOULD HAVE SLAIN HERSELF. Then Sir Tristram dread sore lest he were discovered unto the king that he was there; wherefore he drew him to the strength of the Tower, and armed him in such armour as he had for to fight with them that would withstand him. And so when Sir Tristram saw there was no resistance against him he sent Gouvernail for his horse and his spear, and knightly he rode forth out of the castle openly, that was called the Castle of Tintagil.

Then Sir Tristram made great sorrow, and upon a night

he put his horse from him, and then he unlaced his armour, and then Sir Tristram would go into the wilderness, and brast down the trees and boughs. Thus he there endured a quarter of a year. And then was he naked and waxed lean and poor of flesh; and so he fell in the fellowship of herdmen and shepherds, and daily they would give him some of their meat and drink. And when he did any shrewd deed they would beat him with rods, and so they clipped him with shears and made him like a fool.

And upon a day Dagonet, King Arthur's fool, came into Cornwall with two squires with him; and as they rode through that forest they came by a fair well where Sir Tristram was wont to be; and the weather was hot, and they alighted to drink of that well, and in the meanwhile their horses brake loose. Right so Sir Tristram came unto them, and first he soused Sir Dagonet in that well, and after his squires, and thereat laughed the shepherds; and forthwithal he ran after their horses and brought them again one by one, and right so, wet as they were, he made them leap up and ride their ways.

Now Sir Dagonet deemed that the shepherds had sent that fool to array them so, because that they laughed at them, and so they rode unto the keepers of beasts and all to-beat them. Sir Tristram saw them beat that were wont to give him meat and drink, then he ran thither and gat Sir Dagonet by the head, and gave him such a fall to the earth that he bruised him sore so that he lay still. And then he wrast his sword out of his hand, and therewith he ran to one of his squires and smote off his head, and the other fled. And so Sir Tristram took his way with that sword in his hand, running as he had been wild wood. Then Sir Dagonet

rode to King Mark and told him how he had sped in that forest. And therefore, said Sir Dagonet, beware, King Mark, that thou come not about that well in the forest, for there is a fool naked, and that fool and I fool met together, and he had almost slain me. Ah, said King Mark, that is Sir Matto le Breune, that fell out of his wit because he lost his lady; for when Sir Gaheris smote down Sir Matto and won his lady of him, never since was he in his mind, and that was pity, for he was a good knight.

Then Sir Andred, that was cousin unto Sir Tristram, made a lady that was his paramour to say and to noise it that she was with Sir Tristram or ever he died. And this tale she brought unto King Mark's court, that she buried him by a well, and that or he died he besought King Mark to make his cousin, Sir Andred, king of the country of Liones, of the which Sir Tristram was lord of. All this did Sir Andred because he would have had Sir Tristram's lands. And when King Mark heard tell that Sir Tristram was dead he wept and made great dole. But when Queen Isoud heard of these tidings she made such sorrow that she was nigh out of her mind; and so upon a day she thought to slay herself and never to live after Sir Tristram's death. And so upon a day La Beale Isoud gat a sword privily and bare it into her garden, and there she pight the sword through a plum tree up to the hilt, so that it stuck fast, and it stood breast high. And as she would have run upon the sword and to have slain herself all this espied King Mark, how she kneeled down and said: Sweet Lord Jesu, have mercy upon me, for I may not live after the death of Sir Tristram de Liones, for he was my first love and he shall be the last. And with these words came King Mark and took her in his arms, and then he took up the sword, and bare her away with him into a tower; and there he made her to be kept, and watched her surely, and after that she lay long sick, nigh at the point of death.

HOW SIR TRISTRAM SLEW THE GIANT TAULEAS, AND HOW KING MARK FOUND SIR TRISTRAM NAKED, AND CAUSED HIM TO BE BORNE TO TINTAGIL, AND HOW HE WAS KNOWN BY A BRACHET AND WAS BANISHED FROM CORNWALL FOR THE TERM OF TEN YEARS.

This meanwhile ran Sir Tristram naked in the forest with the sword in his hand, and so he came to an hermitage, and there he laid him down and slept; and in the meanwhile the hermit stole away his sword, and laid meat down by him. Thus was he kept there a ten days; and at the last he departed and came to the herdmen again. And there was a giant in that country that hight Tauleas, and for fear of Sir Tristram more than seven year he durst never much go at large, but for the most part he kept him in a sure castle of his own; and so this Tauleas heard tell that Sir Tristram was dead, by the noise of the court of King Mark. Then this Tauleas went daily at large. And so he happed upon a day he came to the herdmen wandering and langering, and there he set him down to rest among them. The meanwhile there came a knight of Cornwall that led a lady with him, and his name was Sir Dinant; and when the giant saw him he went from the herdmen and hid him under a tree, and so the knight came to that well, and there he alighted to repose him. And as soon as he was from his horse this giant Tauleas came betwixt this knight and his horse, and took the horse and leapt upon him. So forthwith he rode unto Sir Dinant and took him by the collar, and pulled him afore him upon his horse, and there would have stricken off his head. Then the herdmen said unto Sir Tristram: Help yonder knight. Help ye him, said Sir Tristram. We dare not, said the herdmen. Then Sir Tristram was ware of the sword of the knight thereas it lay; and so thither he ran and took up the sword and struck off Sir Tauleas' head, and so he went his way to the herdmen.

Then the knight took up the giant's head and bare it with him unto King Mark, and told him what adventure betid him in the forest, and how a naked man rescued him from the grimly giant, Tauleas. Where had ye this adventure? said King Mark. Forsooth, said Sir Dinant, at the fair fountain in your forest where many adventurous knights meet, and there is the mad man. Well, said King Mark, I will see that wild man. So within a day or two King Mark commanded his knights and his hunters that they should be ready on the morn for to hunt, and so upon the morn he went unto that forest. And when the king came to that well he found there lying by that well a fair naked man, and a sword by him. Then King Mark blew and straked, and therewith his knights came to him; and then the king commanded his knights to: Take that naked man with fairness, and bring him to my castle. So they did safely and fair, and cast mantles upon Sir Tristram, and so led him unto Tintagil; and there they bathed him, and washed him, and gave him hot suppings till they had brought him well to his remembrance; but all this while there was no creature that knew Sir Tristram, nor what man he was.

So it fell upon a day that the queen, La Beale Isoud, heard of such a man, that ran naked in the forest, and how the king had brought him home to the court. Then La Beale Isoud called unto her Dame Bragwaine and said:

Come on with me, for we will go see this man that my lord brought from the forest the last day. So they passed forth, and asked where was the sick man. And then a squire told the queen that he was in the garden taking his rest, and reposing him against the sun.

Then the queen had always a little brachet with her that Sir Tristram gave her the first time that ever she came into Cornwall, and never would that brachet depart from her but if Sir Tristram was nigh thereas was La Beale Isoud; and this brachet was sent from the king's daughter of France unto Sir Tristram for great love. And anon as this little brachet felt a savour of Sir Tristram, she leapt upon him and licked his lears and his ears, and then she whined and quested, and she smelled at his feet and at his hands, and on all parts of his body that she might come to. Ah, my lady, said Dame Bragwaine unto La Beale Isoud. Alas, alas, said she, I see it is mine own lord, Sir Tristram. And thereupon Isoud fell down in a swoon, and so lay a great while. And when she might speak she said: My lord Sir Tristram, blessed be God ye have your life, and now I am sure ye shall be discovered by this little brachet, for she will never leave you. And also I am sure as soon as my lord, King Mark, do know you he will banish you out of the country of Cornwall, or else he will destroy you; for God's sake, mine own lord, grant King Mark his will, and then draw you unto the court of King Arthur, for there are ye beloved, and ever when I may I shall send unto you; and when ye list ye may come to me, and at all times early and late I will be at your commandment, to live as poor a life as ever did queen or lady. O Madam, said Sir Tristram, go from me, for mickle anger and danger have I escaped for your love.

Then the queen departed, but the brachet would not from him; and therewithal came King Mark, and the brachet set upon him, and bayed at them all. Therewithal Sir Andred spake and said: Sir, this is Sir Tristram, I see by the brachet. Nay, said the king, I cannot suppose that. Then the king asked him upon his faith what he was, and what was his name. So God me help, said he, my name is Sir Tristram de Liones; now do by me what ye list. Ah, said King Mark, me repenteth of your recovery. And then he let call his barons to judge Sir Tristram to the death. Then many of his barons would not assent thereto, and in especial Sir Dinas, the Seneschal, and Sir Fergus. And so by the advice of them all Sir Tristram was banished out of the country for ten year, and thereupon he took his oath upon a book before the king and his barons. And so he was made to depart out of the country of Cornwall; and there were many barons brought him unto his ship, of the which some were his friends and some his foes. And in the meanwhile there came a knight of King Arthur's, his name was Dinadan, and his coming was for to seek after Sir Tristram; then they showed him where he was armed at all points going to the ship. Now fair knight, said Sir Dinadan, ere ye pass this court that ye will joust with me I require thee. With a good will, said Sir Tristram, an these lords will give me leave Then the barons granted thereto, and so they ran together, and there Sir Tristram gave Sir Dinadan a fall. And then he prayed Sir Tristram to give him leave to go in his fellowship. Ye shall be right welcome, said then Sir Tristram.

And so they took their horses and rode to their ships together, and when Sir Tristram was in the sea he said: Greet well King Mark and all mine enemies, and say them I will come again when I may; and well am I rewarded for the fighting with Sir Marhaus, and delivered all this country from servage; and well am I rewarded for the fetching and costs of Queen Isoud out of Ireland, and the danger that I was in first and last; and well am I rewarded when I fought with Sir Blamore de Ganis for King Anguish, father unto La Beale Isoud; and well am I rewarded when I smote down the good knight, Sir Lamorak de Galis, at King Mark's request; and well am I rewarded for the slaying of Tauleas, the mighty giant, and many other deeds have I done for him, and now have I my warison. And tell King Mark that many noble knights of the Table Round have spared the barons of this country for my sake. And forthwithal he took the sea.

HOW SIR TRISTRAM AND SIR DINADAN FOUGHT FOR SIR LAUNCELOT AGAINST THIRTY KNIGHTS, AND HOW SIR TRISTRAM RODE TO A TOURNAMENT AND LODGED WITH AN OLD KNIGHT NAMED SIR PELLOUNES, AND OF THE JOUSTING BEFORE THE TOURNAMENT. And at the next landing, fast by the sea, there met with Sir Tristram and with Sir Dinadan, Sir Ector de Maris and Sir Bors de Ganis; and there Sir Ector jousted with Sir Dinadan, and he smote him and his horse down. And then Sir Tristram would have jousted with Sir Bors, and Sir Bors said that he would not joust with no Cornish knights, for they are not called men of worship; and all this was done upon a bridge. And with this came Sir Bleoberis and Sir Driant, and Sir Bleoberis proffered to joust with

Sir Tristram, and there Sir Tristram smote down Sir Bleoberis. Then said Sir Bors de Ganis: I wist never Cornish knight of so great valour nor so valiant as that knight that beareth the trappings embroidered with crowns. And then Sir Tristram and Sir Dinadan departed from them into a forest, and there met them a damosel that came for the love of Sir Launcelot to seek after some noble knights of King Arthur's court for to rescue Sir Launcelot. And so Sir Launcelot was ordained for, by the treason of Queen Morgan le Fay to have slain Sir Launcelot, and for that cause she ordained thirty knights to lie in await for Sir Launcelot, and this damosel knew this treason. And for this cause the damosel came for to seek noble knights to help Sir Launcelot. For that night, or the day after, Sir Launcelot should come where these thirty knights were. And so this damosel met with Sir Bors and Sir Ector and with Sir Driant, and there she told them all four of the treason of Morgan le Fay; and then they promised her that they would be nigh where Sir Launcelot should meet with the thirty knights. And if so be they set upon him we will do rescues as we can.

So the damosel departed, and by adventure the damosel met with Sir Tristram and with Sir Dinadan, and there the damosel told them all the treason that was ordained for Sir Launcelot. Fair damosel, said Sir Tristram, bring me to that same place where they should meet with Sir Launcelot.

So then anon these thirty knights came fast by these four knights, and they were ware of them, and either of other. And so these thirty knights let them pass, for this cause, that they would not wrath them, if case be that they had ado with Sir Launcelot; and the four knights let them pass to this intent, that they would see and behold what they would do with Sir Launcelot. And so the thirty knights passed on and came by Sir Tristram and by Sir Dinadan, and then Sir Tristram cried on high : Lo, here is a knight against you for the love of Sir Launcelot. And there he slew two with one spear and ten with his sword. And then came in Sir Dinadan and he did passing well, and so of the thirty knights there went but ten away, and they fled. All this battle saw Sir Bors de Ganis and his three fellows, and then they saw well it was the same knight that jousted with them at the bridge; then they took their horses and rode unto Sir Tristram, and praised him and thanked him of his good deeds, and they all desired Sir Tristram to go with them to their lodging; and he said : Nay, he would not go to no lodging. Then they all four knights prayed him to tell them his name. Fair lords, said Sir Tristram, as at this time I will not tell you my name.

Then Sir Tristram and Sir Dinadan rode forth their way, and came to a lodging two mile thence with a good man in a priory, and there they were well at ease. And that same night Sir Bors and Sir Bleoberis, and Sir Ector and Sir Driant, abode still in the same place thereas Sir Tristram fought with the thirty knights; and there they met with Sir Launcelot the same night, and had made promise to lodge with Sir Colgrevance the same night.

But anon as the noble knight, Sir Launcelot, heard of the shield of Cornwall, then wist he well that it was Sir Tristram that fought with his enemies. And then Sir Launcelot praised Sir Tristram, and called him the man of most worship in the world. Then Sir Tristram departed and left Sir Dinadan in the priory, for he was so weary and so sore bruised that he might not ride. And on the next day following Sir Tristram met with pursuivants, and they told him that there was made a great cry of tournament between King Carados of Scotland and the King of North Wales, and either should joust against other at the Castle of Maidens; and these pursuivants sought all the country after the good knights, and in especial King Carados let make seeking for Sir Launcelot du Lake, and the King of Northgalis let seek after Sir Tristram de Liones. And at that time Sir Tristram thought to be at that jousts. And then Sir Tristram took his horse and sought lodging, and there he met with a good ancient knight and prayed him to lodge with him. So this old knight's name was Sir Pellounes, and he told of the great tournament that should be at the Castle of Maidens. And there Sir Launcelot and thirty-two knights of his blood had ordained shields of Cornwall. And right so there came one unto Sir Pellounes, and told him that Sir Persides de Bloise was come home; then that knight held up his hands and thanked God of his coming home. And there Sir Pellounes told Sir Tristram that in two years he had not seen his son, Sir Persides. Sir, said Sir Tristram, I know your son well enough for a good knight.

So on a time Sir Tristram and Sir Persides came to their lodging both at once, and so they unarmed them, and put upon them their clothing. And then these two knights each welcomed other. And when Sir Persides understood that Sir Tristram was of Cornwall, he said he was once in Cornwall: And there I jousted afore King Mark; and so it happed me at that time to overthrow ten knights, and then came to me Sir Tristram de Liones and overthrew me, and took my lady away from me, and that shall I never forget, but I shall remember me an ever I see my time. Ah, said Sir Tristram, now I understand that ye hate Sir Tristram. What deem ye, ween ye that Sir Tristram is not able to withstand your malice? Yes, said Sir Persides, I know well that Sir Tristram is a noble knight and a much better knight than I, yet shall I not owe him my good will. Right as they stood thus talking at a bay-window of that castle, they saw many knights riding to and fro toward the tournament. And then was Sir Tristram ware of a likely knight riding upon a great black horse, and a black-covered shield. What knight is that, said Sir Tristram, with the black horse and the black shield? he seemeth a good knight. I know him well, said Sir Persides, he is one of the best knights of the world. Then is it Sir Launcelot, said Tristram. Nay, said Sir Persides, it is Sir Palomides, that is yet unchristened.

Then they saw much people of the country salute Sir Palomides. And within a while after there came a squire of the castle, that told Sir Pellounes that was lord of that castle, that a knight with a black shield had smitten down thirteen knights. Fair brother, said Sir Tristram unto Sir Persides, let us cast upon us cloaks, and let us go see the play. Not so, said Sir Persides, we will not go like knaves thither, but we will ride like men and good knights to withstand our enemies. So they armed them, and took their horses and great spears, and thither they went thereas many knights assayed themselves before the tournament. And anon Sir Palomides saw Sir Persides, and then he sent a squire unto him and said: Go thou to the yonder knight with the green shield and therein a lion of gold, and say him I require him to joust with me, and tell him that my name is Sir Palomides. When Sir Persides understood that request of Sir Palomides, he made him ready, and there anon they met together, but Sir Persides had a fall. Then Sir Tristram dressed him to be revenged upon Sir Palomides, and that saw Sir Palomides that was ready and so was not Sir Tristram, and took him at an advantage and smote him over his horse's tail when he had no spear in his rest. Then stert up Sir Tristram and took his horse lightly, and was wroth out of measure, and sore ashamed of that fall. Then Sir Tristram sent unto Sir Palomides by Gouvernail, and prayed him to joust with him at his request. Nay, said Sir Palomides, as at this time I will not joust with that knight, for I know him better than he weeneth. And if he be wroth he may right it to-morn at the Castle of Maidens, where he may see me and many other knights.

With that came Sir Dinadan, and when he saw Sir Tristram wroth he list not to jape. Lo, said Sir Dinadan, here may a man prove, be a man never so good yet may he have a fall, and he was never so wise but he might be overseen, and he rideth well that never fell. So Sir Tristram was passing wroth, and said to Sir Persides and to Sir Dinadan: I will revenge me. Right so as they stood talking there, there came by Sir Tristram a likely knight riding passing soberly and heavily with a black shield. What knight is that? said Sir Tristram unto Sir Persides. I know him well, said Sir Persides, for his name is Sir Briant of North Wales; so he passed on among other knights of North Wales. And there came in Sir Launcelot du Lake with a shield of the arms of Cornwall, and he sent a squire unto Sir Briant, and required him to joust with him. Well, said Sir Briant, sithen I am required to joust I will do what I may; and there Sir Launcelot smote down Sir Briant from his horse a great fall. And then Sir Tristram marvelled what knight he was that bare the shield of Cornwall. Whatsoever he be, said Sir Dinadan, I warrant you he is of King Ban's blood, the which be knights of the most noble prowess in the world, for to account so many for so many. Then there came two knights of Northgalis, that one hight Hew de la Montaine, and the other Sir Madok de la Montaine, and they challenged Sir Launcelot foot-hot. Sir Launcelot not refusing them but made him ready, with one spear he smote them down both over their horses' croups; and so Sir Launcelot rode his way. By the good lord, said Sir Tristram, he is a good knight that beareth the shield of Cornwall, and meseemeth he rideth in the best manner that ever I saw knight ride.

Then the King of Northgalis rode unto Sir Palomides and prayed him heartily for his sake to joust with that knight that hath done us of Northgalis despite. Sir, said Sir Palomides, I am full loath to have ado with that knight, and cause why is, for as to-morn the great tournament shall be; and therefore I will keep myself fresh by my will. Nay, said the King of Northgalis, I pray you require him of jousts. Sir, said Sir Palomides, I will joust at your request, and require that knight to joust with me, and often I have seen a man have a fall at his own request.

HOW SIR LAUNCELOT JOUSTED WITH PALOMIDES AND OVERTHREW HIM, AND AFTER HE WAS ASSAILED WITH TWELVE KNIGHTS. Then Sir Palomides sent unto Sir Launcelot a squire, and required him of jousts. Fair fellow, said Sir Launcelot, tell me thy lord's name. Sir, said the squire, my lord's name is Sir Palomides, the good knight. In good hour, said Sir Launcelot, for there is no knight that I saw

How Sir Launcelot fought with a fiendly dragon.

How at the Castle of Corbin a maiden bare in the Sangreal and foretold the achievements of Galahad.

How Galahad drew out the sword from the floating stone at Camelot.

How at a great feast that King Mark made came Eliot the harper and sang the lay that Dinadan had made.

How Sir Launcelot was shot by a gentlewoman hunting.

How Mordred was slain by Arthur, and how by him Arthur was hurt to the death.

How Queen Guenever rode a-maying into the woods and fields beside Westminster.

How King Arthur and Queen Guenever went to see the barge that bore the corpse of Elaine the Fair Maiden of Astolat.

this seven years that I had liefer have ado withal than with him. And so either knights made them ready with two great spears. Nay, said Sir Dinadan, ye shall see that Sir Palomides will quit him right well. It may be so, said Sir Tristram, but I undertake that knight with the shield of Cornwall shall give him a fall. I believe it not, said Sir Dinadan. Right so they spurred their horses and feutred their spears, and either hit other, and Sir Palomides brake a spear upon Sir Launcelot, and he sat and moved not; but Sir Launcelot smote him so lightly that he made his horse to avoid the saddle, and the stroke brake his shield and the hauberk, and had he not fallen he had been slain. How now, said Sir Tristram, I wist well by the manner of their riding both that Sir Palomides should have a fall.

Right so Sir Launcelot rode his way, and rode to a well to drink and to repose him, and they of Northgalis espied him whither he rode; and then there followed him twelve knights for to have mischieved him, for this cause that upon the morn at the tournament of the Castle of Maidens that he should not win the victory. So they came upon Sir Launcelot suddenly, and unnethe he might put upon him his helm and take his horse, but they were in hands with him; and then Sir Launcelot gat his spear, and rode through them, and there he slew a knight and brake a spear in his body. Then he drew his sword and smote upon the right hand and upon the left hand, so that within a few strokes he had slain other three knights, and the remnant that abode he wounded them sore, all that did abide. Thus Sir Launcelot escaped from his enemies of North Wales, and then Sir Launcelot rode his way to a friend, and lodged him till on the morn; for he would not the first day have ado in the tournament because of his great labour. And on the first day he was with King Arthur, there as he was set on high upon a scaffold to discern who was best worthy of his deeds. So Sir Launcelot was with King Arthur, and jousted not the first day.

OF THE TOURNAMENT AT THE CASTLE OF MAIDENS, AND OF HOW SIR TRISTRAM, SIR PALOMIDES, AND SIR LAUNCELOT BEHAVED THEM. Now turn we unto Sir Tristram de Liones, that commanded Gouvernail, his servant, to ordain him a black shield with none other remembrance therein. And so Sir Persides and Sir Tristram departed from their host Sir Pellounes, and they rode early toward the tournament, and then they drew them to King Carados' side, of Scotland; and anon knights began the field what of King Northgalis' part, and what of King Carados' part, and there began great party. Then there was hurling and rashing. Right so came in Sir Persides and Sir Tristram, and so they did fare that they put the King of Northgalis aback. Then came in Sir Bleoberis de Ganis and Sir Gaheris with them of Northgalis, and then was Sir Persides smitten down and almost slain, for more than forty horsemen went over him. For Sir Bleoberis did great deeds of arms, and Sir Gaheris failed him not. When Sir Tristram beheld them, and saw them do such deeds of arms he marvelled what they were. Also Sir Tristram thought shame that Sir Persides was so done to; and then he gat a great spear in his hand, and then he rode to Sir Gaheris and smote him down from his horse. And then was Sir Bleoberis wroth, and gat a spear and rode against Sir Tristram in great ire; and there

Sir Tristram met with him, and smote Sir Bleoberis from his horse. So then the King with the Hundred Knights was wroth, and he horsed Sir Bleoberis and Sir Gaheris again, and there began a great medley; and ever Sir Tristram held them passing short, and ever Sir Bleoberis was passing busy upon Sir Tristram; and there came Sir Dinadan against Sir Tristram, and Sir Tristram gave him such a buffet that he swooned in his saddle. Then anon Sir Dinadan came to Sir Tristram and said: Sir, I know thee better than thou weenest; but here I promise thee my troth I will never come against thee more, for I promise thee that sword of thine shall never come on mine helm.

With that came Sir Bleoberis, and Sir Tristram gave him such a buffet that down he laid his head; and then he raught him so sore by the helm that he pulled him under his horse's feet. And then King Arthur blew to lodging. Then Sir Tristram departed to his pavilion, and Sir Dinadan rode with him; and Sir Persides and King Arthur then, and the kings upon both parties, marvelled what knight that was with the black shield. Many said their advice, and some knew him for Sir Tristram, and held their peace and would nought say. So that first day King Arthur, and all the kings and lords that were judges, gave Sir Tristram the prize; howbeit they knew him not, but named him the Knight with the Black Shield.

Then upon the morn Sir Palomides returned from the King of Northgalis, and rode to King Arthur's side, where was King Carados, and the King of Ireland, and Sir Launcelot's kin, and Sir Gawaine's kin. Then will I be with the King of Northgalis, said Sir Tristram, because Sir Palomides will be on King Arthur's side, and else I would not but for his sake. So when King Arthur was come they blew unto the field; and then there began a great party, and so King Carados jousted with the King of the Hundred Knights, and there King Carados had a fall: then was there hurling and rashing, and right so came in knights of King Arthur's, and they bare aback the King of Northgalis' knights.

Then Sir Tristram came in, and began so roughly and so bigly that there was none might withstand him, and thus Sir Tristram dured long. And at the last Sir Tristram fell among the fellowship of King Ban, and there fell upon him Sir Bors de Ganis, and Sir Ector de Maris, and Sir Blamore de Ganis, and many other knights. And then Sir Tristram smote on the right hand and on the left hand, that all lords and ladies spake of his noble deeds. But at the last Sir Tristram should have had the worse had not the King with the Hundred Knights been. And then he came with his fellowship and rescued Sir Tristram, and brought him away from those knights that bare the shields of Cornwall. And then Sir Tristram saw another fellowship by themselves, and there were a forty knights together, and Sir Kay, the Seneschal, was their governor. Then Sir Tristram rode in amongst them, and there he smote down Sir Kay from his horse; and there he fared among those knights like a greyhound among conies.

Then Sir Launcelot found a knight that was sore wounded upon the head. Sir, said Sir Launcelot, who wounded you so sore? Sir, he said, a knight that beareth a black shield, and I may curse the time that ever I met with him, for he is a devil and no man. So Sir Launcelot departed from him and thought to meet with Sir Tristram, and so he rode with his sword drawn in his hand to seek Sir Tristram; and then he espied him how he hurled here and there, and at every stroke Sir Tristram well-nigh smote down a knight. O mercy! said the king, sith the times I bare arms saw I never no knight do so marvellous deeds of arms. And if I should set upon this knight, said Sir Launcelot to himself, I did shame to myself, and therewithal Sir Launcelot put up his sword. And then the King with the Hundred Knights and an hundred more of North Wales set upon the twenty of Sir Launcelot's kin: and they twenty knights held them ever together as wild swine, and none would fail other. And so when Sir Tristram beheld the noblesse of these twenty knights he marvelled of their good deeds, for he saw by their fare and by their rule that they had liefer die than avoid the field. Now truly, said Sir Tristram, well may he be valiant and full of prowess that hath such a sort of noble knights unto his kin, and full like is he to be a noble man that is their leader and governor. He meant it by Sir Launcelot du Lake. So when Sir Tristram had beholden them long he thought shame to see two hundred knights battering upon twenty knights. Then Sir Tristram rode unto the King with the Hundred Knights and said: Sir, leave your fighting with those twenty knights, for ye win no worship of them, ye be so many and they so few; and wit ye well they will not out of the field I see by their cheer and countenance; and worship get ye none an ye slay them. Therefore leave your fighting with them, for I, to increase my worship, I will ride to the twenty knights and help them with all my might and power. Nay, said the King with the Hundred Knights, ye shall not do so; now I see your courage and courtesy I will withdraw my knights for your pleasure, for evermore a good knight will favour another, and like will draw to like.

Then the King with the Hundred Knights withdrew

his knights. And all this while, and long to-fore, Sir Launcelot had watched upon Sir Tristram with a very purpose to have fellowshipped with him. And then suddenly Sir Tristram, Sir Dinadan, and Gouvernail, his man, rode their way into the forest, that no man perceived where they went. So then King Arthur blew unto lodging, and gave the King of Northgalis the prize because Sir Tristram was upon his side. And upon the morn the king blew unto the tournament upon the third day.

So the King of Northgalis and the King with the Hundred Knights, they two encountered with King Carados and with the King of Ireland; and there the King with the Hundred Knights smote down King Carados, and the King of Northgalis smote down the King of Ireland. With that came in Sir Palomides, and when he came he made great work, for by his indented shield he was well known. So came in King Arthur, and did great deeds of arms together, and put the King of Northgalis and the King with the Hundred Knights to the worse. With this came in Sir Tristram with his black shield, and anon he jousted with Sir Palomides, and there by fine force Sir Tristram smote Sir Palomides over his horse's croup. Then King Arthur cried: Knight with the Black Shield, make thee ready to me, and in the same wise Sir Tristram smote King Arthur. And then by force of King Arthur's knights the King and Sir Palomides were horsed again. Then King Arthur with a great eager heart he gat a spear in his hand, and there upon the one side he smote Sir Tristram over his horse. Then foot-hot Sir Palomides came upon Sir Tristram, as he was upon foot, to have overridden him. Then Sir Tristram was ware of him, and there he stooped aside, and with great ire he gat him by the arm, and pulled him down from his horse. Then Sir Palomides lightly arose, and then they dashed together mightily with their swords; and many kings, queens, and lords stood and beheld them. And at the last Sir Tristram smote Sir Palomides upon the helm three mighty strokes, and at every stroke that he gave him he said: This for Sir Tristram's sake. With that Sir Palomides fell to the earth grovelling.

Then came the King with the Hundred Knights, and brought Sir Tristram an horse, and so was he horsed again. By then was Sir Palomides horsed, and with great ire he jousted upon Sir Tristram with his spear as it was in the rest, and gave him a great dash with his sword. Then Sir Tristram avoided his spear, and gat him by the neck with his both hands, and pulled him clean out of his saddle, and so he bare him afore him the length of ten spears, and then in the presence of them all he let him fall at his adventure. Then Sir Tristram was ware of King Arthur with a naked sword in his hand, and with his spear Sir Tristram ran upon King Arthur; and then King Arthur boldly abode him and with his sword he smote a-two his spear, and therewithal Sir Tristram stonied; and so King Arthur gave him three or four strokes or he might get out his sword, and at the last Sir Tristram drew his sword and either assailed other passing hard. With that the great press departed them. Then Sir Tristram rode here and there and did his great pain, that eleven of the good knights of the blood of King Ban, that was of Sir Launcelot's kin, that day Sir Tristram smote down, that all the estates marvelled of his great deeds and all cried upon the Knight with the Black Shield.

Then this cry was so large that Sir Launcelot heard it. And then he gat a great spear in his hand and came towards the cry. Then Sir Launcelot cried: The Knight with the Black Shield, make thee ready to joust with me. When Sir Tristram heard him say so he gat his spear in his hand, and either abashed down their heads, and came together as thunder; and Sir Tristram's spear brake in pieces, and Sir Launcelot by malfortune struck Sir Tristram on the side a deep wound nigh to the death; but yet Sir Tristram avoided not his saddle, and so the spear brake. Therewithal Sir Tristram that was wounded gat out his sword, and he rushed to Sir Launcelot, and gave him three great strokes upon the helm that the fire sprang thereout, and Sir Launcelot abashed his head lowly toward his saddle-bow. And therewithal Sir Tristram departed from the field, for he felt him so wounded that he weened he should have died; and Sir Dinadan espied him and followed him into the forest. Then Sir Launcelot abode and did many marvellous deeds.

So when Sir Tristram was departed by the forest's side he alighted, and unlaced his harness and freshed his wound; then weened Sir Dinadan that he should have died. Nay, nay, said Sir Tristram, Dinadan never dread thee, for I am heart-whole, and of this wound I shall soon be whole, by the mercy of God. By that Sir Dinadan was ware where came Palomides riding straight upon them. And then Sir Tristram was ware that Sir Palomides came to have destroyed him. And so Sir Dinadan gave him warning, and said: Sir Tristram, my lord, ye are so sore wounded that ye may not have ado with him, therefore I will ride against him and do to him what I may, and if I be slain ye may pray for my soul; and in the meanwhile ye may withdraw you and go into the castle, or in the forest, that he shall not meet with you. Sir Tristram smiled and said: I thank you, Sir Dinadan, of your good will, but ye shall wit that I am able to handle him. And then anon hastily he armed him, and took his horse, and a great spear in his hand, and said to Sir Dinadan: Adieu; and rode toward Sir Palomides a soft pace. Then when Sir Palomides saw that, he made countenance to amend his horse, but he did it for this cause, for he abode Sir Gaheris that came after him. And when he was come he rode toward Sir Tristram. Then Sir Tristram sent unto Sir Palomides, and required him to joust with him; and if he smote down Sir Palomides he would do no more to him; and if it so happened that Sir Palomides smote down Sir Tristram, he bade him do his utterance. So they were accorded. Then they met together, and Sir Tristram smote down Sir Palomides that he had a grievous fall, so that he lay still as he had been dead. And then Sir Tristram ran upon Sir Gaheris, and he would not have jousted; but whether he would or not Sir Tristram smote him over his horse's croup, that he lay still as though he had been dead. And then Sir Tristram rode his way and left Sir Persides' squire within the pavilions, and Sir Tristram and Sir Dinadan rode to an old knight's place to lodge them. And that old knight had five sons at the tournament, for whom he prayed God heartily for their coming home.

And when Sir Tristram departed into the forest Sir Launcelot held alway the stour like hard, as a man araged that took no heed to himself, and wit ye well there was many a noble knight against him. And when King Arthur saw Sir Launcelot do so marvellous deeds of arms he then armed him, and took his horse and his armour, and rode into the field to help Sir Launcelot; and so many knights came in with King Arthur. And to make short tale in conclusion, the King of Northgalis and the King of the Hundred Knights were put to the worse; and because Sir Launcelot abode and was the last in the field the prize was given him. But Sir Launcelot would neither for king, queen, nor knight, have the prize, but where the cry was cried through the field: Sir Launcelot, Sir Launcelot hath won the field this day, Sir Launcelot let make another cry contrary: Sir Tristram hath won the field, for he began first, and last he hath endured, and so hath he done the first day, the second, and the third day.

Then all the estates and degrees high and low said of Sir Launcelot great worship, for the honour that he did unto Sir Tristram; and for that honour doing to Sir Tristram he was at that time more praised and renowned than an he had overthrown five hundred knights; and all the people wholly for this gentleness, first the estates both high and low, and after the commonalty cried at once: Sir Launcelot hath won the field, whosoever say nay. Then was Sir Launcelot wroth and ashamed, and so therewithal he rode to King Arthur. Alas, said the king, we are all dismayed that Sir Tristram is thus departed from us. He is one of the noblest knights that ever I saw hold spear or sword in hand, and the most courteoust knight in his fighting. Then King Arthur, Sir Launcelot, and Sir Dodinas le Savage took their horses to seek Sir Tristram, and Sir Persides had told King Arthur where Sir Tristram was in his pavilion. But when they came there, Sir Tristram and Sir Dinadan were gone.

Then King Arthur and Sir Launcelot were heavy, and returned again to the Castle of Maidens making great dole for the hurt of Sir Tristram, and his sudden departing.

OF THE RAGE OF SIR PALOMIDES FOR DESPITE OF SIR TRISTRAM, AND HOW SIR TRISTRAM, SIR DINADAN, AND SIR PALOMIDES LODGED WITH SIR DARRAS, AND HOW SIR DARRAS PUT THEM IN HIS PRISON FOR THE DEATH OF HIS SONS, BUT AT THE LAST HE LET THEM GO. And thus we let pass King Arthur, and a little we will turn unto Sir Palomides, that after he had a fall of Sir Tristram, he was nigh-hand araged out of his wit for despite of Sir Tristram. And so he followed him by adventure. And as he came by a river, in his woodness he would have made his horse to have leapt over; and the horse failed footing and fell in the river, wherefore Sir Palomides was adread lest he should have been drowned; and then he avoided his horse, and swam to the land, and let his horse go down by adventure.

And when he came to the land he took off his harness, and sat roaring and crying as a man out of his mind. Right so came a damosel even by Sir Palomides, that was sent from Sir Gawaine and his brother unto Sir Mordred, that lay sick in the same place with that old knight where Sir Tristram was. For, as the French book saith, Sir Persides hurt so Sir Mordred a ten days afore; and had it not been for the love of Sir Gawaine and his brother, Sir Persides had slain Sir Mordred. And so this damosel came by Sir Palomides, and she and he had language together, the which pleased neither of them; and so the damosel rode her ways till she came to the old knight's place, and there she told that old knight how she met with the woodest knight by adventure that ever she met withal. What bare he in his shield? said Sir Tristram. It was indented with white and black, said the damosel. Ah, said Sir Tristram, that was Sir Palomides, the good knight. For well I know him, said Sir Tristram, for one of the best knights living in this realm. Then that old knight took a little hackney, and rode for Sir Palomides, and brought him unto his own manor; and full well knew Sir Tristram Sir Palomides, but he said but little, for at that time Sir Tristram was walking upon his feet, and well amended of his hurts; and always when Sir Palomides saw Sir Tristram he would behold him full marvellously, and ever him seemed that he had seen him. Then would he say unto Sir Dinadan: An ever I may meet with Sir Tristram he shall not escape mine hands. I marvel, said Sir Dinadan, that ye boast behind Sir Tristram, for it is but late that he was in your hands, and ye in his hands; why would ye not hold him when ye had him? for I saw myself twice or thrice that ye gat but little worship of Sir Tristram. Then was Sir Palomides ashamed.

And then there came a damosel that told Sir Darras that three of his sons were slain at that tournament, and two grievously wounded that they were never like to help themself. And all this was done by a noble knight that bare the black shield, and that was he that bare the prize. Then came there one and told Sir Darras that the same knight was within, him that bare the black shield. Then Sir Darras went unto Sir Tristram's chamber, and there he found his shield and showed it to the damosel. Ah sir, said the damosel, that same is he that slew your three sons. Then without any tarrying Sir Darras put Sir Tristram, and

Sir Palomides, and Sir Dinadan, within a strong prison, and there Sir Tristram was like to have died of great sickness; and every day Sir Palomides would reprove Sir Tristram of old hate betwixt them. And ever Sir Tristram spake fair and said little. So Sir Tristram endured there great pain, for sickness had undertaken him, and that is the greatest pain a prisoner may have. For all the while a prisoner may have his health of body he may endure under the mercy of God and in hope of good deliverance; but when sickness toucheth a prisoner's body, then may a prisoner say all wealth is him bereft, and then he hath cause to wail and to weep. Right so did Sir Tristram when sickness had undertaken him, for then he took such sorrow that he had almost slain himself.

So a damosel came in to them and found them mourning. Then she went unto Sir Darras, and told him how that mighty knight that bare the black shield was likely to die. That shall not be, said Sir Darras, for God defend when knights come to me for succour that I should suffer them to die within my prison. Therefore, said Sir Darras to the damosel, fetch that knight and his fellows afore me. And then anon when Sir Darras saw Sir Tristram brought afore him, he said: Sir knight, me repenteth of thy sickness, for thou art called a full noble knight, and so it seemeth by thee; and wit ye well it shall never be said that Sir Darras shall destroy such a noble knight as thou art in prison, howbeit that thou hast slain three of my sons, whereby I was greatly aggrieved. But now shalt thou go and thy fellows, and your harness and horses have been fair and clean kept, and ye shall go where it liketh you, upon this covenant, that thou, knight, wilt promise me to be good friend to my sons two that be now alive, and also that thou tell me thy name. Sir, said he, as for me, my name is Sir Tristram de Liones, and in Cornwall was I born, and nephew I am unto King Mark. And as for the death of your sons I might not do withal, for an they had been the next kin that I have I might have done none otherwise. And if I had slain them by treason or treachery I had been worthy to have died. All this I consider, said Sir Darras, that all that ye did was by force of knighthood, and that was the cause I would not put you to death. But sith ye be Sir Tristram, the good knight, I pray you heartily to be my good friend and to my sons. Sir, said Sir Tristram, I promise you by the faith of my body, ever while I live I will do you service, for ye have done to us but as a natural knight ought to do. Then Sir Tristram reposed him there till that he was amended of his sickness; and when he was big and strong they took their leave, and every knight took their horses and so departed and rode together till they came to a crossway. Now fellows, said Sir Tristram, here will we depart in sundry ways.

HOW SIR TRISTRAM SAVED SIR PALOMIDES' LIFE, AND HOW THEY PROMISED TO FIGHT TOGETHER WITHIN A FORTNIGHT, AND HOW THEY WERE BOTH SMITTEN DOWN BY A STRONG KNIGHT. Then in every place Sir Tristram asked and demanded after Sir Launcelot, but in no place he could not hear of him whether he were dead or alive; wherefore Sir Tristram made great dole and sorrow. So Sir Tristram rode by a forest, and then was he ware of a fair tower by a marsh on that one side, and on that other side a fair meadow. And there he saw ten knights fighting together. And ever the nearer he came he saw how there was but one knight did battle against nine knights, and that one did so marvellously that Sir Tristram had great wonder that ever one knight might do so great deeds of arms. And then within a little while he had slain half their horses and unhorsed them, and their horses ran in the fields and forest. Then Sir Tristram had so great pity of that one knight that endured so great pain, and ever he thought it should be Sir Palomides, by his shield. And so he rode unto the knights and cried unto them, and bade them cease of their battle, for they did themselves great shame so many knights to fight with one. Then answered the master of those knights, his name was called Breuse Saunce Pité, that was at that time the most mischievoust knight living, and said thus: Sir knight, what have ye ado with us to meddle? and therefore, an ye be wise, depart on your way as ye came, for this knight shall not escape us. That were pity, said Sir Tristram, that so good a knight as he is should be slain so cowardly; and therefore I warn you I will succour him with all my puissance.

So Sir Tristram alighted off his horse because they were on foot, that they should not slay his horse, and then dressed his shield, with his sword in his hand, and he smote on the right hand and on the left hand passing sore, that well-nigh at every stroke he struck down a knight. And when they espied his strokes they fled all with Breuse Saunce Pité unto the tower, and Sir Tristram followed fast after with his sword in his hand, but they escaped into the tower, and shut Sir Tristram without the gate. And when Sir Tristram saw this he returned aback unto Sir Palomides, and found him sitting under a tree sore wounded. Ah, fair knight, said Sir Tristram, well be ye found. Gramercy, said Sir Palomides, of your great goodness, for ye have rescued me of my life, and saved me from my death. What is your name? said Sir Tristram. He said: My name is Sir Palomides. O Jesu, said Sir Tristram, thou hast a fair grace of me this day that I should rescue thee, and thou art the man in the world that I most hate; but now make thee ready, for I will do battle with thee. What is your name? said Sir Palomides. My name is Sir Tristram, your mortal enemy. It may be so, said Sir Palomides; but ye have done over much for me this day that I should fight with you; for inasmuch as ye have saved my life it will be no worship for you to have ado with me, for ye are fresh and I am wounded sore, and therefore, an ye will needs have ado with me, assign me a day and then I shall meet with you without fail. Ye say well, said Sir Tristram, now I assign you to meet me in the meadow by the river of Camelot, where Merlin set the peron. So they were agreed.

Then Sir Tristram asked Sir Palomides why the nine knights did battle with him. For this cause, said Sir Palomides; as I rode upon mine adventures in a forest here beside I espied where lay a dead knight, and a lady weeping beside him. And when I saw her making such dole, I asked her who slew her lord. Sir, she said, the falsest knight of the world now living, and he is the most villain that ever man heard speak of, and his name is Sir Breuse Saunce Pité. Then for pity I made the damosel to leap on her palfrey, and I promised her to be her warrant, and to help her to inter her lord. And so, suddenly, as I came riding by this tower, there came out Sir Breuse Saunce Pité, and suddenly he struck me from my horse. And then or I might recover my horse this Sir Breuse slew the damosel. And so I took my horse again, and I was sore ashamed, and so began the medley betwixt us: and this is the cause wherefore we did this battle. Well, said Sir Tristram, now I understand the manner of your battle, but in any wise have remembrance of your promise that ye have made with me to do battle with me this day fortnight. I shall not fail you, said Sir Palomides. Well, said Sir Tristram, as at this time I will not fail you till that ye be out of the danger of your enemies.

So they mounted upon their horses, and rode together unto that forest, and there they found a fair well, with clear water burbling. Fair sir, said Sir Tristram, to drink of that water have I courage; and then they alighted off their horses. And then were they ware by them where stood a great horse tied to a tree, and ever he neighed. And then were they ware of a fair knight armed, under a tree, lacking no piece of harness, save his helm lay under his head. By the good lord, said Sir Tristram, yonder lieth a well-faring knight; what is best to do? Awake him, said Sir Palomides. So Sir Tristram awaked him with the butt of his spear. And so the knight rose up hastily and put his helm upon his head, and gat a great spear in his hand; and without any more words he hurled unto Sir Tristram, and smote him clean from his saddle to the earth, and hurt him on the left side, that Sir Tristram lay in great peril. Then he walloped farther, and fetched his course, and came hurling upon Sir Palomides, and there he struck him a part through the body, that he fell from his horse to the earth. And then this strange knight left them there, and took his way through the forest. With this Sir Palomides and Sir Tristram were on foot, and gat their horses again, and either asked counsel of other, what was best to do. By my head, said Sir Tristram, I will follow this strong knight that thus hath shamed us. Well, said

Sir Palomides, and I will repose me hereby with a friend of mine. Beware, said Sir Tristram unto Palomides, that ye fail not that day that ye have set with me to do battle, for, as I deem, ye will not hold your day, for I am much bigger than ye. As for that, said Sir Palomides, be it as it be may, for I fear you not, for an I be not sick nor prisoner, I will not fail you; but I have cause to have much more doubt of you that ye will not meet with me, for ye ride after yonder strong knight. And if ye meet with him it is an hard adventure an ever ye escape his hands. Right so Sir Tristram and Sir Palomides departed, and either took their ways diverse.

And by fortune in a meadow Sir Tristram met with Sir Kay, the Seneschal, and Sir Dinadan. What tidings with you, said Sir Tristram, with you knights? Not good, said these knights. Why so? said Sir Tristram; I pray you tell me, for I ride to seek a knight. What cognisance beareth he? said Sir Kay. He beareth, said Sir Tristram, a covered shield close with cloth. By my head, said Sir Kay, that is the same knight that met with us, for this night we were lodged within a widow's house, and there was that knight lodged; and when he wist we were of Arthur's court he spoke great villainy by the king, and specially by the Queen Guenever, and then on the morn was waged battle with him for that cause. And at the first recounter, said Sir Kay, he smote me down from my horse and hurt me passing sore; and when my fellow, Sir Dinadan, saw me smitten down and hurt he would not revenge me, but fled from me; and thus he departed. And then Sir Tristram asked them their names, and so either told other their names. And so Sir Tristram departed from Sir Kay, and from Sir Dinadan, and so he passed through a great forest into a plain, till he was ware of a priory, and there he reposed him with a good man six days. And then he sent his man that hight Gouvernail, and commanded him to go to a city thereby to fetch him new harness; for it was long time afore that that Sir Tristram had been refreshed, his harness was brised and broken. And when Gouvernail, his servant, was come with his apparel, he mounted upon his horse, and rode his way early on the morn. And by sudden adventure Sir Tristram met with Sir Sagramore le Desirous, and with Sir Dodinas le Savage. And these two knights met with Sir Tristram and questioned with him, and asked him if he would joust with them. Fair knights, said Sir Tristram, with a good will I would joust with you, but I have promised at a day set, near hand, to do battle with a strong knight; and therefore I am loath to have ado with you, for an it misfortuned me here to be hurt I should not be able to do my battle which I promised. As for that, said Sagramore, maugre your head, ye shall joust with us or ye pass from us. Well, said Sir Tristram, if ye enforce me thereto I must do what I may. And then they dressed their shields, and came running together with great ire. But through Sir Tristram's great force he struck Sir Sagramore from his horse. Then he hurled his horse farther, and said to Sir Dodinas: Knight, make thee ready; and so through fine force Sir Tristram struck Dodinas from his horse. And when he saw them lie on the earth he took his bridle, and rode forth on his way, and his man Gouvernail with him.

HOW SIR TRISTRAM MET AT THE PERON WITH SIR LAUNCELOT, AND HOW THEY FOUGHT TOGETHER UNKNOWN, AND HOW SIR LAUNCELOT BROUGHT SIR TRISTRAM TO THE COURT, AND OF THE GREAT JOY THAT THE KING AND OTHER MADE FOR THE COMING OF SIR TRISTRAM. Then departed Sir Tristram and rode straight unto Camelot, to the peron that Merlin had made to-fore, where Sir Lanceor, that was the king's son of Ireland, was slain by the hands of Balin. And in that same place was the fair lady Colombe slain, that was love unto Sir Lanceor; for after he was dead she took his sword and thrust it through her body. And by the craft of Merlin he made to inter this knight, Lanceor, and his lady, Colombe, under one stone. And at that time Merlin prophesied that in that same place should fight two the best knights that ever were in Arthur's days, and the best lovers. So when Sir Tristram came to the tomb where Lanceor and his lady were buried he looked about him after Sir Palomides. Then was he ware of a seemly knight came riding against him all in white, with a covered shield. When he came nigh Sir Tristram he said on high: Ye be welcome, sir knight, and well and truly have ye holden your promise. And then they dressed their shields and spears, and came together with all their might of their horses; and they met so fiercely that both their horses and knights fell to the earth, and as fast as they might avoided their horses, and put their shields afore them: and they struck together with bright swords, as men that were of might, and either wounded other wonderly sore, that the blood ran out upon the grass. And thus they fought the space of four hours, that never one would speak to other one word, and of their harness they had hewn off many pieces. I marvel greatly of the strokes my master hath given to your master, said Gouvernail. By my head, said Sir Launcelot's servant, your master hath not given so many but your master has received as many or more. So they stood and wept both, and made great dole when they saw the bright swords over-covered with blood of their bodies.

Then at the last spake Sir Launcelot and said: Knight, thou fightest wonderly well as ever I saw knight, therefore, an it please you, tell me your name. Sir, said Sir Tristram, that is me loath to tell any man my name. Truly, said Sir Launcelot, an I were required I was never loath to tell my name. It is well said, said Sir Tristram, then I require you to tell me your name? Fair knight, he said, my name is Sir Launcelot du Lake. Alas, said Sir Tristram, what have I done! for ye are the man in the world that I love best. Fair knight, said Sir Launcelot, tell me your name? Truly, said he, my name is Sir Tristram de Liones. O Jesu, said Sir Launcelot, what adventure is befallen me! And therewith Sir Launcelot kneeled down and yielded him up his sword. And therewith Sir Tristram kneeled adown, and yielded him up his sword. And so either gave other the degree. And then they both forthwithal went to the stone, and set them down upon it, and took off their helms to cool them, and either kissed other an hundred times. And then anon after they took off their helms and rode to Camelot. And there they met with Sir Gawaine and with Sir Gaheris that had made promise to Arthur never to come again to the court till they had brought Sir Tristram with them.

Return again, said Sir Launcelot, for your quest is done,

for I have met with Sir Tristram: lo, here is his own person! Then was Sir Gawaine glad, and said to Sir Tristram: Ye are welcome, for now have ye eased me greatly of my labour. For what cause, said Sir Gawaine, came ye into this court? Fair sir, said Sir Tristram, I came into this country because of Sir Palomides; for he and I had assigned at this day to have done battle together at the peron, and I marvel I hear not of him.[1] And thus by adventure my lord, Sir Launcelot, and I met together. With this came King Arthur, and when he wist that there was Sir Tristram, then he ran unto him and took him by the hand and said: Sir Tristram, ye are as welcome as any knight that ever came to this court. And when the king had heard how Sir Launcelot and he had foughten, and either had wounded other wonderly sore, then the king made great dole. Then Sir Tristram told the king how he came thither for to have had ado with Sir Palomides. And then he told the king how he had rescued him from the nine knights and Breuse Saunce Pité; and how he found a knight lying by a well, and that knight smote down Sir Palomides and me, but his shield was covered with a cloth. So Sir Palomides left me, and I followed after that knight; and in many places I found where he had slain knights, and forjousted many. By my head, said Sir Gawaine, that same knight smote me down and Sir Bleoberis, and hurt us sore both, he with the covered shield. Ah, said Sir Kay, that knight smote me adown and hurt me passing sore, and fain would I have known him, but I might not. Mercy, said Arthur, what knight was that with the covered shield? I know not, said Sir Tristram; and so said they all. Now,

[1] The cause of this was that Palomides was made prisoner by a lord, so that he could not keep his day.

said King Arthur, then wot I, for it is Sir Launcelot. Then they all looked upon Sir Launcelot and said: Ye have beguiled us with your covered shield. It is not the first time, said Arthur, he hath done so. My lord, said Sir Launcelot, truly wit ye well I was the same knight that bare the covered shield; and because I would not be known that I was of your court I said no worship of your house. That is truth, said Sir Gawaine, Sir Kay, and Sir Bleoberis.

Then King Arthur took Sir Tristram by the hand and went to the Table Round. Then came Queen Guenever and many ladies with her, and all the ladies said at one voice: Welcome, Sir Tristram! Welcome, said the damosels. Welcome, said knights. Welcome, said Arthur, for one of the best knights, and the gentlest of the world, and the man of most worship; for of all manner of hunting thou bearest the prize, and of all measures of blowing thou art the beginning, and of all the terms of hunting and hawking ye are the beginner, of all instruments of music ye are the best; therefore, gentle knight, said Arthur, ye are welcome to this court. And also, I pray you, said Arthur, grant me a boon. It shall be at your commandment, said Tristram. Well, said Arthur, I will desire of you that ye will abide in my court. Sir, said Sir Tristram, thereto is me loath, for I have ado in many countries. Not so, said Arthur, ye have promised it me, ye may not say nay. Sir, said Sir Tristram, I will as ye will. Then went Arthur unto the sieges about the Round Table, and looked in every siege the which were void that lacked knights. And then the king saw in the siege of Marhaus letters that said: This is the siege of the noble knight, Sir Tristram. And then Arthur made Sir Tristram Knight of the Table Round, with great nobley and great feast as might be thought. For Sir Marhaus was slain afore by the hands of Sir Tristram in an island; and that was well known at that time in the court of Arthur, for this Marhaus was a worthy knight. So leave we of Sir Tristram and speak we of King Mark.

HOW FOR THE DESPITE OF SIR TRISTRAM KING MARK CAME WITH TWO KNIGHTS INTO ENGLAND, AND HOW HE SLEW ONE OF THE KNIGHTS, AND HOW HE WAS SCORNED BY SIR LAMORAK AND SIR DINADAN. When Sir Tristram departed out of Cornwall into England King Mark heard of the great prowess that Sir Tristram did there, the which grieved him sore. So he sent on his part men to espy what deeds he did. And the queen sent privily on her part spies to know what deeds he had done, for great love was between them twain. So when the messengers were come home they told the truth as they had heard, that he passed all other knights but if it were Sir Launcelot. Then King Mark was right heavy of these tidings, and as glad was La Beale Isoud. Then in great despite he took with him two good knights and two squires, and disguised himself, and took his way into England, to the intent for to slay Sir Tristram. And one of these two knights hight Bersules, and the other knight was called Amant. So as they rode King Mark asked a knight that he met, where he should find King Arthur. He said: At Camelot. Also he asked that knight after Sir Tristram, whether he heard of him in the court of King Arthur. Wit you well, said that knight, ye shall find Sir Tristram there for a man of as great worship as is now living; for through his prowess he won the tournament of the Castle of Maidens that standeth by the Hard Rock. And sithen he hath won with his own hands thirty knights that were men of great honour. And the last battle that ever he did he fought with Sir Launcelot; and that was a marvellous battle. And not by force Sir Launcelot brought Sir Tristram to the court, and of him King Arthur made passing great joy, and so made him Knight of the Table Round; and his seat was where the good knight's, Sir Marhaus, seat was. Then was King Mark passing sorry when he heard of the honour of Sir Tristram; and so they departed.

Then said King Mark unto his two knights: Now will I tell you my counsel: ye are the men that I trust most to alive, and I will that ye wit my coming hither is to this intent, for to destroy Sir Tristram by wiles or by treason; and it shall be hard if ever he escape our hands. Alas, said Sir Bersules, what mean you? for ye be set in such a way ye are disposed shamefully; for Sir Tristram is the knight of most worship that we know living, and therefore I warn you plainly I will never consent to do him to the death; and therefore I will yield my service, and forsake you. When King Mark heard him say so, suddenly he drew his sword and said: Ah, traitor; and smote Sir Bersules on the head, that the sword went to his teeth. When Amant, the knight, saw him do that villainous deed, and his squires, they said it was foul done, and mischievously: Wherefore we will do thee no more service, and wit ye well, we will appeach thee of treason afore Arthur. Then was King Mark wonderly wroth and would have slain Amant; but he and the two squires held them together, and set nought by his malice. When King Mark saw he might not be revenged on them, he said thus unto the knight, Amant: Wit thou well, an thou appeach me of treason I shall thereof defend me afore King Arthur; but I require thee that thou tell not my name, that I am King Mark, whatsomever come of me. As for that, said Sir Amant, I will not discover your name; and so they departed, and Amant and his fellows took the body of Bersules and buried it.

Then King Mark rode till he came to a fountain, and there he rested him, and stood in a doubt whether he would ride to Arthur's court or none, or return again to his country. And as he thus rested him by that fountain there came by him a knight well armed on horseback; and he alighted, and tied his horse until a tree, and set him down by the brink of the fountain; and there he made great languor and dole, and made the dolefullest complaint of love that ever man heard; and all this while was he not ware of King Mark. And this was a great part of his complaint: he cried and wept, saying: O fair Queen of Orkney, King Lot's wife, and mother of Sir Gawaine, and to Sir Gaheris, and mother to many other, for thy love I am in great pains. Then King Mark arose and went near him and said: Fair knight, ye have made piteous complaint. Truly, said the knight, it is an hundred part more ruefuller than my heart can utter. I require you, said King Mark, tell me your name. Sir, said he, as for my name I will not hide it from no knight that beareth a shield, and my name is Sir Lamorak de Galis. But when Sir Lamorak heard King Mark speak, then wist he well by his speech that he was a Cornish knight. Sir, said Sir Lamorak, I understand by your tongue ye be of Cornwall, wherein there dwelleth the shamefullest king that is now living, for he is a great enemy to all good knights; and that proveth well, for he hath chased out of that country Sir Tristram, that is the worshipfullest knight that now is living, and all knights speak of him worship; and for jealousness of his queen he hath chased him out of his country. It is pity, said Sir Lamorak, that ever any such false knight-coward as King Mark is, should be matched with such a fair lady and good as La Beale Isoud is, for all the world of him speaketh shame, and of her worship that any queen may have. I have not ado in this matter, said King Mark, neither nought will I speak thereof.

Then there came Sir Dinadan, and saluted them both. And when he wist that King Mark was a knight of Cornwall he reproved him for the love of King Mark a thousand fold more than did Sir Lamorak. Then he proffered to joust with King Mark. And he was full loath thereto, but Sir Dinadan edged him so, that he jousted with Sir Lamorak. And Sir Lamorak smote King Mark so sore that he bare him on his spear end over his horse's tail. And then King Mark arose again, and followed after Sir Lamorak. But Sir Dinadan would not joust with Sir Lamorak, but he told King Mark that Sir Lamorak was Sir Kay, the Seneschal. That is not so, said King Mark, for he is much bigger than Sir Kay; and so he followed and overtook him, and bade him abide. What will you do? said Sir Lamorak. Sir, he said, I will fight with a sword, for ye have shamed me with a spear; and therewith they dashed together with swords, and Sir Lamorak suffered him and forbare him. And King Mark was passing hasty, and smote thick strokes. Sir Lamorak saw he would not stint, and waxed somewhat wroth, and doubled his strokes, for he was one of the noblest knights of the world; and he beat him so on the helm that his head hung nigh on the saddle bow. When Sir Lamorak saw him fare so, he said: Sir knight, what cheer? meseemeth ye have nigh your fill of fighting, it were pity to do you any more harm, for ye are but a mean knight, therefore I give you leave to go where ye list. Gramercy, said King Mark, for ye and I be not matches.

HOW KING MARK SLEW SIR AMANT WRONGFULLY TO-FORE KING ARTHUR, AND SIR LAUNCELOT FETCHED KING MARK AGAIN TO KING ARTHUR. Then King Mark rode as fast as he might unto Camelot; and the same day he found there Amant, the knight, ready, that afore Arthur had appealed him of treason; and so, lightly the king commanded them to do battle. And by misadventure King Mark smote Amant through the body. And yet was Amant in the righteous quarrel. And right so he took his horse and departed from the court for dread of Sir Dinadan, that he would tell Sir Tristram and Sir Palomides what he was. Then were there maidens that La Beale Isoud had sent to Sir Tristram, that knew Sir Amant well.

Then by the license of King Arthur they went to him and spake with him; for while the truncheon of the spear stuck in his body he spake: Ah, fair damosels, said Amant, recommend me unto La Beale Isoud, and tell her that I am slain for the love of her and of Sir Tristram. And there he told the damosels how cowardly King Mark had slain him, and Sir Bersules, his fellow. And for that deed I appealed him of treason, and here am I slain in a righteous quarrel; and all was because Sir Bersules and I would not consent by treason to slay the noble knight, Sir Tristram. Then the two maidens cried aloud that all the court might hear it, and said: O sweet Lord Jesu, that knowest all hid things, why sufferest thou so false a traitor to vanquish and slay a true knight that fought in a righteous quarrel? Then anon it was sprung to the king, and the queen, and to all the lords, that it was King Mark that had slain Sir Amant, and Sir Bersules aforehand; wherefore they did their battle. Then was King Arthur wroth out of measure, and so were all the other knights. But when Sir Tristram knew all the matter he made great dole and sorrow out of measure, and wept for sorrow for the loss of the noble knights, Sir Bersules and Sir Amant.

When Sir Launcelot espied Sir Tristram weep he went hastily to King Arthur, and said: Sir, I pray you give me leave to return again to yonder false king and knight. I pray you, said King Arthur, fetch him again, but I would not that ye slew him, for my worship. Then Sir Launcelot armed him in all haste, and mounted upon a great horse, and took a spear in his hand and rode after King Mark. And from thence a three mile English Sir Launcelot overtook him, and bade him: Turn recreant king and knight, for whether thou wilt or not thou shalt go with me to King Arthur's court. King Mark returned and looked upon Sir Launcelot, and said: Fair sir, what is your name? Wit thou well, said he, my name is Sir Launcelot, and therefore defend thee. And when King Mark wist that it was Sir Launcelot, and came so fast upon him with a spear, he cried then aloud: I yield me to thee, Sir Launcelot, honourable knight. But Sir Launcelot would not hear him, but came fast upon him. King Mark saw that, and made no defence, but tumbled adown out of his saddle to the earth as a sack, and there he lay still, and cried Sir Launcelot mercy. Arise, recreant knight and king. I will not fight, said King Mark, but whither that ye will I will go with you. Alas, alas, said

Sir Launcelot, that I may not give thee one buffet for the love of Sir Tristram and of La Beale Isoud, and for the two knights that thou hast slain traitorly. And so he mounted upon his horse and brought him to King Arthur; and there King Mark alighted in that same place, and threw his helm from him upon the earth, and his sword, and fell flat to the earth of King Arthur's feet, and put him in his grace and mercy. So God me help, said Arthur, ye are welcome in a manner, and in a manner ye are not welcome. In this manner ye are welcome, that ye come hither maugre thy head, as I suppose. That is truth, said King Mark, and else I had not been here, for my lord, Sir Launcelot, brought me hither through his fine force, and to him am I yolden to as recreant. Well, said Arthur, ye understand ye ought to do me service, homage, and fealty. And never would ye do me none, but ever ye have been against me, and a destroyer of my knights; now, how will ye acquit you? Sir, said King Mark, right as your lordship will require me, unto my power, I will make a large amends. For he was a fair speaker, and false thereunder. Then for great pleasure of Sir Tristram, to make them twain accorded, the king withheld King Mark as at that time, and made a broken love-day between them.

HOW KING ARTHUR MADE A JOUSTING, AND HOW SIR LAMORAK CAME IN, AND OVERTHREW SIR GAWAINE, AND HOW KING ARTHUR MADE KING MARK TO BE ACCORDED WITH SIR TRISTRAM AND THEY RODE TOGETHER TO CORNWALL. Then within three days after the king let make a jousting at a priory. And there made them ready many knights of the Round Table, for Sir Gawaine and his brethren made them ready to joust; but Tristram, Launcelot, nor Dinadan, would not joust, but suffered Sir Gawaine, for the love of King Arthur, with his brethren, to win the gree if they might. Then on the morn they apparelled them to joust, Sir Gawaine and his four brethren, and did there great deeds of arms. And Sir Ector de Maris did marvellously well, but Sir Gawaine passed all that fellowship; wherefore King Arthur and all the knights gave Sir Gawaine the honour at the beginning.

Right so King Arthur was ware of a knight and two squires, the which came out of a forest side, with a shield covered with leather, and then he came slyly and hurtled here and there, and anon with one spear he had smitten down two knights of the Round Table. Then with this hurtling he lost the covering of his shield: then was the king and all other ware that he bare a red shield. See where rideth a stout knight, said King Arthur, he with the red shield. And there was noise and crying: Beware the Knight with the Red Shield. So within a little while he had overthrown three brethren of Sir Gawaine's. Truly, said King Arthur, meseemeth yonder is the best jouster that ever I saw. With that he saw him encounter with Sir Gawaine, and he smote him down with so great force that he made his horse to avoid the saddle. How now, said the king, Sir Gawaine hath a fall; well were me an I knew what knight he were with the red shield. I know him well, said Dinadan, but as at this time ye shall not know his name. By my head, said Sir Tristram, he jousted better than Sir Palomides, and if ye list to know his name, wit ye well his name is Sir Lamorak de Galis.

As they stood thus talking, Sir Gawaine and he encountered together again, and there he smote Sir Gawaine from his horse, and brised him sore. And in the sight of King Arthur he smote down twenty knights, beside Sir Gawaine and his brethren. And so clearly was the prize given him as a knight peerless. Then slyly and marvellously Sir Lamorak withdrew him from all the fellowship into the forest side. All this espied King Arthur, for his eye went never from him. Then the king, Sir Launcelot, Sir Tristram, and Sir Dinadan, took their hackneys, and rode straight after the good knight, Sir Lamorak de Galis, and there found him. And thus said the king: Ah, fair knight, well be ye found. When he saw the king he put off his helm and saluted him, and when he saw Sir Tristram he alighted down off his horse and ran to him to take him by the thighs, but Sir Tristram would not suffer him, but he alighted or that he came, and either took other in arms, and made great joy of other. The king was glad, and also was all the fellowship of the Round Table, except Sir Gawaine and his brethren. And when they wist that he was Sir Lamorak, they had great despite at him, and were wonderly wroth with him that he had put Gawaine to dishonour that day.

Then Gawaine called privily in council all his brethren, and to them said thus: Fair brethren, here may ye see, whom that we hate King Arthur loveth, and whom that we love he hateth. And wit ye well, my fair brethren, that this Sir Lamorak will never love us, because we slew his father, King Pellinore, for we deemed that he slew our father, King of Orkney. And for the despite of Pellinore, Sir Lamorak did us a shame to our mother, therefore I will be revenged. Sir, said Sir Gawaine's brethren, let see how ye will or may be revenged, and ye shall find us ready. Well, said Gawaine, hold you still and we shall espy our time.

Now pass we our matter, and leave we Sir Gawaine, and speak of King Arthur, that on a day said unto King Mark: Sir, I pray you give me a gift that I shall ask you. Sir, said King Mark, I will give you whatsomever ye desire an it be in my power. Sir, gramercy, said Arthur. This I will ask you, that ye will be good lord unto Sir Tristram, for he is a man of great honour; and that ye will take him with you into Cornwall, and let him see his friends, and there cherish him for my sake. Sir, said King Mark, I promise you by the faith of my body, and by the faith that I owe to God and to you, I shall worship him for your sake in all that I can or may. Sir, said Arthur, and I will forgive you all the evil will that ever I owed you, an so be that you swear that upon a book before me. With a good will, said King Mark; and so he there sware upon a book afore him and all his knights, and therewith King Mark and Sir Tristram took either other by the hands hard knit together. But for all this King Mark thought falsely, as it proved after, for he put Sir Tristram in prison, and cowardly would have slain him.

Then soon after King Mark took his leave to ride into Cornwall, and Sir Tristram made him ready to ride with him, whereof the most part of the Round Table were wroth and heavy, and in especial Sir Launcelot, and Sir Lamorak, and Sir Dinadan, were wroth out of measure. For well they wist King Mark would slay or destroy Sir Tristram. Alas, said Dinadan, that my lord, Sir Tristram, shall depart. And Sir Tristram took such sorrow that he was amazed like a fool. Alas, said Sir Launcelot unto King Arthur, what have ye done, for ye shall lose the most man of worship that ever came into your court. It was his own desire, said Arthur, and therefore I might not do withal, for I have done all that

I can and made them at accord. Accord, said Sir Launcelot, fie upon that accord, for ye shall hear that he shall slay Sir Tristram, or put him in a prison, for he is the most coward and the villainest king and knight that is now living.

And therewith Sir Launcelot departed, and came to King Mark, and said to him thus: Sir king, wit thou well the good knight Sir Tristram shall go with thee. Beware, I rede thee, of treason, for an thou mischief that knight by any manner of falsehood or treason, by the faith I owe to God and to the order of knighthood, I shall slay thee with mine own hands. Sir Launcelot, said the king, over-much have ye said to me, and I have sworn and said over largely afore King Arthur in hearing of all his knights, that I shall not slay nor betray him. It were to me over-much shame to break my promise. Ye say well, said Sir Launcelot, but ye are called so false and full of treason that no man may believe you. Forsooth it is known well wherefore ye came into this country, and for none other cause but for to slay Sir Tristram. So with great dole King Mark and Sir Tristram rode together, for it was by Sir Tristram's will and his means to go with King Mark, and all was for the intent to see La Beale Isoud, for without the sight of her Sir Tristram might not endure.

HOW SIR PERCIVALE WAS MADE KNIGHT OF KING ARTHUR, AND HOW A DUMB MAID SPAKE, AND BROUGHT HIM TO THE ROUND TABLE. So when King Mark and Sir Tristram were departed from the court there was made great dole and sorrow for the departing of Sir Tristram. Then the king and his knights made no manner of joys eight days after. And at the eight days' end there came to the court a knight with a young squire with him. And when this knight was unarmed, he went to the king and required him to make the young squire a knight. Of what lineage is he come? said King Arthur. Sir, said the knight, he is the son of King Pellinore, that did you some time good service, and he is a brother unto Sir Lamorak de Galis, the good knight. Well, said the king, for what cause desire ye that of me that I should make him knight? Wit you well, my lord the king, that this young squire is brother to me as well as to Sir Lamorak, and my name is Aglavale. Sir Aglavale, said Arthur, for the love of Sir Lamorak, and for his father's love, he shall be made knight to-morrow. Now tell me, said Arthur, what is his name? Sir, said the knight, his name is Percivale de Galis. So on the morn the king made him knight in Camelot. But the king and all the knights thought it would be long ere that he proved a good knight.

Then at the dinner, when the king was set at the table, and every knight after he was of prowess, the king commanded him to be set among mean knights; and so was Sir Percivale set as the king commanded. Then was there a maiden in the queen's court that was come of high blood, and she was dumb and never spake word. Right so she came straight into the hall, and went unto Sir Percivale, and took him by the hand and said aloud, that the king and all the knights might hear it: Arise, Sir Percivale, the noble knight and God's knight, and go with me; and so he did. And there she brought him to the right side of the Siege Perilous, and said, Fair knight, take here thy siege, for that siege appertaineth to thee and to none other. Right so she departed and asked a priest. And as she was confessed and houselled then she died. Then the king and all the court made great joy of Sir Percivale.

HOW AT A GREAT FEAST THAT KING MARK MADE AN HARPER CAME AND SANG A LAY OF SIR DINADAN'S AGAINST KING MARK.

Then there came a knight out of Cornwall, his name was Fergus, a fellow of the Round Table. And there he told the king and Sir Launcelot good tidings of Sir Tristram, and there were brought goodly letters, and how he left him in the castle of Tintagil. Then came the damosel that brought goodly letters unto King Arthur and unto Sir Launcelot, and there she had passing good cheer of the king, and of the Queen Guenever, and of Sir Launcelot. Then they wrote goodly letters again. But Sir Launcelot bade ever Sir Tristram beware of King Mark, for ever he called him in his letters King Fox, as who saith, he fareth all with wiles and treason. Whereof Sir Tristram in his heart thanked Sir Launcelot. Then the damosel went unto La Beale Isoud, and bare her letters from the king and from Sir Launcelot, whereof she was in passing great joy. Fair damosel, said La Beale Isoud, how fareth my Lord Arthur, and the Queen Guenever, and the noble knight, Sir Launcelot? She answered, and to make short tale: Much the better that ye and Sir Tristram be in joy. God reward them, said La Beale Isoud, for Sir Tristram suffereth great pain for me, and I for him.

So the damosel departed, and brought letters to King Mark. And when he had read them, and understood them, he was wroth with Sir Tristram, for he deemed that he had sent the damosel unto King Arthur. For Arthur and Launcelot in a manner threated King Mark. And as King Mark read these letters he deemed treason by Sir Tristram.

Then privily and secretly he sent letters unto King Arthur, and unto Queen Guenever, and unto Sir Launcelot. So the varlet departed, and found the king and the queen in Wales, at Carlion. And as the king and the queen were at mass the varlet came with the letters. And when mass was done the king and the queen opened the letters privily by themselves. And the beginning of the king's letters spake wonderly short unto King Arthur, and bade him entermete with himself and with his wife, and of his knights; for he was able enough to rule and keep his wife.

When King Arthur understood the letter, he mused of many things, and thought on his sister's words, Queen Morgan le Fay, that she had said betwixt Queen Guenever and Sir Launcelot. And in this thought he studied a great while. Then he bethought him again how his sister was his own enemy, and that she hated the queen and Sir Launcelot, and so he put all that out of his thought. Then King Arthur read the letter again, and the latter clause said that King Mark took Sir Tristram for his mortal enemy; wherefore he put Arthur out of doubt he would be revenged of Sir Tristram. Then was King Arthur wroth with King Mark. And when Queen Guenever read her letter and understood it, she was wroth out of measure, for the letter spake shame by her and by Sir Launcelot. And so privily she sent the letter unto Sir Launcelot. And when he wist the intent of the letter he was so wroth that he laid him down on his bed to sleep, whereof Sir Dinadan was ware, for it was his manner to be privy with all good knights. And as Sir Launcelot slept he stole the letter out of his hand, and read it word by word. And then he made great sorrow for anger. And so Sir Launcelot awaked, and went to a window, and read the letter again, the which made him angry.

Sir, said Dinadan, wherefore be ye angry? discover your heart to me: forsooth ye wot well I owe you good will, howbeit I am a poor knight and a servitor unto you and to all good knights. For though I be not of worship myself I love all those that be of worship. It is truth, said Sir Launcelot, ye are a trusty knight, and for great trust I will shew you my counsel. And when Dinadan understood all, he said: This is my counsel: set you right nought by these threats, for King Mark is so villainous, that by fair speech shall never man get of him. But ye shall see what I shall do; I will make a lay for him, and when it is made I shall make an harper to sing it afore him. So anon he went and made it, and taught it an harper that hight Eliot. And when he knew it, he taught it to many harpers. And so by the will of Sir Launcelot, and of Arthur, the harpers went straight into Wales, and into Cornwall, to sing the lay that Sir Dinadan made by King Mark, the which was the worst lay that ever harper sang with harp or with any other instruments.

And at a great feast that King Mark made came Eliot the harper with the lay that Dinadan had made, and secretly brought it unto Sir Tristram, and told him the lay that Dinadan had made by King Mark. And when Sir Tristram heard it, he said: That Dinadan can make wonderly well and ill, thereas it shall be. Sir, said Eliot, dare I sing this song afore King Mark? Yea, on my peril, said Sir Tristram, for I shall be thy warrant. Then at the meat came in Eliot the harper, and because he was a curious harper men heard him sing the same lay that Dinadan had made, the which spake the most villainy by King Mark of his treason that ever man heard.

When the harper had sung his song to the end King Mark was wonderly wroth, and said: Thou harper, how durst thou be so bold on thy head to sing this song afore me. Sir, said Eliot, wit you well I am a minstrel, and I must do as I am commanded of these lords that I bear the arms of. And sir, wit ye well that Sir Dinadan, a knight of the Table Round, made this song, and made me to sing it afore you. Thou sayest well, said King Mark, and because thou art a minstrel thou shalt go quit, but I charge thee hie thee fast out of my sight. So the harper departed and went to Sir Tristram, and told him how he had sped. Then Sir Tristram let make letters as goodly as he could to Launcelot and to Sir Dinadan. And so he let conduct the harper out of the country. But to say that King Mark was wonderly wroth, he was, for he deemed that the lay that was sung afore him was made by Sir Tristram's counsel, wherefore he thought to slay him and all his well-willers in that country.

HOW BY TREASON SIR TRISTRAM WAS BROUGHT TO A TOURNAMENT FOR TO HAVE BEEN SLAIN, AND HOW HE WAS PUT IN PRISON, AND HOW HE AND LA BEALE ISOUD CAME TO ENGLAND AND WERE LODGED BY SIR LAUNCELOT AT JOYOUS GARD. Then there was cried by the coasts of Cornwall a great tournament and jousts, and all was done by Sir Galahalt the haut prince and King Bagdemagus, to the intent to slay Launcelot, or else utterly destroy him and shame him, because Sir Launcelot had always the higher degree; therefore this prince and this king made this jousts against Sir Launcelot. And thus their counsel was discovered unto King Mark, whereof he was full glad.

Then King Mark bethought him that he would have Sir Tristram unto that tournament disguised that no man should know him, to that intent that the haut prince should ween that Sir Tristram were Sir Launcelot. So at these jousts came in Sir Tristram. And at that time Sir Launcelot was not there, but when they saw a knight disguised do such deeds of arms, they weened it had been Sir Launcelot. And in especial King Mark said it was Sir Launcelot plainly. Then they set upon him, both King Bagdemagus, and the haut prince, and their knights, that it was wonder that ever Sir Tristram might endure that pain. Notwithstanding for all the pain that he had, Sir Tristram won the degree at that tournament, and there he hurt many knights and brised them, and they hurt him and brised him wonderly sore. So when the jousts were all done they knew well that it was Sir Tristram de Liones; and all that were on King Mark's party were glad that Sir Tristram was hurt, and the remnant were sorry of his hurt; for Sir Tristram was not so behated as was Sir Launcelot within the realm of England.

Then came King Mark unto Sir Tristram and said: Fair nephew, I am sorry of your hurts. Gramercy my lord, said Sir Tristram. Then King Mark made Sir Tristram to be put in an horse bier in great sign of love, and said: Fair cousin, I shall be your leech myself. And so he rode forth with Sir Tristram, and brought him to a castle by daylight. And then King Mark made Sir Tristram to eat. And then after he gave him a drink, the which as soon as he had drunk he fell asleep. And when it was night he made him to be carried to another castle, and there he put him in a strong prison, and there he ordained a man and a woman to give him his meat and drink. So there he was a great while.

When Queen Isoud understood that Sir Tristram was in prison she made as great sorrow as ever made lady or gentlewoman. Then Sir Tristram sent a letter unto La Beale Isoud, and prayed her to be his good lady; and if it pleased her to make a vessel ready for her and him, he would go with her unto the realm of Logris, that is this land. When La Beale Isoud understood Sir Tristram's letters and his intent, she sent him another, and bade him be of good comfort, for she would do make the vessel ready, and all thing to purpose.

Then La Beale Isoud sent unto Sir Dinas, and to Sadok, and prayed them in anywise to take King Mark, and put him in prison, unto the time that she and Sir Tristram were departed unto the realm of Logris. When Sir Dinas the Seneschal understood the treason of King Mark he promised her again, and sent her word that King Mark should be put in prison. And as they devised it so it was done. And then Sir Tristram was delivered out of prison; and anon in all the haste Queen Isoud and Sir Tristram went and took their counsel with that they would have with them when they departed.

Then La Beale Isoud and Sir Tristram took their vessel, and came by water into this land. And so they were not in this land four days but there came a cry of a jousts and tournament that King Arthur let make. When Sir Tristram heard tell of that tournament he disguised himself, and La Beale Isoud, and rode unto that tournament. And when he came there he saw many knights joust and tourney; and so Sir Tristram dressed him to the range, and to make short conclusion, he overthrew fourteen knights of the Round

Table. When Sir Launcelot saw these knights thus overthrown, Sir Launcelot dressed him to Sir Tristram. That saw La Beale Isoud how Sir Launcelot was come into the field. Then La Beale Isoud sent unto Sir Launcelot a ring, and bade him wit that it was Sir Tristram de Liones. When Sir Launcelot understood that there was Sir Tristram he was full glad, and would not joust. Then Sir Launcelot espied whither Sir Tristram went, and after him he rode; and then either made of other great joy. And so Sir Launcelot brought Sir Tristram and La Beale Isoud unto Joyous Gard, that was his own castle, that he had won with his own hands. And there Sir Launcelot put them in to wield for their own. And wit ye well that castle was garnished and furnished for a king and a queen royal there to have sojourned. And Sir Launcelot charged all his people to honour them and love them as they would do himself.

So Sir Launcelot departed unto King Arthur; and then he told Queen Guenever how he that jousted so well at the last tournament was Sir Tristram. And there he told her how he had with him La Beale Isoud maugre King Mark, and so Queen Guenever told all this unto King Arthur. When King Arthur wist that Sir Tristram was escaped and come from King Mark, and had brought La Beale Isoud with him, then was he passing glad. So because of Sir Tristram King Arthur let make a cry, that on May Day should be a jousts before the castle of Lonazep; and that castle was fast by Joyous Gard. And thus Arthur devised, that all the knights of this land, and of Cornwall, and of North Wales, should joust against all these countries, Ireland, Scotland, and the remnant of Wales, and the country of Gore, and Surluse, and of Listinoise, and they of Northumberland, and all they that held lands of Arthur on this half the sea. When this cry was made many knights were glad and many were unglad. Sir, said Launcelot unto Arthur, by this cry that ye have made ye will put us that be about you in great jeopardy, for there be many knights that have great envy to us; therefore when we shall meet at the day of jousts there will be hard shift among us. As for that, said Arthur, I care not; there shall we prove who shall be best of his hands. So when Sir Launcelot understood wherefore King Arthur made this jousting, then he made such purveyance that La Beale Isoud should behold the jousts in a secret place that was honest for her estate.

Now turn we unto Sir Tristram and to La Beale Isoud, how they made great joy daily together with all manner of mirths that they could devise; and every day Sir Tristram would go ride a-hunting, for Sir Tristram was that time called the best chaser of the world, and the noblest blower of an horn of all manner of measures; for as books report, of Sir Tristram came all the good terms of venery and hunting, and all the sizes and measures of blowing of an horn; and of him we had first all the terms of hawking, and which were beasts of chase and beasts of venery, and which were vermins, and all the blasts that long to all manner of games. First to the uncoupling, to the seeking, to the rechate, to the flight, to the death, and to strake, and many other blasts and terms, that all manner of gentlemen have cause to the world's end to praise Sir Tristram, and to pray for his soul.

HOW BY THE COUNSEL OF LA BEALE ISOUD SIR TRISTRAM RODE ARMED, AND HOW HE MET WITH SIR PALOMIDES, AND SIR BREUSE SAUNCE PITÉ BEGUILED THREE GOOD KNIGHTS. So on a day La Beale Isoud said unto Sir Tristram: I marvel me much, said she, that ye remember not yourself, how ye be here in a strange country, and here be many perilous knights; and well ye wot that King Mark is full of treason; and that ye will ride thus to chase and to hunt unarmed; ye might be destroyed. My fair lady and my love, I cry you mercy, I will no more do so. So then Sir Tristram rode daily a-hunting armed, and his men bearing his shield and his spear. So on a day a little afore the month of May, Sir Tristram chased an hart passing eagerly, and so the hart passed by a fair well. And then Sir Tristram alighted and put off his helm to drink of that burbly water. Right so he heard and saw the Questing Beast come to the well. When Sir Tristram saw that beast he put on his helm, for he deemed he should hear of Sir Palomides, for that beast was his quest. Right so Sir Tristram saw where came a knight armed, upon a noble courser, and he saluted him, and they spake of many things; and this knight's name was Breuse Saunce Pité. And right so withal there came unto them the noble knight Sir Palomides, and either saluted other, and spake fair to other.

Fair knights, said Sir Palomides, I can tell you tidings. What is that? said those knights. Sirs, wit ye well that King Mark is put in prison by his own knights, and all was for love of Sir Tristram; for King Mark had put Sir Tristram in prison, and Queen La Beale Isoud delivered him, and went clearly away with him into this realm; and all this while King Mark, the false traitor, is in prison. Is this truth? said Palomides; then shall we hastily hear of Sir Tristram. And as for to say that I love La Beale Isoud I dare make good that I do, and that she hath my service above all other ladies, and shall have the term of my life.

And right so as they stood talking they saw afore them where came a knight all armed, on a great horse, and one of his men bare his shield, and the other his spear. And anon as that knight espied them he gat his shield and his spear and dressed him to joust. Fair fellows, said Sir Tristram, yonder is a knight will joust with us, let see which of us shall encounter with him, for I see well he is of the court of King Arthur. It shall not be long or he be met withal, said Sir Palomides, for I found never no knight in my quest of this glasting beast, but an he would joust I never refused him. As well may I, said Breuse Saunce Pité, follow that beast as ye. Then shall ye do battle with me, said Palomides.

So Sir Palomides dressed him unto that other knight, Sir Bleoberis, that was a full noble knight, nigh kin unto Sir Launcelot. And so they met so hard that Sir Palomides fell to the earth, horse and all. Then Sir Bleoberis cried aloud and said thus: Make thee ready thou false traitor knight, Breuse Saunce Pité, for wit thou certainly I will have ado with thee to the utterance for the noble knights and ladies that thou hast falsely betrayed. When this false knight and traitor, Breuse Saunce Pité, heard him say so, he took his horse by the bridle and fled his way as fast as ever his horse might run, for sore he was of him afeard. When Sir Bleoberis saw him flee he followed fast after, through thick and through thin. And by fortune as Sir Breuse fled, he saw even afore him three knights of the Table Round, of the which the one hight Sir Ector de Maris, the other hight Sir Percivale de Galis, the third hight Sir Harry le Fise Lake, a good knight and an hardy. And as for Sir Percivale, he was called that time of his time one of the best knights of the world, and the best assured. When Breuse saw these knights he rode straight unto them, and cried unto them and prayed them of rescues. What need have ye? said Sir Ector. Ah, fair knights, said Sir Breuse, here followeth me the most traitor knight, and most coward, and most of villainy; his name is Breuse Saunce Pité, and if he may get me he will slay me without mercy and pity. Abide with us, said Sir Percivale, and we shall warrant you.

Then were they ware of Sir Bleoberis that came riding all that he might. Then Sir Ector put himself forth to joust afore them all. When Sir Bleoberis saw that they were four knights and he but himself, he stood in a doubt whether he would turn or hold his way. Then he said to himself: I am a knight of the Table Round, and rather than I should shame mine oath and my blood I will hold my way whatsoever fall thereof. And then Sir Ector dressed his spear, and smote either other passing sore, but Sir Ector fell to the earth. That saw Sir Percivale, and he dressed his horse toward him all that he might drive, but Sir Percivale had such a stroke that horse and man fell to the earth. When Sir Harry saw that they were both to the earth then he said to himself: Never was Breuse of such prowess. So Sir Harry dressed his horse, and they met together so strongly that both the horses and knights fell to the earth, but Sir Bleoberis' horse began to recover again. That saw Breuse and he came hurtling, and smote him over and over, and would have slain him as he lay on the ground. Then Sir Harry le Fise Lake arose lightly, and took the bridle of Sir Breuse's horse, and said: Fie for shame! strike never a knight when he is at the earth, for this knight may be called no shameful knight of his deeds, for yet as men may see thereas he lieth on the ground he hath done worshipfully, and put to the worse passing good knights. Therefore will I not let, said Sir Breuse. Thou shalt not choose, said Sir Harry, as at this time. Then when Sir Breuse saw that he might not choose nor have his will he spake fair. Then Sir Harry let him go. And then anon he made his horse to run over Sir Bleoberis, and rashed him to the earth like if he would have slain him. When Sir Harry saw him do so villainously he cried: Traitor knight, leave off for shame. And as Sir Harry would have taken his horse to fight with Sir Breuse, then Sir Breuse ran upon him as he was half upon his horse, and smote him down, horse and man, to the earth, and had near slain Sir Harry, the good knight. That saw Sir Percivale, and then he cried: Traitor knight, what dost thou? And when Sir Percivale was upon his horse Sir Breuse took his horse and fled all that ever he might, and Sir Percivale and Sir Harry followed after him fast, but ever the longer they chased the farther were they behind.

Then they turned again and came to Sir Ector de Maris and to Sir Bleoberis. Ah, fair knights, said Bleoberis, why have ye succoured that false knight and traitor? Why, said Sir Harry, what knight is he? for well I wot it is a false knight, said Sir Harry, and a coward and a felonious knight. Sir, said Bleoberis, he is the most coward knight, and a devourer of ladies and a destroyer of good knights, and especially of Arthur's. What is your name? said Sir Ector. My name is Sir Bleoberis de Ganis. Alas, fair cousin, said Ector, forgive it me, for I am Sir Ector de Maris. Then Sir Percivale and Sir Harry made great joy that they met with Bleoberis, but all they were heavy that Sir Breuse was escaped them, whereof they made great dole.

Right so as they stood thus there came Sir Palomides, and when he saw the shield of Bleoberis lie on the earth, then said Palomides: He that oweth that shield let him dress him to me, for he smote me down here fast by at a fountain, and therefore I will fight with him on foot. I am ready, said Bleoberis, here to answer thee, for wit thou well, sir knight, it was I, and my name is Bleoberis de Ganis. Well art thou met, said Palomides, and wit thou well my name is Palomides the Saracen; and either of them hated other to the death. Sir Palomides, said Ector, wit thou well there is neither thou nor none knight that beareth the life that slayeth any of our blood but he shall die for it; therefore an thou list to fight go seek Sir Launcelot or Sir Tristram, and there shall ye find your match. With them have I met, said Palomides, but I had never no worship of them. Was there never no manner of knight, said Sir Ector, but they that ever matched with you? Yes, said Palomides, there was the third, a good knight as any of them, and of his age he was the best that ever I found; for an he might have lived till he had been an hardier man there liveth no knight now such, and his name was Sir Lamorak de Galis. And as he had jousted at a tournament there he overthrew me and thirty knights more, and there he won the degree. And at his departing there met him Sir Gawaine and his brethren, and with great pain they slew him feloniously, unto all good knights' great damage. Anon as Sir Percivale heard that his brother was dead, Sir

Lamorak, he fell over his horse's mane swooning, and there he made the greatest dole that ever made knight. And when Sir Percivale arose he said: Alas, my good and noble brother Sir Lamorak, now shall we never meet, and I trow in all the wide world a man may not find such a knight as he was of his age; and it is too much to suffer the death of our father King Pellinore, and now the death of our good brother Sir Lamorak.

Then in the meanwhile there came a varlet from the court of King Arthur, and told them of the great tournament that should be at Lonazep, and how these lands, Cornwall and Northgalis, should be against all them that would come.

HOW SIR TRISTRAM MET WITH SIR DINADAN, AND OF THEIR DEVICES, AND HOW SIR DINADAN WAS SENT FOR BY LA BEALE ISOUD, AND HOW SIR TRISTRAM IN JOUSTING WITH SIR PALOMIDES WAS KNOWN BY SIR DINADAN. Now turn we unto Sir Tristram, that as he rode a-hunting he met with Sir Dinadan, that was come into that country to seek Sir Tristram. Then Sir Dinadan told Sir Tristram his name, but Sir Tristram would not tell him his name, wherefore Sir Dinadan was wroth. For such a foolish knight as ye are, said Sir Dinadan, I saw but late this day lying by a well, and he fared as he slept; and there he lay like a fool grinning, and would not speak, and his shield lay by him, and his horse stood by him; and well I wot he was a lover. Ah, fair sir, said Sir Tristram, are ye not a lover? Mary, fie on that craft! said Sir Dinadan. That is evil said, said Sir Tristram, for a knight may never be of prowess but if he be a lover. It is well said, said Sir Dinadan; now tell me your name, sith ye be a lover, or else I shall do battle with you. As for that, said Sir Tristram, it is no reason to fight with me but I tell you my name; and as for that my name shall ye not wit as at this time. Fie for shame, said Dinadan, art thou a knight and durst not tell thy name to me? therefore I will fight with thee. As for that, said Sir Tristram, I will be advised, for I will not do battle but if me list. And if I do battle, said Sir Tristram, ye are not able to withstand me. Fie on thee, coward, said Sir Dinadan.

And thus as they hoved still, they saw a knight come riding against them. Lo, said Sir Tristram, see where cometh a knight riding, will joust with you. Anon, as Sir Dinadan beheld him he said: That is the same doted knight that I saw lie by the well, neither sleeping nor waking. Well, said Sir Tristram, I know that knight well with the covered shield of azure, he is the king's son of Northumberland, his name is Epinegris; and he is as great a lover as I know, and he loveth the king's daughter of Wales, a full fair lady. And now I suppose, said Sir Tristram, an ye require him he will joust with you, and then shall ye prove whether a lover be a better knight, or ye that will not love no lady. Well, said Dinadan, now shalt thou see what I shall do. Therewithal Sir Dinadan spake on high and said: Sir knight, make thee ready to joust with me, for it is the custom of errant knights one to joust with other. Sir, said Epinegris, is that the rule of you errant knights for to make a knight to joust, will he or nill? As for that, said Dinadan, make thee ready, for here is for me. And therewithal they spurred their horses and met together so hard that Epinegris smote down Sir Dinadan. Then Sir Tristram rode to Sir Dinadan and said: How now, meseemeth the lover hath well sped. Fie on thee, coward, said Sir Dinadan, and if thou be a good knight revenge me. Nay, said Sir Tristram, I will not joust as at this time, but take your horse and let us go hence. Defend me, said Sir Dinadan, from thy fellowship, for I never sped well since I met with thee: and so they departed. Well, said Sir Tristram, peradventure I could tell you tidings of Sir Tristram. God defend me, said Dinadan, from thy fellowship, for Sir Tristram were mickle the worse an he were in thy company: and then they departed. Sir, said Sir Tristram, yet it may happen I shall meet with you in other places.

So rode Sir Tristram unto Joyous Gard, and told La Beale Isoud of all his adventure, as ye have heard to-fore. And when she heard him tell of Sir Dinadan: Sir, said she, is not that he that made the song by King Mark? That same is he, said Sir Tristram, for he is the best bourder and japer, and a noble knight of his hands, and the best fellow that I know, and all good knights love his fellowship. Alas, sir, said she, why brought ye not him with you? Have ye no care, said Sir Tristram, for he rideth to seek me in this country; and therefore he will not away till he have met with me. And there Sir Tristram told La Beale Isoud how Sir Dinadan held against all lovers. Right so there came in a varlet and told Sir Tristram how there was come an errant knight into the town, with such colours upon his shield. That is Sir Dinadan, said Sir Tristram; wit ye what ye shall do, said Sir Tristram: send ye for him, my Lady Isoud, and I will not be seen, and ye shall hear the merriest knight that ever ye spake withal, and the maddest talker; and I pray you heartily that ye make him good cheer.

Then anon La Beale Isoud sent into the town, and prayed

Sir Dinadan that he would come into the castle and repose him there with a lady. With a good will, said Sir Dinadan; and so he mounted upon his horse and rode into the castle; and there he alighted, and was unarmed, and brought into the castle. Anon La Beale Isoud came unto him, and either saluted other; then she asked him of whence that he was. Madam, said Dinadan, I am of the court of King Arthur, and knight of the Table Round, and my name is Sir Dinadan. What do ye in this country? said La Beale Isoud. Madam, said he, I seek Sir Tristram the good knight, for it was told me that he was in this country. It may well be, said La Beale Isoud, but I am not ware of him. Madam, said Dinadan, I marvel of Sir Tristram and mo other lovers, what aileth them to be so mad and so sotted upon women. Why, said La Beale Isoud, are ye a knight and be no lover? it is shame to you: wherefore ye may not be called a good knight but if ye make a quarrel for a lady. Defend me, said Dinadan, for the joy of love is too short, and the sorrow thereof, and what cometh thereof, dureth over long. Ah, said La Beale Isoud, say ye not so, for here fast by was the good knight Sir Bleoberis, that fought with three knights at once for a damosel's sake, and he won her afore the King of Northumberland. It was so, said Sir Dinadan, for I know him well for a good knight and a noble, and come of noble blood; for all be noble knights of whom he is come of, that is Sir Launcelot du Lake.

Now I pray you, said La Beale Isoud, tell me will you fight for my love with three knights that do me great wrong? and insomuch as ye be a knight of King Arthur's I require you to do battle for me. Then Sir Dinadan said: I shall say you ye be as fair a lady as ever I saw any, and much fairer than is my lady Queen Guenever, but wit ye well at one word, I will not fight for you with three knights. Then Isoud laughed, and had good game at him. So he had all the cheer that she might make him, and there he lay all that night. And on the morn early Sir Tristram armed him, and La Beale Isoud gave him a good helm; and then he promised her that he would meet with Sir Dinadan, and they two would ride together into Lonazep, where the tournament should be: And there shall I make ready for you where ye shall see the tournament. Then departed Sir Tristram with two squires that bare his shield and his spears that were great and long.

Then after that Sir Dinadan departed, and rode his way a great pace until he had overtaken Sir Tristram. And when Sir Dinadan had overtaken him he knew him anon, and he hated the fellowship of him above all other knights. Ah, said Sir Dinadan, art thou that coward knight that I met with yesterday? keep thee, for thou shalt joust with me maugre thy head. Well, said Sir Tristram, and I am loath to joust. And so they let their horses run, and Sir Tristram missed of him a-purpose, and Sir Dinadan brake a spear upon Sir Tristram, and therewith Sir Dinadan dressed him to draw out his sword. Not so, said Sir Tristram, why are ye so wroth? I will not fight. Fie on thee, coward, said Dinadan, thou shamest all knights. As for that, said Sir Tristram, I care not, for I will wait upon you and be under your protection; for because ye are so good a knight ye may save me. The devil deliver me of thee, said Sir Dinadan, for thou art as goodly a man of arms and of thy person as ever I saw, and the most coward that ever I saw What wilt thou do with those great spears that thou carriest with thee? I shall give them, said Sir Tristram, to some good knight when I come to the tournament; and if I see you do best, I shall give them to you.

So thus as they rode talking they saw where came an errant knight afore them, that dressed him to joust. Lo, said Sir Tristram, yonder is one will joust; now dress thee to him. Ah, shame betide thee, said Sir Dinadan. Nay, not so, said Tristram, for that knight beseemeth a shrew. Then shall I, said Sir Dinadan. And so they dressed their shields and their spears, and they met together so hard that the other knight smote down Sir Dinadan from his horse. Lo, said Sir Tristram, it had been better ye had left. Fie on thee, coward, said Sir Dinadan. Then Sir Dinadan started up and gat his sword in his hand, and proffered to do battle on foot. Whether in love or in wrath? said the other knight. Let us do battle in love, said Sir Dinadan. What is your name, said that knight, I pray you tell me. Wit ye well my name is Sir Dinadan. Ah, Dinadan, said that knight, and my name is Gareth, the youngest brother unto Sir Gawaine. Then either made of other great cheer, for this Gareth was the best knight of all the brethren, and he proved a good knight. Then they took their horses, and there they spake of Sir Tristram, how such a coward he was; and every word Sir Tristram heard and laughed them to scorn.

Then were they ware where came a knight afore them well horsed and well armed, and he made him ready to joust. Fair knights, said Sir Tristram, look betwixt you who shall joust with yonder knight, for I warn you I will not have ado with him. Then shall I, said Sir Gareth. And so they encountered together, and there that knight smote down Sir Gareth over his horse's croup. How now, said Sir Tristram unto Sir Dinadan, dress thee now and revenge the good knight

Gareth. That shall I not, said Sir Dinadan, for he hath stricken down a much bigger knight than I am. Ah, said Sir Tristram, now Sir Dinadan, I see and feel well your heart faileth you, therefore now shall ye see what I shall do. And then Sir Tristram hurtled unto that knight, and smote him quite from his horse. And when Sir Dinadan saw that, he marvelled greatly; and then he deemed that it was Sir Tristram.

Then this knight that was on foot pulled out his sword to do battle. What is your name? said Sir Tristram. Wit ye well, said that knight, my name is Sir Palomides. What knight hate ye most? said Sir Tristram. Sir knight, said he, I hate Sir Tristram to the death, for an I may meet with him the one of us shall die. Ye say well, said Sir Tristram, and wit ye well that I am Sir Tristram de Liones, and now do your worst. When Sir Palomides heard him say so he was astonied. And then he said thus: I pray you, Sir Tristram, forgive me all mine evil will, and if I live I shall do you service above all other knights that be living; and whereas I have owed you evil will me sore repenteth. I wot not what aileth me, for meseemeth that ye are a good knight, and none other knight that named himself a good knight should not hate you; therefore I require you, Sir Tristram, take no displeasure at mine unkind words. Sir Palomides, said Sir Tristram, ye say well, and well I wot ye are a good knight, for I have seen ye proved; and many great enterprises have ye taken upon you, and well achieved them; therefore, said Sir Tristram, an ye have any evil will to me, now may ye right it, for I am ready at your hand. Not so, my lord Sir Tristram, I will do you knightly service in all thing as ye will command. And right so I will take you, said Sir Tristram. And so they rode forth on their ways talking of many things. O my lord Sir Tristram, said Dinadan, foul have ye mocked me, for God knoweth I came into this country for your sake, and by the advice of my lord Sir Launcelot; and yet would not Sir Launcelot tell me the certainty of you, where I should find you. Truly, said Sir Tristram, Sir Launcelot wist well where I was, for I abode within his own castle.

HOW THEY APPROACHED THE CASTLE LONAZEP, AND HOW THEY TALKED OF THE DEATH OF SIR LAMORAK, AND HOW ON HUMBER BANK THEY FOUND A SHIP, WHEREIN LAY THE BODY OF KING HERMANCE. Thus they rode until they were ware of the Castle Lonazep. And then were they ware of four hundred tents and pavilions, and marvellous great ordinance. So God me help, said Sir Tristram, yonder I see the greatest ordinance that ever I saw. Sir, said Palomides, meseemeth that there was as great an ordinance at the Castle of Maidens upon the rock, where ye won the prize, for I saw myself where ye for-jousted thirty knights. Sir, said Dinadan, and in Surluse, at that tournament that Galahalt of the Long Isles made, the which there dured seven days, was as great a gathering as is here, for there were many nations. Who was the best? said Sir Tristram. Sir, it was Sir Launcelot du Lake and the noble knight, Sir Lamorak de Galis, and Sir Launcelot won the degree. I doubt not, said Sir Tristram, but he won the degree, so he had not been overmatched with many knights; and of the death of Sir Lamorak, said Sir Tristram, it was over great pity, for I dare say he was the cleanest mighted man and the best winded of his age that was alive; for I knew him that he was the biggest knight that ever I met withal, but if it were Sir Launcelot. Alas, said Sir Tristram, full woe is me for his death. And if they were not the cousins of my lord Arthur that slew him, they should die for it, and all those that were consenting to his death. And for such things, said Sir Tristram, I fear to draw unto the court of my lord Arthur; I will that ye wit it, said Sir Tristram unto Gareth.

Sir, I blame you not, said Gareth, for well I understand the vengeance of my brethren Sir Gawaine, Agravaine, Gaheris, and Mordred. But as for me, said Sir Gareth, I meddle not of their matters, therefore there is none of them that loveth me. And for I understand they be murderers of good knights I left their company; and God would I had been by, said Gareth, when the noble knight, Sir Lamorak, was slain. Now as Jesu be my help, said Sir Tristram, it is well said of you, for I had liefer than all the gold betwixt this and Rome I had been there. Y-wis, said Palomides, and so would I had been there, and yet had I never the degree at no jousts nor tournament thereas he was, but he put me to the worse, or on foot or on horseback; and that day that he was slain he did the most deeds of arms that ever I saw knight do in all my life days. And when him was given the degree by my lord Arthur, Sir Gawaine and his three brethren, Agravaine, Gaheris, and Sir Mordred, set upon Sir Lamorak in a privy place, and there they slew his horse. And so they fought with him on foot more than three hours, both before him and behind him; and Sir Mordred gave him his death wound behind him at his back, and all to-hew him: for one of his squires told me that saw it. Fie upon treason, said Sir Tristram, for it killeth my heart to hear this tale. So it doth mine, said Gareth; brethren as they be mine I shall never love them, nor draw in their fellowship for that deed.

So thus they rode until that they came to Humber bank, where they heard a cry and a doleful noise. Then were they ware in the wind where came a rich vessel covered over with red silk, and the vessel landed fast by them. Therewith Sir Tristram alighted and his knights. And so Sir Tristram went afore and entered into that vessel. And when he came within he saw a fair bed richly covered, and thereupon lay a dead seemly knight, all armed save the head, was all be-bled with deadly wounds upon him, the which seemed to be a passing good knight. How may this be, said Sir Tristram, that this knight is thus slain? Then Sir Tristram was ware of a letter in the dead knight's hand. Master mariners, said Sir Tristram, what meaneth that letter? Sir, said they, in that letter ye shall hear and know how he was slain, and for what cause, and what was his name. But sir, said the mariners, wit ye well that no man shall take that letter and read it but if he be a good knight, and that he will faithfully promise to revenge his death, else shall there be no knight see that letter open. Wit ye well, said Sir Tristram, that some of us may revenge his death as well as other, and if it be so as ye mariners say his death shall be revenged. And therewith Sir Tristram took the letter out of the knight's hand, and it said thus: Hermance, king and lord of the Red City, I send unto all knights errant, recommending unto you noble knights of Arthur's court. I beseech them all among them to find one knight that will fight for my sake with two brethren that I brought up of nought, and feloniously and traitorly they have slain me; wherefore I beseech one good knight to revenge my death. And he that revengeth my death I will that he have my Red City and all my castles.

Sir, said the mariners, wit ye well this king and knight that here lieth was a full worshipful man and of full great prowess, and full well he loved all manner knights errants. Here is a piteous case, said Sir Tristram, and full fain would I take this enterprise upon me; but I have made such a promise that needs I must be at this great tournament, or else I am shamed. For well I wot for my sake in especial my lord Arthur let make this jousts and tournament in this country; and well I wot that many worshipful people will be there at that tournament for to see me; therefore I fear me to take this enterprise upon me that I shall not come again by time to this jousts. Sir, said Palomides, I pray you give me this enterprise, and ye shall see me achieve it worshipfully, other else I shall die in this quarrel. Well, said Sir Tristram, and this enterprise I give you, with this, that ye be with me at this tournament that shall be as this day seven night. Sir, said Palomides, I promise you that I shall be with you by that day if I be unslain or unmaimed.

HOW PALOMIDES WENT FOR TO FIGHT WITH TWO BRETHREN FOR THE DEATH OF KING HERMANCE, AND SLEW THEM, AND CAME UNTO JOYOUS GARD. Then Sir Palomides sailed even long Humber to the coasts of the sea, where was a fair castle. And at that time it was early in the morning, afore day. Then the mariners went unto Sir Palomides that slept fast. Sir knight, said the mariners, ye must arise, for here is a castle there ye must go into. I assent me, said Sir Palomides; and therewithal he arrived. And then he blew his horn that the mariners had given him. And when they within the castle heard that horn they put forth many knights; and there they stood upon the walls, and said with one voice: Welcome be ye to this castle. And then it waxed clear day, and Sir Palomides entered into the castle. And within a while he was served with many divers meats. Then Sir Palomides heard about him much weeping and great dole. What may this mean? said Sir Palomides; I love not to hear such a sorrow, and fain I would know what it meaneth. Then there came afore him one whose name was Sir Ebel, that said thus: Wit ye well, sir knight, this dole and sorrow is here made every day, and for this cause: we had a king that hight Hermance, and he was King of the Red City, and this king that was lord was a noble knight, large and liberal of his expense; and in the world he loved nothing so much as he did errant knights of King Arthur's court, and all jousting, hunting, and all manner of knightly games; for so kind a king and knight had never the rule of poor people as he was; and because of his goodness and gentleness we bemoan him, and ever shall. And all kings and estates may beware by our lord, for he was destroyed in his own default; for had he cherished them of his blood he had yet lived with great riches and rest: but all estates may beware by our king. But alas, said Ebel, that we shall give all other warning by his death.

Tell me, said Palomides, and in what manner was your lord slain, and by whom. Sir, said Sir Ebel, our king brought up of children two men that now are perilous knights; and these two knights our king had so in charity, that he loved no man nor trusted no man of his blood, nor none other that was about him. And by these two knights our king was governed, and so they ruled him peaceably and his lands, and never would they suffer none of his blood to have no rule with our king. And also he was so free and so gentle, and they so false and deceivable, that they ruled him peaceably; and that espied the lords of our king's blood, and departed from him unto their own livelihood. Then when these two traitors understood that they had driven all the lords of his blood from him, they were not pleased with that rule, but then they thought to have more, as ever it is an old saw: Give a churl rule and thereby he will not be sufficed; for whatsomever he be that is ruled by a villain born, and the lord of the soil to be a gentleman born, the same villain shall destroy all the gentlemen about him: therefore all estates and lords, beware whom ye take about you. And if ye be a knight of King Arthur's court remember this tale, for this is the end and conclusion. My lord and king rode unto the forest hereby by the advice of these traitors, and there he chased at the red deer, armed at all pieces full like a good knight; and so for labour he waxed dry, and then he alighted, and drank at a well. And when he was alighted, by the assent of these two traitors, that one that hight Helius he suddenly smote our king through the body with a spear, and so they left him there. And when they were departed, then by fortune I came to the well, and found my lord and king wounded to the death. And when I heard his complaint, I let bring him to the water side, and in that same ship I put him alive; and when my lord King Hermance was in that vessel, he required me for the true faith I owed unto him for to write a letter in this manner.

Recommending unto King Arthur and to all his knights errant, beseeching them all that insomuch as I, King Hermance, King of the Red City, thus am slain by felony and treason, through two knights of mine own, and of mine own bringing up and of mine own making, that some worshipful knight will revenge my death, insomuch I have been ever to my power well willing unto Arthur's court. And who that will adventure his life with these two traitors for my sake in one battle, I, King Hermance, King of the Red City, freely give him all my lands and rents that ever I wielded in my life. This letter, said Ebel, I wrote by my lord's commandment, and then he received his Creator; and when he was dead, he commanded me or ever he were cold to put that letter fast in his hand. And then he commanded me to put forth that same vessel down Humber, and I should give these mariners in commandment never to stint until that they came unto Logris, where all the noble knights shall assemble at this time. And there shall some good knight have pity on me to revenge my death, for there was never king nor lord falslier nor traitorlier slain than I am here to my death. Thus was the complaint of our King Hermance. Now, said Sir Ebel, ye know all how our lord was betrayed, we require you for God's sake have pity upon his death, and worshipfully revenge his death, and then may ye wield all these lands. For we all wit well that an ye may slay these two traitors, the Red City and all those that be therein will take you for their lord.

Truly, said Sir Palomides, it grieveth my heart for to hear you tell this doleful tale; and to say the truth I saw the same letter that ye speak of, and one of the best knights on the earth read that letter to me, and by his commandment I came hither to revenge your king's death; and therefore have done, and let me wit where I shall find those traitors, for I shall never be at ease in my heart till I be in hands with them. Sir, said Sir Ebel, then take your ship again, and that ship must bring you unto the Delectable Isle, fast by the Red City, and we in this castle shall pray for you, and abide your again-coming.

So Sir Palomides took his ship, and arrived up at the Delectable Isle. And in the meanwhile Sir Hermind that was the king's brother, he arrived up at the Red City, and there he told them how there was come a knight of King Arthur's to avenge King Hermance's death: And his name is Sir Palomides, the good knight, that for the most part he followeth the beast Glatisant. Then all the city made great joy, for mickle had they heard of Sir Palomides, and of his noble prowess. So let they ordain a messenger, and sent unto the two brethren, and bade them to make them ready, for there was a knight come that would fight with them both. So the messenger went unto them where they were at a castle there beside; and there he told them how there was a knight come of King Arthur's court to fight with them both at once. He is welcome, said they; but tell us, we pray you, if it be Sir Launcelot or any of his blood? He is none of that blood, said the messenger. Then we care the less, said the two brethren, for with none of the blood of Sir Launcelot we keep not to have ado withal. Wit ye well, said the messenger, that his name is Sir Palomides, that yet is unchristened, a noble knight. Well, said they, an he be now unchristened he shall never be christened. So they appointed to be at the city within two days.

So within the third day there came to the city these two brethren, the one hight Helius, the other hight Helake, the which were men of great prowess; howbeit that they were false and full of treason, and but poor men born, yet were they noble knights of their hands. And with them they brought forty knights, to that intent that they should be big enough for the Red City. Thus came the two brethren with great bobaunce and pride, for they had put the Red City in fear and damage. Then they were brought to the lists, and Sir Palomides came into the place and said thus: Be ye the two brethren, Helius and Helake, that slew your king and lord, Sir Hermance, by felony and treason, for whom that I am come hither to revenge his death? Wit thou well, said Sir Helius and Sir Helake, that we are the same knights that slew King Hermance; and wit thou well, Sir Palomides Saracen, that we shall handle thee so ere thou depart that thou shalt wish that thou wert christened. It may well be, said Sir Palomides, for yet I would not die or I were christened; and yet so am I not afeard of you both, but I trust to God that I shall die a better christian man than any of you both; and doubt ye not, said Sir Palomides, either ye or I shall be left dead in this place.

Then they departed, and the two brethren came against Sir Palomides, and he against them, as fast as their horses might run. And by fortune Sir Palomides smote Helake through his shield and through the breast more than a fathom. All this while Sir Helius held up his spear, and for pride and orgulité he would not smite Sir Palomides with his spear; but when he saw his brother lie on the earth, and saw he might not help himself, then he said unto Sir Palomides: Help thyself. And therewith he came hurtling unto Sir Palomides with his spear, and smote him quite from his saddle. Then Sir Helius rode over Sir Palomides twice or thrice. And therewith Sir Palomides was ashamed, and gat the horse of Sir Helius by the bridle, and therewithal the horse areared, and Sir Palomides halp after, and so they fell both to the earth; but anon Sir Helius stert up lightly, and there he smote Sir Palomides a great stroke upon the helm, that he kneeled upon his own knee. Then they lashed together many sad strokes, and traced and traversed, now backward, now sideling, hurtling together like two boars, and that same time they fell both grovelling to the earth.

Thus they fought still without any reposing two hours, and never breathed; and then Sir Palomides waxed faint and weary, and Sir Helius waxed passing strong, and doubled his strokes, and drove Sir Palomides overthwart and endlong all the field, that they of the city when they saw Sir Palomides in this case they wept and cried, and made great dole, and the other party made as great joy. Alas, said the men of the city, that this noble knight should thus be slain for our king's sake. And as they were thus weeping and crying, Sir Palomides that had suffered an hundred strokes, that it was wonder that he stood on his feet, at the last Sir Palomides beheld as he might the common people, how they wept for him; and then he said to himself: Ah, fie for shame, Sir Palomides, why hangest thou thy head so low; and therewith he bare up his shield, and looked Sir Helius in the visage, and he smote him a great stroke upon the helm, and after that another and another. And then he smote Sir Helius with such a might that he fell to the earth grovelling; and then he raced off his helm from his head, and there he smote him such a buffet that he departed his head from the body. And then were the people of the city the joyfullest people that might be. So they brought him to his lodging with great solemnity, and there all the people became his men. And then Sir Palomides prayed them all to take keep unto all the lordship of King Hermance:

For, fair sirs, wit ye well I may not as at this time abide with you, for I must in all haste be with my lord King Arthur at the Castle of Lonazep, the which I have promised. Then was the people full heavy at his departing, for all that city proffered Sir Palomides the third part of their goods so that he would abide with them; but in no wise as at that time he would not abide.

And so Sir Palomides departed, and so he came unto the castle thereas Sir Ebel was lieutenant. And when they in the castle wist how Sir Palomides had sped, there was a joyful company; and so Sir Palomides departed, and came to the castle of Lonazep. And when he wist that Sir Tristram was not there he took his way over Humber, and came unto Joyous Gard, whereas Sir Tristram was and La Beale Isoud; and there Sir Tristram talked unto Sir Palomides of his battle, how he sped at the Red City, and as ye have heard afore so was it ended. Truly, said Sir Tristram, I am glad ye have well sped, for ye have done worshipfully. Well, said Sir Tristram, we must forward to-morn. And then he devised how it should be; and Sir Tristram devised to send his two pavilions to set them fast by the well of Lonazep, and therein shall be the queen La Beale Isoud. It is well said, said Sir Dinadan, but when Sir Palomides heard of that his heart was ravished out of measure: notwithstanding he said but little. So when they came to Joyous Gard Sir Palomides would not have gone into the castle, but as Sir Tristram took him by the finger, and led him into the castle. And when Sir Palomides saw La Beale Isoud he was ravished so that he might scarce speak. So they went unto meat, but Palomides might not eat, and there was all the cheer that might be had. And on the morn they were apparelled to ride toward Lonazep, and came to the well where Sir Tristram's two pavilions were set; and there they alighted, and there they saw many pavilions and great array.

OF THE TOURNAMENT AT LONAZEP, AND HOW THE PRIZE ON THE FIRST DAY WAS GIVEN TO SIR PALOMIDES. Now upon what party, said Tristram, is it best we be withal as to-morn? Sir, said Palomides, ye shall have mine advice to be against King Arthur as to-morn, for on his party will be Sir Launcelot and many good knights of his blood with him. And the more men of worship that they be, the more worship we shall win. That is full knightly spoken, said Sir Tristram; and right so as ye counsel me, so will we do. So that night they were lodged with the best. And on the morn when it was day they were arrayed all in green trappings, shields and spears, and La Beale Isoud in the same colour, and her three damosels. And right so these four knights came into the field endlong and through. And so they led La Beale Isoud thither as she should stand and behold all the jousts in a bay window; but always she was wimpled that no man might see her visage. And then these four knights rode straight unto the party of the King of Scots.

Then came therein two brethren, cousins unto Sir Gawaine, the one hight Sir Edward, that other hight Sir Sadok, the which were two good knights; and they asked of King Arthur that they might have the first jousts, for they were of Orkney. I am pleased, said King Arthur. Then Sir Edward encountered with the King of Scots, in whose party was Sir

Tristram and Sir Palomides; and Sir Edward smote the King of Scots quite from his horse, and Sir Sadok smote down the King of North Wales, and gave him a wonder great fall, that there was a great cry on King Arthur's party, and that made Sir Palomides passing wroth. And so Sir Palomides dressed his shield and his spear, and with all his might he met with Sir Edward of Orkney, that he smote him so hard that his horse might not stand on his feet, and so they hurtled to the earth; and then with the same spear Sir Palomides smote down Sir Sadok over his horse's croup.

This meanwhile there came into the place Sir Tristram upon a black horse, and or ever he stint he smote down with one spear four good knights of Orkney that were of the kin of Sir Gawaine; and Sir Gareth and Sir Dinadan everych of them smote down a good knight. Then Sir Tristram made to horse again the two kings that Edward and Sadok had unhorsed at the beginning. And then Sir Tristram drew his sword and rode into the thickest of the press against them of Orkney; and there he smote down knights, and rashed off helms, and pulled away their shields, and hurtled down many knights: he fared so that Sir Arthur and all knights had great marvel when they saw one knight do so great deeds of arms. And Sir Palomides failed not upon the other side, but did so marvellously well that all men had wonder. But ever Sir Tristram did so much deeds of arms that they of Orkney waxed weary of him, and so withdrew them unto Lonazep.

Then was the cry of heralds and all manner of common people: The Green Knight hath done marvellously, and beaten all them of Orkney. And there the heralds numbered that Sir Tristram that sat upon the black horse had smitten down with spears and swords thirty knights; and

Sir Palomides had smitten down twenty knights, and the most part of these fifty knights were of the house of King Arthur, and proved knights. This is a great shame to us, said Arthur unto Sir Launcelot, to see four knights beat so many knights of mine; and therefore make you ready, for we will have ado with them. Sir, said Launcelot, wit ye well that these are two passing good knights, and great worship were it not to us now to have ado with them, for they have this day sore travailed. As for that, said Arthur, I will be avenged; and therefore take with you Sir Bleoberis and Sir Ector, and I will be the fourth, said Arthur. Sir, said Launcelot, ye shall find me ready, and my brother Sir Ector, and my cousin Sir Bleoberis. And so when they were ready and on horseback: Now choose, said Sir Arthur unto Sir Launcelot, with whom that ye will encounter withal. Sir, said Launcelot, I will meet with the green knight upon the black horse (that was Sir Tristram); and my cousin Sir Bleoberis shall match the green knight upon the white horse (that was Sir Palomides); and my brother Sir Ector shall match with the green knight upon the white horse (that was Sir Gareth). Then must I, said Sir Arthur, have ado with the green knight upon the grisled horse (and that was Sir Dinadan). Now every man take heed to his fellow, said Sir Launcelot. And so they trotted on together, and there encountered Sir Launcelot against Sir Tristram. So Sir Launcelot smote Sir Tristram so sore upon the shield that he bare horse and man to the earth; but Sir Launcelot weened that it had been Sir Palomides, and so he passed forth. And then Sir Bleoberis encountered with Sir Palomides, and he smote him so hard upon the shield that Sir Palomides and his white horse rustled to the earth. Then Sir Ector de

Maris smote Sir Gareth so hard that down he fell off his horse. And the noble King Arthur encountered with Sir Dinadan, and he smote him quite from his saddle. And then the noise turned awhile how the green knights were slain down.

When the King of Northgalis saw that Sir Tristram had a fall, then he remembered him how great deeds of arms Sir Tristram had done. Then he made ready many knights, for the custom and cry was such, that what knight were smitten down, and might not be horsed again by his fellows, outher by his own strength, that as that day he should be prisoner unto the party that had smitten him down. So came in the King of Northgalis, and he rode straight unto Sir Tristram; and when he came nigh him he alighted down suddenly and betook Sir Tristram his horse, and said thus: Noble knight, I know thee not of what country that thou art, but for the noble deeds that thou hast done this day take there my horse, and let me do as well I may; for thou art better worthy to have mine horse than I myself. Gramercy, said Sir Tristram, and if I may I shall quite you: look that ye go not far from us, and as I suppose, I shall win you another horse. And therewith Sir Tristram mounted upon his horse, and there he met with King Arthur, and he gave him such a buffet upon the helm with his sword that King Arthur had no power to keep his saddle. And then Sir Tristram gave the King of Northgalis King Arthur's horse. Then was there great press about King Arthur for to horse him again; but Sir Palomides would not suffer King Arthur to be horsed again, but ever Sir Palomides smote on the right hand and on the left hand mightily as a noble knight. And this meanwhile Sir Tristram rode through the thickest of the press, and smote down knights on the right hand and on the left hand, and raced off helms, and so passed forth unto his pavilions, and left Sir Palomides on foot; and Sir Tristram changed his horse and disguised himself all in red, horse and harness.

And when the queen La Beale Isoud saw that Sir Tristram was unhorsed, and she wist not where he was, then she wept greatly. But Sir Tristram, when he was ready, came dashing lightly into the field, and then La Beale Isoud espied him. And so he did great deeds of arms; with one spear, that was great, Sir Tristram smote down five knights or ever he stint. Then Sir Launcelot espied him readily, that it was Sir Tristram, and then he repented him that he had smitten him down; and so Sir Launcelot went out of the press to repose him and lightly he came again. And now when Sir Tristram came into the press, through his great force he put Sir Palomides upon his horse, and Sir Gareth, and Sir Dinadan, and then they began to do marvellously; but Sir Palomides nor none of his two fellows knew not who had holpen them on horseback again. But ever Sir Tristram was nigh them and succoured them, and they knew not him, because he was changed into red armour. And all this while Sir Launcelot was away.

So when La Beale Isoud knew Sir Tristram again upon his horse-back she was passing glad, and then she laughed and made good cheer. And as it happened, Sir Palomides looked up toward her where she lay in the window, and he espied how she laughed; and therewith he took such a rejoicing that he smote down, what with his spear and with his sword, all that ever he met; for through the sight of her he was so enamoured in her love that he seemed at that time, that an both Sir Tristram and Sir Launcelot had been both against him they should have won no worship of him. And in his heart, as the book saith, Sir Palomides wished that with his worship he might have ado with Sir Tristram before all men, because of La Beale Isoud. Then Sir Palomides began to double his strength, and he did so marvellously that all men had wonder of him, and ever he cast up his eye unto La Beale Isoud. And when he saw her make such cheer he fared like a lion, that there might no man withstand him. And then Sir Tristram beheld him, how that Sir Palomides bestirred him; and then he said unto Sir Dinadan: Sir Palomides is a passing good knight and a well enduring, but such deeds saw I him never do, nor never heard I tell that ever he did so much in one day. It is his day, said Dinadan; and he would say no more unto Sir Tristram; but to himself he said: An if ye knew for whose love he doth all those deeds of arms, soon would Sir Tristram abate his courage. Alas, said Sir Tristram, that Sir Palomides is not christened. So said King Arthur, and so said all those that beheld him. Then all people gave him the prize, as for the best knight that day, that he passed Sir Launcelot or Sir Tristram. Well, said Dinadan to himself, all this worship that Sir Palomides hath here this day he may thank the Queen Isoud, for had she been away this day Sir Palomides had not gotten the prize this day.

Right so came into the field Sir Launcelot du Lake, and saw and heard the noise and cry and the great worship that Sir Palomides had. He dressed him against Sir Palomides, with a great mighty spear and a long, and thought to smite him down. And when Sir Palomides saw Sir Launcelot come upon him so fast, he ran upon Sir Launcelot as fast with his sword as he might; and as Sir Launcelot should have stricken him he smote his spear aside, and smote it a-two with his sword. And Sir Palomides rashed unto Sir Launcelot, and thought to have put him to a shame; and with his sword he smote his horse's neck that Sir Launcelot rode upon, and then Sir Launcelot fell to the earth. Then was the cry huge and great: See how Sir Palomides the Saracen hath smitten down Sir Launcelot's horse. Right then were there many knights wroth with Sir Palomides because he had done that deed; therefore many knights held there against that it was unknightly done in a tournament to kill an horse wilfully, but that it had been done in plain battle, life for life.

When Sir Ector de Maris saw Sir Launcelot his brother have such a despite, and so set on foot, then he gat a spear eagerly, and ran against Sir Palomides, and he smote him so hard that he bare him quite from his horse. That saw Sir Tristram, that was in red harness, and he smote down Sir Ector de Maris quite from his horse. Then Sir Launcelot dressed his shield upon his shoulder, and with his sword naked in his hand, and so came straight upon Sir Palomides fiercely and said: Wit thou well thou hast done me this day the greatest despite that ever any worshipful knight did to me in tournament or in jousts, and therefore I will be avenged upon thee, therefore take keep to yourself. Ah, mercy, noble knight, said Palomides, and forgive me mine unkindly deeds, for I have no power nor might to withstand you, and I have done so much this day that well I wot I did never so much, nor never shall in my life-days; and therefore, most noble knight, I require thee spare me as at this day, and I promise you I shall ever be your knight while I live: an ye put me from my worship now, ye put me from the greatest worship that ever I had or ever shall have in my life-days. Well, said Sir Launcelot, I see, for to say thee sooth, ye have done marvellously well this day; and I understand a part for whose love ye do it, and well I wot that love is a great mistress. And if my lady were here, as she nis not, wit you well, said Sir Launcelot, ye should not bear away the worship. But beware your love be not discovered, for an Sir Tristram may know it ye will repent it; and sithen my quarrel is not here, ye shall have this day the worship as for me; considering the great travail and pain that ye have had this day, it were no worship for me to put you from it. And therewithal Sir Launcelot suffered Sir Palomides to depart.

Then Sir Launcelot by great force and might gat his own horse maugre twenty knights. So when Sir Launcelot was horsed he did many marvels, and so did Sir Tristram, and Sir Palomides in like wise. And then the king let blow to lodging; and because Sir Palomides began first, and never he went nor rode out of the field to repose, but ever he was doing marvellously well either on foot or on horseback, and longest during, King Arthur and all the kings gave Sir Palomides the honour and the gree as for that day.

HOW KING ARTHUR AND SIR LAUNCELOT CAME TO SEE LA BEALE ISOUD, AND HOW PALOMIDES SMOTE DOWN KING ARTHUR, AND OF THE SECOND DAY OF THE TOURNAMENT AND OF THE TREASON OF SIR PALOMIDES TO SIR TRISTRAM. So on the morn Sir Tristram was ready, and La Beale Isoud with Sir Palomides and Sir Gareth. And so they rode all in green full freshly beseen unto the forest. And Sir Tristram left Sir

Dinadan sleeping in his bed. And so as they rode it happed the king and Launcelot stood in a window, and saw Sir Tristram ride and Isoud. Sir, said Launcelot, yonder rideth the fairest lady of the world except your queen, Dame Guenever. Who is that? said Sir Arthur. Sir, said he, it is Queen Isoud that, out-taken my lady your queen, she is makeless. Take your horse, said Arthur, and array you at all rights as I will do, and I promise you, said the king, I will see her. Then anon they were armed and horsed, and either took a spear and rode unto the forest. Sir, said Launcelot, it is not good that ye go too nigh them, for wit ye well these are two as good knights as now are living, and therefore, sir, I pray you be not too hasty. For peradventure there will be some knights be displeased an we come suddenly upon them. As for that, said Arthur, I will see her, for I take no force whom I grieve. Sir, said Launcelot, ye put yourself in great jeopardy. As for that, said the king, we will take the adventure. Right so anon the king rode even to her, and saluted her, and said: God you save. Sir, said she, ye are welcome. Then the king beheld her, and liked her wonderly well.

With that came Sir Palomides unto Arthur, and said: Uncourteous knight, what seekest thou here? thou art uncourteous to come upon a lady thus suddenly, therefore withdraw thee. Sir Arthur took none heed of Sir Palomides' words, but ever he looked still upon Queen Isoud. Then was Sir Palomides wroth, and therewith he took a spear, and came hurtling upon King Arthur, and smote him down with a spear. When Sir Launcelot saw that despite of Sir Palomides, he said to himself: I am loath to have ado with yonder knight, and not for his own sake but for Sir Tristram. And one thing I am sure of, if I smite down Sir Palomides

I must have ado with Sir Tristram, and that were overmuch for me to match them both, for they are two noble knights; notwithstanding, whether I live or I die, needs must I revenge my lord, and so will I, whatsomever befall of me. And therewith Sir Launcelot cried to Sir Palomides: Keep thee from me. And then Sir Launcelot and Sir Palomides rushed together with two spears strongly, but Sir Launcelot smote Sir Palomides so hard that he went quite out of his saddle, and had a great fall. When Sir Tristram saw Sir Palomides have that fall, he said to Sir Launcelot: Sir knight, keep thee, for I must joust with thee. As for to joust with me, said Sir Launcelot, I will not fail you, for no dread I have of you; but I am loath to have ado with you an I might choose, for I will that ye wit that I must revenge my special lord that was unhorsed unwarly and unknightly. And therefore, though I revenged that fall, take ye no displeasure therein, for he is to me such a friend that I may not see him shamed.

Anon Sir Tristram understood by his person and by his knightly words that it was Sir Launcelot du Lake, and verily Sir Tristram deemed that it was King Arthur, he that Sir Palomides had smitten down. And then Sir Tristram put his spear from him, and put Sir Palomides again on horseback, and Sir Launcelot put King Arthur on horseback and so departed. Ye did not worshipfully, said Sir Tristram unto Palomides, when ye smote down that knight so suddenly as ye did. And wit ye well ye did yourself great shame, for the knights came hither of their gentleness to see a fair lady; and that is every good knight's part, to behold a fair lady; and ye had not ado to play such masteries afore my lady. Wit thou well it will turn to anger, for he that ye smote down was King Arthur, and that other was the good knight Sir Launcelot. But I shall not forget the words of Sir Launcelot when that he called him a man of great worship, thereby I wist that it was King Arthur. And as for Sir Launcelot, an there had been five hundred knights in the meadow, he would not have refused them, and yet he said he would refuse me. By that again I wist that it was Sir Launcelot, for ever he forbeareth me in every place, and showeth me great kindness; and of all knights, I out-take none, say what men will say, he beareth the flower of all chivalry, say it him whosomever will. An he be well angered, and that him list to do his utterance without any favour, I know him not alive but Sir Launcelot is over hard for him, be it on horseback or on foot. I may never believe, said Palomides, that King Arthur will ride so privily as a poor errant knight. Ah, said Sir Tristram, ye know not my lord Arthur, for all knights may learn to be a knight of him. And therefore ye may be sorry, said Sir Tristram, of your unkindly deeds to so noble a king. And a thing that is done may not be undone, said Palomides. Then Sir Tristram sent Queen Isoud unto her lodging in the priory, there to behold all the tournament.

Then there was a cry unto all knights, that when they heard an horn blow they should make jousts as they did the first day. And like as the brethren Sir Edward and Sir Sadok began the jousts the first day, Sir Uwaine the king's son Urien and Sir Lucanere de Buttelere began the jousts the second day. And at the first encounter Sir Uwaine smote down the King's son of Scots; and Sir Lucanere ran against the King of Wales, and they brake their spears all to pieces; and they were so fierce both, that they hurtled together that both fell to the earth.

When Sir Tristram saw them so begin, he said to Palomides: How feel ye yourself? may ye do this day as ye did yesterday? Nay, said Palomides, I feel myself so weary, and so sore bruised of the deeds of yesterday, that I may not endure as I did yesterday. That me repenteth, said Sir Tristram, for I shall lack you this day. Sir Palomides said: Trust not to me, for I may not do as I did. All these words said Palomides for to beguile Sir Tristram. Sir, said Sir Tristram unto Sir Gareth, then must I trust upon you; wherefore I pray you be not far from me to rescue me. An need be, said Sir Gareth, I shall not fail you in all that I may do. Then Sir Palomides rode by himself; and then in despite of Sir Tristram he put himself in the thickest press among them of Orkney, and there he did so marvellously deeds of arms that all men had wonder of him, for there might none stand him a stroke.

When Sir Tristram saw Sir Palomides do such deeds, he marvelled and said to himself: He is weary of my company. So Sir Tristram beheld him a great while and did but little else, for the noise and cry was so huge and great that Sir Tristram marvelled from whence came the strength that Sir Palomides had there in the field. Sir, said Sir Gareth unto Sir Tristram, let me know this day what ye be; and wonder ye not so upon Sir Palomides, for he enforceth himself to win all the worship and honour from you. I may well believe it, said Sir Tristram. And sithen I understand his evil will and his envy, ye shall see, if that I enforce myself, that the noise shall be left that now is upon him.

Then Sir Tristram rode into the thickest of the press, and then he did so marvellously well, and did so great deeds of arms, that all men said that Sir Tristram did double so much deeds of arms as Sir Palomides had done aforehand. And then the noise went plain from Sir Palomides, and all the people cried upon Sir Tristram.

But when Sir Palomides heard the noise and the cry was turned from him, he rode out on a part and beheld Sir Tristram. And when Sir Palomides saw Sir Tristram do so marvellously well he wept passingly sore for despite, for he wist well he should no worship win that day; for well knew Sir Palomides, when Sir Tristram would put forth his strength and his manhood, he should get but little worship that day.

Then Sir Tristram rode privily out of the press, that none espied him but La Beale Isoud and Sir Palomides, for they two would not let off their eyes upon Sir Tristram. And when Sir Tristram came to his pavilions he found Sir Dinadan in his bed asleep. Awake, said Tristram, ye ought to be ashamed so to sleep when knights have ado in the field. Then Sir Dinadan arose lightly and said: What will ye that I shall do? Make you ready, said Sir Tristram, to ride with me into the field. So when Sir Dinadan was armed he looked upon Sir Tristram's helm and on his shield, and when he saw so many strokes upon his helm and upon his shield he said: In good time was I thus asleep, for had I been with you I must needs for shame there have followed you, more for shame than any prowess that is in me, that I see well now by those strokes that I should have been truly beaten as I was yesterday. Leave your japes, said Sir Tristram, and come off, that we were in the field again. What, said Sir Dinadan, is your heart up? yesterday ye fared as though ye had dreamed. So then Sir Tristram was arrayed in black harness. What aileth you this day? said Dinadan, meseemeth ye be wilder than ye were yesterday. Then smiled Sir Tristram and said to Dinadan: Await well upon me; if ye see me overmatched look that ye be ever behind me, and I shall make you ready way by God's grace. So Sir Tristram and Sir Dinadan took their horses. All this espied Sir Palomides, both their going and their coming, and so did La Beale Isoud, for she knew Sir Tristram above all other.

Then when Sir Palomides saw that Sir Tristram was disguised, then he thought to do him a shame. So Sir Palomides rode to a knight that was sore wounded, that sat under a fair well from the field. Sir knight, said Sir Palomides, I pray you to lend me your armour and your shield, for mine is over-well known in this field, and that hath done me great damage; and ye shall have mine armour and my shield that is as sure as yours. I will well, said the knight, that ye have mine armour and my shield, if they may do you any avail. So Sir Palomides armed him hastily in that knight's armour and his shield that shone as any crystal or silver, and so he came riding into the field. And then there was neither Sir Tristram nor none of King Arthur's party that knew Sir Palomides. And right so as Sir Palomides was come into the field Sir Tristram smote down three knights, even in the sight of Sir Palomides. And then Sir Palomides rode against Sir Tristram, and either met other with great spears, that they brast to their hands. And then they dashed together with swords eagerly. Then Sir Tristram had marvel what knight he was that did battle so knightly with him. Then was Sir Tristram wroth, for he felt him passing strong, so that he deemed he might not have ado with the remnant of the knights, because of the strength of Sir Palomides. So they lashed together and gave many sad strokes together, and many knights marvelled what knight he might be that so encountered with the black knight, Sir Tristram. Full well knew La Beale Isoud that there was Sir Palomides that fought with Sir Tristram, for she espied all in her window where that she stood, as Sir Palomides changed his harness with the wounded knight. And then she began to weep so heartily for the despite of Sir Palomides that there she swooned.

Then came in Sir Launcelot with the knights of Orkney. And when the other party had espied Sir Launcelot, they cried: Return, return, here cometh Sir Launcelot du Lake. So there came knights and said: Sir Launcelot, ye must needs fight with yonder knight in the black harness (that was Sir Tristram), for he hath almost overcome that good knight that fighteth with him with the silver shield (that was Sir Palomides). Then Sir Launcelot rode betwixt Sir Tristram and Sir Palomides, and Sir Launcelot said to Palomides: Sir knight, let me have the battle, for ye have need to be reposed. Sir Palomides knew Sir Launcelot well, and so did Sir Tristram, but because Sir Launcelot was a far hardier knight than himself therefore he was glad, and suffered Sir Launcelot to fight with Sir Tristram. For well wist he that Sir Launcelot knew not Sir Tristram, and there he hoped that Sir Launcelot should beat or shame Sir Tristram, whereof Sir Palomides was full fain. And so Sir Launcelot gave Sir Tristram many sad strokes, but Sir Launcelot knew not Sir Tristram, but Sir Tristram knew well Sir Launcelot. And thus they fought long together, that La Beale Isoud was well-nigh out of her mind for sorrow.

Then Sir Dinadan told Sir Gareth how that knight in the black harness was Sir Tristram: And this is Launcelot that fighteth with him, that must needs have the better of him, for Sir Tristram hath had too much travail this day.

Then let us smite him down, said Sir Gareth. So it is better that we do, said Sir Dinadan, than Sir Tristram be shamed, for yonder hoveth the strong knight with the silver shield to fall upon Sir Tristram if need be. Then forthwithal Gareth rushed upon Sir Launcelot, and gave him a great stroke upon his helm so hard that he was astonied. And then came Sir Dinadan with a spear, and he smote Sir Launcelot such a buffet that horse and all fell to the earth. Fie for shame, said Sir Tristram to Sir Gareth and Sir Dinadan, why did ye smite down so good a knight as he is, and namely when I had ado with him? now ye do yourself great shame, and him no disworship; for I held him reasonable hot, though ye had not holpen me.

Then came Sir Palomides that was disguised, and smote down Sir Dinadan from his horse. Then Sir Launcelot, because Sir Dinadan had smitten him aforehand, assailed Sir Dinadan passing sore, and Sir Dinadan defended him mightily. But well understood Sir Tristram that Sir Dinadan might not endure Sir Launcelot, wherefore Sir Tristram was sorry. Then came Sir Palomides fresh upon Sir Tristram. And when Sir Tristram saw him come, he thought to deliver him at once, because that he would help Sir Dinadan, because he stood in great peril with Sir Launcelot. Then Sir Tristram hurtled unto Sir Palomides and gave him a great buffet, and then Sir Tristram gat Sir Palomides and pulled him down underneath him. And so fell Sir Tristram with him; and Sir Tristram leapt up lightly and left Sir Palomides, and went betwixt Sir Launcelot and Dinadan, and then they began to do battle together.

Right so Sir Dinadan gat Sir Tristram's horse, and said on high that Sir Launcelot might hear it: My lord Sir Tristram, take your horse. And when Sir Launcelot heard him name Sir Tristram: Alas! said Launcelot, what have I done? I am dishonoured. Ah, my lord Sir Tristram, said Launcelot, why were ye disguised? ye have put yourself in great peril this day; but I pray you noble knight to pardon me, for an I had known you we had not done this battle. Sir, said Sir Tristram, this is not the first kindness ye showed me. So they were both horsed again.

Then all the people on the one side gave Sir Launcelot the honour and the degree, and on the other side all the people gave to the noble knight Sir Tristram the honour and the degree; but Launcelot said nay thereto: For I am not worthy to have this honour, for I will report me unto all knights that Sir Tristram hath been longer in the field than I, and he hath smitten down many more knights this day than I have done. And therefore I will give Sir Tristram my voice and my name, and so I pray all my lords and fellows so to do. Then there was the whole voice of dukes and earls, barons and knights, that Sir Tristram this day is proved the best knight.

HOW SIR TRISTRAM DEPARTED WITH LA BEALE ISOUD, AND HOW PALOMIDES FOLLOWED AND EXCUSED HIM, AND HOW KING ARTHUR AND SIR LAUNCELOT CAME UNTO THEIR PAVILIONS AS THEY SAT AT SUPPER, AND OF SIR PALOMIDES. Then they blew unto lodging, and Queen Isoud was led unto her pavilions. But wit you well she was wroth out of measure with Sir Palomides, for she saw all his treason from the beginning to the ending. And all this while neither Sir Tristram, neither Sir Gareth nor Dinadan, knew not of the treason of Sir Palomides; but afterward ye shall hear that there befell the greatest debate betwixt Sir Tristram and Sir Palomides that might be.

So when the tournament was done, Sir Tristram, Gareth, and Dinadan, rode with La Beale Isoud to these pavilions. And ever Sir Palomides rode with them in their company disguised as he was. But when Sir Tristram had espied him that he was the same knight with the shield of silver that held him so hot that day: Sir knight, said Sir Tristram, wit ye well here is none that hath need of your fellowship, and therefore I pray you depart from us. Sir Palomides answered again as though he had not known Sir Tristram: Wit you well, sir knight, from this fellowship will I never depart, for one of the best knights of the world commanded me to be in this company, and till he discharge me of my service I will not be discharged. By that Sir Tristram knew that it was Sir Palomides. Ah, Sir Palomides, said the noble knight Sir Tristram, are ye such a knight? Ye have been named wrong, for ye have long been called a gentle knight, and as this day ye have showed me great ungentleness, for ye had almost brought me unto my death. But, as for you, I suppose I should have done well enough, but Sir Launcelot with you was overmuch; for I know no knight living but Sir Launcelot is over good for him, an he will do his uttermost. Alas, said Sir Palomides, are ye my lord Sir Tristram? Yea, sir, and that ye know well enough. By my knighthood, said Palomides, until now I knew you not; I weened that ye had been the King of Ireland, for well I wot ye bare his arms. His arms I bare, said Sir Tristram, and that will I stand by, for I won them once in a field of a full noble knight, his name was Sir Marhaus; and with great pain I won that knight, for there was none other recover, but Sir Marhaus died through false leeches; and yet was he never yolden to me. Sir, said Palomides, I weened ye had been turned upon Sir Launcelot's party, and that caused me to turn. Ye say well, said Sir Tristram, and so I take you, and I forgive you.

So then they rode into their pavilions; and when they were alighted they unarmed them and washed their faces and hands, and so went unto meat, and were set at their table. But when Isoud saw Sir Palomides she changed then her colours, and for wrath she might not speak. Anon Sir Tristram espied her countenance and said: Madam, for what cause make ye us such cheer? we have been sore travailed this day. Mine own lord, said La Beale Isoud, be ye not displeased with me, for I may none otherwise do; for I saw this day how ye were betrayed and nigh brought to your death. Truly, sir, I saw every deal, how and in what wise, and therefore, sir, how should I suffer in your presence such a felon and traitor as Sir Palomides; for I saw him with mine eyes, how he beheld you when ye went out of the field. For ever he hoved still upon his horse till he saw you come in againward. And then forthwithal I saw him ride to the hurt knight, and changed harness with him, and then straight I saw him how he rode into the field. And anon as he had found you he encountered with you, and thus wilfully Sir Palomides did battle with you; and as for him, sir, I was not greatly afraid, but I dread sore Launcelot, that knew you not. Madam, said Palomides, ye may say whatso ye will, I may not contrary you, but by my knighthood I knew not Sir Tristram. Sir Palomides, said Sir Tristram, I will take your excuse, but well I wot ye spared me but little; but all is pardoned on my part. Then La Beale Isoud held down her head and said no more at that time.

And therewithal two knights armed came unto the pavilion, and there they alighted both, and came in armed at all pieces. Fair knights, said Sir Tristram, ye are to blame to come thus armed at all pieces upon me while we are at our meat; if ye would anything when we were in the field there might ye have eased your hearts. Not so, said the one of those knights, we come not for that intent; but wit ye well Sir Tristram, we be come hither as your friends. And I am come here, said the one, for to see you, and this knight is come for to see La Beale Isoud. Then said Sir Tristram: I require you do off your helms that I may see you. That will we do at your desire, said the knights. And when their helms were off, then, said Sir Tristram unto La Beale Isoud, Madam arise, for here is my lord, King Arthur. Then the king and the queen kissed, and Sir Launcelot and Sir Tristram braced either other in arms, and then there was joy without measure; and at the request of La Beale Isoud, King Arthur and Launcelot were unarmed, and then there was merry talking. Madam, said Sir Arthur, it is many a day sithen that I have desired to see you, for ye have been praised so far; and now I dare say ye are the fairest that ever I saw, and Sir Tristram is as fair and as good a knight as any that I know; therefore me seemeth ye are well beset together. Sir, God thank you, said the noble knight, Sir Tristram, and Isoud; of your great goodness and largess ye are peerless. Thus they talked of many things and of all the whole jousts. But for what cause, said

King Arthur, were ye, Sir Tristram, against us? Ye are a knight of the Table Round; of right ye should have been with us. Sir, said Sir Tristram, here is Dinadan, and Sir Gareth your own nephew, caused me to be against you. My lord Arthur, said Gareth, I may well bear the blame, but it were Sir Tristram's own deeds. That may I repent, said Dinadan, for this unhappy Sir Tristram brought us to this tournament, and many great buffets he caused us to have. Then the king and Launcelot laughed that they might not sit.

What knight was that, said Arthur, that held you so short, this with the shield of silver? Sir, said Sir Tristram, here he sitteth at this board. What, said Arthur, was it Sir Palomides? Wit ye well it was he, said La Beale Isoud. Truly, said Arthur, that was unknightly done of you of so good a knight, for I have heard many people call you a courteous knight. Sir, said Palomides, I knew not Sir Tristram, for he was so disguised. It may well be, said Launcelot, for I knew not Sir Tristram; but I marvel why ye turned on our party. That was done for the same cause, said Palomides. As for that, said Sir Tristram, I have pardoned him, and I would be right loath to leave his fellowship, for I love right well his company: so they left off and talked of other things.

And in the evening King Arthur and Sir Launcelot departed unto their lodging; but wit ye well Sir Palomides had envy heartily, for all that night he had never rest in his bed, but wailed and wept out of measure. So on the morn Sir Tristram, Gareth, and Dinadan arose early, and then they went unto Sir Palomides' chamber, and there they found him fast asleep, for he had all night watched, and it was seen upon his cheeks that he had wept full sore. Say nothing, said Sir Tristram, for I am sure he hath taken anger and sorrow for the rebuke that I gave to him, and La Beale Isoud.

HOW SIR TRISTRAM AND SIR PALOMIDES DID THE THIRD DAY OF THE TOURNAMENT, AND HOW SIR TRISTRAM TURNED TO KING ARTHUR'S SIDE, AND OF THE SORROW OF SIR PALOMIDES. Then Sir Tristram let call Sir Palomides, and bade him make him ready, for it was time to go to the field. When they were ready they were armed, and clothed all in red, both Isoud and all they; and so they led her passing freshly through the field, into the priory where was her lodging. And then they heard three blasts blow, and every king and knight dressed him unto the field. And the first that was ready to joust was Sir Palomides and Sir Kainus le Strange, a knight of the Table Round. And so they two encountered together, but Sir Palomides smote Sir Kainus so hard that he smote him quite over his horse's croup. And forthwithal Sir Palomides smote down another knight, and brake then his spear, and pulled out his sword and did wonderly well. And then the noise began greatly upon Sir Palomides. Lo, said King Arthur, yonder Palomides beginneth to play his pageant. Truly, said Arthur, he is a passing good knight. And right as they stood talking thus, in came Sir Tristram as thunder, and he encountered with Sir Kay the Seneschal, and there he smote him down quite from his horse; and with that same spear Sir Tristram smote down three knights more, and then he pulled out his sword and did marvellously. Then the noise and cry changed from Sir Palomides and turned to Sir Tristram, and all the people cried: O Tristram, O Tristram. And then was Sir Palomides clean forgotten.

Then Sir Arthur and Sir Launcelot took their horses and dressed them, and gat into the thickest of the press. And there Sir Tristram unknowing smote down King Arthur, and then Sir Launcelot would have rescued him, but there were so many upon Sir Launcelot that they pulled him down from his horse. And then the King of Ireland and the King of Scots with their knights did their pain to take King Arthur and Sir Launcelot prisoner. When Sir Launcelot heard them say so, he fared as it had been an hungry lion, for he fared so that no knight durst nigh him.

Then came Sir Ector de Maris, and he bare a spear against Sir Palomides, and brast it upon him all to shivers. And then Sir Ector came again and gave Sir Palomides such a dash with a sword that he stooped down upon his saddle bow. And forthwithal Sir Ector pulled down Sir Palomides under his feet; and then Sir Ector de Maris gat Sir Launcelot du Lake an horse, and brought it to him, and bade him mount upon him; but Sir Palomides leapt afore and gat the horse by the bridle, and leapt into the saddle. So God me help, said Launcelot, ye are better worthy to have that horse than I. Then Sir Ector brought Sir Launcelot another horse. Gramercy, said Launcelot unto his brother. And so when he was horsed again, with one spear he smote down four knights. And then Sir Launcelot brought to King Arthur one of the best of the four horses. Then Sir Launcelot with King Arthur and a few of his knights of Sir Launcelot's kin did marvellous deeds; for that time, as the book recordeth, Sir Launcelot smote down and pulled down thirty knights. Notwithstanding the other party held them so fast together that King Arthur and his knights were overmatched. And when Sir Tristram saw that, what labour King Arthur and his knights, and in especial the noble deeds that Sir Launcelot did with his own hands, he marvelled greatly.

Then Sir Tristram called unto him Sir Palomides, Sir Gareth, and Sir Dinadan, and said thus to them: My fair fellows, wit ye well that I will turn unto King Arthur's party, for I saw never so few men do so well, and it will be shame unto us knights that be of the Round Table to see our lord King Arthur, and that noble knight Sir Launcelot, to be dishonoured. It will be well done, said Sir Gareth and Sir Dinadan. Do your best, said Palomides, for I will not change my party that I came in withal. That is for my sake, said Sir Tristram; God speed you in your journey. And so departed Sir Palomides from them. Then Sir Tristram, Gareth, and Dinadan, turned with Sir Launcelot. And then Sir Launcelot smote down the King of Ireland quite from his horse; and so Sir Launcelot smote down the King of Scots, and the King of Wales; and then Sir Arthur ran unto Sir Palomides and smote him quite from his horse; and then Sir Tristram bare down all that he met, and Sir Gareth and Sir Dinadan did there as noble knights; then all the parties began to flee. Alas, said Palomides, that ever I should see this day, for now have I lost all the worship that I won; and then Sir Palomides went his way wailing, and so withdrew him till he came to a well, and there he put his horse from him, and did off his armour, and wailed and wept like as he had been a wood man. Then many knights gave the prize to Sir Tristram, and there were many that gave the prize unto Sir Launcelot. Fair lords, said Sir Tristram, I thank you of the honour ye would give me, but I pray you heartily that ye would give your voice to Sir Launcelot, for by my faith, said Sir Tristram, I will give Sir Launcelot my voice. But Sir Launcelot would not have it, and so the prize was given betwixt them both.

Then every man rode to his lodging, and Sir Bleoberis and Sir Ector rode with Sir Tristram and La Beale Isoud unto their pavilions. Then as Sir Palomides was at the well wailing and weeping, there came by him fleeing the kings of Wales and of Scotland, and they saw Sir Palomides in that arage. Alas, said they, that so noble a man as ye be should be in this array. And then those kings gat Sir Palomides' horse again, and made him to arm him and mount upon his horse, and so he rode with them, making great dole. So when Sir Palomides came nigh the pavilions thereas Sir Tristram and La Beale Isoud was in, then Sir Palomides prayed the two kings to abide him there the while that he spake with Sir Tristram. And when he came to the port of the pavilions, Sir Palomides said on high: Where art thou, Sir Tristram de Liones? Sir, said Dinadan, that is Palomides. What, Sir Palomides, will ye not come in here among us? Fie on thee, traitor, said Palomides, for wit you well an it were daylight as it is night I should slay thee, mine own hands. And if ever I may get thee, said Palomides, thou shalt die for this day's deed. Sir Palomides, said Sir Tristram, ye wite me with wrong, for had ye done as I did ye had won worship. But sithen ye give me so large warning I shall be well ware of you. Fie on thee, traitor, said Palomides, and therewith departed.

Then on the morn Sir Tristram, Bleoberis, and Sir Ector de Maris, Sir Gareth, Sir Dinadan, what by water and what by land, they brought La Beale Isoud unto Joyous Gard, and there reposed them a seven night, and made all the mirths and disports that they could devise. And King Arthur and his knights drew unto Camelot, and Sir Palomides rode with the two kings; and ever he made the greatest dole that any man could think, for he was not all only so dolorous for the departing from La Beale Isoud, but he was a part as sorrowful to depart from the fellowship of Sir Tristram; for Sir Tristram was so kind and so gentle that when Sir Palomides remembered him thereof he might never be merry.

HOW ON A DAY SIR TRISTRAM DEPARTED UNARMED AND MET WITH SIR PALOMIDES, AND HOW THEY SMOTE EACH OTHER, AND HOW SIR PALOMIDES FORBARE HIM, AND HOW SIR TRISTRAM GAT HARNESS OF A HURT KNIGHT AND OVERTHREW SIR PALOMIDES AND MADE HIM BE CHRISTENED.

And so on a day Sir Tristram was riding with no more harness of war but his spear and his sword, and saw afore him where Sir Palomides had stricken down a knight, and almost wounded him to the death. Then Sir Tristram repented him that he was not armed, and then he hoved still. With that Sir Palomides knew Sir Tristram, and cried on high: Sir Tristram, now be we well met, for ere we depart we will redress our old sores. As for that, said Sir Tristram, there was yet never Christian man might make his boast that ever I fled from him; and wit ye well, Sir Palomides, thou that art a Saracen shall never make thy boast that Sir Tristram de Liones shall flee from thee. And therewith Sir Tristram made his horse to run, and with all his might he came straight upon Sir Palomides, and brast his spear upon him an hundred pieces. And forthwithal Sir Tristram drew his sword. And then he turned his horse and struck at Palomides six great strokes upon his helm; and then Sir Palomides stood still, and beheld Sir Tristram, and marvelled of his woodness, and of his folly. And then Sir Palomides said to himself: An Sir Tristram were armed, it were hard to cease him of this battle, and if I turn again and slay him I am ashamed wheresomever that I go.

Then Sir Tristram spake and said: Thou coward knight, what castest thou to do; why wilt thou not do battle with me? for have thou no doubt I shall endure all thy malice. Ah, Sir Tristram, said Palomides, full well thou wottest I may not fight with thee for shame, for thou art here naked and I am armed, and if I slay thee, dishonour shall be mine. Now, I require you, tell me a question that I shall say to you. Tell me what it is, said Sir Tristram, and I shall answer you the truth. I put case, said Sir Palomides, that ye were armed at all rights as well as I am, and I naked as ye be, what would you do to me now, by your true knighthood? Ah, said Sir Tristram, now I understand thee well, Sir Palomides, for now must I say mine own judgment, and as God me bless, that I shall say shall not be said for no fear that I have of thee. But this is all: wit, Sir Palomides, as at this time thou shouldest depart from me, for I would not have ado with thee. No more will I, said Palomides, and therefore ride forth on thy way. As for that I may choose, said Sir Tristram, either to ride or to abide. But Sir Palomides, said Sir Tristram, I marvel of one thing, that thou that art so good a knight, that thou wilt not be christened, and thy brother, Sir Safere, hath been christened many a day.

As for that, said Sir Palomides, I may not yet be christened, for one avow that I have made many years agone; howbeit in my heart I believe in Jesu Christ and his mild mother Mary; but I have but one battle to do, and when that is done I will be baptised with a good will. By my head, said Tristram, as for one battle thou shalt not seek it no longer. For God defend, said Sir Tristram, that through my default thou shouldst longer live thus a Saracen. For yonder is a knight that ye, Sir Palomides, have hurt and smitten down; now help me that I were armed in his armour, and I shall soon fulfil thine avows. As ye will, said Palomides, so it shall be.

So they rode both unto that knight that sat upon a bank, and then Sir Tristram saluted him, and he weakly saluted him again. Sir knight, said Sir Tristram, I require you tell me your right name. Sir, he said, my name is Sir Galleron of Galway, and knight of the Table Round. Truly, said Sir Tristram, I am right heavy of your hurts; but this is all, I must pray you to lend me all your whole armour, for ye see I am unarmed, and I must do battle with this knight. Sir, said the hurt knight, ye shall have it with a good will; but ye must beware, for I warn you that knight is wight. Sir, said Galleron, I pray you tell me your name, and what is that knight's name that hath beaten me. Sir, as for my name it is Sir Tristram de Liones, and as for the knight's name that hath hurt you it is Sir Palomides, brother to the good knight Sir Safere, and yet is Sir Palomides unchristened. Alas, said Sir Galleron, that is pity that so good a knight and so noble a man of arms should be unchristened. Either he shall slay me, said Sir Tristram, or I him, but that he shall be christened or ever we depart insunder. My lord Sir Tristram, said Sir Galleron, your renown and worship is well known through many realms, and God save you this day from shenship and shame.

Then Sir Tristram unarmed Galleron, the which was a noble knight, and had done many deeds of arms, and he was a large knight of flesh and bone. And when he was unarmed he stood upon his feet, for he was brised in the back with a spear; yet so as Sir Galleron might, he armed Sir Tristram. And then Sir Tristram mounted upon his own horse, and in his hand he gat Sir Galleron's spear; and therewithal Sir Palomides was ready. And so they came hurtling together, and either smote other in midst of their shields; and therewithal Sir Palomides' spear brake, and Sir Tristram smote down the horse; and Sir Palomides, as soon as he might, avoided his horse, and dressed his shield, and pulled out his sword. That saw Sir Tristram, and therewithal he alighted and tied his horse to a tree.

And then they came together as two wild boars, lashing together, tracing and traversing as noble men that oft had been well proved in battle; but ever Sir Palomides dread the might of Sir Tristram, and therefore he suffered him to breathe him. Thus they fought more than two hours, but often Sir Tristram smote such strokes at Sir Palomides that he made him to kneel; and Sir Palomides brake and cut away many pieces of Sir Tristram's shield; and then Sir Palomides wounded Sir Tristram, for he was a well fighting man. Then Sir Tristram was wood wroth out of measure, and rushed upon Sir Palomides with such a might that Sir Palomides fell grovelling to the earth; and therewithal he leapt up lightly upon his feet, and then Sir Tristram wounded Palomides sore through the shoulder. And ever Sir Tristram fought still in like hard, and Sir Palomides failed not, but gave him many sad strokes. And at the last Sir Tristram doubled his strokes, and by fortune Sir Tristram smote Sir Palomides' sword out of his hand, and if Sir Palomides had stooped for his sword he had been slain.

Then Palomides stood still and beheld his sword with a sorrowful heart. How now, said Sir Tristram unto Palomides, now have I thee at advantage as thou haddest me this day; but it shall never be said in no court, nor among good knights, that Sir Tristram shall slay any knight that is weaponless; and therefore take thou thy sword, and let us make an end of this battle. As for to do this battle, said Palomides, I dare right well end it; but I have no great lust to fight no more. And for this cause, said Palomides: mine offence to you is not so great but that we may be friends. All that I have offended is and was for the love of La Beale Isoud. And as for her, I dare say she is peerless above all other ladies, and also I proffered her never no dishonour; and by her I have gotten the most part of my worship. And sithen I offended never as to her own person, and as for the offence that I have done, it was against your own person, and for that offence ye have given me this day many sad strokes, and some I have given you again; and now I dare say I felt never man of your might, nor so well breathed, but if it were Sir Launcelot du Lake; wherefore I require you, my lord, forgive me all that I have offended unto you; and this same day have me to the next church, and first let me be clean confessed, and after see you now that I be truly baptised. And then will we all ride together unto the court of Arthur, that we be there at the high feast. Now take your horse, said Sir Tristram, and as ye say so it shall be, and all thine evil will God forgive it you, and I do. And here within this mile is the Suffragan of Carlisle that shall give you the sacrament of baptism.

Then they took their horses and Sir Galleron rode with them. And when they came to the Suffragan Sir Tristram told him their desire. Then the Suffragan let fill a great vessel with water, and when he had hallowed it he then confessed clean Sir Palomides, and Sir Tristram and Sir Galleron were his godfathers. And then soon after they departed, riding toward Camelot, where King Arthur and Queen Guenever was, and for the most part all the knights of the Round Table. And so the king and all the court were glad that Sir Palomides was christened. And at the same feast in came Galahad and sat in the Siege Perilous. And so therewithal departed and dissevered all the knights of the Round Table. And Sir Tristram returned again unto Joyous Gard, and Sir Palomides followed the Questing Beast.

OF SIR LAUNCELOT AND DAME ELAINE

HOW SIR LAUNCELOT HOLP A DOLOROUS LADY FROM HER PAIN, AND FOUGHT WITH A DRAGON, AND OF THE BEGETTING OF SIR GALAHAD.

Now leave we Sir Tristram de Liones, and speak we of Sir Launcelot du Lake, and of Sir Galahad, Sir Launcelot's son, how he was born, and in what manner, as the book of French rehearseth. Afore the time that Sir Galahad was born, there came in an hermit unto King Arthur upon Whitsunday, as the knights sat at the Table Round. And when the hermit saw the Siege Perilous, he asked the king and all the knights why that siege was void. Sir Arthur and all the knights answered: There shall never none sit in that siege but one, but if he be destroyed. Then said the hermit: Wot ye what is he? Nay, said Arthur and all the knights, we wot not who is he that shall sit therein. Then wot I, said the hermit, for he that shall sit there is unborn, and this same year he shall be born that shall sit there in that Siege Perilous, and he shall win the Sangreal. When this hermit had made this mention he departed from the court of King Arthur.

And then after this feast Sir Launcelot rode on his adventure, till on a time by adventure he passed over the bridge of Corbin; and there he saw the fairest tower that ever he saw, and there-under was a fair town full of people; and all the people, men and women, cried at once: Welcome, Sir Launcelot du Lake, the flower of all knighthood, for by thee all we shall be holpen out of danger. What mean ye, said Sir Launcelot, that ye cry so upon me? Ah, fair knight, said they all, here is within this tower a dolorous lady that hath been there in pains many winters and days, for ever she boileth in scalding water; and but late, said all the people, Sir Gawaine was here and he might not help her, and so he left her in pain. So may I, said Sir Launcelot, leave her in pain as well as Sir Gawaine did. Nay, said the people, we know well that it is Sir Launcelot that shall deliver her. Well, said Launcelot, then shew me what I shall do.

Then they brought Sir Launcelot into the tower; and when he came to the chamber thereas this lady was, the doors of iron unlocked and unbolted. And so Sir Launcelot went into the chamber that was as hot as any stew. And there Sir Launcelot took the fairest lady by the hand that ever he saw, and she was naked as a needle; and by enchantment Queen Morgan le Fay and the Queen of Northgalis had put her there in that pains, because she was called the fairest lady of that country; and there she had been five years, and never might she be delivered out of her great pains unto the time the best knight of the world had taken her by the hand. Then the people brought her clothes. And when she was arrayed, Sir Launcelot thought she was the fairest lady of the world, but if it were Queen Guenever.

Then this lady said to Sir Launcelot: Sir, if it please you will ye go with me hereby into a chapel that we may give loving and thanking unto God? Madam, said Sir Launcelot, come on with me, I will go with you. So when they came there and gave thankings to God all the people, both learned and lewd, gave thankings unto God and him, and said: Sir knight, since ye have delivered this lady, ye shall deliver us from a serpent there is here in a tomb. Then Sir Launcelot took his shield and said: Bring me thither, and what I may do unto the pleasure of God and you I will do. So when Sir Launcelot came thither he saw written upon the tomb letters of gold that said thus: Here shall come a leopard of king's blood, and he shall slay this serpent, and this leopard shall engender a lion in this foreign country, the which lion shall pass all other knights. So then Sir Launcelot lift up the tomb, and there came out an horrible and a fiendly dragon, spitting fire out of his mouth. Then Sir Launcelot drew his sword and fought with the dragon long, and at the last with great pain Sir Launcelot slew that dragon.

Therewithal came King Pelles, the good and noble knight, and saluted Sir Launcelot, and he him again. Fair knight, said the king, what is your name? I require you of your knighthood tell me! Sir, said Launcelot, wit you well my name is Sir Launcelot du Lake. And my name is, said the king, Pelles, king of the foreign country, and cousin nigh unto Joseph of Aramathie. And then either of them made much of other, and so they went into the castle to take their repast. And anon there came in a dove at a window, and in her mouth there seemed a little censer of gold. And therewithal there was such a savour as all the spicery of the world had been there. And forthwithal there was upon the table all manner of meats and drinks that they could think upon. So came in a damosel passing fair and young, and she bare a vessel of gold betwixt her hands; and thereto the king kneeled devoutly, and said his prayers, and so did all that were there. Then, said Sir Launcelot, What may this mean? This is, said the king, the richest thing that any man hath living. And when this thing goeth about, the Round Table shall be broken; and wit thou well, said the king, this is the holy Sangreal that ye have here seen. So the king and Sir Launcelot led their life the most part of that day. And fain would King Pelles have found the mean to have had Sir Launcelot to love his daughter, fair Elaine. And for this intent: the king knew well that Sir Launcelot should have a child by his daughter, the which should be named Sir Galahad the good knight, by whom all the foreign country should be brought out of danger, and by him the Holy Greal should be achieved.

Then came forth a lady that hight Dame Brisen, and she said unto the king: Sir, wit ye well Sir Launcelot loveth no lady in the world but all only Queen Guenever; and therefore work ye by counsel, and I shall make him to see your daughter, and he shall not wit but that he seeth Queen Guenever. O fair lady, Dame Brisen, said the king, hope ye to bring this about? Sir, said she, upon pain of my life let me deal. For this Brisen was one of the greatest enchantresses that was at that time in the world living. Then anon by Dame Brisen's wit she made one to come to Sir Launcelot that he knew well. And this man brought him a ring from Queen Guenever like as it had come from her, and such one as she was wont for the most part to wear; and when Sir

Launcelot saw that token wit ye well he was never so fain. Where is my lady? said Sir Launcelot. In the Castle of Case, said the messenger, but five mile hence. Then Sir Launcelot thought to be there the same night. And then this Brisen by the commandment of King Pelles let send Elaine to this castle with twenty-five knights unto the Castle of Case. Then Sir Launcelot against night rode unto that castle, and there anon he was received worshipfully with such people, to his seeming, as were about Queen Guenever.

So when Sir Launcelot was alighted, then Dame Brisen brought him a cup full of wine; and anon as he had drunken that wine he was so assotted that he weened that maiden Elaine had been Queen Guenever. Wit you well that Sir Launcelot was glad, and so was that lady Elaine, for well she knew that of them should be born Galahad that should prove the best knight of the world; and all the windows and holes of that chamber were stopped that no manner of day might be seen. And then Sir Launcelot remembered him, and he arose up and went to the window.

And anon as he had unshut the window the enchantment was gone; then he knew himself that he had been deceived. Alas, he said, that I have lived so long; now I am shamed. So then he gat his sword in his hand and said: Thou traitress, what art thou? thou shalt die right here of my hands. Then this fair lady Elaine kneeled down afore Sir Launcelot, and said: Fair courteous knight, come of king's blood, I require you have mercy upon me, and as thou art renowned the most noble knight of the world, slay me not, for I shall have a son by thee that shall be the most noblest knight of the world. Ah, false traitress, said Sir Launcelot, why hast thou betrayed me? anon tell me what thou art. Sir, she said, I am Elaine, the daughter of King Pelles. Well, said Sir Launcelot, I will forgive you this deed; and therewith he took her up in his arms, and kissed her, for she was as fair a lady, and thereto lusty and young, and as wise, as any was that time living. I may not wite this to you, said Sir Launcelot; but her that made this enchantment upon me as between you and me, an I may find her, that same Lady Brisen, she shall lose her head for witchcrafts, for there was never knight deceived so as I am this night. And so Sir Launcelot arrayed him, and armed him, and took his leave mildly at that lady young Elaine, and so he departed. Then she said: My lord Sir Launcelot, I beseech you see me as soon as ye may, for I have obeyed me unto the prophecy that my father told me. And by his commandment to fulfil this prophecy I have given the greatest riches and the fairest flower that ever I had, and that is my maidenhood that I shall never have again; and therefore, gentle knight, owe me your goodwill.

And so Sir Launcelot arrayed him and was armed, and took his leave mildly at that young lady Elaine; and so he departed, and rode till he came to the Castle of Corbin, where her father was. And as fast as her time came she was delivered of a fair child, and they christened him Galahad; and wit ye well that child was well kept and well nourished, and he was named Galahad because Sir Launcelot was so named at the fountain stone; and after that the Lady of the Lake confirmed him Sir Launcelot du Lake.

Then after this lady was delivered and churched, there came a knight unto her, his name was Sir Bromel la Pleche, the which was a great lord; and he had loved that lady long, and he evermore desired her to wed her; and so by no mean she could put him off, till on a day she said to Sir Bromel: Wit thou well, sir knight, I will not love you, for my love is set upon the best knight of the world. Who is he? said Sir Bromel. Sir, she said, it is Sir Launcelot du Lake that I love and none other, and therefore woo me no longer. Ye say well, said Sir Bromel, and sithen ye have told me so much, ye shall have but little joy of Sir Launcelot, for I shall slay him wheresomever I meet him. Sir, said the Lady Elaine, do to him no treason. Wit ye well, my lady, said Bromel, and I promise you this twelvemonth I shall keep the pont of Corbin for Sir Launcelot's sake, that he shall neither come nor go unto you, but I shall meet with him.

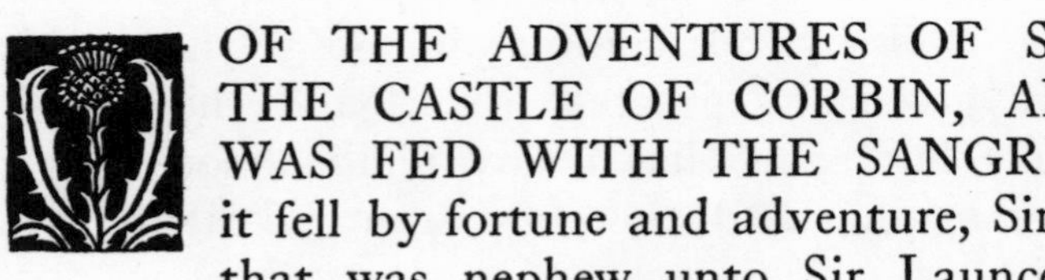

OF THE ADVENTURES OF SIR BORS AT THE CASTLE OF CORBIN, AND HOW HE WAS FED WITH THE SANGREAL. Then as it fell by fortune and adventure, Sir Bors de Ganis, that was nephew unto Sir Launcelot, came over that bridge; and there Sir Bromel and Sir Bors jousted, and Sir Bors smote Sir Bromel such a buffet that he bare him over his horse's croup. And then Sir Bromel, as an hardy knight, pulled out his sword, and dressed his shield to do battle with Sir Bors. And then Sir Bors alighted and avoided his horse, and there they dashed together many sad strokes; and long thus they fought, till at the last Sir Bromel was laid to the earth, and there Sir Bors began to unlace his helm to slay him. Then Sir Bromel cried Sir Bors mercy, and yielded him. Upon this covenant thou shalt have thy life, said Sir Bors, so thou go unto Sir Launcelot upon Whitsunday that next cometh, and yield thee unto him as knight recreant. I will do it, said Sir Bromel, and that he sware upon the cross of the sword. And so Sir Bors let him depart, and rode unto King Pelles, that was within Corbin.

And when the king and Elaine his daughter wist that Sir Bors was nephew unto Sir Launcelot, they made him great cheer. Then said Dame Elaine: We marvel where Sir Launcelot is, for he came never here but once. Marvel not, said Sir Bors, for this half year he hath been in prison with Queen Morgan le Fay, King Arthur's sister. Alas, said Dame Elaine, that me repenteth. And ever Sir Bors beheld that child in her arms, and ever him seemed it was passing like Sir Launcelot. Truly, said Elaine, wit ye well this is his child. Then Sir Bors wept for joy, and he prayed to God it might prove as good a knight as his father was. And so came in a white dove, and she bare a little censer of gold in her mouth, and there was all manner of meats and drinks; and a maiden bare that Sangreal, and she said openly: Wit you well, Sir Bors, that this child is Galahad, that shall sit in the Siege Perilous, and achieve the Sangreal, and he shall be much better than ever was Sir Launcelot du Lake, that is his own father. And then they kneeled down and made their devotions, and there was such a savour as all the spicery in the world had been there. And when the dove took her flight, the maiden vanished with the Sangreal as she came.

Sir, said Sir Bors unto King Pelles, this castle may be named the Castle Adventurous, for here be many strange adventures. That is sooth, said the king, for well may this place be called the adventurous place, for there come but few knights here that go away with any worship; be he never so strong, here he may be proved; and but late Sir Gawaine, the good knight, gat but little worship here. For I let you wit, said King Pelles, here shall no knight win no worship but if he be of worship himself and of good living, and that loveth God and dreadeth God, and else he getteth no worship here, be he never so hardy. That is a wonderful thing, said Sir Bors. What ye mean in this country I wot not, for ye have many strange adventures, and therefore I will lie in this castle this night. Ye shall not do so, said King Pelles, by my counsel, for it is hard an ye escape without a shame. I shall take the adventure that will befall me, said Sir Bors. Then I counsel you, said the king, to be confessed clean. As for that, said Sir Bors, I will be shriven with a good will. So Sir Bors was confessed, and for all women Sir Bors was a virgin, save for one, that was the daughter of King Brangoris, and their child hight Elaine, and save for her Sir Bors was a clean maiden.

And so Sir Bors was led unto bed in a fair large chamber, and many doors were shut about the chamber. When Sir Bors espied all those doors, he avoided all the people, for he might have nobody with him; but in no wise Sir Bors would unarm him, but so he laid him down upon the bed. And right so he saw come in a light, that he might well see a spear great and long that came straight upon him pointling, and to Sir Bors seemed that the head of the spear brent like a taper. And anon, ere Sir Bors wist, the spear head smote him into the shoulder an handbreadth in deepness, and that wound grieved Sir Bors passing sore. And then he laid him down again for pain; and anon therewithal there came a knight armed with his shield on his shoulder and his sword in his hand, and he bade Sir Bors: Arise, sir knight, and fight with me. I am sore hurt, he said, but yet I shall not fail thee. And then Sir Bors started up and dressed his shield; and then they lashed together mightily a great while; and at the last Sir Bors bare him backward until that he came unto a chamber door, and there that knight went into that chamber and rested him a great while. And when he had reposed him he came out freshly again, and began new battle with Sir Bors mightily and strongly.

Then Sir Bors thought he should no more go into that chamber to rest him, and so Sir Bors dressed him betwixt the knight and that chamber door, and there Sir Bors smote him down, and then that knight yielded him. What is your name? said Sir Bors. Sir, said he, my name is Pedivere of the Straight Marches. So Sir Bors made him to swear at Whitsunday next coming to be at the court of King Arthur, and yield him there as a prisoner as an overcome knight by the hands of Sir Bors. So thus departed Sir Pedivere of the Straight Marches. And then Sir Bors laid him down to rest, and then he heard and felt much noise in that chamber; and then Sir Bors espied that there came in, he wist not whether at the doors nor windows, shot of arrows and of quarrels so thick that he marvelled, and many fell upon him and hurt him in the bare places.

And then Sir Bors was ware where came in an hideous lion; so Sir Bors dressed him unto the lion, and anon the lion bereft him his shield, and with his sword Sir Bors smote off the lion's head. Right so Sir Bors forthwithal saw a dragon in the court passing horrible, and there seemed letters of gold written in his forehead; and Sir Bors thought that the letters made a signification of King Arthur. Right so there came an horrible leopard and an old, and there they fought long, and did great battle together. And at the last the dragon spit out of his mouth as it had been an hundred dragons; and lightly all the small dragons slew the old dragon and tare him all to pieces.

Anon withal there came an old man into the hall, and he sat him down in a fair chair, and there seemed to be two adders about his neck; and then the old man had an harp, and there he sang an old song how Joseph of Aramathie came into this land. Then when he had sung, the old man bade Sir Bors go from thence. For here shall ye have no more adventures; and full worshipfully have ye done, and better shall ye do hereafter. And then Sir Bors seemed that there came the whitest dove with a little golden censer in her mouth. And anon therewithal the tempest ceased and passed, that afore was marvellous to hear. So was all that court full of good savours. Then Sir Bors saw four children bearing four fair tapers, and an old man in the midst of the children with a censer in his one hand, and a spear in his other hand, and that spear was called the Spear of Vengeance.

Now, said that old man to Sir Bors, go ye to your cousin, Sir Launcelot, and tell him of this adventure the which had been most convenient for him of all earthly knights; but sin is so foul in him he may not achieve such holy deeds, for had not been his sin he had passed all the knights that ever were in his days; and tell thou Sir Launcelot, of all worldly adventures he passeth in manhood and prowess all other, but in these spiritual matters he shall have many his better. And then Sir Bors saw four gentlewomen come by him, purely beseen: and he saw where that they entered into a chamber where was great light as it were a summer light; and the women kneeled down afore an altar of silver with four pillars, and as it had been a bishop kneeled down afore that table of silver. And as Sir Bors looked over his head he saw a sword like silver, naked, hoving over his head, and the clearness thereof smote so in his eyes that as at that time Sir Bors was blind; and there he heard a voice that said: Go hence, thou Sir Bors, for as yet thou art not worthy for to be in this place. And then he went backward to his bed till on the morn. And on the morn King Pelles made great joy of Sir Bors; and then he departed and rode to Camelot, and there he found Sir Launcelot du Lake, and told him of the adventures that he had seen with King Pelles at Corbin.

So the noise sprang in Arthur's court that Launcelot had a child by Elaine, the daughter of King Pelles, wherefore Queen Guenever was wroth, and gave many rebukes to Sir Launcelot, and called him false knight. And then Sir Launcelot told the queen all, and how he was made to meet her by enchantment in likeness of the queen. So the queen held Sir Launcelot excused. And as the book saith, King Arthur had been in France, and had made war upon the mighty King Claudas, and had won much of his lands. And when the king was come again he let cry a great feast, that all lords and ladies of all England should be there, but if it were such as were rebellious against him.

HOW DAME ELAINE, GALAHAD'S MOTHER, CAME IN GREAT ESTATE UNTO CAMELOT, AND HOW SIR LAUNCELOT BEHAVED HIM THERE. And when Dame Elaine, the daughter of King Pelles, heard of this feast she went to her father and required him that he would give her leave to ride to that feast. The king answered: I will well ye go thither, but in any wise as ye love me and will have my blessing, that ye be well beseen in the richest wise; and look that ye spare not for no cost; ask and ye shall have all that you needeth. Then by the advice of Dame Brisen, her maiden, all thing was apparelled unto the purpose, that there was never no lady more richlier beseen. So she rode with twenty knights, and ten ladies, and gentlewomen, to the number of an hundred horses. And when she came to Camelot, King Arthur and Queen Guenever said, and all the knights, that Dame Elaine was the fairest and the best beseen lady that ever was seen in that court. And anon as King Arthur wist that she was come he met her and saluted her, and so did the most part of all the knights of the Round Table, both Sir Tristram, Sir Bleoberis, and Sir Gawaine, and many more that I will not rehearse. But when Sir Launcelot saw her he was so ashamed, and that because he drew his sword on her, that he would not salute her nor speak to her; and yet Sir Launcelot thought she was the fairest woman that ever he saw in his life-days.

But when Dame Elaine saw Sir Launcelot that would not speak unto her she was so heavy that she weened her heart would have to-brast; for wit you well, out of measure she loved him. And then Elaine said unto her woman, Dame Brisen: The unkindness of Sir Launcelot slayeth me near. Ah, peace, madam, said Dame Brisen, I will undertake that he shall come to you, an ye would hold you still. That were me liefer, said Dame Elaine, than all the gold that is above the earth. Let me deal, said Dame Brisen. So when Elaine was brought unto Queen Guenever either made other good cheer by countenance, but nothing with hearts. But all men and women spake of the beauty of Dame Elaine, and of her great riches.

Then the queen commanded that Dame Elaine should sleep in a chamber nigh her chamber, and all under one roof; and so it was done as the queen commanded. Then the queen sent for Sir Launcelot and bade him come to her: Or else I am sure, said the queen, that ye will go to your lady, Dame Elaine, by whom ye had Galahad. Ah, madam, said Sir Launcelot, never say ye so, for that was against my will. Then, said the queen, look that ye come to me when I send for you. Madam, said Launcelot, I shall not fail you, but I shall be ready at your commandment. This bargain was soon done and made between them, but Dame Brisen knew it by her crafts, and told it to her lady, Dame Elaine. Alas, said she, how shall I do? Let me deal, said Dame Brisen, for I shall bring him by the hand even to you, and he shall ween that I am Queen Guenever's messenger. Now well is me, said Dame Elaine, for all the world I love not so much as I do Sir Launcelot.

So then Dame Brisen came to Sir Launcelot and said: Sir Launcelot du Lake, my lady, Queen Guenever, awaiteth upon you. O my fair lady, said Sir Launcelot, I am ready to go with you where ye will have me. So Sir Launcelot took his sword in his hand; and then Dame Brisen took him by the finger and led him to her lady, Dame Elaine; and then she departed and left them together. Wit ye well the lady was glad, and so was Sir Launcelot, for he weened that it was the queen.

Then Queen Guenever sent one of her women unto Sir Launcelot; and when she came there she found he was away; so she came to the queen and told her all. Alas, said the queen, where is that false knight become? Then the queen was nigh out of her wit, and then she writhed and weltered as a mad woman, and at the last the queen met with Sir Launcelot; and thus she said: False traitor knight that thou art, look thou never abide in my court, and not so hardy, thou false traitor knight that thou art, that ever thou come in my sight. Alas, said Sir Launcelot; and therewith he took such an heartly sorrow at her words that he fell down to the floor in a swoon. And therewithal Queen Guenever departed. And when Sir Launcelot awoke of his swoon, he leapt out at a bay window into a garden, and there with thorns he was all to-scratched in his visage and his body; and so he ran forth he wist not whither, and was wild wood as ever was man; and so he ran two year, and never man might have grace to know him.

HOW DAME ELAINE WAS COMMANDED BY QUEEN GUENEVER TO AVOID THE COURT, AND HOW SIR LAUNCELOT BECAME MAD, AND OF THE SORROW OF QUEEN GUENEVER. Now turn we unto Queen Guenever and to the fair Lady Elaine. When Dame Elaine heard the queen so to rebuke Sir Launcelot, and also she saw how he swooned, and how he leaped out at a bay window, then she said unto Queen Guenever: Madam, ye are greatly to blame for Sir Launcelot, for now have ye lost him, for I saw and heard by his countenance that he is mad for ever. Alas, madam, ye do great sin, and to yourself great dishonour, for ye have a lord of your own, and therefore it is your part to love him; for there is no queen in this world hath such another king as ye have. And, if ye were not, I might have the love of my lord Sir Launcelot; and cause I have to love him for

I am his, and by him I have borne a fair son, and his name is Galahad, and he shall be in his time the best knight of the world. Dame Elaine, said the queen, when it is daylight I charge you and command you to avoid my court; and for the love ye owe unto Sir Launcelot discover not his counsel, for an ye do, it will be his death. As for that, said Dame Elaine, I dare undertake he is marred for ever, and that have ye made; for ye, nor I, are like to rejoice him; for he made the most piteous groans when he leapt out at yonder bay window that ever I heard man make. Alas, said fair Elaine, and alas, said the Queen Guenever, for now I wot well we have lost him for ever.

So on the morn Dame Elaine took her leave to depart, and she would no longer abide. Then King Arthur brought her on her way with mo than an hundred knights through a forest. And by the way she told Sir Bors de Ganis all how it betid, and how Sir Launcelot leapt out at a window, araged out of his wit. Alas, said Sir Bors, where is my lord, Sir Launcelot, become? Sir, said Elaine, I wot never. Alas, said Sir Bors, betwixt you both ye have destroyed that good knight. As for me, said Dame Elaine, I said never nor did never thing that should in any wise displease him, but with the rebuke that Queen Guenever gave him I saw him swoon to the earth; and when he awoke he took his sword in his hand and leapt out at a window with the grisliest groan that ever I heard man make. Now farewell, Dame Elaine, said Sir Bors, and hold my lord Arthur with a tale as long as ye can, for I will turn again to Queen Guenever and give her a hete; and I require you, as ever ye will have my service, make good watch and espy if ever ye may see my lord Sir Launcelot. Truly, said fair Elaine, I shall do all that I may do, for as fain would I know and wit where he is become, as you, or any of his kin, or Queen Guenever; and cause great enough have I thereto as well as any other. And wit ye well, said fair Elaine to Sir Bors, I would lose my life for him rather than he should be hurt; but alas, I cast me never for to see him, and the chief causer of this is Dame Guenever. Madam, said Dame Brisen, the which had made the enchantment before betwixt Sir Launcelot and her, I pray you heartily, let Sir Bors depart, and hie him with all his might as fast as he may to seek Sir Launcelot, for I warn you he is clean out of his mind; and yet he shall be well holpen an but by miracle.

Then wept Dame Elaine, and so did Sir Bors de Ganis; and so they departed, and Sir Bors rode straight unto Queen Guenever. And when she saw Sir Bors she wept as she were wood. Fie on your weeping, said Sir Bors de Ganis, for ye weep never but when there is no bote. Alas, said Sir Bors, that ever Sir Launcelot's kin saw you, for now have ye lost the best knight of our blood, and he that was all our leader and our succour; and I dare say and make it good that all kings, christian nor heathen, may not find such a knight, for to speak of his nobleness and courtesy, with his beauty and his gentleness. Alas, said Sir Bors, what shall we do that be of his blood? Alas, said Sir Ector de Maris. Alas, said Lionel.

And when the queen heard them say so she fell to the earth in a dead swoon. And then Sir Bors took her up, and dawed her; and when she was awaked she kneeled afore the three knights, and held up both her hands, and besought them to seek him. And spare not for no goods but that he be found, for I wot he is out of his mind. And

Sir Bors, Sir Ector, and Sir Lionel departed from the queen, for they might not abide no longer for sorrow. And then the queen sent them treasure enough for their expenses, and so they took their horses and their armour, and departed. And then they rode from country to country, in forests, and in wilderness, and in wastes; and ever they laid watch both at forests and at all manner of men as they rode, to hearken and spere after him, as he that was a naked man, in his shirt, with a sword in his hand. And thus they rode nigh a quarter of a year, endlong and overthwart, in many places, forests and wilderness, and oft-times were evil lodged for his sake; and yet for all their labour and seeking could they never hear word of him. And wit you well these three knights were passing sorry.

Then at the last Sir Bors and his fellows met with a knight that hight Sir Melion de Tartare. Now fair knight, said Sir Bors, whither be ye away? for they knew either other afore time. Sir, said Melion, I am in the way toward the court of King Arthur. Then we pray you, said Sir Bors, that ye will tell my lord Arthur, and my lady, Queen Guenever, and all the fellowship of the Round Table, that we cannot in no wise hear tell where Sir Launcelot is become. Then Sir Melion departed from them, and said that he would tell the king, and the queen, and all the fellowship of the Round Table, as they had desired him. So when Sir Melion came to the court of King Arthur he told the king, and the queen, and all the fellowship of the Round Table, what Sir Bors had said of Sir Launcelot. Then Sir Gawaine, Sir Uwaine, Sir Sagramore le Desirous, Sir Aglovale, and Sir Percivale de Galis took upon them by the great desire of King Arthur, and in especial by the queen, to seek throughout all England,

Wales, and Scotland, to find Sir Launcelot, and with them rode eighteen knights mo to bear them fellowship; and wit ye well, they lacked no manner of spending; and so were they three and twenty knights.

And thus as these noble knights rode together, they by one assent departed, and then they rode by two, by three, and by four, and by five, and ever they assigned where they should meet. And so Sir Aglovale and Sir Percivale rode together unto their mother that was a queen in those days. And when she saw her two sons, for joy she wept tenderly. And then she said: Ah, my dear sons, when your father was slain he left me four sons, of the which now be twain slain. And for the death of my noble son, Sir Lamorak, shall my heart never be glad. And then she kneeled down upon her knees to-fore Aglovale and Sir Percivale, and besought them to abide at home with her. Ah, sweet mother, said Sir Percivale, we may not, for we be come of king's blood of both parties, and therefore, mother, it is our kind to haunt arms and noble deeds. Alas, my sweet sons, then she said, for your sakes I shall lose my liking and lust, and then wind and weather I may not endure, what for the death of your father, King Pellinore, that was shamefully slain by the hands of Sir Gawaine, and his brother, Sir Gaheris: and they slew him not manly but by treason. Ah, my dear sons, this is a piteous complaint for me of your father's death, considering also the death of Sir Lamorak, that of knighthood had but few fellows. Now, my dear sons, have this in your mind. Then there was but weeping and sobbing in the court when they should depart, and she fell a-swooning in midst of the court.

HOW SIR PERCIVALE SOUGHT FOR SIR LAUNCELOT, HOW HE FOUGHT WITH SIR ECTOR, AND HOW THEY WERE BOTH MADE WHOLE BY THE COMING OF THE SANGREAL. Then Sir Percivale and Sir Aglovale rode into many countries, ever inquiring after Sir Launcelot, but never they could hear of him; and at the last they came to a castle that hight Cardican, and there they were lodged together. And privily about midnight Sir Percivale came to Aglovale's squire and said: Arise and make thee ready, for ye and I will ride away secretly. Sir, said the squire, I would full fain ride with you where ye would have me, but an my lord, your brother, take me he will slay me. As for that care thou not, for I shall be thy warrant.

And so Sir Percivale rode till it was after noon, and then he came upon a bridge of stone, and there he found a knight that was bound with a chain fast about the waist unto a pillar of stone. O fair knight, said that bound knight, I require thee loose me of my bonds. What knight are ye, said Sir Percivale, and for what cause are ye so bound? Sir, I shall tell you, said that knight: I am a knight of the Table Round, and my name is Sir Persides; and thus by adventure I came this way, and here I lodged in this castle at the bridge foot, and therein dwelleth an uncourteous lady; and because she proffered me to be her paramour, and I refused her, she set her men upon me suddenly or ever I might come to my weapon; and thus they bound me, and here I wot well I shall die but if some man of worship break my bands. Be ye of good cheer, said Sir Percivale, and because ye are a knight of the Round Table as well as I, I trust to God to break your bands. And therewith Sir Percivale pulled out his sword and struck at the chain with such a might that he cut a-two the chain, and through Sir Persides' hauberk and hurt him a little. That was a mighty stroke as ever I felt one, said Sir Persides, for had not the chain been ye had slain me.

And therewithal Sir Persides saw a knight coming out of a castle all that ever he might fling. Beware, sir, said Sir Persides, yonder cometh a man that will have ado with you. Let him come, said Sir Percivale. And so he met with that knight in midst of the bridge; and Sir Percivale gave him such a buffet that he smote him quite from his horse and over a part of the bridge, that, had not been a little vessel under the bridge, that knight had been drowned. And then Sir Percivale took the knight's horse and made Sir Persides to mount up him; and so they rode unto the castle, and bade the lady deliver Sir Persides' servants, or else he would slay all that ever he found; and so for fear she delivered them all. Then was Sir Percivale ware of a lady that stood in that tower. Ah, madam, said Sir Percivale, what use and custom is that in a lady to destroy good knights but if they will be your paramour? Forsooth this is a shameful custom of a lady, and if I had not a great matter in my hand I should fordo your evil customs.

And so Sir Persides brought Sir Percivale unto his own castle, and there he made him great cheer all that night. And on the morn, when Sir Percivale had heard mass and broken his fast, he bade Sir Persides ride unto King Arthur: And tell the king how that ye met with me; and tell my brother, Sir Aglovale, how I rescued you; and bid him seek not after me, for I am in the quest to seek Sir Launcelot du Lake, and though he seek me he shall not find me; and tell him I will never see him, nor the court, till I have found Sir Launcelot. And so Sir Persides departed from Sir Percivale, and then he rode unto King Arthur, and told there of Sir Percivale. And when Sir Aglovale heard him speak of his brother Sir Percivale, he said: He departed from me unkindly.

And now will we turn unto Sir Percivale that rode long; and in a forest he met a knight with a broken shield and a broken helm; and as soon as either saw other readily they made them ready to joust, and so hurtled together with all the might of their horses, and met together so hard, that Sir Percivale was smitten to the earth. And then Sir Percivale arose lightly, and cast his shield on his shoulder and drew his sword, and bade the other knight: Alight, and do we battle unto the uttermost. Will ye more? said that knight. And therewith he alighted, and put his horse from him; and then they came together an easy pace, and there they lashed together with noble swords, and sometime they struck and sometime they foined, and either gave other many great wounds. Thus they fought near half a day, and never rested but right little, and there was none of them both that had less wounds than fifteen, and they bled so much that it was marvel they stood on their feet. But this knight that fought with Sir Percivale was a proved knight and a wise-fighting knight, and Sir Percivale was young and strong, not knowing in fighting as the other was.

Then Sir Percivale spoke first, and said: Sir knight, hold thy hand a while still, for we have fought for a simple matter and quarrel overlong, and therefore I require thee tell me thy name, for I was never or this time matched. So God me help, said that knight, and never or this time was there never knight that wounded me so sore as thou hast done, and yet have I fought in many battles; and now shalt thou wit that I am a knight of the Table Round, and my name is Sir Ector de Maris, brother unto the good knight, Sir Launcelot du Lake. Alas, said Sir Percivale, and my name is Sir Percivale de Galis that hath made my quest to seek Sir Launcelot, and now I am sure that I shall never finish my quest, for ye have slain me with your hands. It is not so, said Sir Ector, for I am slain by your hands, and may not live. Therefore I require you, said Sir Ector unto Sir Percivale, ride ye hereby to a priory, and bring me a priest that I may receive my Saviour, for I may not live. And when ye come to the court of King Arthur tell not my brother, Sir Launcelot, how that ye slew me, for then he would be your mortal enemy, but ye may say that I was slain in my quest as I sought him. Alas, said Sir Percivale, ye say that never will be, for I am so faint for bleeding that I may unnethe stand, how should I then take my horse?

Then they made both great dole out of measure. This will not avail, said Sir Percivale. And then he kneeled down and made his prayer devoutly unto Almighty Jesu, for he was one of the best knights of the world that at that time was, in whom the very faith stood most in. Right so there came by the holy vessel of the Sangreal with all manner of sweetness and savour; but they could not readily see who that bare that vessel, but Sir Percivale had a glimmering of the vessel and of the maiden that bare it, for he was a perfect clean maiden. And forthwithal they both were as whole of hide and limb as ever they were in their life-days: then they gave thankings to God with great mildness. O Jesu, said Sir Percivale, what may this mean, that we be thus healed, and right now we were at the point of dying? I wot full well, said Sir Ector, what it is; it is an holy vessel that is borne by a maiden, and therein is part of the holy blood of our Lord Jesu Christ, blessed mote he be. But it may not be seen, said Sir Ector, but if it be by a perfect man. Truly, said Sir Percivale, I saw a damosel, as me thought, all in white, with a vessel in both her hands, and forthwithal I was whole.

So then they took their horses and their harness, and amended their harness as well as they might that was broken; and so they mounted upon their horses, and rode talking together. And there Sir Ector de Maris told Sir Percivale how he had sought his brother, Sir Launcelot, long, and never could hear witting of him: In many strange adventures have I been in this quest. And so either told other of their adventures.

OF THE MADNESS OF SIR LAUNCELOT, AND HOW HE WAS HEALED BY THE SANGREAL. And now leave we off a while of Sir Ector and of Sir Percivale, and speak we of Sir Launcelot that suffered and endured many sharp showers, that ever ran wild wood from place to place, and lived by fruit and such as he might get, and drank water two year; and other clothing had he but little but his shirt and his breech. Thus as Sir Launcelot wandered here and there he came in a fair meadow where he found a pavilion; and there by, upon a tree, there hung a white shield, and two swords hung thereby, and two spears leaned there by a tree. And when Sir Launcelot saw the swords, anon he leapt to the one sword, and took it in his hand, and drew it out. And then he lashed at the shield, that all the meadow rang of the dints, that he gave such a noise as ten knights had foughten together.

Then came forth a dwarf, and leapt unto Sir Launcelot, and would have had the sword out of his hand. And then Sir Launcelot took him by the both shoulders and threw him to the ground upon his neck, that he had almost broken his neck; and therewithal the dwarf cried help. Then came forth a likely knight, and well apparelled in scarlet furred with minever. And anon as he saw Sir Launcelot he deemed that he should be out of his wit. And then he said with fair speech: Good man, lay down that sword, for as meseemeth thou hadst more need of sleep and of warm clothes than to wield that sword. As for that, said Sir Launcelot, come not too nigh, for an thou do, wit thou well I will slay thee.

And when the knight of the pavilion saw that, he stert backward within the pavilion. And then the dwarf armed him lightly; and so the knight thought by force and might to take the sword from Sir Launcelot, and so he came stepping out; and when Sir Launcelot saw him come so all armed with his sword in his hand, then Sir Launcelot flew to him with such a might, and hit him upon the helm such a buffet, that the stroke troubled his brains, and therewith the sword brake in three. And the knight fell to the earth as he had been dead, the blood brasting out of his mouth, the nose, and the ears. And then Sir Launcelot ran into the pavilion, and rushed even into the warm bed; and there was a lady in that bed, and she gat her smock, and ran out of the pavilion. And when she saw her lord lie at the ground like to be dead, then she cried and wept as she had been mad. Then with her noise the knight awaked out of his swoon, and looked up weakly with his eyes; and then he asked her, where was that mad man that had given him such a buffet: For such a buffet had I never of man's hand. Sir, said the dwarf, it is not worship to hurt him, for he is a man out of his wit; and doubt ye not he hath been a man of great worship, and for some heartly sorrow that he hath taken, he is fallen mad; and me beseemeth, said the dwarf, he resembleth much unto Sir Launcelot, for him I saw at the great tournament beside Lonazep. Jesu defend, said that knight, that ever that noble knight, Sir Launcelot, should be in such a plight; but whatsomever he be, said that knight, harm will I none do him. And this knight's name was Bliant. Then he said unto the dwarf: Go thou fast on horseback, unto my brother Sir Selivant, that is at the Castle Blank, and tell him of mine adventure, and bid him bring with him an horse litter, and then will we bear this knight unto my castle.

So the dwarf rode fast, and he came again and brought Sir Selivant with him, and six men with an horse litter; and so they took up the feather bed with Sir Launcelot, and so carried all away with them unto the Castle Blank, and he never awaked till he was within the castle. And then they bound his hands and his feet, and gave him good meats and good drinks, and brought him again to his strength and his fairness; but in his wit they could not bring him again, nor to know himself. Thus was Sir Launcelot there more than a year and a half, honestly arrayed and fair faren withal.

Then upon a day this lord of that castle, Sir Bliant, took his arms, on horseback, with a spear, to seek adventures.

And as he rode in a forest there met with him two knights adventurous, the one was Breuse Saunce Pité, and his brother, Sir Bertelot; and these two ran both at once upon Sir Bliant, and brake their spears upon his body. And then they drew out swords and made great battle, and fought long together. But at the last Sir Bliant was sore wounded, and felt himself faint; and then he fled on horseback toward his castle. And as they came hurling under the castle whereas Sir Launcelot lay in a window, he saw how two knights laid upon Sir Bliant with their swords. And when Sir Launcelot saw that, yet as wood as he was he was sorry for his lord, Sir Bliant. And then Sir Launcelot brake the chains from his legs and off his arms, and in the breaking he hurt his hands sore; and so Sir Launcelot ran out at a postern, and there he met with the two knights that chased Sir Bliant; and there he pulled down Sir Bertelot with his bare hands from his horse, and therewithal he wrothe his sword out of his hand; and so he leapt unto Sir Breuse, and gave him such a buffet upon the head that he tumbled backward over his horse's croup. And when Sir Bertelot saw there his brother have such a fall, he gat a spear in his hand, and would have run Sir Launcelot through: that saw Sir Bliant, and struck off the hand of Sir Bertelot. And then Sir Breuse and Sir Bertelot gat their horses and fled away.

When Sir Selivant came and saw what Sir Launcelot had done for his brother, then he thanked God, and so did his brother, that ever they did him any good. But when Sir Bliant saw that Sir Launcelot was hurt with the breaking of his irons, then was he heavy that ever he bound him. Bind him no more, said Sir Selivant, for he is happy and gracious. Then they made great joy of Sir Launcelot, and they bound him no more; and so he abode there an half year and more. And on the morn early Sir Launcelot was ware where came a great boar with many hounds nigh him. But the boar was so big there might no hounds tear him; and the hunters came after, blowing their horns, both upon horseback and some upon foot; and then Sir Launcelot was ware where one alighted and tied his horse to a tree, and leaned his spear against the tree.

So came Sir Launcelot and found the horse bounden till a tree, and a spear leaning against a tree, and a sword tied to the saddle bow; and then Sir Launcelot leapt into the saddle and gat that spear in his hand, and then he rode after the boar; and then Sir Launcelot was ware where the boar set his back to a tree fast by an hermitage. Then Sir Launcelot ran at the boar with his spear, and therewith the boar turned him nimbly, and rove out the lungs and the heart of the horse, so that Launcelot fell to the earth; and, or ever Sir Launcelot might get from the horse, the boar rove him on the brawn of the thigh up to the hough bone. And then Sir Launcelot was wroth, and up he gat upon his feet, and drew his sword, and he smote off the boar's head at one stroke. And therewithal came out the hermit, and saw him have such a wound. Then the hermit came to Sir Launcelot and bemoaned him, and would have had him home unto his hermitage; but when Sir Launcelot heard him speak, he was so wroth with his wound that he ran upon the hermit to have slain him, and the hermit ran away. And when Sir Launcelot might not overget him, he threw his sword after him, for Sir Launcelot might go no further for bleeding; then the hermit turned again, and asked Sir Launcelot how he was hurt. Fellow, said Sir Launcelot, this boar hath bitten me sore. Then come with me, said the hermit, and I shall heal you. Go thy way, said Sir Launcelot, and deal not with me.

Then the hermit ran his way, and there he met with a good knight with many men. Sir, said the hermit, here is fast by my place the goodliest man that ever I saw, and he is sore wounded with a boar, and yet he hath slain the boar. But well I wot, said the hermit, and he be not holpen, that goodly man shall die of that wound, and that were great pity. Then that knight at the desire of the hermit gat a cart, and in that cart that knight put the boar and Sir Launcelot, for Sir Launcelot was so feeble that they might right easily deal with him; and so Sir Launcelot was brought unto the hermitage, and there the hermit healed him of his wound. But the hermit might not find Sir Launcelot's sustenance, and so he impaired and waxed feeble, both of his body and of his wit: for the default of his sustenance he waxed more wooder than he was aforehand.

And then upon a day Sir Launcelot ran his way into the forest; and by adventure he came to the city of Corbin, where Dame Elaine was, that bare Galahad, Sir Launcelot's son. And so when he was entered into the town he ran through the town to the castle; and then all the young men of that city ran after Sir Launcelot, and there they threw turves at him, and gave him many sad strokes. And ever as Sir Launcelot might overreach any of them, he threw them so that they would never come in his hands no more; for of some he brake the legs and the arms, and so fled into the castle; and then came out knights and squires and rescued Sir Launcelot. And when they beheld him and looked upon his person, they thought they saw never so goodly a man. And when they saw so many wounds upon him, all they deemed that he had been a man of worship. And then they ordained him clothes to his body, and straw underneath him, and a little house. And then every day they would throw him meat, and set him drink, but there was but few would bring him meat to his hands.

So it befell that King Pelles had a nephew, his name was Castor; and so he desired of the king to be made knight, and so at the request of this Castor the king made him knight at the feast of Candlemas. And when Sir Castor was made knight, that same day he gave many gowns. And then Sir Castor sent for the fool — that was Sir Launcelot. And when he was come afore Sir Castor, he gave Sir Launcelot a robe of scarlet and all that longed unto him. And when Sir Launcelot was so arrayed like a knight, he was the seemliest man in all the court, and none so well made. So when he saw his time he went into the garden, and there Sir Launcelot laid him down by a well and slept. And so at afternoon Dame Elaine and her maidens came into the garden to play them; and as they roamed up and down one of Dame Elaine's maidens espied where lay a goodly man by the well sleeping, and then she brought Dame Elaine where he lay. And when that she beheld him, anon she fell in remembrance of him, and knew him verily for Sir Launcelot; and therewithal she fell a-weeping so heartily that she sank even to the earth; and when she had thus wept a great while, then she arose and called her maidens and said she was sick.

And so she yede out of the garden, and she went straight to her father, and there she took him apart by herself; and then she said: O father, now have I need of your help, and but if that ye help me farewell my good days for ever. What is that, daughter? said King Pelles. Sir, she said, thus is it: in your garden I went for to sport, and there, by the well, I found Sir Launcelot du Lake sleeping. I may not believe that, said King Pelles. Sir, she said, truly he is there, and meseemeth he should be distract out of his wit. Then hold you still, said the king, and let me deal. Then the king called to him such as he most trusted, a four persons, and Dame Elaine, his daughter. And when they came to the well and beheld Sir Launcelot, anon Dame Brisen knew him. Sir, said Dame Brisen, we must be wise how we deal with him, for this knight is out of his mind, and if we awake him rudely what he will do we all know not; but ye shall abide, and I shall throw such an enchantment upon him that he shall not awake within the space of an hour; and so she did.

Then within a little while after, the king commanded that all people should avoid, that none should be in that way there as the king would come. And so when this was done, these four men and these ladies laid hand on Sir Launcelot, and so they bare him into a tower, and so into a chamber where was the holy vessel of the Sangreal, and by force Sir Launcelot was laid by that holy vessel; and there came an holy man and unhilled that vessel, and so by miracle and by virtue of that holy vessel Sir Launcelot was healed and recovered. And when that he was awaked he groaned and sighed, and complained greatly that he was passing sore.

HOW SIR LAUNCELOT, AFTER THAT HE WAS WHOLE AND HAD HIS MIND, HE WAS ASHAMED, AND HOW HE CAME TO THE JOYOUS ISLE. And when Sir Launcelot saw King Pelles and Elaine, he waxed ashamed and said thus: O Lord Jesu, how came I here? for God's sake, my lord, let me wit how I came here. Sir, said Dame Elaine, into this country ye came like a madman, clean out of your wit, and here have ye been kept as a fool; and no creature here knew what ye were, until by fortune a maiden of mine brought me unto you whereas ye lay sleeping by a well, and anon as I verily beheld you I knew you. And then I told my father, and so were ye brought afore this holy vessel, and by the virtue of it thus were ye healed. O Jesu, mercy, said Sir Launcelot; if this be sooth, how many there be that know of my woodness! So God me help, said Elaine, no more but my father, and I, and Dame Brisen. Now for Christ's love, said Sir Launcelot, keep it in counsel, and let no man know it in the world, for I am sore ashamed that I have been thus miscarried; for I am banished out of the country of Logris for ever, that is for to say the country of England.

And so Sir Launcelot lay more than a fortnight or ever that he might stir for soreness. And then upon a day he said unto Dame Elaine these words: Lady Elaine, for your sake I have had much travail, care, and anguish; it needeth not to rehearse it, ye know how. Notwithstanding I know well I have done foul to you when that I drew my sword to you, to have slain you. And all was the cause, that ye and Dame Brisen deceived me. Now will ye for my love, said Sir Launcelot, go unto your father and get me a place of him wherein I may dwell? for in the court of King Arthur may I never come. Sir, said Dame Elaine, I will live and die with you, and only for your sake; and if my life might not avail you and my death might avail you, wit you well I would die for your sake. And I will go to my father, and I am sure there is nothing that I can desire of him but I shall have it. And where ye be, my lord Sir Launcelot, doubt ye not but I will be with you with all the service that I may do. So forthwithal she went to her father and said, Sir, my lord, Sir Launcelot, desireth to be here by you in some castle of yours. Well daughter, said the king, sith it is his desire to abide in these marches he shall be in the Castle of Bliant, and there shall ye be with him, and twenty of the fairest ladies that be in the country, and they shall all be of the great blood, and ye shall have ten knights with you; for, daughter, I will that ye wit we all be honoured by the blood of Sir Launcelot.

Then went Dame Elaine unto Sir Launcelot, and told him all how her father had devised for him and her. And then, after this, King Pelles with ten knights, and Dame Elaine, and twenty ladies, rode unto the Castle of Bliant that stood in an island beclosed in iron, with a fair water deep and large. And when they were there Sir Launcelot let call it the Joyous Isle; and there was he called none otherwise but Le Chevaler Mal Fet, the knight that hath trespassed. Then Sir Launcelot let make him a shield all of sable, and a queen crowned in the midst, all of silver, and a knight clean armed kneeling afore her. And every day once, for any mirths that all the ladies might make him, he would once every day look toward the realm of Logris, where King Arthur and Queen Guenever was. And then would he fall upon a weeping as his heart should to-brast.

So it fell that time Sir Launcelot heard of a jousting fast by his castle, within three leagues. Then he called unto him a dwarf, and he bade him go unto that jousting: And or ever the knights depart, look thou make there a cry, in hearing of all the knights, that there is one knight in the Joyous Isle, that is the Castle of Bliant, and say his name is Le Chevaler Mal Fet, that will joust against knights that will come. And who that putteth that knight to the worse shall have a fair maid and a gerfalcon.

OF A GREAT TOURNEYING IN THE JOYOUS ISLE, AND HOW SIR LAUNCELOT FOUGHT WITH SIR PERCIVALE, AND HOW THEY RETURNED TO KING ARTHUR'S COURT. So when this cry was made, unto Joyous Isle drew knights to the number of five hundred; and wit ye well there was never seen in Arthur's days one knight that did so much deeds of arms as Sir Launcelot did three days together; for as the book maketh truly mention, he had the better of all the five hundred knights, and there was not one slain of them. And after that Sir Launcelot made them all a great feast.

And in the meanwhile came Sir Percivale de Galis and Sir Ector de Maris under that castle that was called the Joyous Isle. And as they beheld that gay castle they would have gone to that castle, but they might not for the broad water, and bridge could they find none. Then they saw on the other side a lady with a sperhawk on her hand, and Sir Percivale called unto her, and asked that lady who was in that castle. Fair knights, she said, here within this castle is the fairest lady in this land, and her name is Elaine. Also we have in this castle the fairest knight and the mightiest man that is I dare say living, and he calleth himself Le Chevaler Mal Fet. How came he into these marches? said Sir Percivale. Truly, said the damosel, he came into this country like a mad man, with dogs and boys chasing him through the city of Corbin, and by the holy vessel of the Sangreal he was brought into his wit again; but he will not do battle with no knight, but by underne or by noon. And if ye list to come into the castle, said the lady, ye must ride unto the further side of the castle and there shall ye find a vessel that will bear you and your horse. Then they departed, and came unto the vessel. And then Sir Percivale alighted, and said to Sir Ector de Maris: Ye shall abide me here until that I wit what manner a knight he is; for it were shame unto us, inasmuch as he is but one knight, an we should both do battle with him. Do ye as ye list, said Sir Ector, and here I shall abide you until that I hear of you.

Then passed Sir Percivale the water, and when he came to the castle gate he bade the porter: Go thou to the good knight within the castle, and tell him here is come an errant knight to joust with him. Sir, said the porter, ride ye within the castle, and there is a common place for jousting, that lords and ladies may behold you. So anon as Sir Launcelot had warning he was soon ready; and there Sir Percivale and Sir Launcelot encountered with such a might, and their spears were so rude, that both the horses and the knights fell to the earth. Then they avoided their horses, and flang out noble swords, and hewed away cantels of their shields, and hurtled together with their shields like two boars, and either wounded other passing sore. At the last Sir Percivale spake first when they had foughten there more than

A Rackham

two hours. Fair knight, said Sir Percivale, I require thee tell me thy name, for I met never with such a knight. Sir, said Sir Launcelot, my name is Le Chevaler Mal Fet. Now tell me your name, said Sir Launcelot, I require you, gentle knight. Truly, said Sir Percivale, my name is Sir Percivale de Galis, that was brother unto the good knight, Sir Lamorak de Galis, and King Pellinore was our father, and Sir Aglovale is my brother. Alas, said Sir Launcelot, what have I done to fight with you that art a knight of the Round Table, that sometime was your fellow?

And therewithal Sir Launcelot kneeled down upon his knees, and threw away his shield and his sword from him. When Sir Percivale saw him do so he marvelled what he meant. And then thus he said: Sir knight, whatsomever thou be, I require thee upon the high order of knighthood, tell me thy true name. Then he said: So God me help, my name is Sir Launcelot du Lake, King Ban's son of Benoy. Alas, said Sir Percivale, what have I done? I was sent by the queen for to seek you, and so I have sought you nigh this two year, and yonder is Sir Ector de Maris, your brother, abideth me on the other side of the yonder water. Now, I pray you, said Sir Percivale, forgive me mine offence that I have here done. It is soon forgiven, said Sir Launcelot.

Then Sir Percivale sent for Sir Ector de Maris; and when Sir Launcelot had a sight of him, he ran unto him and took him in his arms; and then Sir Ector kneeled down, and either wept upon other, that all had pity to behold them. Then came Dame Elaine, and she there made them great cheer as might lie in her power.

Then it befell upon a day Sir Ector and Sir Percivale came to Sir Launcelot and asked him what he would do, and whether he would go with them unto King Arthur or not. Nay, said Sir Launcelot, that may not be by no mean, for I was so entreated at the court that I cast me never to come there more. Sir, said Sir Ector, I am your brother, and ye are the man in the world that I love most; and if I understood that it were your disworship, ye may understand I would never counsel you thereto; but King Arthur and all his knights, and in especial Queen Guenever, made such dole and sorrow that it was marvel to hear and see. And ye must remember the great worship and renown that ye be of, how that ye have been more spoken of than any other knight that is now living; for there is none that beareth the name now but ye and Sir Tristram. Therefore brother, said Sir Ector, make you ready to ride to the court with us, and I dare say there was never knight better welcome to the court than ye; and I wot well and can make it good, said Sir Ector, it hath cost my lady, the queen, twenty thousand pound the seeking of you. Well brother, said Sir Launcelot, I will do after your counsel, and ride with you.

So then they took their horses and made them ready, and took their leave at King Pelles and at Dame Elaine. And when Sir Launcelot should depart Dame Elaine made great sorrow. My lord, Sir Launcelot, said Dame Elaine, at this same feast of Pentecost shall your son and mine, Galahad, be made knight, for he is fully now fifteen winter old. Do as ye list, said Sir Launcelot; God give him grace to prove a good knight. As for that, said Dame Elaine, I doubt not he shall prove the best man of his kin except one. Then shall he be a man good enough, said Sir Launcelot.

HOW SIR LAUNCELOT WITH SIR PERCIVALE AND SIR ECTOR CAME TO THE COURT, AND OF THE GREAT JOY OF HIM.

Then they departed, and within five days' journey they came to Camelot, that is called in English, Winchester. And when Sir Launcelot was come among them, the king and all the knights made great joy of him. And there Sir Percivale de Galis and Sir Ector de Maris began and told the whole adventures: that Sir Launcelot had been out of his mind the time of his absence, and how he called himself Le Chevaler Mal Fet, the knight that had trespassed; and in three days Sir Launcelot smote down five hundred knights. And ever as Sir Ector and Sir Percivale told these tales of Sir Launcelot, Queen Guenever wept as she should have died. Then the queen made great cheer. I marvel, said King Arthur, for what cause ye, Sir Launcelot, went out of your mind. I and many others deem it was for the love of fair Elaine, the daughter of King Pelles, by whom ye are noised that ye have a child, and his name is Galahad, and men say he shall do marvels. My lord, said Sir Launcelot, if I did any folly I have that I sought. And therewithal the king spake no more. But all Sir Launcelot's kin knew for whom he went out of his mind. And then there were great feasts made and great joy; and many great lords and ladies, when they heard that Sir Launcelot was come to the court again, they made great joy.

OF SIR GALAHAD AND THE QUEST OF THE HOLY GRAIL

HOW AT THE VIGIL OF THE FEAST OF PENTECOST A DAMOSEL DESIRED SIR LAUNCELOT FOR TO COME AND DUB A KNIGHT, AND OF THE MARVELLOUS ADVENTURE OF THE SWORD IN A STONE. At the vigil of Pentecost, when all the fellowship of the Round Table were come unto Camelot and there heard their service, and the tables were set ready to the meat, right so entered into the hall a full fair gentlewoman on horseback, that had ridden full fast, for her horse was all besweated. Then she there alighted, and came before the king and saluted him; and he said: Damosel, God thee bless. Sir, said she, I pray you say me where Sir Launcelot is. Yonder ye may see him, said the king. Then she went unto Launcelot and said: Sir Launcelot, I salute you on King

Pelles' behalf, and I require you come on with me hereby into a forest. Then Sir Launcelot asked her with whom she dwelled. I dwell, said she, with King Pelles. What will ye with me? said Launcelot. Ye shall know, said she, when ye come thither. Well, said he, I will gladly go with you. So Sir Launcelot bade his squire saddle his horse and bring his arms; and in all haste he did his commandment.

Then came the queen unto Launcelot, and said: Will ye leave us at this high feast? Madam, said the gentlewoman, wit ye well he shall be with you to-morn by dinner time. If I wist, said the queen, that he should not be with us here to-morn he should not go with you by my good will. Right so departed Sir Launcelot with the gentlewoman, and rode until that he came into a forest and into a great valley, where they saw an abbey of nuns; and there was a squire ready and opened the gates, and so they entered and descended off their horses; and there came a fair fellowship about Sir Launcelot, and welcomed him, and were passing glad of his coming. And then they led him unto the Abbess's chamber and unarmed him; and right so he was ware upon a bed lying two of his cousins, Sir Bors and Sir Lionel, and then he waked them; and when they saw him they made great joy. Sir, said Sir Bors unto Sir Launcelot, what adventure hath brought you hither, for we weened to-morn to have found you at Camelot? Truly, said Sir Launcelot, a gentlewoman brought me hither, but I know not the cause.

In the meanwhile that they thus stood talking together, therein came twelve nuns that brought with them Galahad, the which was passing fair and well made, that unnethe in the world men might not find his match: and all those ladies wept. Sir, said they all, we bring you here this child the which we have nourished, and we pray you to make him a knight, for of a more worthier man's hand may he not receive the order of knighthood. Sir Launcelot beheld the young squire and saw him seemly and demure as a dove, with all manner of good features, that he weened of his age never to have seen so fair a man of form. Then said Sir Launcelot: Cometh this desire of himself? He and all they said Yea. Then shall he, said Sir Launcelot, receive the high order of knighthood as to-morn at the reverence of the high feast. That night Sir Launcelot had passing good cheer; and on the morn at the hour of prime, at Galahad's desire, he made him knight and said: God make him a good man, for of beauty faileth you not as any that liveth.

Now fair sir, said Sir Launcelot, will ye come with me unto the court of King Arthur? Nay, said he, I will not go with you as at this time. Then Sir Launcelot departed from them and took his two cousins with him, and so they came unto Camelot by the hour of underne on Whitsunday. By that time the king and the queen were gone to the minster to hear their service. Then the king and the queen were passing glad of Sir Bors and Sir Lionel, and so was all the fellowship. So when the king and all the knights were come from service, the barons espied in the sieges of the Round Table all about, written with golden letters: Here ought to sit he, and he ought to sit here. And thus they went so long till that they came to the Siege Perilous, where they found letters newly written of gold which said: Four hundred winters and four and fifty accomplished after the passion of our Lord Jesu Christ ought this siege to be fulfilled.

Then all they said: This is a marvellous thing and an adventurous. In the name of God, said Sir Launcelot; and then he accompted the term of the writing from the birth of our Lord unto that day. It seemeth me, said Sir Launcelot, this siege ought to be fulfilled this same day, for this is the feast of Pentecost after the four hundred and four and fifty year; and if it would please all parties, I would none of these letters were seen this day, till he be come that ought to enchieve this adventure. Then made they to ordain a cloth of silk, for to cover these letters in the Siege Perilous.

Then the king bade haste unto dinner. Sir, said Sir Kay the Steward, if ye go now unto your meat ye shall break your old custom of your court, for ye have not used on this day to sit at your meat or that ye have seen some adventure. Ye say sooth, said the king, but I had so great joy of Sir Launcelot and of his cousins, which be come to the court whole and sound, so that I bethought me not of mine old custom. So, as they stood speaking, in came a squire and said unto the king: Sir, I bring unto you marvellous tidings. What be they? said the king. Sir, there is here beneath at the river a great stone which I saw fleet above the water, and therein I saw sticking a sword. The king said: I will see that marvel. So all the knights went with him, and when they came to the river they found there a stone fleeting, as it were of red marble, and therein stuck a fair rich sword, and in the pommel thereof were precious stones wrought with subtle letters of gold. Then the barons read the letters which said in this wise: Never shall man take me hence, but only he by whose side I ought to hang, and he shall be the best knight of the world.

When the king had seen the letters, he said unto Sir

Launcelot: Fair Sir, this sword ought to be yours, for I am sure ye be the best knight of the world. Then Sir Launcelot answered full soberly: Certes, sir, it is not my sword; also, Sir, wit ye well I have no hardiness to set my hand to it, for it longeth not to hang by my side. Also, who that assayeth to take the sword and faileth of it, he shall receive a wound by that sword that he shall not be whole long after. And I will that ye wit that this same day shall the adventures of the Sangreal, that is called the Holy Vessel, begin.

HOW SIR GAWAINE ASSAYED TO DRAW OUT THE SWORD, AND HOW AN OLD MAN BROUGHT IN GALAHAD, AND SET HIM IN THE SIEGE PERILOUS, AND HOW HE DREW OUT THE SWORD. Now, fair nephew, said the king unto Sir Gawaine, assay ye, for my love. Sir, he said, save your good grace I shall not do that. Sir, said the king, assay to take the sword and at my commandment. Sir, said Gawaine, your commandment I will obey. And therewith he took up the sword by the handles, but he might not stir it. I thank you, said the king to Sir Gawaine. My lord Sir Gawaine, said Sir Launcelot, now wit ye well this sword shall touch you so sore that ye shall will ye had never set your hand thereto for the best castle of this realm. Sir, he said, I might not withsay mine uncle's will and commandment. But when the king heard this he repented it much, and said unto Sir Percivale that he should assay, for his love. And he said: Gladly, for to bear Sir Gawaine fellowship. And therewith he set his hand on the sword and drew it strongly, but he might not move it. Then were there no mo that durst be so hardy to set their hands thereto. Now may ye go to your dinner, said Sir Kay unto the king, for a marvellous adventure have ye seen. So the king and all went unto the court, and every knight knew his own place, and set him therein, and young men that were knights served them.

So when they were served, and all sieges fulfilled save only the Siege Perilous, anon there befell a marvellous adventure, that all the doors and windows of the palace shut by themself. Not for then the hall was not greatly darked; and therewith they were all abashed both one and other. Then King Arthur spake first and said: Fair fellows and lords, we have seen this day marvels, but ere night I suppose we shall see greater marvels.

In the meanwhile came in a good old man, and an ancient, clothed all in white, and there was no knight knew from whence he came. And with him he brought a young knight, both on foot, in red arms, without sword or shield, save a scabbard hanging by his side. And these words he said: Peace be with you, fair lords. Then the old man said unto Arthur: Sir, I bring here a young knight, the which is of king's lineage, and of the kindred of Joseph of Aramathie, whereby the marvels of this court, and of strange realms, shall be fully accomplished.

The king was right glad of his words, and said unto the good man: Sir, ye be right welcome, and the young knight with you. Then the old man made the young man to unarm him, and he was in a coat of red sendal, and bare a mantle upon his shoulder that was furred with ermine, and put that upon him. And the old knight said unto the young knight: Sir, follow me. And anon he led him unto the Siege Perilous, where beside sat Sir Launcelot; and the good man lift up the cloth, and found there letters that said thus: This is the siege of Galahad, the haut prince. Sir, said the old knight, wit ye well that place is yours. And then he set him down surely in that siege. And then he said to the old man: Sir, ye may now go your way, for well have ye done that ye were commanded to do; and recommend me unto my grandsire, King Pelles, and unto my lord Petchere, and say them on my behalf, I shall come and see them as soon as ever I may. So the good man departed; and there met him twenty noble squires, and so took their horses and went their way.

Then all the knights of the Table Round marvelled greatly of Sir Galahad, that he durst sit there in that Siege Perilous, and was so tender of age; and wist not from whence he came but all only by God; and said: This is he by whom the Sangreal shall be enchieved, for there sat never none but he, but he were mischieved. Then Sir Launcelot beheld his son and had great joy of him. Then Bors told his fellows: Upon pain of my life this young knight shall come unto great worship. This noise was great in all the court, so that it came to the queen. Then she had marvel what knight it might be that durst adventure him to sit in the Siege Perilous. Many said unto the queen he resembled much unto Sir Launcelot. I may well suppose, said the queen, that he is son of Sir Launcelot and King Pelles' daughter, and his name is Galahad. I would fain see him, said the queen, for he must needs be a noble man, for so is his father, I report me unto all the Table Round.

So when the meat was done that the king and all were risen, the king went unto the Siege Perilous and lift up the cloth, and found there the name of Galahad; and then he shewed it unto Sir Gawaine, and said: Fair nephew, now have we among us Sir Galahad, the good knight that shall worship us all; and upon pain of my life he shall enchieve the Sangreal, right as Sir Launcelot hath done us to understand. Then came King Arthur unto Galahad and said: Sir, ye be welcome, for ye shall move many good knights to the quest of the Sangreal, and ye shall enchieve that never knights might bring to an end. Then the king took him by the hand, and went down from the palace to shew Galahad the adventures of the stone.

The queen heard thereof, and came after with many ladies, and shewed them the stone where it hoved on the water. Sir, said the king unto Sir Galahad, here is a great marvel as ever I saw, and right good knights have assayed and failed. Sir, said Galahad, that is no marvel, for this adventure is not theirs but mine; and for the surety of this sword I brought none with me, for here by my side hangeth the scabbard. And anon he laid his hand on the sword, and lightly drew it out of the stone, and put it in the sheath, and said unto the king: Now it goeth better than it did aforehand. Now have I that sword that sometime was the good knight's, Balin le Savage, and he was a passing good man of his hands; and with this sword he slew his brother Balan, and that was great pity, for he was a good knight, and either slew other through a dolorous stroke that Balin gave unto my grandfather King Pelles, the which is not yet whole, nor not shall be till I heal him.

HOW A DAMOSEL ANNOUNCED TO KING ARTHUR THAT THE SANGREAL SHOULD APPEAR IN HIS HOUSE, AND HOW KING ARTHUR HAD ALL HIS KNIGHTS TOGETHER FOR TO JOUST OR THEY DEPARTED, AND HOW THE SANGREAL APPEARED AS THEY SAT AT SUPPER, AND HOW ALL THE KNIGHTS TOOK UPON THEM THE QUEST, AND OF THE SORROW OF THE KING AND QUEEN AT THEIR DEPARTING. Therewith the king and all espied where came riding down the river a lady on a white palfrey toward them. Then she saluted the king and the queen, and asked if that Sir Launcelot was there. And then he answered himself: I am here, fair lady. Then she said all with weeping: How your great doing is changed sith this day in the morn. Damosel, why say you so? said Launcelot. I say you sooth, said the damosel, for ye were this day the best knight of the world, but who should say so now, he should be a liar, for there is now one better than ye, and well it is proved by the adventures of the sword whereto ye durst not set to your hand; and that is the change and leaving of your name. Wherefore I make unto you a remembrance, that ye shall not ween from henceforth that ye be the best knight of the world. As touching unto that, said Launcelot, I know well I was never the best. Yes, said the damosel, that were ye, and are yet, of any sinful man of the world. And, Sir king, Nacien, the hermit, sendeth thee word, that thee shall befall the greatest worship that ever befell king in Britain; and I say you wherefore, for this day the Sangreal shall appear in thy house and shall feed thee and all thy fellowship of the Round Table. So she departed and went that same way that she came.

Now, said the king, I am sure at this quest of the Sangreal shall all ye of the Table Round depart, and never shall I see you again whole together; therefore I will see you all whole together in the meadow of Camelot to joust and to tourney, that after your death men may speak of it that such good knights were wholly together such a day. As unto that counsel and at the king's request they accorded all, and took on their harness that longed unto jousting. But all this moving of the king was for this intent, for to see Galahad proved; for the king deemed he should not lightly come again unto the court after his departing. So were they assembled in the meadow, both more and less. Then Sir Galahad, by the prayer of the king and the queen, did upon him a noble jesseraunce, and also he did on his helm, but shield would he take none for no prayer of the king. And then Sir Gawaine and other knights prayed him to take a spear. Right so he did; and the queen was in a tower with all her ladies, for to behold that tournament. Then Sir Galahad dressed him in midst of the meadow, and began to break spears marvellously, that all men had wonder of him; for he there surmounted all other knights, for within a while he had defouled many good knights of the Table Round save twain, that was Sir Launcelot and Sir Percivale.

Then the king, at the queen's request, made him to alight and to unlace his helm, that the queen might see him in the visage. When she beheld him she said: Soothly I dare well say that Sir Launcelot is his father, for never two men resembled more in likeness, therefore it nis no marvel though he be of great prowess. So a lady that stood by the queen said: Madam, ought he of right to be so good a knight? Yea, forsooth, said the queen, for he is of all parties come of the best knights of the world and of the highest lineage; for Sir Launcelot is come but of the eighth degree from our Lord Jesu Christ, and Sir Galahad is of the ninth degree from our Lord Jesu Christ, therefore I dare say they be the greatest gentlemen of the world.

And then the king and all estates went home unto Camelot, and so went to evensong to the great minster, and so after upon that to supper, and every knight sat in his own place as they were toforehand. Then anon they heard cracking and crying of thunder, that them thought the place should all to-drive. In the midst of this blast entered a sunbeam more clearer by seven times than ever they saw day, and all they were alighted of the grace of the Holy Ghost. Then began every knight to behold other, and either saw other, by their seeming, fairer than ever they saw afore. Not for then there was no knight might speak one word a great while, and so they looked every man on other as they had been dumb. Then there entered into the hall the Holy Grail covered with white samite, but there was none might see it, nor who bare it. And there was all the hall fulfilled with good odours, and every knight had such meats and drinks as he best loved in this world. And when the Holy Grail had been borne through the hall, then the holy vessel departed suddenly, that they wist not where it became: then had they all breath to speak. And then the king yielded thankings to God, of His good grace that he had sent them. Certes, said the king, we ought to thank our Lord Jesu greatly for that He hath shewed us this day, at the reverence of this high feast of Pentecost.

Now, said Sir Gawaine, we have been served this day of what meats and drinks we thought on; but one thing beguiled us, we might not see the Holy Grail, it was so preciously covered. Wherefore I will make here avow, that to-morn, without longer abiding, I shall labour in the quest of the Sangreal, that I shall hold me out a twelvemonth and a day, or more if need be, and never shall I return again unto the court till I have seen it more openly than it hath been seen here; and if I may not speed I shall return again as he that may not be against the will of our Lord Jesu Christ.

When they of the Table Round heard Sir Gawaine say so, they arose up the most part and made such avows as Sir Gawaine had made. Anon as King Arthur heard this he was greatly displeased, for he wist well they might not again-say their avows. Alas, said King Arthur unto Sir Gawaine, ye have nigh slain me with the avow and promise that ye have made; for through you ye have bereft me the fairest fellowship and the truest of knighthood that ever were seen together in any realm of the world; for when they depart from hence I am sure they all shall never meet more in this world, for there shall die many in the quest. And so it forthinketh me a little, for I have loved them as well as my life, wherefore it shall grieve me right sore, the departition of this fellowship: for I have had an old custom to have them in my fellowship. And therewith the tears fell in his eyes.

When the queen, ladies, and gentlewomen, wist these tidings, they had such sorrow and heaviness that there might no tongue tell it, for those knights had held them in honour and chierté. But among all other Queen Guenever made great sorrow. I marvel, said she, my lord would suffer them to depart from him. Thus was all the court troubled for the departition of those knights.

After this the queen came unto Galahad and asked him of whence he was, and of what country. He told her of whence he was. And son unto Launcelot, she said he was. As to that he said neither yea nor nay. So God me help, said the queen, of your father ye need not to shame you, for he is the goodliest knight, and of the best men of the world come, and of the strain, of all parties, of kings. Wherefore ye ought of right to be, of your deeds, a passing good man; and certainly, she said, ye resemble him much. Then Sir Galahad was a little ashamed and said: Madam, sith ye know in certain, wherefore do ye ask it me? for he that is my father shall be known openly and all betimes. And then they went to rest them. And in the honour of the highness of Galahad he was led into King Arthur's chamber, and there rested in his own bed.

And as soon as it was day the king arose, for he had no rest of all that night for sorrow. Then he went unto Gawaine and to Sir Launcelot that were arisen for to hear mass. And then the king again said: Ah Gawaine, Gawaine, ye have betrayed me; for never shall my court be amended by you, but ye will never be sorry for me as I am for you. And therewith the tears began to run down by his visage. And therewith the king said: Ah, knight Sir Launcelot, I require thee thou counsel me, for I would that this quest were undone, an it might be. Sir, said Sir Launcelot, ye saw yesterday so many worthy knights that then were sworn that they may not leave it in no manner of wise. That wot I well, said the king, but it shall so heavy me at their departing that I wot well there shall no manner of joy remedy me. And then the king and the queen went unto the minster. So anon Launcelot and Gawaine commanded their men to bring their arms. And when they all were armed save their shields and their helms, then they came to their fellowship, which were all ready in the same wise, for to go to the minster to hear their service.

Then after the service was done the king would wit how many had undertaken the quest of the Holy Grail; and to accompt them he prayed them all. Then found they by the tale an hundred and fifty, and all were knights of the Round Table. And then they put on their helms and departed, and recommended them all wholly unto the queen; and there was weeping and great sorrow. Then the queen departed into her chamber and held her, so that no man should perceive her great sorrows. When Sir Launcelot missed the queen he went to her chamber, and when she saw him she cried aloud: O Launcelot, Launcelot, ye have betrayed me and put me to the death, for to leave thus my lord. Ah, madam, I pray you be not displeased, for I shall come again as soon as I may with my worship. Alas, said she, that ever I saw you; but he that suffered upon the cross for all mankind, he be unto you good conduct and safety, and to all the whole fellowship.

Right so departed Sir Launcelot, and found his fellowship that abode his coming. And so they mounted upon their horses and rode through the streets of Camelot; and there was weeping of rich and poor, and the king turned away and might not speak for weeping.

HOW GALAHAD GAT HIM A SHIELD, AND HOW THEY SPED THAT PRESUMED TO TAKE DOWN THE SAID SHIELD, AND HOW KING EVELAKE HAD RECEIVED THAT SHIELD OF JOSEPH OF ARAMATHIE. Now rideth Sir Galahad yet without shield, and so he rode four days without any adventure. And at the fourth day after evensong he came to a White Abbey, and there he was received with great reverence, and led unto a chamber, and there was he unarmed; and then was he ware of two knights of the Table Round, one was Sir Bagdemagus, and that other was Sir Uwaine. And when they saw him they went unto Galahad and made of him great solace, and so they went unto supper. Sirs, said Sir Galahad, what adventure brought you hither? Sir, said they, it is told us that within this place is a shield that no man may bear about his neck but he be mischieved outher dead within three days, or maimed for ever. Ah sir, said King Bagdemagus, I shall it bear to-morrow for to assay this adventure. In the name of God, said Sir Galahad. Sir, said Bagdemagus, an I may not enchieve the adventure of this shield ye shall take it upon you, for I am sure ye shall not fail. Sir, said Galahad, I right well agree me thereto, for I have no shield. So on the morn they arose and heard mass. Then Bagdemagus asked where the adventurous shield was. Anon a monk led him behind an altar where the shield hung as white as any snow, but in the midst was a red cross. Sir, said the monk, this shield ought not to be hanged about no knight's neck but he be the worthiest knight of the world; therefore I counsel you knights to be well advised. Well, said Bagdemagus, I wot well that I am not the best knight of the world, but yet I shall assay to bear it, and so bare it out of the minster. And then he said unto Galahad: An it please you, abide here still, till ye wit how that I speed. I shall abide you, said Galahad. Then King Bagdemagus took with him a good squire, to bring tidings unto Sir Galahad how he sped.

Then when they had ridden a two mile and came to a fair valley afore an hermitage, then they saw a knight come from that part in white armour, horse and all; and he came as fast as his horse might run, and his spear in his rest, and Bagdemagus dressed his spear against him and brake it upon the white knight. But the other struck him so hard that he brast the mails, and sheef him through the right shoulder, for the shield covered him not as at that time; and so he bare him from his horse. And therewith he alighted and took the white shield from him, saying: Knight, thou hast done thyself great folly, for this shield ought not to be borne but by him that shall have no peer that liveth. And then he came to Bagdemagus' squire and said: Bear this shield unto the good knight Sir Galahad, that thou left in the abbey, and greet him well by me. Sir, said the squire, what is your name? Take thou no heed of my name, said the knight, for it is not for thee to know, nor for none earthly man. Now, fair sir, said the squire, at the reverence of Jesu Christ, tell me for what cause this shield may not be borne but if the bearer thereof be mischieved. Now sith thou hast conjured me so, said the knight, this shield behoveth unto no man but unto Galahad. And the squire went unto Bagdemagus and asked whether he were sore wounded or not. Yea forsooth, said he, I shall escape hard from the death. Then he fetched his horse, and brought him with great pain unto an abbey. Then was he taken down softly and unarmed, and laid in a bed, and there was looked to his wounds. And as the book telleth, he lay there long, and escaped hard with the life.

Sir Galahad, said the squire, that knight that wounded Bagdemagus sendeth you greeting, and bade that ye should bear this shield, wherethrough great adventures should befall. Now blessed be God and fortune, said Galahad. And then he asked his arms, and mounted upon his horse, and hung the white shield about his neck, and commended them unto God. And Sir Uwaine said he would bear him fellowship if it pleased him. Sir, said Galahad, that may ye not, for I must go alone, save this squire shall bear me fellowship: and so departed Uwaine.

Then within a while came Galahad thereas the White Knight abode him by the hermitage, and everych saluted other courteously. Sir, said Galahad, by this shield be many marvels fallen. Sir, said the knight, it befell after the passion of our Lord Jesu Christ thirty-two year, that Joseph of Aramathie, the gentle knight, the which took down our Lord off the holy Cross, at that time he departed from Jerusalem with a great party of his kindred with him. And so he laboured till that they came to a city that hight Sarras. And at that same hour that Joseph came to Sarras there was a king that hight Evelake, that had great war against the Saracens, and in especial against one Saracen, the which was King Evelake's cousin, a rich king and a mighty, which marched nigh this land, and his name was called Tolleme la Feintes. So on a day these two met to do battle. Then Joseph, the son of Joseph of Aramathie, went to King Evelake and told him he should be discomfit and slain, but if he left his belief of the old law and believed upon the new law. And then there he shewed him the right belief of the Holy Trinity, to the which he agreed unto with all his heart; and there this shield was made for King Evelake, in the name of Him that died upon the Cross. And then through his good belief he had the better of King Tolleme. For when Evelake was in the battle there was a cloth set afore the shield, and when he was in the greatest peril he let put away the cloth, and then his enemies saw a figure of a man on the Cross, wherethrough they all were discomfit. And so it befell that a man of King Evelake's was smitten his hand off, and bare that hand in his other hand; and Joseph called that man unto him and bade him go with good devotion touch the Cross. And as soon as that man had touched the Cross with his hand it was as whole as ever it was to-fore. Then soon after there fell a great marvel, that the cross of the shield at one time vanished away that no man wist where it became. And then King Evelake was baptised, and for the most part all the people of that city. So, soon after Joseph would depart, and King Evelake would go with him, whether he wold or nold. And so by fortune they came into this land, that at that time was called Great Britain; and there they found a great felon paynim, that put Joseph into prison. And so by fortune tidings came unto a worthy man that hight Mondrames, and he assembled all his people for the great renown he had heard of Joseph; and so he came into the land of Great Britain and disherited this felon paynim and consumed him, and therewith delivered Joseph out of prison. And after that all the people were turned to the Christian faith.

Not long after that Joseph was laid in his deadly bed.

And when King Evelake saw that he made much sorrow, and said: For thy love I have left my country, and sith ye shall depart out of this world, leave me some token of yours that I may think on you. Joseph said: That will I do full gladly; now bring me your shield that I took you when ye went into battle against King Tolleme. Then Joseph bled sore at the nose, so that he might not by no mean be staunched. And there upon that shield he made a cross of his own blood. Now may ye see a remembrance that I love you, for ye shall never see this shield but ye shall think on me, and it shall be always as fresh as it is now. And never shall man bear this shield about his neck but he shall repent it, unto the time that Galahad, the good knight, bear it; and the last of my lineage shall have it about his neck, that shall do many marvellous deeds. Now, said King Evelake, where shall I put this shield, that this worthy knight may have it? Ye shall leave it thereas Nacien, the hermit, shall be put after his death; for thither shall that good knight come the fifteenth day after that he shall receive the order of knighthood. And so that day that they set is this time that ye have his shield, and in the same abbey lieth Nacien, the hermit. And then the White Knight vanished away.

HOW SIR GALAHAD DESTROYED THE WICKED CUSTOM OF THE CASTLE OF MAIDENS, AND HOW HE MET WITH SIR LAUNCELOT AND SIR PERCIVALE AND SMOTE THEM DOWN. Now departed Galahad, and rode many journeys forward and backward, as adventure would lead him. And at the last Sir Galahad came unto a mountain where he found an old chapel, and found there nobody, for all, all was desolate; and there he kneeled to-fore the altar, and besought God of wholesome counsel. So as he prayed he heard a voice that said: Go thou now, thou adventurous knight, to the Castle of Maidens, and there do thou away the wicked customs.

When Sir Galahad heard this he thanked God, and took his horse; and he had not ridden but half a mile, he saw in the valley afore him a strong castle with deep ditches, and there ran beside it a fair river that hight Severn; and there he met with a man of great age, and either saluted other, and Galahad asked him the castle's name. Fair sir, said he, it is the Castle of Maidens. That is a cursed castle, said Galahad, and all they that be conversant therein, for all pity is out thereof, and all hardiness and mischief is therein. Therefore, I counsel you, sir knight, to turn again. Sir, said Galahad, wit you well I shall not turn again. Then looked Sir Galahad on his arms that nothing failed him, and then he put his shield afore him; and anon there met him seven fair maidens, the which said unto him: Sir knight, ye ride here in a great folly, for ye have the water to pass over. Why should I not pass the water? said Galahad. So rode he away from them and met with a squire that said: Knight, those knights in the castle defy you, and defenden you ye go no further till that they wit what ye would. Fair sir, said Galahad, I come for to destroy the wicked custom of this castle. Sir, an ye will abide by that ye shall have enough to do. Go you now, said Galahad, and haste my needs.

Then the squire entered into the castle. And anon after there came out of the castle seven knights, and all were brethren. And when they saw Galahad they cried:

Knight, keep thee, for we assure thee nothing but death. Why, said Galahad, will ye all have ado with me at once? Yea, said they, thereto mayst thou trust. Then Galahad put forth his spear and smote the foremost to the earth, that near he brake his neck. And therewithal the other smote him on his shield great strokes, so that their spears brake. Then Sir Galahad drew out his sword, and set upon them so hard that it was marvel to see it, and so through great force he made them to forsake the field; and Galahad chased them till they entered into the castle, and so passed through the castle at another gate.

And there met Sir Galahad an old man clothed in religious clothing, and said: Sir, have here the keys of this castle. Then Sir Galahad opened the gates, and saw so much people in the streets that he might not number them, and all said: Sir, ye be welcome, for long have we abiden here our deliverance. Then came to him a gentlewoman and said: These knights be fled, but they will come again this night, and here to begin again their evil custom. What will ye that I shall do? said Galahad. Sir, said the gentlewoman, that ye send after all the knights hither that hold their lands of this castle, and make them to swear for to use the customs that were used heretofore of old time. I will well, said Galahad. And there she brought him an horn of ivory, bounden with gold richly, and said: Sir, blow this horn which will be heard two mile about this castle. When Sir Galahad had blown the horn he set him down upon a bed.

Then came a priest to Galahad, and said: Sir, it is past a seven year agone that these seven brethren came into this castle, and harboured with the lord of this castle, that hight the Duke Lianour, and he was lord of all this country. And when they espied the duke's daughter, that was a full fair woman, then by their false covin they made debate betwixt themselves, and the duke of his goodness would have departed them, and there they slew him and his eldest son. And then they took the maiden and the treasure of the castle. And then by great force they held all the knights of this castle against their will under their obeissance, and in great service and truage, robbing and pilling the poor common people of all that they had. So it happened on a day the duke's daughter said: Ye have done unto me great wrong to slay mine own father, and my brother, and thus to hold our lands: not for then, she said, ye shall not hold this castle for many years, for by one knight ye shall be overcome. Thus she prophesied seven years agone. Well, said the seven knights, sithen ye say so, there shall never lady nor knight pass this castle but they shall abide maugre their heads, or die therefore, till that knight be come by whom we shall lose this castle. And therefore is it called the Maidens' Castle, for they have devoured many maidens. Now, said Galahad, is she here for whom this castle was lost? Nay, sir, said the priest, she was dead within these three nights after that she was thus enforced; and sithen have they kept her younger sister, which endureth great pains with many other ladies.

By this were the knights of the country come, and then he made them do homage and fealty to the king's daughter, and set them in great ease of heart. And in the morn there came one to Galahad and told him how that Gawaine, Gareth, and Uwaine, had slain the seven brethren. I suppose well, said Sir Galahad, and took his armour and his horse, and commended them unto God.

So when Sir Galahad was departed from the Castle of Maidens he rode till he came to a waste forest, and there he met with Sir Launcelot and Sir Percivale, but they knew him not, for he was new disguised. Right so Sir Launcelot, his father, dressed his spear and brake it upon Sir Galahad, and Galahad smote him so again that he smote down horse and man. And then he drew his sword, and dressed him unto Sir Percivale, and smote him so on the helm, that it rove to the coif of steel; and had not the sword swerved Sir Percivale had been slain, and with the stroke he fell out of his saddle. This jousts was done to-fore the hermitage where a recluse dwelled. And when she saw Sir Galahad ride, she said: God be with thee, best knight of the world. Ah certes, said she, all aloud that Launcelot and Percivale might hear it, an yonder two knights had known thee as well as I do they would not have encountered with thee. When Sir Galahad heard her say so he was adread to be known: therewith he smote his horse with his spurs and rode a great pace froward them. Then perceived they both that he was Galahad; and up they gat on their horses, and rode fast after him, but in a while he was out of their sight.

And then Sir Launcelot rode overthwart and endlong in a wild forest, and held no path but as wild adventure led him. And at the last he came to a stony cross which departed two ways in waste land; and by the cross was a stone that was of marble, but it was so dark that Sir Launcelot might not wit what it was. Then Sir Launcelot looked by him, and saw an old chapel, and there he weened to have found people; and Sir Launcelot tied his horse till a tree, and there he did off his shield and hung it upon a tree, and then went to the chapel door, and found it waste and broken. And within he found a fair altar, full richly arrayed with cloth of clean silk, and there stood a fair clean candlestick, which bare six great candles, and the candlestick was of silver. And when Sir Launcelot saw this light he had great will for to enter into the chapel, but he could find no place where he might enter; then was he passing heavy and dismayed. Then he returned and came to his horse and did off his saddle and bridle, and let him pasture, and unlaced his helm, and ungirt his sword, and laid him down to sleep upon his shield to-fore the cross.

HOW SIR LAUNCELOT, HALF SLEEPING AND HALF WAKING, SAW A SICK MAN HEALED WITH THE SANGREAL, AND HOW A VOICE SPAKE TO SIR LAUNCELOT, AND HOW HE WAS SHRIVEN, AND HOW A GOOD MAN GAVE HIM A HAIR SHIRT TO WEAR, AND HOW HE WAS OVERCOME AT A JOUSTING AND AT LAST CAME TO A RIVER. And so he fell asleep; and half waking and sleeping he saw come by him two palfreys all fair and white, the which bare a litter, therein lying a sick knight. And when he was nigh the cross he there abode still. All this Sir Launcelot saw and beheld, for he slept not verily; and he heard him say: O sweet Lord, when shall this sorrow leave me? and when shall the holy vessel come by me, wherethrough I shall be blessed? For I have endured thus long for little trespass. A full great while complained the knight thus, and always Sir Launcelot heard it. With that Sir Launcelot saw the candlestick with the six tapers come before the cross, and he saw nobody that brought it. Also there came a table of silver, and the holy vessel of the Sangreal, which Launcelot had seen aforetime in King Pescheour's house. And therewith the sick knight set him up, and held up both his hands, and said: Fair sweet Lord, which is here within this holy vessel; take heed unto me that I may be whole of this malady. And therewith on his hands and on his knees he went so nigh that he touched the holy vessel and kissed it, and anon he was whole; and then he said: Lord God, I thank thee, for I am healed of this sickness.

So when the holy vessel had been there a great while it went unto the chapel with the chandelier and the light, so that Launcelot wist not where it was become; for he was overtaken with sin that he had no power to rise again the holy vessel; wherefore after that many men said of him shame, but he took repentance after that. Then the sick knight dressed him up and kissed the cross; anon his squire brought him his arms, and asked his lord how he did. Certes, said he, I thank God right well, through the holy vessel I am healed. But I have marvel of this sleeping knight that had no power to awake when this holy vessel was brought hither. I dare right well say, said the squire, that he dwelleth in some deadly sin whereof he was never confessed. By my faith, said the knight, whatsomever he be he is unhappy, for as I deem he is of the fellowship of the Round Table, the which is entered into the quest of the Sangreal. Sir, said the squire, here I have brought you all your arms save your helm and your sword, and therefore by mine assent now may ye take this knight's helm and his sword: and so he did. And when he was clean armed he took Sir Launcelot's horse, for he was better than his; and so departed they from the cross.

Then anon Sir Launcelot waked, and set him up, and bethought him what he had seen there, and whether it were dreams or not. Right so heard he a voice that said: Sir Launcelot, more harder than is the stone, and more bitter than is the wood, and more naked and barer than is the leaf of the fig tree; therefore go thou from hence, and withdraw thee from this holy place. And when Sir Launcelot heard this he was passing heavy and wist not what to do, and so departed sore weeping, and cursed the time that he was born. For then he deemed never to have had worship more. For those words went to his heart. Then Sir Launcelot went to the cross and found his helm, his sword, and his horse taken away. And then he called himself a very wretch, and most unhappy of all knights; and there he said: My sin and my wickedness have brought me unto great dishonour. For when I sought worldly adventures for worldly desires, I ever enchieved them and had the better in every place, and never was I discomfit in no quarrel, were it right or wrong. And now I take upon me the adventures of holy things, and now I see and understand that mine old sin hindereth me and shameth me, so that I had no power to stir nor speak when the holy blood appeared afore me. So thus he sorrowed till it was day, and heard the fowls sing: then somewhat he was comforted. But when Sir Launcelot missed his horse and his harness then he wist well God was displeased with him.

Then he departed from the cross on foot into a forest; and so by prime he came to an high hill, and found an hermitage and a hermit therein which was going unto mass.

And then Launcelot kneeled down and cried on Our Lord mercy for his wicked works. So when mass was done Launcelot called the hermit, and prayed him for charity for to hear his life. With a good will, said the good man. Sir, said he, be ye of King Arthur's court and of the fellowship of the Round Table? Yea forsooth, and my name is Sir Launcelot du Lake that hath been right well said of, and now my good fortune is changed, for I am the most wretch of the world. The hermit beheld him and had marvel how he was so abashed. Sir, said the hermit, ye ought to thank God more than any knight living, for He hath caused you to have more worldly worship than any knight that now liveth. And for your presumption to take upon you in deadly sin for to be in His presence, where His flesh and His blood was, that caused you ye might not see it with worldly eyes; for He will not appear where such sinners be, but if it be unto their great hurt and unto their great shame; and there is no knight living now that ought to give God so great thank as ye, for He hath given you beauty, seemliness, and great strength above all other knights; and therefore ye are the more beholding unto God than any other man, to love Him and dread Him, for your strength and manhood will little avail you an God be against you.

Then Sir Launcelot wept with heavy cheer, and said: Now I know well ye say me sooth. Sir, said the good man, hide none old sin from me. Truly, said Sir Launcelot, that were me full loath to discover. For this fourteen year I never discovered one thing that I have used, and that may I now wite my shame and my disadventure. And then he told there that good man all his life. And how he had loved a queen unmeasurably and out of measure long. And all my great deeds of arms that I have done, I did for the most part for the queen's sake, and for her sake would I do battle were it right or wrong; and never did I battle all only for God's sake, but for to win worship and to cause me to be the better beloved, and little or nought I thanked God of it. Then Sir Launcelot said: I pray you counsel me. I will counsel you, said the hermit, if ye will ensure me that ye will never come in that queen's fellowship as much as ye may forbear. And then Sir Launcelot promised him he nold, by the faith of his body. Look that your heart and your mouth accord, said the good man, and I shall ensure you ye shall have more worship than ever ye had.

Then the good man enjoined Sir Launcelot such penance as he might do and to sewe knighthood, and so assoiled him, and when he had kept Sir Launcelot three days, he gat him an horse, an helm, and a sword. And then Sir Launcelot departed about the hour of noon. And then he saw a little house. And when he came near he saw a chapel, and there beside he saw an old man that was clothed all in white fuil richly; and then Sir Launcelot said: God save you. God keep you, said the good man, and make you a good knight. Be ye not Sir Launcelot? Yea, sir, said he. What seek ye in this country? Sir, said Sir Launcelot, I go to seek the adventures of the Sangreal. Well, said he, seek it ye may well, but though it were here ye shall have no power to see it no more than a blind man should see a bright sword, and that is long on your sin, and else ye were more abler than any man living. And then Sir Launcelot began to weep, and said: Father, what shall I do? Now, said the good man, I require you take this hair that was an holy man's and put it next thy skin, and it shall prevail thee greatly. Sir, and I will do it, said Sir Launcelot. Also I charge you that ye eat no flesh as long as ye be in the quest of the Sangreal, nor ye shall drink no wine, and that ye hear mass daily an ye may do it. So he took the hair and put it upon him, and so departed at evensong-time. Then he rode till that he came to a Cross, and took that for his host as for that night, and made his prayers unto the Cross that he never fall in deadly sin again. And on the morn he took his horse and rode till midday; and there by adventure he met with the same knight that took his horse, his helm, and his sword, when he slept when the Sangreal appeared afore the Cross. When Sir Launcelot saw him he saluted him not fair, but cried on high: Knight, keep thee, for thou hast done to me great unkindness. And then they put afore them their spears, and Sir Launcelot came so fiercely upon him that he smote him and his horse down to the earth, that he had nigh broken his neck. Then Sir Launcelot took the knight's horse that was his own aforehand, and descended from the horse he sat upon, and mounted upon his own horse, and tied the knight's own horse to a tree, that he might find that horse when that he was arisen.

Then Sir Launcelot rode into a forest, and held no highway. And as he looked afore him he saw a fair plain, and beside that a fair castle, and afore the castle were many pavilions of silk and of divers hue. And him seemed that he saw there five hundred knights riding on horseback; and there were two parties: they that were of the castle were all on black horses and their trappings black, and they that were without were all on white horses and trappings, and everych hurtled to other that it marvelled Sir Launcelot. And at the last him thought they of the castle were put to the worse.

Then thought Sir Launcelot for to help there the weaker party in increasing of his chivalry. And so Sir Launcelot thrust in among the party of the castle, and smote down a knight, horse and man, to the earth. And then he rashed here and there, and did marvellous deeds of arms. And then he drew out his sword, and struck many knights to the earth, so that all those that saw him marvelled that ever one knight might do so great deeds of arms. But always the white knights held them nigh about Sir Launcelot, for to tire him and wind him. But at the last, as a man may not ever endure, Sir Launcelot waxed so faint of fighting and travailing, and was so weary of his great deeds, that he might not lift up his arms for to give one stroke, so that he weened never to have borne arms; and then they all took and led him away into a forest, and there made him to alight and to rest him. And then all the fellowship of the castle were overcome for the default of him. Then they said all unto Sir Launcelot: Blessed be God that ye be now of our fellowship, for we shall hold you in our prison; and so they left him with few words. And then Sir Launcelot made great sorrow, For never or now was I never at tournament nor jousts but I had the best, and now I am shamed; and then he said: Now I am sure that I am more sinfuller than ever I was.

Thus he rode sorrowing, and half a day he was out of despair, till that he came into a deep valley, and there he saw a river and an high mountain. And through the water he must needs pass, the which was hideous; and then in the name of God he took it with good heart. And when he came over he saw an armed knight, horse and man black as any bear; without any word he smote Sir Launcelot's horse to the earth; and so he passed on, he wist not where he was become. And then he took his helm and his shield, and thanked God of his adventure.

HOW SIR PERCIVALE FOUND KING EVELAKE, AND HOW HE WAS RESCUED FROM TWENTY KNIGHTS BY SIR GALAHAD, AND HOW THE FIEND DISGUISED AS THE LADY OF A SHIP BEGUILED HIM, AND OF HIS PENANCE. Now saith the tale that, when Sir Launcelot was ridden after Sir Galahad, Sir Percivale rode till he was ware of an house closed well with walls and deep ditches, and there he knocked at the gate and was let in, and he alighted and was led unto a chamber, and soon he was unarmed. And there he had right good cheer all that night; and on the morn he heard his mass, and in the monastery he found a priest ready at the altar. And on the right side he saw a pew closed with iron, and behind the altar he saw a rich bed and a fair, as of cloth of silk and gold.

Then Sir Percivale espied that therein was a man or a woman, for the visage was covered; then he left off his looking and heard his service. And when it came to the sacring, he that lay within that parclos dressed him up, and uncovered his head; and then him beseemed a passing old man, and he had a crown of gold upon his head, and his shoulders were naked and uncovered unto his middle. And then Sir Percivale espied his body was full of great wounds, both on the shoulders, arms, and visage. And ever he held up his hands against Our Lord's body, and cried: Fair, sweet Father, Jesu Christ, forget not me. And so he lay down, but always he was in his prayers and orisons; and him seemed to be of the age of three hundred winter. And when the mass was done the priest took Our Lord's body and bare it to the sick king. And when he had used it he did off his crown, and commanded the crown to be set on the altar.

Then Sir Percivale asked one of the brethren what he was. Sir, said the good man, ye have heard much of Joseph of Aramathie, how he was sent by Jesu Christ into this land for to teach and preach the holy Christian faith; and therefore he suffered many persecutions the which the enemies of Christ did unto him, and in the city of Sarras he converted a king whose name was Evelake. And so this king came with Joseph into this land, and ever he was busy to be thereas the Sangreal was; and on a time he nighed it so nigh that Our Lord was displeased with him, but ever he followed it more and more, till God struck him almost blind. Then this king cried mercy, and said: Fair Lord, let me never die till the good knight of my blood of the ninth degree be come, that I may see him openly that he shall enchieve the Sangreal, that I may kiss him.

When the king thus had made his prayers he heard a voice that said: Heard be thy prayers, for thou shalt not die till he have kissed thee. And when that knight shall come the clearness of your eyes shall come again, and thou shalt see openly, and thy wounds shall be healed, and erst shall they never close. And this befell of King Evelake, and this same king hath lived this three hundred winters this holy life, and men say the knight is in the court that shall heal him. Sir, said the good man, I pray you tell me what knight that ye be, and if ye be of King Arthur's court and of the Table Round. Yea forsooth, said he, and my name is Sir Percivale de Galis. And when the good man understood his name he made great joy of him.

And then Sir Percivale departed and rode till the hour of noon. And he met in a valley about a twenty men of arms, which bare in a bier a knight deadly slain. And when they saw Sir Percivale they asked him of whence he was. And he answered: Of the court of King Arthur. Then they cried all at once: Slay him. Then Sir Percivale smote the first to the earth and his horse upon him. And then seven of the knights smote upon his shield all at once, and the remnant slew his horse so that he fell to the earth. So had they slain him, or taken him, had not the good knight, Sir Galahad, with the red arms, come there by adventure into those parts. And when he saw all those knights upon one knight he cried: Save me that knight's life. And then he dressed him toward the twenty men of arms as fast as his horse might drive, with his spear in the rest, and smote the foremost horse and man to the earth. And when his spear was broken he set his hand to his sword, and smote on the right hand and on the left hand that it was marvel to see, and at every stroke he smote one down or put him to a rebuke, so that they would fight no more but fled to a thick forest, and Sir Galahad followed them.

And when Sir Percivale saw him chase them so, he made great sorrow that his horse was away. And then he wist well it was Sir Galahad. And then he cried aloud: Ah fair knight, abide and suffer me to do thankings unto thee, for much have ye done for me. But ever Sir Galahad rode so fast that at the last he passed out of his sight.

Then Sir Percivale came to a rough water and saw a ship

come rowing in the sea, as all the wind of the world had driven it. And so it drove under a rock. And when Sir Percivale saw this he hied him thither, and found the ship covered with silk more blacker than any bear, and therein was a gentlewoman of great beauty, and she was clothed richly that none might be better. And when she saw Sir Percivale she said: Who brought you in this wilderness where ye be never like to pass hence? for ye shall die here for hunger and mischief and be eaten with wild beasts; and ye be a young man and a goodly knight, and I shall help you an ye will. What are ye, said Sir Percivale, that proffered me thus great kindness? I am, said she, a gentlewoman that am disherited, which was sometime the richest woman of the world. Damosel, said Sir Percivale, who hath disherited you? for I have great pity of you. Sir, said she, I dwelled with the greatest man of the world, and he made me so fair and so clear that there was none like me; and of that great beauty I had a little pride more than I ought to have had. Also I said a word that pleased him not. And then he would not suffer me to be any longer in his company, and so drove me from mine heritage, and so disherited me, and he had never pity of me nor of none of my council, nor of my court. And sithen, sir knight, it hath befallen me so, through me and mine I have taken from him many of his men, and made them to become my men. For they ask never nothing of me but I give it them, that and much more. Thus I and all my servants war against him night and day. Therefore I know now no good knight, nor no good man, but I get them on my side an I may. And for that I know that thou art a good knight, I beseech you to help me; and for ye be a fellow of the Round Table, wherefore ye ought not to fail no gentlewoman which is disherited, an she besought you of help.

Then Sir Percivale promised her all the help that he might; and then she thanked him. And at that time the weather was hot. Then she called unto her a gentlewoman and bade her bring forth a pavilion; and so she did, and pight it upon the gravel. Sir, said she, now may ye rest you in this heat of the day. Then he thanked her, and she put off his helm and his shield, and there he slept a great while. And then he awoke and asked her if she had any meat, and she said: Yea, also ye shall have enough. And so there was set enough upon the table, and thereon so much that he had marvel, for there was all manner of meats that he could think on. Also he drank there the strongest wine that ever he drank, him thought, and therewith he was a little chafed more than he ought to be; with that he beheld the gentlewoman, and him thought she was the fairest creature that ever he saw. And then Sir Percivale proffered her love, and prayed her that she would be his. Then she refused him, in a manner, when he required her, for the cause he should be the more ardent on her, and ever he ceased not to pray her of love. And when she saw him well enchafed, then she said: Sir Percivale, wit you well I shall not fulfil your will but if ye swear from henceforth ye shall be my true servant, and to do nothing but that I shall command you. Will ye ensure me this as ye be a true knight? Yea, said he, fair lady, by the faith of my body. Well, said she, now shall ye do with me whatso it please you; and now wit ye well ye are the knight in the world that I have most desire to.

And then Sir Percivale by adventure and grace saw his sword lie on the ground naked, in whose pommel was a red cross and the sign of the crucifix therein, and bethought him on his knighthood, and then he made a sign of the cross in his forehead, and there with the pavilion turned up-so-down, and then it changed unto a smoke, and a black cloud, and then he was adread and cried aloud: Fair sweet Father, Jesu Christ, ne let me not be shamed, the which was nigh lost had not thy good grace been. And then he looked into a ship, and saw her enter therein, which said: Sir Percivale, ye have betrayed me. And so she went with the wind roaring and yelling, that it seemed all the water brent after her. Then Sir Percivale made great sorrow, and drew his sword unto him, saying: Sithen my flesh will be my master I shall punish it; and therewith he rove himself through the thigh that the blood stert about him, and said: O good Lord, take this in recompensation of that I have done against thee, my Lord. So then he clothed him and armed him, and called himself a wretch, saying: How nigh was I lost, and to have lost that I should never have gotten again, that was my virginity, for that may never be recovered after it is once lost. And then he stopped his bleeding wound with a piece of his shirt.

Thus as he made his moan he saw a ship come from Orient covered within and without with white samite. Then Sir Percivale took his arms, and entered into the ship, and so departed from thence.

HOW SIR BORS RESCUED A DAMOSEL RATHER THAN HIS BROTHER SIR LIONEL, AND HOW THEREAFTER SIR LIONEL WOULD FIGHT WITH SIR BORS, BUT SIR BORS WOULD NOT. Now turn we to Sir Bors that when he was departed from Camelot rode into a forest, and there befell him a marvellous adventure. So he met at the departing of two ways two knights that led Lionel, his brother, all naked, bounden upon a strong hackney, and his hands bounden to-fore his breast. And everych of them held in his hands thorns wherewith they went beating him so sore that the blood trailed down more than in an hundred places of his body, so that he was all blood to-fore and behind, but he said never a word; as he which was great of heart he suffered all that ever they did to him, as though he had felt none anguish.

Anon Sir Bors dressed him to rescue him that was his brother; and so he looked upon the other side of him, and saw a knight which brought a fair gentlewoman, and would have set her in the thickest place of the forest for to have been the more surer out of the way from them that sought him. And she, which was nothing assured, cried with an high voice: Saint Mary, succour your maid. And anon she espied where Sir Bors came riding. And when she came nigh him she deemed him a knight of the Round Table, whereof she hoped to have some comfort; and then she conjured him: By the faith that ye owe unto Him in whose service thou art entered in, and for the faith ye owe unto the high order of knighthood, and for the noble King Arthur's sake, that I suppose made thee knight, that thou help me, and suffer me not to be shamed of this knight. When Bors heard her say thus he had so much sorrow there he nist not what to do. For if I let my brother be in adventure he must be slain, and that would I not for all the earth. And if I help not the maid she is shamed for ever, and also she shall lose her virginity the which she shall never get again.

Then lift he up his eyes and said weeping: Fair sweet Lord Jesu Christ, whose liege man I am, keep Lionel, my brother, that these knights slay him not, and for pity of you, and for Mary's sake, I shall succour this maid.

Then dressed he him unto the knight the which had the gentlewoman, and then he cried: Sir knight, let your hand off that maiden, or ye be but dead. And then he set down the maiden, and was armed at all pieces save he lacked his spear. Then he dressed his shield, and drew out his sword, and Bors smote him so hard that it went through his shield and habergeon on the left shoulder. And through great strength he beat him down to the earth, and at the pulling out of Bors' spear there he swooned. Then came Bors to the maid and said: How seemeth it you? of this knight ye be delivered at this time. Now sir, said she, I pray you lead me thereas this knight had me. So shall I do gladly: and took the horse of the wounded knight, and set the gentlewoman upon him, and so brought her as she desired.

Then Sir Bors rode after Lionel, his brother, by the trace of their horses. Thus he rode seeking a great while, and then he turned to an hermitage that was in the entry of a forest.

And when he was come thither he found there Sir Lionel, his brother, which sat all armed at the entry of the chapel door for to abide there harbour till on the morn that a tournament should be. And when Sir Bors saw him he had great joy of him, that it were marvel to tell of his joy. And then he alighted off his horse, and said: Fair sweet brother, when came ye hither? Anon as Lionel saw him he said: Ah Bors, ye may not make none avaunt, but as for you I might have been slain; when ye saw two knights leading me away beating me, ye left me for to succour a gentlewoman, and suffered me in peril of death; for never erst ne did no brother to another so great an untruth. And for that misdeed now I ensure you but death, for well have ye deserved it; therefore keep thee from henceforward, and that shall ye find as soon as I am armed. When Sir Bors understood his brother's wrath he kneeled down to the earth and cried him mercy, holding up both his hands, and prayed him to forgive him his evil will. Nay, said Lionel, that shall never be an I may have the higher hand, that I make mine avow to God, thou shalt have death for it, for it were pity ye lived any longer.

Right so he went in and took his harness, and mounted upon his horse, and came to-fore him and said: Bors, keep thee from me, for I shall do to thee as I would to a felon or a traitor, for ye be the untruest knight that ever came out of so worthy an house as was King Bors de Ganis which was our father; therefore start upon thy horse, and so shall ye be most at your advantage. And but if ye will I will run upon you thereas ye stand upon foot, and so the shame shall be mine and the harm yours, but of that shame ne reck I nought.

HOW WHEN SIR BORS WOULD NOT FIGHT WITH HIM SIR LIONEL WOULD HAVE SLAIN HIM, AND HOW HE SLEW A HERMIT AND SIR COLGREVANCE WHO WOULD HAVE SAVED SIR BORS, AND HOW SIR BORS AND SIR LIONEL WERE PARTED BY A CLOUD. When Sir Bors saw that he must fight with his brother or else to die, he nist what to do; then his heart counselled him not thereto, inasmuch as Lionel was born or he, wherefore he ought to bear him reverence; yet kneeled he down afore Lionel's horse's feet, and said: Fair sweet brother, have mercy upon me and slay me not, and have in remembrance the great love which ought to be between us twain. What Sir Bors said to Lionel he recked not, for the fiend had brought him in such a will that he should slay him. Then when Lionel saw he would none other, and that he would not have risen to give him battle, he rashed over him so that he smote Bors with his horse, feet upward, to the earth, and hurt him so sore that he swooned of distress, the which he felt in himself to have died without confession. So when Lionel saw this, he alighted off his horse to have smitten off his head. And so he took him by the helm, and would have rent it from his head. Then came the hermit running unto him, which was a good man and of great age, and well had heard all the words that were between them, and so fell down upon Sir Bors.

Then he said to Lionel: Ah gentle knight, have mercy upon me and on thy brother, for if thou slay him thou shalt be dead of sin, and that were sorrowful, for he is one of the worthiest knights of the world, and of the best conditions. So God me help, said Lionel, sir priest, but if ye flee from him I shall slay you, and he shall never the sooner be quit. Certes, said the good man, I have liefer ye slay me than him, for my death shall not be great harm, not half so much as of his. Well, said Lionel, I am greed; and set his hand to his sword and smote him so hard that his head went backward. Not for that he restrained him of his evil will, but took his brother by the helm, and unlaced it to have stricken off his head, and had slain him without fail, but so it happed, Colgrevance, a fellow of the Round Table, came at that time thither as Our Lord's will was. And when he saw the good man slain he marvelled much what it might be. And then he beheld Lionel would have slain his brother, and knew Sir Bors, which he loved right well. Then stert he down and took Lionel by the shoulders, and drew him strongly aback from Bors, and said: Lionel, will ye slay your brother, one of the worthiest knights of the world? and that should no good man suffer. Why, said Lionel, will ye let me? therefore if ye entermete you in this I shall slay you, and him after. Why, said Colgrevance, is this sooth that ye will slay him? Slay him will I, said he, whoso say the contrary, for he hath done so much against me that he hath well deserved it. And so ran upon him, and would have smitten him through the head, and Sir Colgrevance ran betwixt them, and said: An ye be so hardy to do so more, we two shall meddle together.

When Lionel understood his words he took his shield afore him, and asked him what that he was. And he told him, Colgrevance, one of his fellows. Then Lionel defied him, and gave him a great stroke through the helm. Then he drew his sword, for he was a passing good knight, and defended him right manfully. So long dured the battle that Bors rose up all anguishly, and beheld how Colgrevance, the good knight, fought with his brother for his quarrel; then was he full sorry and heavy, and thought if Colgrevance slew him that was his brother he should never have joy; and if his brother slew Colgrevance the shame should ever be his. Then would he have risen to have departed them, but he had not so much might to stand on foot; so he abode him so long till Colgrevance had the worse, for Lionel was of great chivalry and right hardy, for he had pierced the hauberk and the helm, that he abode but death, for he had lost much of his blood that it was marvel that he might stand upright. Then beheld he Sir Bors which sat dressing him upward and said: Ah, Bors, why come ye not to cast me out of peril of death, wherein I have put me to succour you which were right now nigh the death? Certes, said Lionel, that shall not avail you, for none of you shall bear other's warrant, but that ye shall die both of my hand. When Bors heard that, he did so much, he rose and put on his helm. Then perceived he first the hermit-priest which was slain, then made he a marvellous sorrow upon him.

Then oft Colgrevance cried upon Sir Bors: Why will ye let me die here for your sake? if it please you that I die for you the death, it will please me the better for to save a worthy man. With that word Sir Lionel smote off the helm from his head. Then Colgrevance saw that he might not escape; then he said: Fair sweet Jesu, that I have misdone have mercy upon my soul, for such sorrow that my heart suffereth for goodness, and for alms deed that I would have done here, be to me aligement of penance unto my soul's health. At these words Lionel smote him so sore that he bare him to the earth. So when he had slain Colgrevance he ran upon his brother as a fiendly man, and gave him such a stroke that he made him stoop. And he that was full of humility prayed him for God's love to leave this battle: For an it befell, fair brother, that I slew you or ye me, we should be dead of that sin. Never God me help but if I have on you mercy, an I may have the better hand. Then drew Bors his sword, all weeping, and said: Fair brother, God knoweth mine intent. Ah, fair brother, ye have done full evil this day to slay such an holy priest the which never trespassed. Also ye have slain a gentle knight, and one of our fellows. And well wot ye that I am not afeard of you greatly, but I dread the wrath of God, and this is an unkindly war, therefore God show miracle upon us both. Now God have mercy upon me though I defend my life against my brother. With that Bors lift up his hand and would have smitten his brother.

And then he heard a voice that said: Flee Bors, and touch him not, or else thou shalt slay him. Right so alighted a cloud betwixt them in likeness of a fire and a marvellous flame, that both their two shields brent. Then were they sore afraid, that they fell both to the earth, and lay there a great while in a swoon. And when they came to themself, Bors saw that his brother had no harm; then he held up both his hands, for he dread God had taken vengeance upon him. With that he heard a voice say: Bors, go hence, and bear thy brother no longer fellowship, but take thy way anon right to the sea, for Sir Percivale abideth thee there. Then he said to his brother: Fair sweet brother, forgive me for God's love all that I have trespassed unto you. Then he answered: God forgive it thee and I do gladly.

So Sir Bors departed from him and rode the next way to the sea. And at the last by fortune he came to an abbey which was nigh the sea. That night Bors rested him there; and in his sleep there came a voice to him and bade him go to the sea. Then he stert up and made a sign of the cross in the midst of his forehead, and took his harness, and made ready his horse, and mounted upon him; and at a broken wall he rode out, and rode so long till that he came to the sea. And on the strand he found a ship covered all with white samite, and he alighted, and betook him to Jesu Christ. And as soon as he entered into the ship, the ship departed into the sea, and went so fast that him seemed the ship went flying, but it was soon dark so that he might know no man, and so he slept till it was day. Then he awaked, and saw in midst of the ship a knight lie all armed save his helm. Then knew he that it was Sir Percivale of Wales, and then he made of him right great joy; and either told other of their temptations, as ye have heard to-forehand. So went they downward in the sea, one while backward, another while forward, and everych comforted other, and oft were in their prayers. Then said Sir Percivale: We lack nothing but Galahad, the good knight.

HOW SIR GALAHAD FOUGHT AT A TOURNAMENT, AND OF THE STROKE THAT HE GAVE SIR GAWAINE, AND HOW HE RODE WITH A DAMOSEL AND CAME TO A SHIP WHEREIN WERE SIR BORS AND SIR PERCIVALE.

Now saith this story, when Galahad had rescued Percivale from the twenty knights, he went then into a waste forest wherein he rode many journeys; and he found many adventures the which he brought to an end, whereof the story maketh here no mention. Then he took his way to the sea on a day, and it befell as he passed by a castle where was a wonder tournament, but they without had done so much that they within were put to the worse, yet were they within good knights enough. When Galahad saw that those within were at so great a mischief that men slew them at the entry of the castle, then he thought to help them, and put a spear forth and smote the first that he fell to the earth, and the spear brake to pieces. Then he drew his sword and smote thereas they were thickest, and so he did wonderful deeds of arms that all they marvelled. Then it happed that Gawaine and Sir Ector de Maris were with the knights without. But when they espied the white shield with the red cross the one said to the other: Yonder is the good knight, Sir Galahad, the haut prince: now he should be a great fool which should meet with him to fight. So by adventure he came by Sir Gawaine, and he smote him so hard that he clave his helm and the coif of iron unto his head, so that Gawaine fell to the earth; but the stroke was so great that it slanted down to the earth and carved the horse's shoulder in two.

When Ector saw Gawaine down he drew him aside, and thought it no wisdom for to abide Galahad, and also for natural love, that he was his uncle. Thus through his great hardiness he beat aback all the knights without. And then they within came out and chased them all about. But when Galahad saw there would none turn again he stole away privily, so that none wist where he was become. Now by my head, said Gawaine to Ector, now are the wonders true that were said of Launcelot du Lake, that the sword which stuck in the stone should give me such a buffet that I would not have it for the best castle in this world; and soothly now it is proved true, for never ere had I such a stroke of man's hand. Sir, said Ector, meseemeth your quest is done. And yours is not done, said Gawaine, but mine is done, I shall seek no further. Then Gawaine was borne into a castle and unarmed him, and laid him in a rich bed, and a leech found that he might live, and to be whole within a month. Thus Gawaine and Ector abode together, for Sir Ector would not away till Gawaine were whole.

And the good knight, Galahad, rode so long till he came that night to the Castle of Carboneck; and it befell him thus that he was benighted in an hermitage. So the good man was fain when he saw he was a knight-errant. Then when they were at rest there came a gentlewoman knocking at the door, and called Galahad, and so the good man came to the door to wit what she would. Then she called the hermit: Sir Ulfin, I am a gentlewoman that would speak with the knight which is with you. Then the good man awaked Galahad, and bade him: Arise, and speak with a gentlewoman that seemeth hath great need of you. Then Galahad went to her and asked her what she would. Galahad, said she, I will that ye arm you, and mount upon your horse and follow me, for I shall show you within these three days the highest adventure that ever any knight saw. Anon Galahad armed him, and took his horse, and commended him to God, and bade the gentlewoman go, and he would follow thereas she liked.

So she rode as fast as her palfrey might bear her, till that she came to the sea; and there they found the ship where Bors and Percivale were in, the which cried on the ship's board: Sir Galahad, ye be welcome, we have abiden you long. And when he heard them he asked them what they were. Sir, said she, leave your horse here, and I shall leave mine; and took their saddles and their bridles with them, and made a cross on them, and so entered into the ship. And the two knights received them both with great joy, and everych knew other; and so the wind arose, and drove them through the sea in a marvellous pace. And within a while it dawned.

By then the ship went from the land of Logris, and by adventure it arrived up betwixt two rocks passing great and marvellous; but there they might not land, for there was a swallow of the sea, save there was another ship, and upon it they might go without danger. Go we thither, said the gentlewoman, and there shall we see adventures, for so is Our Lord's will. And when they came thither they found the ship rich enough, but they found neither man nor woman therein. But they found in the end of the ship two fair letters written, which said a dreadful word and a marvellous: Thou man, which shall enter into this ship, beware thou be in steadfast belief, for I am Faith, and therefore beware how thou enterest, for an thou fail I shall not help thee. Then said the gentlewoman: Percivale, wot ye what I am? Certes, said he, nay, to my witting. Wit ye well, said she, that I am thy sister, which am daughter of King Pellinore, and therefore wit ye well ye are the man in the world that I most love; and if ye be not in perfect belief of Jesu Christ enter not in no manner of wise, for then should ye perish the ship, for he is so perfect he will suffer no sinner in him. When Percivale understood that she was his very sister he was inwardly glad, and said: Fair sister, I shall enter therein, for if I be a miscreature, or an untrue knight, there shall I perish.

HOW SIR GALAHAD, SIR BORS, AND SIR PERCIVALE ENTERED INTO THE SHIP, AND OF A FAIR BED THEREIN, AND OF A SWORD, AND OF HOW KING PELLES HAD BEEN MAIMED FOR DRAWING IT. In the meanwhile Galahad blessed him, and entered therein; and then next the gentlewoman, and then Sir Bors and Sir Percivale. And when they were in, it was so marvellous fair and rich that they marvelled; and in midst of the ship was a fair bed, and Galahad went thereto, and found there a crown of silk. And at the feet was a sword, rich and fair, and it was drawn out of the sheath half a foot and more; and the sword was of divers fashions, and the pommel was of stone, and there was in him all manner of colours that any man might find, and everych of the colours had divers virtues.

Then Galahad beheld the sword and saw letters like blood that said: Let see who shall assay to draw me out of my sheath, but if he be more hardier than any other; and who that draweth me, wit ye well that he shall never fail of shame of his body, or to be wounded to the death. By my faith, said Galahad, I would draw this sword out of the sheath, but the offending is so great that I shall not set my hand thereto. Now sirs, said the gentlewoman, wit ye well that the drawing of this sword is warned to all men save all only to you. In the name of God, said Galahad, ye are right wise of these works.

Sir, said she, there was a king that hight Pelles, the maimed king. And while he might ride he supported much Christendom and Holy Church. So upon a day he hunted in a wood of his which lasted unto the sea; and at the last he lost his hounds and his knights save only one: and there he and his knight went till that they came toward Ireland, and there he found the ship. And when he saw the letters and understood them, yet he entered, for he was right perfect of his life, but his knight had none hardiness to enter; and there found he this sword, and drew it out as much as ye may see. So therewith entered a spear wherewith he was smitten him through both the thighs, and never sith might he be healed, nor nought shall to-fore we come to him. Thus, said she, was not King Pelles, your grandsire, maimed for his hardiness? In the name of God, damosel, said Galahad.

HOW SIR GALAHAD GRIPPED THE SWORD, AND OF THE CUSTOM OF A CASTLE, AND HOW SIR PERCIVALE'S SISTER BLED A DISH FULL OF BLOOD FOR TO HEAL A LADY, WHEREFORE SHE DIED; AND HOW THAT HER BODY WAS PUT IN A SHIP. Now let me begin, said Galahad, to grip this sword for to give you courage; but wit ye well it longeth no more to me than it doth to you. And then he gripped about it with his fingers a great deal; and then she girt him about the middle with the sword. Now reck I not though I die, for now I hold me one of the blessed maidens of the world, which hath made the worthiest knight of the world. Damosel, said Galahad, ye have done so much that I shall be your knight all the days of my life.

Then they went from that ship, and went to the other. And anon the wind drove them into the sea a great pace, but they had no victuals: but it befell that they came on the morn to a castle, and passed by. So there came a knight armed after them and said: Lords, hark what I shall say to you. This gentlewoman that ye lead with you is a maid? Sir, said she, a maid I am. Then he took her by the bridle and said: By the Holy Cross, ye shall not escape me to-fore ye have yolden the custom of this castle. Let her go, said Percivale, ye be not wise, for a maid in what place she cometh is free. So in the meanwhile there came out a ten or twelve knights armed, out of the castle, and with them came gentlewomen which held a dish of silver. And then they said: This gentlewoman must yield us the custom of this castle. Sir, said a knight, what maid passeth hereby shall give this dish full of blood of her right arm. Blame have ye, said Galahad, that brought up such customs, and so God me save, I ensure you of this gentlewoman ye shall fail while that I live. So God me help, said Percivale, I had liefer be slain. And I also, said Sir Bors. By my troth, said the knight, then shall ye die, for ye may not endure against us though ye were the best knights of the world.

Then let they run each to other, and the three fellows beat the ten knights, and then set their hands to their swords and beat them down and slew them. Then there came out of the castle a three score knights armed. Fair lords, said the three fellows, have mercy on yourself and have not ado with us. Nay, fair lords, said the knights of the castle, we counsel you to withdraw you, for ye be the best knights of the world, and therefore do no more, for ye have done enough. We will let you go with this harm, but we must needs have the custom. Certes, said Galahad, for nought speak ye. Well, said they, will ye die? We be not yet come thereto, said Galahad. Then began they to meddle together, and Galahad, with the strange girdles, drew his sword, and smote on the right hand and on the left hand, and slew what that ever abode him, and did such marvels that there was none that saw him but weened he had been none earthly man, but a monster. And his two fellows halp him passing well, and so they held the journey everych in like hard till it was night: then must they needs depart.

So came in a good knight, and said to the three fellows:

If ye will come in to-night and take such harbour as here is ye shall be right welcome, and we shall ensure you by the faith of our bodies, and as we be true knights, to leave you in such estate to-morrow as we find you, without any falsehood. And as soon as ye know of the custom we dare say ye will accord therefore. For God's love, said the gentlewoman, go thither and spare not for me. Go we, said Galahad; and so they entered into the chapel. And when they were alighted they made great joy of them. So within a while the three knights asked the custom of the castle and wherefore it was. What it is, said they, we will say you sooth.

There is in this castle a gentlewoman which we and this castle is hers, and many other. So it befell many years agone there fell upon her a malady; and when she had lain a great while she fell unto a measle, and of no leech she could have no remedy. But at the last an old man said an she might have a dish full of blood of a maid and a clean virgin in will and in work, and a king's daughter, that blood should be her health, and for to anoint her withal; and for this thing was this custom made. Now, said Percivale's sister, fair knights, I see well that this gentlewoman is but dead. Certes, said Galahad, an ye bleed so much ye may die. Truly, said she, an I die for to heal her I shall get me great worship and soul's health, and worship to my lineage, and better is one harm than twain. And therefore there shall be no more battle, but to-morn I shall yield you your custom of this castle. And then there was great joy more than there was to-fore, for else had there been mortal war upon the morn; notwithstanding she would none other, whether they wold or nold.

That night were the three fellows eased with the best;

and on the morn they heard mass, and Sir Percivale's sister bade bring forth the sick lady. So she was, the which was evil at ease. Then said she: Who shall let me blood? So one came forth and let her blood, and she bled so much that the dish was full. Then she lift up her hand and blessed her; and then she said to the lady: Madam, I am come to the death for to make you whole, for God's love pray for me. With that she fell in a swoon. Then Galahad and his two fellows start up to her, and lift her up and staunched her, but she had bled so much that she might not live. Then she said when she was awaked: Fair brother Percivale, I die for the healing of this lady, so I require you that ye bury me not in this country, but as soon as I am dead put me in a boat at the next haven, and let me go as adventure will lead me; and as soon as ye three come to the City of Sarras, there to enchieve the Holy Grail, ye shall find me under a tower arrived, and there bury me in the spiritual place; for I say you so much, there Galahad shall be buried, and ye also, in the same place.

Then Percivale understood these words, and granted it her, weeping. And then said a voice: Lords and fellows, to-morrow at the hour of prime ye three shall depart everych from other, till the adventure bring you to the Maimed King. Then asked she her Saviour; and as soon as she had received it the soul departed from the body. So the same day was the lady healed, when she was anointed withal. Then Sir Percivale made a letter of all that she had holpen them as in strange adventures, and put it in her right hand, and so laid her in a barge, and covered it with black silk; and so the wind arose, and drove the barge from the land, and all knights beheld it till it was out of their sight. Then they drew all to the castle, and so forthwith there fell a sudden tempest and a thunder, lightning, and rain, as all the earth would have broken. So half the castle turned up-so-down. So it passed evensong or the tempest was ceased.

HOW SIR LAUNCELOT ENTERED INTO THE SHIP WHERE SIR PERCIVALE'S SISTER LAY DEAD, AND HOW HE CAME TO A CASTLE AND WAS BEFORE THE DOOR OF A CHAMBER WHEREIN WAS THE SANGREAL. Now saith the history, that when Launcelot was come to the water of Mortoise, as it is rehearsed before, he was in great peril, and so he laid him down and slept, and took the adventure that God would send him. So when he was asleep there came a vision unto him and said: Launcelot, arise up and take thine armour, and enter into the first ship that thou shalt find. And when he heard these words he start up and saw great clearness about him. And then he lifted up his hand and blessed him, and so took his arms and made him ready; and so by adventure he came by a strand, and found a ship the which was without sail or oar. And as soon as he was within the ship there he felt the most sweetness that ever he felt, and he was fulfilled with all thing that he thought on or desired. Then he said: Fair sweet Father, Jesu Christ, I wot not in what joy I am, for this joy passeth all earthly joys that ever I was in. And so in this joy he laid him down to the ship's board, and slept till day. And when he awoke he found there a fair bed, and therein lying a gentlewoman dead, the which was Sir Percivale's sister. And as Launcelot devised her, he espied in her right hand a writ, the which he read, the which told him all the adventures that ye have heard to-fore, and of what lineage she was come.

Then the wind arose, and drove Launcelot more than a month throughout the sea, where he slept but little, but prayed to God that he might see some tidings of the Sangreal. So it befell on a night, at midnight, he arrived afore a castle, on the back side, which was rich and fair, and there was a postern opened toward the sea, and was open without any keeping, save two lions kept the entry; and the moon shone clear. Anon Sir Launcelot heard a voice that said: Launcelot, go out of this ship and enter into the castle, where thou shalt see a great part of thy desire. Then he ran to his arms, and so armed him, and so went to the gate and saw the lions. Then set he hand to his sword and drew it. Then there came a dwarf suddenly, and smote him on the arm so sore that the sword fell out of his hand. Then heard he a voice say: O man of evil faith and poor belief, wherefore trowest thou more on thy harness than in thy Maker, for He might more avail thee than thine armour, in whose service thou art set. Then said Launcelot: Fair Father Jesu Christ, I thank thee of Thy great mercy that Thou reprovest me of my misdeed; now see I well that ye hold me for your servant. Then took he again his sword and put it up in his sheath, and made a cross in his forehead, and came to the lions, and they made semblaunt to do him harm. Notwithstanding he passed by them without hurt, and entered into the castle to the chief fortress, and there were they all at rest. Then Launcelot entered in so armed, for he found no gate nor door but it was open. And at the last he found a chamber whereof the door was shut, and he set his hand thereto to have opened it, but he might not.

Then he enforced him mickle to undo the door. Then

he listened and heard a voice which sang so sweetly that it seemed none earthly thing; and him thought the voice said: Joy and honour be to the Father of Heaven. Then Launcelot kneeled down to-fore the chamber, for well wist he that there was the Sangreal within that chamber. Then said he: Fair sweet Father, Jesu Christ, if ever I did thing that pleased Thee, Lord for Thy pity ne have me not in despite for my sins done aforetime, and that Thou show me something of that I seek. And with that he saw the chamber door open, and there came out a great clearness, that the house was as bright as all the torches of the world had been there.

So came he to the chamber door, and would have entered. And anon a voice said to him: Flee, Launcelot, and enter not, for thou oughtest not to do it; and if thou enter thou shalt for-think it. Then he withdrew him aback right heavy. Then looked he up in the midst of the chamber, and saw a table of silver, and the Holy Vessel, covered with red samite, and many angels about it, whereof one held a candle of wax burning, and the other held a cross, and the ornaments of an altar. And before the Holy Vessel he saw a good man clothed as a priest. And it seemed that he was at the sacring of the mass. And it seemed to Launcelot that above the priest's hands were three men, whereof the two put the youngest by likeness between the priest's hands; and so he lifted it up right high, and it seemed to show so to the people. And then Launcelot marvelled not a little, for him thought the priest was so greatly charged of the figure that him seemed that he should fall to the earth. And when he saw none about him that would help him, then came he to the door a great pace, and said: Fair Father Jesu Christ, ne take it for no sin though I help the good man which hath great need of help.

Right so entered he into the chamber, and came toward the table of silver; and when he came nigh he felt a breath, that him thought it was intermeddled with fire, which smote him so sore in the visage that him thought it brent his visage; and therewith he fell to the earth, and had no power to arise, as he that was so araged, that had lost the power of his body, and his hearing, and his seeing. Then felt he many hands about him, which took him up and bare him out of the chamber door, without any amending of his swoon, and left him there, seeming dead to all people.

So upon the morrow when it was fair day they within were arisen, and found Launcelot lying afore the chamber door. All they marvelled how that he came in, and so they looked upon him, and felt his pulse to wit whether there were any life in him; and so they found life in him, but he might not stand nor stir no member that he had. And so they took him by every part of the body, and bare him into a chamber, and laid him in a rich bed, far from all folk; and so he lay four days. Then the one said he was alive, and the other said, Nay. In the name of God, said an old man, for I do you verily to wit he is not dead, but he is so full of life as the mightiest of you all; and therefore I counsel you that he be well kept till God send him life again.

HOW AFTER THAT SIR LAUNCELOT HAD LAIN FOUR-AND-TWENTY DAYS AND NIGHTS AS A DEAD MAN, IT WAS TOLD HIM THAT HE HAD ACHIEVED ALL HE MIGHT OF THE QUEST OF THE SANGREAL, AND HE RETURNED TO KING ARTHUR'S COURT. In such manner they kept Launcelot four-and-twenty days and all so many nights, that ever he lay still as a dead man; and at the twenty-fifth day befell him after midday that he opened his eyes. And when he saw folk he made great sorrow, and said: Why have ye awaked me, for I was more at ease than I am now. O Jesu Christ, who might be so blessed that might see openly thy great marvels of secretness there where no sinner may be! What have ye seen? said they about him. I have seen, said he, so great marvels that no tongue may tell, and more than any heart can think.

Then they told him how he had lain there four-and-twenty days and nights. Then him thought it was punishment for the four-and-twenty years that he had been a sinner, wherefore Our Lord put him in penance four-and-twenty days and nights. Then looked Sir Launcelot afore him, and saw the hair which he had borne nigh a year, for that he for-thought him right much that he had broken his promise unto the hermit, which he had avowed to do. Then they asked how it stood with him. Forsooth, said he, I am whole of body, thanked be Our Lord; therefore, sirs, for God's love tell me where I am. Then said they all that he was in the castle of Carbonek.

Therewith came a gentlewoman and brought him a shirt of small linen cloth, but he changed not there, but took the hair to him again. Sir, said they, the quest of the Sangreal is achieved now right in you, that never shall ye see of the Sangreal no more than ye have seen. Now I thank God, said Launcelot, of His great mercy of that I have seen, for it sufficeth me; for as I suppose no man in this world hath lived better than I have done to enchieve that I have done. And therewith he took the hair and clothed him in it, and above that he put a linen shirt, and after a robe of scarlet, fresh and new. And when he was so arrayed they marvelled all, for they knew him that he was Launcelot, the good knight. And then they said all: O my lord Sir Launcelot, be that ye? And he said: Truly I am he.

Then came word to King Pelles that the knight that had lain so long dead was Sir Launcelot. Then was the king right glad, and went to see him. And when Launcelot saw him come he dressed him against him, and there made the king great joy of him. And there the king told him tidings that his fair daughter was dead. Then Launcelot was right heavy of it, and said: Sir, me forthinketh the death of your daughter, for she was a full fair lady, fresh and young. And well I wot she bare the best knight that is now on the earth, or that ever was sith God was born. So the king held him there four days, and on the morrow he took his leave at King Pelles and at all the fellowship, and thanked them of their great labour.

So Sir Launcelot departed, and took his arms, and said he would go see the realm of Logris, which I have not seen in twelve months. And therewith he commended the king to God, and so rode through many realms. And at the last he came to a white abbey, and there they made him that night great cheer; and on the morn he rose and heard mass. And a fore an altar he found a rich tomb, which was newly made; and then he took heed, and saw the sides written with gold which said: Here lieth King Bagdemagus of Gore, which King Arthur's nephew slew; and named him, Sir Gawaine. Then was not he a little sorry, for Launcelot loved him much more than any other, and had it been any other than Gawaine he should not have escaped from death to life; and said to himself: Ah Lord God, this is a great hurt unto King Arthur's court, the loss of such a man. And then he departed and came to the abbey where Galahad won the white shield with the red cross; and there had he great cheer all that night.

And on the morn he turned unto Camelot, where he found King Arthur and the queen. But many of the knights of the Round Table were slain and destroyed, more than half. And all the court was passing glad of Sir Launcelot, and the king asked him many tidings of his son Galahad. And there Launcelot told the king of his adventures that had befallen him since he departed. And also he told him of the adventures of Galahad, Percivale, and Bors, which that he knew by the letter of the dead damosel, and as Galahad had told him. Now God would, said the king, that they were all three here. That shall never be, said Launcelot, for two of them shall ye never see, but one of them shall come again.

Now leave we this story and speak of Galahad.

HOW GALAHAD CAME TO KING MORDRAINS, AND HOW SIR PERCIVALE AND SIR BORS MET WITH HIM, AND HOW THEY CAME TO THE CASTLE OF CARBONEK.

Now, saith the story, Galahad rode many journeys in vain. And at the last he came to the abbey where King Mordrains was, and when he heard that, he thought he would abide to see him. And upon the morn, when he had heard mass, Galahad came unto King Mordrains, and anon the king saw him, the which had lain blind of long time. And then he dressed him against him, and said: Galahad, the servant of Jesu Christ, whose coming I have abiden so long, now embrace me and let me rest on thy breast, so that I may rest between thine arms, for thou art a clean virgin above all knights, as the flower of the lily in whom virginity is signified, and thou art the rose the which is the flower of all good virtues, and in colour of fire. For the fire of the Holy Ghost is taken so in thee that my flesh which was all dead of oldness is become young again. When Galahad heard his words, then he embraced him and all his body. Then said he: Fair Lord Jesu Christ, now I have my will. Now I require thee, in this point that I am in, thou come and visit me. And anon Our Lord heard his prayer: therewith the soul departed from the body.

And then Galahad put him in the earth as a king ought to be, and so departed and rode till that he came to the Maimed King. And ever followed Percivale, asking where he had been. So on a day it befell that they came out of a great forest, and there they met at traverse with Sir Bors, the which rode alone. It is none need to tell if they were glad; and them he saluted, and they yielded him honour and good adventure, and everych told other. Then said Bors: It is mo than a year and an half that I ne lay ten times where men dwelled, but in wild forests and in mountains, but God was ever my comfort.

Then rode they a great while till that they came to the castle of Carbonek. And when they were entered within the castle King Pelles knew them; then there was great joy, for they wist well by their coming that they had fulfilled the quest of the Sangreal. Then Eliazar, King Pelles' son, brought to-fore them the broken sword wherewith Joseph was stricken through the thigh. Then Bors set his hand thereto, if that he might have soldered it again; but it would not be. Then he took it to Percivale, but he had no more power thereto than he. Now have ye it again, said Percivale to Galahad, for an it be ever enchieved by any bodily man ye must do it. And then he took the pieces and set them together, and they seemed that they had never been broken, and as well as it had been first forged. And when they within espied that the adventure of the sword was enchieved, then they gave the sword to Bors, for it might not be better set; for he was a good knight and a worthy man.

And a little afore even the sword arose great and marvellous, and was full of great heat that many men fell for dread. And anon alighted a voice among them, and said: They that ought not to sit at the table of Jesu Christ arise, for now shall very knights be fed. So they went thence, all save King Pelles and Eliazar, his son, the which were holy men, and a maid which was his niece; and so these three fellows and they three were there, no mo. Anon they saw knights all armed came in at the hall door, and did off their helms and their arms, and said unto Galahad: Sir, we have hied right much for to be with you at this table where the holy meat shall be departed. Then said he: Ye be welcome, but of whence be ye? So three of them said they were of Gaul, and other three said they were of Ireland, and the other three said they were of Denmark. So as they sat thus there came out a bed of tree, of a chamber, the which four gentlewomen brought; and in the bed lay a good man sick, and a crown of gold upon his head; and there in the midst of the place they set him down, and went again their way. Then he lifted up his head, and said: Galahad, Knight, ye be welcome, for much have I desired your coming, for in such pain and in such anguish I have been long. But now I trust to God the term is come that my pain shall be allayed, that I shall pass out of this world so as it was promised me long ago. Therewith a voice said: There be two among you that be not in the quest of the Sangreal, and therefore depart ye.

HOW GALAHAD AND HIS FELLOWS WERE FED OF THE HOLY SANGREAL, AND HOW OUR LORD APPEARED TO THEM, AND HOW GALAHAD ANOINTED THE MAIMED KING, AND HOW THEY DEPARTED AND TOOK SHIP AND CAME TO THE CITY OF SARRAS, AND FOUND THERE THE SHIP WITH THE BODY OF PERCIVALE'S SISTER. Then King Pelles and his son departed. And therewithal beseemed them that there came a man, and four angels from heaven, clothed in likeness of a bishop, and had a cross in his hand; and these four angels bare him up in a chair, and set him down before the table of silver whereupon the Sangreal was; and it seemed that he had in midst of his forehead letters the which said: See ye here Joseph, the first bishop of Christendom, the same which Our Lord succoured in the city of Sarras in the spiritual place. Then the knights marvelled, for that bishop was dead more than three hundred year to-fore. O knights, said he, marvel not, for I was sometime an earthly man. With that they heard the chamber door open, and there they saw angels; and two bare candles of wax, and the third a towel, and the fourth a spear which bled marvellously, that three drops fell within a box which he held with his other hand. And they set the candles upon the table, and the third the towel upon the vessel, and the fourth the holy spear even upright upon the vessel. And then the bishop made semblaunt as though he would have gone to the sacring of the mass. And then he took an ubblie which was made in likeness of bread. And at the lifting up there came a figure in likeness of a child, and the visage was as red and as bright as any fire, and smote himself into the bread, so that they all saw it that the bread was formed of a fleshly man; and then he put it into the Holy Vessel again, and then he did that longed to a priest to do to a mass. And then he went to Galahad and kissed him, and bade him go and kiss his fellows: and so he did anon. Now, said he, servants of Jesu Christ, ye shall be fed afore this table with sweet meats that never knights tasted. And when he had said, he vanished away. And they set them at the table in great dread, and made their prayers.

Then looked they and saw a man come out of the Holy Vessel, that had all the signs of the passion of Jesu Christ, bleeding all openly, and said: My knights, and my servants, and my true children, which be come out of deadly life into spiritual life, I will now no longer hide me from you, but ye shall see now a part of my secrets and of my hidden things: now hold and receive the high meat which ye have so much desired. Then took he himself the Holy Vessel and came to Galahad; and he kneeled down, and there he received his Saviour, and after him so received all his fellows; and they thought it so sweet that it was marvellous to tell. Then said he to Galahad: Son, wottest thou what I hold betwixt my hands? Nay, said he, but if ye will tell me. This is, said he, the holy dish wherein I ate the lamb on Sheer-Thursday. And now hast thou seen that thou most desired to see, but yet hast thou not seen it so openly as thou shalt see it in the city of Sarras in the spiritual place. Therefore thou must go hence and bear with thee this Holy Vessel; for this night it shall depart from the realm of Logris, that it shall never be seen more here. And wottest thou wherefore? For he is not served nor worshipped to his right by them of this land, for they be turned to evil living; therefore I shall disherit them of the honour which I have done them. And therefore go ye three to-morrow unto the sea, where ye shall find your ship ready, and with you take the sword with the strange girdles, and no more with you but Sir Percivale and Sir Bors. Also I will that ye take with you of the blood of this spear for to anoint the Maimed King, both his legs and all his body, and he shall have his health. Sir, said Galahad, why shall not these other fellows go with us? For this cause: for right as I departed my apostles one here and another there, so I will that ye depart; and two of you shall die in my service, but one of you shall come again and tell tidings. Then gave he them his blessing and vanished away.

And Galahad went anon to the spear which lay upon the table, and touched the blood with his fingers, and came after to the Maimed King and anointed his legs. And therewith he clothed him anon, and started upon his feet out of his bed as an whole man, and thanked Our Lord that He had healed him. And that was not to the worldward, for anon he yielded him to a place of religion of white monks, and was a full holy man. That same night about midnight came a voice among them which said: My sons and not my chief sons, my friends and not my warriors, go ye hence where ye hope best to do and as I bade you. And anon in all haste they took their harness and departed. But the three knights of Gaul, one of them hight Claudine, King Claudas' son, and the other two were great gentlemen. Then prayed Galahad to everych of them, that if they come to King Arthur's court that they should salute my lord, Sir Launcelot, my father, and all the fellowship of the Round Table; and prayed them if that they came on that part that they should not forget it.

Right so departed Galahad, Percivale and Bors with him; and so they rode three days, and then they came to a rivage, and found the ship whereof the tale speaketh of to-fore. And when they came to the board they found in the midst the table of silver which they had left with the Maimed King, and the Sangreal which was covered with red samite. Then were they glad to have such things in their fellowship; and so they entered and made great reverence thereto; and Galahad fell in his prayer long time to Our Lord, that at what time he asked, that he should pass out of this world. So much he prayed till a voice said to him: Galahad, thou shalt have thy request; and when thou askest the death of thy body thou shalt have it, and then shalt thou find the life of the soul. Percivale heard this, and prayed him, of fellowship that was between them, to tell him wherefore he asked such things. That shall I tell you, said Galahad; the other day when we saw a part of the adventures of the Sangreal I was in such a joy of heart, that I trow never man was that was earthly. And therefore I wot well, when my body is dead my soul shall be in great joy to see the blessed Trinity every day, and the majesty of Our Lord, Jesu Christ.

So long were they in the ship that they said to Galahad: Sir, in this bed ought ye to lie, for so saith the scripture. And so he laid him down and slept a great while; and when he awaked he looked afore him and saw the city of Sarras. And as they would have landed they saw the ship wherein Percivale had put his sister in. Truly, said Percivale, in the name of God, well hath my sister holden us covenant. Then took they out of the ship the table of silver, and he took it to Percivale and to Bors, to go to-fore, and Galahad came behind. And right so they went to the city, and at the gate of the city they saw an old man crooked. Then Galahad called him and bade him help to bear this heavy thing. Truly, said the old man, it is ten year ago that I might not go but with crutches. Care thou not, said Galahad, and arise up and shew thy good will. And so he assayed, and found himself as whole as ever he was. Then ran he to the table, and took one part against Galahad. And anon arose there great noise in the city, that a cripple was made whole by knights marvellous that entered into the city.

HOW THEY BURIED PERCIVALE'S SISTER AND WERE PUT IN PRISON BY THE KING OF THE CITY, AND HOW THEY WERE FED WITH THE SANGREAL AND HOW GALAHAD WAS MADE KING, AND HOW GALAHAD AND PERCIVALE DIED. Then anon after, the three knights went to the water, and brought up into the palace Percivale's sister, and buried her as richly as a king's daughter ought to be. And when the king of the city, which was cleped Estorause, saw the fellowship, he asked them of whence they were, and what thing it was that they had brought upon the table of silver. And they told him the truth of the Sangreal, and the power which that God had sent there. Then the king was a tyrant, and was come of the line of paynims, and took them and put them in prison in a deep hole.

But as soon as they were there Our Lord sent them the Sangreal, through whose grace they were always fulfilled while that they were in prison. So at the year's end it befell that this King Estorause lay sick, and felt that he should die. Then he sent for the three knights, and they came afore him; and he cried them mercy of that he had done to them, and they forgave it him goodly; and he died anon. When the king was dead all the city was dismayed, and wist not who might be their king. Right so as they were in counsel there came a voice among them, and bade them choose the youngest knight of them three to be their king: For he shall well maintain you and all yours. So they made Galahad king by all the assent of the holy city, and else they would have slain him. And when he was come to behold the land, he let make above the table of silver a chest of gold and of precious stones, that covered the Holy Vessel. And every day early the three fellows would come afore it, and make their prayers.

Now at the year's end, and the self day after Galahad had borne the crown of gold, he arose up early and his fellows, and came to the palace, and saw to-fore them the Holy Vessel, and a man kneeling on his knees in likeness of a bishop, that had about him a great fellowship of angels, as it had been Jesu Christ himself; and then he arose and began a mass of Our Lady. And when he came to the sacrament of the mass, and had done, anon he called Galahad, and said to him: Come forth the servant of Jesu Christ, and thou shalt see that thou hast much desired to see. And then he began to tremble right hard when the deadly flesh began to behold the spiritual things. Then he held up his hands toward heaven and said: Lord, I thank thee, for now I see that that hath been my desire many a day. Now, blessed Lord, would I not longer live, if it might please thee, Lord. And therewith the good man took Our Lord's body betwixt his hands, and proffered it to Galahad, and he received it right gladly and meekly. Now wottest thou what I am? said the good man. Nay, said Galahad. I am Joseph of Aramathie, the which Our Lord hath sent here to thee to bear thee fellowship; and wottest thou wherefore that he hath sent me more than any other? For thou hast resembled me in two things; in that thou hast seen the marvels of the Sangreal, in that thou hast been a clean maiden, as I have been and am.

And when he had said these words Galahad went to Percivale and kissed him, and commended him to God; and so he went to Sir Bors and kissed him, and commended him to God, and said: Fair lord, salute me to my lord, Sir Launcelot, my father, and as soon as ye see him, bid him remember of this unstable world. And therewith he kneeled down to-fore the table and made his prayers, and then suddenly his soul departed to Jesu Christ, and a great multitude of angels bare his soul up to heaven, that the two fellows might well behold it. Also the two fellows saw come from heaven an hand, but they saw not the body. And then it came right to the vessel, and took it and the spear, and so bare it up to heaven. Sithen was there never man so hardy to say that he had seen the Sangreal.

When Percivale and Bors saw Galahad dead they made as much sorrow as ever did two men. And if they had not been good men they might lightly have fallen in despair. And the people of the country and of the city were right heavy. And then he was buried; and as soon as he was buried Sir Percivale yielded him to an hermitage out of the city, and took a religious clothing. And Bors was alway with him, but never changed he his secular clothing, for that he purposed him to go again into the realm of Logris. Thus a year and two months lived Sir Percivale in the hermitage a full holy life, and then passed out of this world; and Bors let bury him by his sister and by Galahad in the spiritualities.

When Bors saw that he was in so far countries as in the parts of Babylon he departed from Sarras, and armed him and came to the sea, and entered into a ship; and so it befell him in good adventure he came into the realm of Logris; and he rode so fast till he came to Camelot where the king was. And then was there great joy made of him in the court, for they weened all he had been dead, forasmuch as he had been so long out of the country. And when they had eaten, the king made great clerks to come afore him, that they should chronicle of the high adventures of the good knights. When Bors had told him of the adventures of the Sangreal, such as had befallen him and his three fellows, that was Launcelot, Percivale, Galahad, and himself, there Launcelot told the adventures of the Sangreal that he had seen. All this was made in great books, and put up in almeries at Salisbury. And anon Sir Bors said to Sir Launcelot: Galahad, your own son, saluted you by me, and after you King Arthur and all the court, and so did Sir Percivale, for I buried them with mine own hands in the city of Sarras. Also, Sir Launcelot, Galahad prayed you to remember of this unsiker world. Now I trust to God, said Launcelot, his prayer shall avail me.

OF LAUNCELOT, GUENEVER, AND KING ARTHUR

HOW LAUNCELOT FELL TO HIS OLD LOVE AGAIN, BUT WITHDREW HIM FROM GUENEVER TO ESCHEW SLANDER, AND HOW THE QUEEN COMMANDED HIM TO AVOID THE COURT. So after the quest of the Sangreal was fulfilled, and all knights that were left alive were come again unto the Table Round, as the book of the Sangreal maketh mention, then was there great joy in the court; and in especial King Arthur and Queen Guenever made great joy of the remnant that were come home, and passing glad was the king and the queen of Sir Launcelot and of Sir Bors, for they had been passing long away in the quest of the Sangreal.

Then, as the book saith, Sir Launcelot began to resort unto Queen Guenever again, and forgat the promise and the perfection that he made in the quest, and so they loved together more hotter than they did to-forehand, that many in the court spake of it, and in especial Sir Agravaine, Sir Gawaine's brother, for he was ever open-mouthed.

So befell that Sir Launcelot had many resorts of ladies and damosels that daily resorted unto him, that besought him to be their champion, and in all such matters of right Sir Launcelot applied him daily to do for the pleasure of Our Lord, Jesu Christ. And ever as much as he might he withdrew him from the company and fellowship of Queen Guenever, for to eschew the slander and noise; wherefore the queen waxed wroth with Sir Launcelot. And upon a day she called Sir Launcelot unto her chamber, and said thus: Sir Launcelot, I see and feel daily that thy love beginneth to slake, for thou hast no joy to be in my presence, but ever thou art of this court, and quarrels and matters thou hast nowadays for ladies and gentlewomen more than ever thou wert wont to have aforehand.

Ah madam, said Launcelot, in this ye must hold me excused for divers causes; one is, I was but late in the quest of the Sangreal; and I thank God of his great mercy, and never of my desert, that I saw in that my quest as much as ever saw any sinful man, and so was it told me. And if I had not had my privy thoughts to return to your love again as I do, I had seen as great mysteries as ever saw my son Galahad, outher Percivale, or Sir Bors; and therefore, madam, I was but late in that quest. Wit ye well, madam, it may not be yet lightly forgotten the high service in whom I did my diligent labour. Also, madam, wit ye well that there be many men speak of our love in this court, and have you and me greatly in await, as Sir Agravaine and Sir Mordred; and madam, wit ye well I dread them more for your sake than for any fear I have of them myself, for I may happen to escape and rid myself in a great need, where ye must abide all that will be said unto you. And then if that ye fall in any distress through wilful folly, then is there none other remedy or help but by me and my blood. And wit ye well, madam, the boldness of you and me will bring us to great shame and slander; and that were me loath, to see you dishonoured. And that is the cause I take upon me more for to do for damosels and maidens than ever I did to-fore, that men should understand my joy and my delight is my pleasure to have ado for damosels and maidens.

All this while the queen stood still and let Sir Launcelot say what he would. And when he had all said she brast out a-weeping, and so she sobbed and wept a great while. And when she might speak she said: Launcelot, now I well understand that thou art a false recreant knight and lovest and holdest other ladies, and by me thou hast disdain and scorn. For wit thou well, she said, now I understand thy falsehood, and therefore shall I never love thee no more. And never be thou so hardy to come in my sight; and right here I discharge thee this court, that thou never come within it; and I forfend thee my fellowship, and upon pain of thy head that thou see me no more. Right so Sir Launcelot departed with great heaviness, that unnethe he might sustain himself for great dole-making.

Then he called Sir Bors, Sir Ector de Maris, and Sir Lionel, and told them how the queen had forfended him the court, and so he was in will to depart into his own country. Fair sir, said Sir Bors de Ganis, ye shall not depart out of this land by mine advice. Ye must remember in what honour ye are renowned, and called the noblest knight of the world; and many great matters ye have in hand. And women in their hastiness will do ofttimes that sore repenteth them; and therefore by mine advice ye shall take your horse, and ride to the good hermit here beside Windsor, that sometime was a good knight, his name is Sir Brasias, and there shall ye abide till I send you word of better tidings.

And then the noble knight, Sir Launcelot, departed with right heavy cheer suddenly, that none earthly creature wist of him, nor where he was become, but Sir Bors. So when Sir Launcelot was departed, the queen outward made no manner of sorrow in showing, to none of his blood, nor to none other. But wit ye well, inwardly, as the book saith, she took great thought, but she bare it out with a proud countenance as though she felt nothing nor danger.

HOW AT A DINNER THAT THE QUEEN MADE THERE WAS A KNIGHT EN-POISONED, WHICH SIR MADOR LAID ON THE QUEEN, AND APPEACHED HER FOR IT AND HOW SIR BORS TOOK ON HIM TO FIGHT FOR THE QUEEN UPON CONDITION. And then the queen let make a privy dinner in London unto the knights of the Round Table. And all was for to show outward that she had as great joy in all other knights of the Table Round as she had in Sir Launcelot. All only at that dinner she had Sir Gawaine and his brethren, that is for to say Sir Agravaine, Sir Gaheris, Sir Gareth, and Sir Mordred. Also there was Sir Bors de Ganis, Sir Blamore de Ganis, Sir Bleoberis de Ganis, Sir Galihud, Sir Galihodin, Sir Ector de Maris, Sir Lionel, Sir Palomides, Sir Safere his brother, Sir La Cote Male Taile, Sir Persant, Sir Ironside, Sir Brandiles, Sir Kay le Seneschal, Sir Mador de la Porte, Sir Patrise, a knight of Ireland, Aliduk, Sir Astamore, and Sir Pinel le Savage, the which was cousin to Sir Lamorak de Galis, the good knight that Sir Gawaine and his brethren slew by treason. And so these four-and-twenty knights should dine with the queen in a privy place by themself, and there was made a great feast of all manner of dainties.

But Sir Gawaine had a custom that he used daily at dinner and at supper, that he loved well all manner of fruit, and in especial apples and pears. And therefore whosomever dined or feasted Sir Gawaine would commonly purvey for good fruit for him, and so did the queen for to please Sir Gawaine; she let purvey for him all manner of fruit, for Sir Gawaine was a passing hot knight of nature. And this Pinel hated Sir Gawaine because of his kinsman Sir Lamorak de Galis; and therefore for pure envy and hate Sir Pinel enpoisoned certain apples for to enpoison Sir Gawaine. And so this was well unto the end of the meat; and so it befell by misfortune a good knight named Patrise, cousin unto Sir Mador de la Porte, to take a poisoned apple. And when he had eaten it he swelled so till he brast, and there Sir Patrise fell down suddenly dead among them.

Then every knight leapt from the board ashamed, and araged for wrath, nigh out of their wits. For they wist not what to say; considering Queen Guenever made the feast and dinner, they all had suspicion unto her. My lady, the queen, said Gawaine, wit ye well, madam, that this dinner was made for me, for all folks that know my condition understand that I love well fruit, and now I see well I had near been slain; therefore, madam, I dread me lest ye will be shamed. Then the queen stood still and was sore abashed, that she nist not what to say. This shall not so be ended, said Sir Mador de la Porte, for here have I lost a full noble knight of my blood; and therefore upon this shame and despite I will be revenged to the utterance. And there openly Sir Mador appealed the queen of the death of his cousin, Sir Patrise. Then stood they all still, that none would speak a word against him, for they all had great suspicion unto the queen because she let make that dinner. And the queen was so abashed that she could none other ways do, but wept so heartily that she fell in a swoon. With this noise and cry came to them King Arthur, and when he wist of that trouble he was a passing heavy man.

And ever Sir Mador stood still afore the king, and ever he appealed the queen of treason; for the custom was such that time that all manner of shameful death was called treason. Fair lords, said King Arthur, me repenteth of this trouble, but the case is so I may not have ado in this matter, for I must be a rightful judge; and that repenteth me that I may not do battle for my wife, for as I deem this deed came never by her. And therefore I suppose she shall not be all distained, but that some good knight shall put his body in jeopardy for my queen rather than she shall be brent in a wrong quarrel. And therefore, Sir Mador, be not so hasty, for it may happen she shall not be all friendless; and therefore desire thou thy day of battle, and she shall purvey her of some good knight that shall answer you, or else it were to me great shame, and to all my court.

My gracious lord, said Sir Mador, ye must hold me excused, for though ye be our king in that degree, ye are but a knight as we are, and ye are sworn unto knighthood as well as we; and therefore I beseech you that ye be not displeased, for there is none of the four-and-twenty knights that were bidden to this dinner but all they have great suspicion unto the queen. What say ye all, my lords? said Sir Mador. Then they answered by and by that they could not excuse the queen, forwhy she made the dinner, and either it must come by her or by her servants. Alas, said the queen, I made this dinner for a good intent, and never for none evil, so Almighty God help me in my right, as I was never purposed to do such evil deeds, and that I report me unto God.

My lord, the king, said Sir Mador, I require you as ye be a righteous king give me a day that I may have justice. Well, said the king, I give the day this day fifteen days that thou be ready armed on horseback in the meadow beside Westminster. And if it so fall that there be any knight to encounter with you, there mayst thou do the best, and God speed the right. And if it so fall that there be no knight at that day, then must my queen be burnt, and there she shall be ready to have her judgment. I am answered, said Sir Mador. And every knight went where it liked them.

So when the king and the queen were together the king asked the queen how this case befell. The queen answered: So God me help, I wot not how or in what manner. Where is Sir Launcelot? said King Arthur; an he were here he would not grudge to do battle for you. Sir, said the queen, I wot not where he is, but his brother and his kinsmen deem that he be not within this realm. That me repenteth, said King Arthur, for an he were here he would soon stint this strife. Then I will counsel you, said the king, send unto Sir Bors, that he will do battle for you for Sir Launcelot's sake, and upon my life he will not refuse you. For well I see, said the king, that none of these four-and-twenty knights that were with you at your dinner where Sir Patrise was slain, will do battle for you, nor none of them will say well of you, and that shall be a great slander for you in this court. Alas, said the queen, and I may not do withal; but now I miss Sir Launcelot, for an he were here he would put me soon to my heart's ease. What aileth you, said the king, ye cannot keep Sir Launcelot upon your side? For wit ye well, said the king, who that hath Sir Launcelot upon his party hath the most man of worship in the world upon his side. Now go your way, said the king unto the queen, and require Sir Bors to do battle for you for Sir Launcelot's sake.

So the queen departed from the king, and sent for Sir Bors into her chamber. And when he was come she besought him of succour. Madam, said he, what would ye that I did? for I may not with my worship have ado in this matter, because I was at the same dinner, for dread that any of those knights would have me in suspicion. Also, madam, said Sir Bors, now miss ye Sir Launcelot, for he would not have failed you, neither in right nor in wrong, as ye have well proved when ye have been in danger; and now ye have driven him out of this country, by whom ye and all we were daily worshipped; therefore, madam, I marvel how ye dare for shame require me to do any thing for you, in so much ye have chased him out of your country by whom we were borne up and honoured. Alas, fair knight, said the queen, I put me wholly in your grace, and all that is done amiss I will amend as ye will counsel me. And therewith she kneeled down upon both her knees, and besought Sir Bors to have mercy upon her: Outher I shall have a shameful death, and thereto I never offended.

Right so came King Arthur, and found the queen kneeling afore Sir Bors; then Sir Bors pulled her up, and said: Madam, ye do me great dishonour. Ah, gentle knight, said the king, have mercy upon my queen, courteous knight, for I am now in certain she is untruly defamed. And therefore, courteous knight, said the king, promise her to do battle for her: I require you for the love of Sir Launcelot. My lord, said Sir Bors, ye require me the greatest thing that any man may require me; and wit ye well if I grant to do battle for the queen I shall wrath many of my fellowship of the Table Round. But as for that, said Bors, I will grant my lord that for my lord Sir Launcelot's sake, and for your sake I will at that day be the queen's champion, unless that there come by adventure a better knight than I am to do battle for her. Will ye promise me this, said the king, by your faith? Yea sir, said Sir Bors, of that I will not fail you, nor her both, but if there come a better knight than I am, and then shall he have the battle. Then was the king and the queen passing glad, and so departed, and thanked him heartily.

So then Sir Bors departed secretly upon a day, and rode unto Sir Launcelot, there as he was with the hermit, Sir Brasias, and told him of all their adventure. Ah Jesu, said Sir Launcelot, this is come happily as I would have it, and therefore I pray you make you ready to do battle, but look that ye tarry till ye see me come, as long as ye may. For I am sure Mador is an hot knight when he is enchafed, for the more ye suffer him the hastier will he be to battle. Sir, said Bors, let me deal with him; doubt ye not ye shall have all your will. Then departed Sir Bors from him and came to the court again. Then was it noised in all the court that Sir Bors should do battle for the queen; wherefore many knights were displeased with him, that he would take upon him to do battle in the queen's quarrel; for there were but few knights in all the court but they deemed the queen was in the wrong, and that she had done that treason.

HOW AT THE DAY SIR BORS MADE HIM READY FOR TO FIGHT FOR THE QUEEN, BUT SIR LAUNCELOT DISCHARGED HIM, AND OVERCAME SIR MADOR, AND HOW THE TRUTH WAS KNOWN BY THE DAMOSEL OF THE LAKE. The day came on fast that the battle should be, and the king and the queen and all manner of knights that were there at that time drew them unto the meadow beside Westminster. And so when the king was come with the queen and many knights of the Round Table, then the queen was put there in the Constable's ward, and a great fire made about an iron stake, that an Sir Mador de la Porte had the better, she should be burnt: such custom was used in those days, that neither for favour, neither for love nor affinity, there should be none other but righteous judgment, as well upon a king as upon a knight, and as well upon a queen as upon another poor lady.

So in this meanwhile came in Sir Mador de la Porte, and took his oath afore the king, that the queen did this treason until his cousin Sir Patrise, and unto his oath he would prove it with his body, hand for hand, who that would say the contrary. Right so came in Sir Bors de Ganis, and said: That as for Queen Guenever she is in the right, and that will I make good with my hands that she is not culpable of this treason that is put upon her. Then make thee ready, said Sir Mador, and we shall prove whether thou be in the right or I. Sir Mador, said Sir Bors, wit thou well I know you for a good knight. Not for then I shall not fear you so greatly, but I trust to God I shall be able to withstand your malice. But thus much have I promised my lord Arthur and my lady the queen, that I shall do battle for her in this case to the uttermost, unless that there come a better knight than I am and discharge me. Is that all? said Sir Mador, either come thou off and do battle with me, or else say nay. Take your horse, said Sir Bors, and as I suppose, ye shall not tarry long but ye shall be answered.

Then either departed to their tents and made them ready to horseback as they thought best. And anon Sir Mador came into the field with his shield on his shoulder and his spear in his hand; and so rode about the place crying unto Arthur: Bid your champion come forth an he dare. Then was Sir Bors ashamed and took his horse and came to the lists' end. And then was he ware where came from a wood there fast by a knight all armed, upon a white horse, with a strange shield of strange arms; and he came riding all that he might run, and so he came to Sir Bors, and said thus: Fair knight, I pray you be not displeased, for here must a better knight than ye are have this battle: therefore I pray you withdraw you. For wit ye well I have had this day a right great journey, and this battle ought to be mine, and so I promised you when I spake with you last, and with all my heart I thank you of your good will. Then Sir Bors rode unto King Arthur and told him how there was a knight come that would have the battle for to fight for the queen. What knight is he? said the king. I wot not, said Sir Bors, but such covenant he made with me to be here this day. Now my lord, said Sir Bors, here am I discharged.

Then the king called to that knight, and asked him if he would fight for the queen. Then he answered to the king: Therefore came I hither, and therefore, sir king, he said, tarry me no longer, for I may not tarry. For anon as I have finished this battle I must depart hence, for I have ado many matters elsewhere. For wit you well, said that knight, this is dishonour to you all knights of the Round Table, to see and know so noble a lady and so courteous a queen as Queen Guenever is, thus to be rebuked and shamed amongst you. Then they all marvelled what knight that might be that so took the battle upon him. For there was not one that knew him, but if it were Sir Bors.

Then said Sir Mador de la Porte unto the king: Now let me wit with whom I shall have ado withal. And then they rode to the lists' end, and there they couched their spears, and ran together with all their might, and Sir Mador's spear brake all to pieces, but the other's spear held, and bare Sir Mador's horse and all backward to the earth a great fall. But mightily and suddenly he avoided his horse and put his shield afore him, and then drew his sword, and bade the other knight alight and do battle with him on foot. Then that knight descended from his horse lightly like a valiant man, and put his shield afore him and drew his sword; and so they came eagerly unto battle, and either gave other many great strokes. But at the last this knight smote Sir Mador grovelling upon the earth, and the knight stepped near him to have pulled Sir Mador flatling upon the ground; and therewith suddenly Sir Mador arose, and in his rising he smote that knight through the thick of the thighs that the blood ran out fiercely. And when he felt himself so wounded, and saw his blood, he let him arise upon his feet. And then he gave him such a buffet upon the helm that he fell to the earth flatling, and therewith he strode to him to have pulled off his helm off his head. And then Sir Mador prayed that knight to save his life, and so he yielded him as overcome, and released the queen of his quarrel. I will not grant thee thy life, said that knight, only that thou freely release the queen for ever, and that no mention be made upon Sir Patrise's tomb that ever Queen Guenever consented to that treason. All this shall be done, said Sir Mador, I clearly discharge my quarrel for ever.

Then the knights parters of the lists took up Sir Mador, and led him to his tent, and the other knight went straight to the stair-foot where sat King Arthur; and by that time was the queen come to the king, and either kissed other heartily. And when the king saw that knight, he stooped down to him, and thanked him, and in likewise did the queen; and the king prayed him to put off his helmet, and to repose him, and to take a sop of wine. And then he put off his helm to drink, and then every knight knew him that it was Sir Launcelot du Lake. Anon as the king wist that, he took the queen in his hand, and yode unto Sir Launcelot, and said: Sir, grand merci of your great travail that ye have had this day for me and for my queen. My lord, said Sir Launcelot, wit ye well I ought of right ever to be in your quarrel, and in my lady the queen's quarrel, to do battle; for ye are the man that gave me the high order of knighthood, and that day my lady, your queen, did me great worship, and else I had been shamed; for that same day ye made me knight, through my hastiness I lost my sword, and my lady, your queen, found it, and lapped it in her train, and gave me my sword when I had need thereto, and else had I been shamed among all knights; and therefore, my lord Arthur, I promised her at that day ever to be her knight in right or in wrong. Grand merci, said the king, for this journey; and wit ye well, said the king, I shall acquit your goodness.

And ever the queen beheld Sir Launcelot, and wept so tenderly that she sank almost to the ground for sorrow that he had done to her so great goodness, where she shewed him great unkindness. Then the knights of his blood drew unto him, and there either of them made great joy of other. And so came all the knights of the Table Round that were there at that time, and welcomed him. And then Sir Mador was had to leech-craft, and Sir Launcelot was healed of his wound. And then there was made great joy and mirths in that court.

And so it befell that the damosel of the lake, her name was Nimue, the which wedded the good knight Sir Pelleas, when she heard how the queen was an-angered for the death of Sir Patrise, then she told it openly that she was never guilty; and there she disclosed by whom it was done, and named him, Sir Pinel; and for what cause he did it; and so the queen was excused, and the knight Pinel fled into his country. And then Sir Mador sued daily and long, to have the queen's good grace; and so by the means of Sir Launcelot he caused him to stand in the queen's good grace, and all was forgiven.

HOW KING ARTHUR LET CRY A TOURNAMENT AT CAMELOT OR WINCHESTER, AND HOW SIR LAUNCELOT, RIDING THITHER, LODGED AT ASTOLAT, AND RECEIVED A SLEEVE TO WEAR ON HIS HELM AT REQUEST OF A MAID. Thus it passed on till our Lady Day, Assumption. Within a fifteen days of that feast the king let cry a great jousts and a tournament that should be at that day at Camelot, that is Winchester; and the king let cry that he and the King of Scots would joust against all that would come against them. And when this cry was made, thither came many knights. So there came thither the King of Northgalis, and King Anguish of Ireland, and the King with the Hundred Knights, and Galahad, the haut prince, and the King of Northumberland, and many other noble dukes and earls of divers countries. So King Arthur made him ready to depart to these jousts, and would have had the queen with him; but at that time she would not, she said, for she was sick and might not ride at that time. And many deemed the queen would not be there because of Sir Launcelot du Lake; for Sir Launcelot would not ride with the king, for he said that he was not whole of the wound the which Sir Mador had given him. Wherefore the king was heavy and passing wroth. And so he departed toward Winchester with his fellowship; and so by the way the king lodged in a town called Astolat, that is now in English called Guildford, and there the king lay in the castle.

So when the king was departed the queen called Sir Launcelot to her, and said thus: Sir Launcelot, ye are greatly to blame thus to hold you behind my lord; what, trow ye, what will your enemies and mine say and deem? nought else but, See how Sir Launcelot holdeth him ever behind the king, and so doth the queen, for that they would be together. And thus will they say, said the queen to Sir Launcelot, have ye no doubt thereof.

Madam, said Sir Launcelot, I allow your wit; it is of late come since ye were wise. And therefore, madam, at this time I will be ruled by your counsel, and this night I will take my rest, and to-morrow by time I will take my way toward Winchester. But wit you well, said Sir Launcelot to the queen, that at that jousts I will be against the king, and against all his fellowship. Ye may there do as ye list, said the queen, but by my counsel ye shall not be against your king and your fellowship. For therein be full many hard knights of your blood, as ye wot well enough, it needeth not to rehearse them. Madam, said Sir Launcelot, I pray you that ye be not displeased with me, for I will take the adventure that God will send me.

And so upon the morn early Sir Launcelot heard mass and brake his fast, and so took his leave of the queen and departed. And then he rode so much until he came to Astolat, that is Guildford; and there it happed him in the eventide he came to an old baron's place that hight Sir Bernard of Astolat. And as Sir Launcelot entered into his lodging, King Arthur espied him as he did walk in a garden beside the castle, how he took his lodging, and knew him full well. It is well, said King Arthur unto the knights that were with him in that garden beside the castle, I have now espied one knight that will play his play at the jousts to the which we be gone toward; I undertake he will do marvels. Who is that, we pray you tell us? said many knights that were there at that time. Ye shall not wit for me, said the king, as at this time. And so the king smiled, and went to his lodging.

So when Sir Launcelot was in his lodging, and unarmed him in his chamber, the old baron came to him making his reverence, and welcomed him in the best manner; but the old knight knew not Sir Launcelot. Fair sir, said Sir Launcelot to his host, I would pray you to lend me a shield that were not openly known, for mine is well known. Sir, said his host, ye shall have your desire, for meseemeth ye be one of the likeliest knights of the world, and therefore I shall shew you friendship. Sir, wit you well I have two sons that were but late made knights, and the eldest hight Sir Tirre, and he was hurt that same day he was made knight, that he may not ride, and his shield ye shall have; for that is not known I dare say but here, and in no place else. And my youngest son hight Lavaine, and if it please you, he shall ride with you unto that jousts, and he is of his age strong and wight; for much my heart giveth unto you that ye should be a noble knight, therefore I pray you, tell me your name, said Sir Bernard. As for that, said Sir Launcelot, ye must hold me excused as at this time, and if God give me grace to speed well at the jousts I shall come again and tell you. But I pray you, said Sir Launcelot, in any wise let me have your son, Sir Lavaine, with me, and that I may have his brother's shield. All this shall be done, said Sir Bernard.

This old baron had a daughter that was called that time the Fair Maiden of Astolat. And ever she beheld Sir Launcelot wonderfully, and her name was Elaine le Blank. So thus as she came to and fro she was so hot in her love that she besought Sir Launcelot to wear upon him at the jousts a token of hers. Fair damosel, said Sir Launcelot, an if I grant you that, ye may say I do more for your love than ever I did for lady or damosel. Then he remembered him he would go to the jousts disguised. And because he had never before that time borne no manner of token of no damosel, then he bethought him that he would bare one of her, that none of his blood thereby might know him, and then he said: Fair maiden, I will grant you to wear a token of yours upon mine helmet, and therefore what it is, shew it me. Sir, she said, it is a red sleeve of mine, of scarlet, well embroidered with great pearls: and so she brought it him. So Sir Launcelot received it, and said: Never did I erst so much for no damosel. And then Sir Launcelot betook the fair maiden his shield in keeping, and prayed her to keep that until that he came again; and so that night he had merry rest and great cheer, for ever the damosel Elaine was about Sir Launcelot all the while she might be suffered.

OF THE TOURNEY AT WINCHESTER, AND HOW SIR LAUNCELOT WAS SORE WOUNDED. So upon a day, on the morn, King Arthur and all his knights departed, for the king had tarried there three days to abide his noble knights. And so when the king was ridden, Sir Launcelot and Sir Lavaine made them ready to ride, and either of them had white shields, and the red sleeve Sir Launcelot let carry with him. And so they took their leave at Sir Bernard, the old baron, and at his daughter, the Fair Maiden of Astolat. And then they rode so long till that they came to Camelot, that time called Winchester; and there was great press of kings, dukes, earls, and barons, and many noble knights. But there Sir Launcelot was lodged privily by the means of Sir Lavaine with a rich burgess, that no man in that town was ware what they were. And so they reposed them there till our Lady Day, Assumption, as the great feast should be. So then trumpets blew unto the field, and King Arthur was set on high upon a scaffold to behold who did best. But, as the French book saith, King Arthur would not suffer Sir Gawaine to go from him; for never had Sir Gawaine the better, an Sir Launcelot were in the field; and many times was Sir Gawaine rebuked when Launcelot came into any jousts disguised.

Then Sir Launcelot and Sir Lavaine came in at the thickest of the press, and there Sir Launcelot smote down Sir Brandiles, Sir Sagramore, Sir Dodinas, Sir Kay, Sir Griflet, and all this he did with one spear; and Sir Lavaine smote down Sir Lucan de Butler and Sir Bedevere. And then Sir Launcelot gat another spear, and there he smote down Sir Agravaine, Sir Gaheris, and Sir Mordred, and Sir Meliot de Logris; and Sir Lavaine smote Ozanna le Cure Hardy. And then Sir Launcelot drew his sword, and there he smote on the right hand and on the left hand, and by great force he unhorsed Sir Safere, Sir Epinogris, and Sir Galleron; and then the knights of the Table Round withdrew them aback, after they had gotten their horses as well as they might. What knight is yonder, said Sir Gawaine, that doth so marvellous deeds of arms in that field? I wot well what he is, said King Arthur, but as at this time I will not name him. Sir, said Sir Gawaine, I would say it were Sir Launcelot by his riding and his buffets that I see him deal, but ever meseemeth it should not be he, for that he beareth the red sleeve upon his head; for I wist him never bear token at no jousts, of lady nor gentlewoman. Let him be, said King Arthur, he will be better known, and do more, or ever he depart.

Then the party that was against King Arthur were well comforted, and then they held them together that beforehand were sore rebuked. Then Sir Bors, Sir Ector de Maris, and Sir Lionel called unto them the knights of their blood, as Sir Blamore de Ganis, Sir Bleoberis, Sir Aliduke, Sir Galihud, Sir Galihodin, Sir Bellangere le Beuse. So these nine knights of Sir Launcelot's kin thrust in mightily, for they were all noble knights; and they, of great hate and despite that they had unto him, thought to rebuke that noble knight Sir Launcelot, and Sir Lavaine, for they knew them not; and so they came hurling together, and smote down many knights of Northgalis and of Northumberland. And when Sir Launcelot saw them fare so, he gat a spear in his hand; and there encountered with him all at once Sir Bors, Sir Ector, and Sir Lionel, and all they three smote him at once with their spears. And with force of themselves they smote Sir Launcelot's horse to the earth; and by misfortune Sir Bors smote Sir Launcelot through the shield into the side, and the spear brake, and the head left still in his side.

When Sir Lavaine saw his master lie on the ground, he ran to the King of Scots and smote him to the earth; and by great force he took his horse, and brought him to Sir Launcelot, and maugre of them all he made him to mount upon that horse. And then Launcelot gat a spear in his hand, and there he smote Sir Bors, horse and man, to the earth. In the same wise he served Sir Ector and Sir Lionel; and Sir Lavaine smote down Sir Blamore de Ganis. And there Sir Launcelot with his sword smote down and pulled down, as the French book maketh mention, mo than thirty knights, and the most part were of the Table Round; and Sir Lavaine did full well that day, for he smote down ten knights of the Table Round.

Mercy, said Sir Gawaine to Arthur, I marvel what knight that he is with the red sleeve. Sir, said King Arthur, he will be known or he depart. And then the king blew unto lodging, and the prize was given by heralds unto the knight with the white shield that bare the red sleeve. Then came the King with the Hundred Knights, the King of Northgalis, and the King of Northumberland, and Sir Galahad, the haut prince, and said unto Sir Launcelot: Fair knight, God bless thee, for much have ye done this day for us, therefore we pray you that ye will come with us that ye may receive the honour and the prize as ye have worshipfully deserved it. My fair lords, said Sir Launcelot, wit you well if I have deserved thanks I have sore bought it, and that me repenteth, for I am like never to escape with my life; therefore, fair lords, I pray you that ye will suffer me to depart where me liketh, for I am sore hurt. I take none force of none honour, for I had liefer to repose me than to be lord of all the world. And therewithal he groaned piteously, and rode a great wallop away-ward from them until he came under a wood's side.

And when he saw that he was from the field nigh a mile, that he was sure he might not be seen, then he said with an high voice: O gentle knight, Sir Lavaine, help me that this truncheon were out of my side, for it sticketh so sore that it nigh slayeth me. O mine own lord, said Sir Lavaine, I would fain do that might please you, but I dread me sore an I pull out the truncheon that ye shall be in peril of death. I charge you, said Sir Launcelot, as ye love me, draw it out. And therewithal he descended from his horse, and right so did Sir Lavaine; and forthwithal Sir Lavaine drew the truncheon out of his side, and he gave a great shriek and a marvellous grisly groan, and the blood brast out nigh a pint at once, that at the last he sank down, and so swooned pale and deadly. Alas, said Sir Lavaine, what shall I do? And then he turned Sir Launcelot into the wind, but so he lay there nigh half an hour as he had been dead.

And so at the last Sir Launcelot cast up his eyes, and said: O Lavaine, help me that I were on my horse, for here is fast by within this two mile a gentle hermit that sometime was a full noble knight and a great lord of possessions. And for great goodness he hath taken him to wilful poverty, and forsaken many lands, and his name is Sir Baudwin of Brittany, and he is a full noble surgeon and a good leech. Now let see, help me up that I were there; for ever my heart giveth me that I shall never die of my cousin-germain's hands. And then with great pain Sir Lavaine halp him upon his horse. And then they rode a great wallop together, and ever Sir Launcelot bled that it ran down to the earth; and so by fortune they came to that hermitage, the which was under a wood, and a great cliff on the other side, and a fair water running under it. And then Sir Lavaine beat on the gate with the butt of his spear, and cried fast: Let in for Jesu's sake.

And there came a fair child to them, and asked them what they would. Fair son, said Sir Lavaine, go and pray thy lord, the hermit, for God's sake to let in here a knight that is full sore wounded; and this day, tell thy lord, I saw him do more deeds of arms than ever I heard say that any man did. So the child went in lightly, and then he brought the hermit, the which was a passing good man. When Sir Lavaine saw him he prayed him for God's sake of succour. What knight is he? said the hermit. Is he of the house of King Arthur, or not? I wot not, said Sir Lavaine, what is he, nor what is his name, but well I wot I saw him do marvellously this day as of deeds of arms. On whose party was he? said the hermit. Sir, said Sir Lavaine, he was this day against King Arthur, and there he won the prize of all the knights of the Round Table. I have seen the day, said the hermit, I would have loved him the worse because he was against my lord, King Arthur, for sometime I was one of the fellowship of the Round Table, but I thank God now I am otherwise disposed. But where is he? let me see him. Then Sir Lavaine brought the hermit to him.

HOW SIR LAUNCELOT WAS BROUGHT TO AN HERMIT FOR TO BE HEALED, AND HOW IT BECAME KNOWN THAT IT WAS HE THAT BARE THE RED SLEEVE, AND OF THE ANGER OF THE QUEEN. And when the hermit beheld him, as he sat leaning upon his saddle-bow ever bleeding piteously, and ever the knight-hermit thought that he should know him, but he could not bring him to knowledge because he was so pale for bleeding. What knight are ye, said the hermit, and where were ye born? My fair lord, said Sir Launcelot, I am a stranger and a knight adventurous, that laboureth throughout many realms for to win worship. Then the hermit advised him better, and saw by a wound on his cheek that he was Sir Launcelot. Alas, said the hermit, mine own lord why hide you your name from me? Forsooth I ought to know you of right, for ye are the most noblest knight of the world, for well I know you for Sir Launcelot. Sir, said he, sith ye know me, help me an ye may, for God's sake, for I would be out of this pain at once, either to death or to life. Have ye no doubt, said the hermit, ye shall live and fare right well. And so the hermit called to him two of his servants, and so he and his servants bare him into the hermitage, and lightly unarmed him, and laid him in his bed. And then anon the hermit staunched his blood, and made him to drink good wine, so that Sir Launcelot was well refreshed and knew himself; for in those days it was not the guise of hermits as is nowadays, for there were none hermits in those days but that they had been men of worship and of prowess; and those hermits held great household, and refreshed people that were in distress.

Now turn we unto King Arthur, and leave we Sir Launcelot in the hermitage. So when the kings were come together on both parties, and the great feast should be holden, King Arthur asked the King of Northgalis and their fellowship, where was that knight that bare the red sleeve: Bring him afore me that he may have his laud, and honour, and the prize, as it is right. Then spake Sir Galahad, the haut prince, and the King with the Hundred Knights: We suppose that knight is mischieved, and that he is never like to see you nor none of us all, and that is the greatest pity that ever we wist of any knight. Alas, said Arthur, how may this be? is he so hurt? What is his name? said King Arthur. Truly, said they all, we know not his name, nor from whence he came, nor whither he would. Alas, said the king, these be to me the worst tidings that came to me this seven year, for I would not for all the lands I wield to know and wit it were so that that noble knight were slain. Know ye him? said they all. As for that, said Arthur, whether I know him or know him not, ye shall not know for me what man he is, but Almighty Jesu send me good tidings of him. And so said they all. By my head, said Sir Gawaine, if it so be that the good knight be so sore hurt, it is great damage and pity to all this land, for he is one of the noblest knights that ever I saw in a field handle a spear or a sword; and if he may be found I shall find him, for I am sure he nis not far from this town.

Right so Sir Gawaine took a squire with him upon hackneys, and rode all about Camelot within six or seven mile, but so he came again and could hear no word of him. Then within two days King Arthur and all the fellowship returned unto London again. And so as they rode by the way it happed Sir Gawaine at Astolat to lodge with Sir Bernard thereas was Sir Launcelot lodged. And so as Sir Gawaine was in his chamber to repose him, Sir Bernard, the old baron, came unto him, and his daughter Elaine, to cheer him and to ask him what tidings, and who did best at that tournament of Winchester. So God me help, said Sir Gawaine, there were two knights that bare two white shields, but the one of them bare a red sleeve upon his head, and certainly he was one of the best knights that ever I saw joust in field. For I dare say, said Sir Gawaine, that one knight with the red sleeve smote down forty knights of the Table Round, and his fellow did right well and worshipfully. Now blessed be God, said the Fair Maiden of Astolat, that that knight sped so well, for he is the man in the world that I first loved, and truly he shall be last that ever I shall love. Now, fair maid, said Sir Gawaine, is that good knight your love? Certainly sir, said she, wit ye well he is my love. Then know ye his name? said Sir Gawaine. Nay truly, said the damosel, I know not his name nor from whence he cometh, but to say that I love him, I promise you and God that I love him. How had ye knowledge of him first? said Sir Gawaine.

Then she told him as ye have heard to-fore, and how her father betook him her brother to do him service, and how her father lent him her brother's, Sir Tirre's, shield: And here with me he left his own shield. For what cause did he so? said Sir Gawaine. For this cause, said the damosel, for his shield was too well known among many noble knights. Ah, fair damosel, said Sir Gawaine, please it you let me have a sight of that shield. Sir, said she, it is in my chamber, covered with a case, and if ye will come with me ye shall see it. Not so, said Sir Bernard to his daughter, let send for it.

So when the shield was come, Sir Gawaine took off the case, and when he beheld that shield he knew anon that it was Sir Launcelot's shield, and his own arms. Ah Jesu mercy, said Sir Gawaine, now is my heart more heavier than ever it was to-fore. Why? said Elaine. For I have great cause, said Sir Gawaine. Is that knight that oweth this shield your love? Yea truly, said she, my love he is; God would I were his love. So God me speed, said Sir Gawaine, fair damosel ye have right, for an he be your love ye love the most honourable knight of the world, and the man of most worship. But I dread me, said Sir Gawaine, that ye shall never see him in this world, and that is great pity that ever was of earthly knight. Alas, said she, how may this be, is he slain? I say not so, said Sir Gawaine, but wit ye well he is grievously wounded, by all manner of signs, and by men's sight more likelier to be dead than to be alive; and wit ye well he is the noble knight, Sir Launcelot, for by this shield I know him. Alas, said the Fair Maiden of Astolat, how may this be, and what was his hurt? Truly, said Sir Gawaine, the man in the world that loved him best hurt him so; and I dare say, said Sir Gawaine, an that knight that hurt him knew the very certainty that he had hurt Sir Launcelot, it would be the most sorrow that ever came to his heart.

Now fair father, said then Elaine, I require you give me leave to ride and to seek him, or else I wot well I shall go out of my mind, for I shall never stint till that I find him and my brother, Sir Lavaine. Do as it liketh you, said her father, for me sore repenteth of the hurt of that noble knight. Right so the maid made her ready, and before Sir Gawaine, making great dole.

Then on the morn Sir Gawaine came to King Arthur, and told him how he had found Sir Launcelot's shield in the keeping of the Fair Maiden of Astolat. So the king and all came to London, and there Sir Gawaine openly disclosed to all the court that it was Sir Launcelot that jousted best.

And when Sir Bors heard that, wit ye well he was an heavy man, and so were all his kinsmen. But when Queen Guenever wist that Sir Launcelot bare the red sleeve of the Fair Maiden of Astolat she was nigh out of her mind for wrath. And then she sent for Sir Bors de Ganis in all the haste that might be. So when Sir Bors was come to-fore the queen, then she said: Ah, Sir Bors, have ye heard say how falsely Sir Launcelot hath betrayed me? Alas madam, said Sir Bors, I am afeard he hath betrayed himself and us all. No force, said the queen, though he be destroyed, for he is a false traitor-knight. Madam, said Sir Bors, I pray you say ye not so, for wit you well I may not hear such language of him. Why, Sir Bors, said she, should I not call him traitor when he bare the red sleeve upon his head at Winchester, at the great jousts? Madam, said Sir Bors, that sleeve-bearing repenteth me sore, but I dare say he did it to none evil intent, but for this cause he bare the red sleeve that none of his blood should know him. For ere then we, nor none of us all, never knew that ever he bare token or sign of maid, lady, ne gentlewoman. Fie on him, said the queen, for I heard Sir Gawaine say before my lord Arthur that it were marvel to tell the great love that is between the Fair Maiden of Astolat and him. Madam, said Sir Bors, I may not warn Sir Gawaine to say what it pleased him; but I dare say, as for my lord, Sir Launcelot, that he loveth no lady, gentlewoman, nor maid, but all he loveth in like much. And therefore madam, said Sir Bors, ye may say what ye will, but wit ye well I will haste me to seek him, and find him wheresomever he be, and God send me good tidings of him. And so leave we them there, and speak we of Sir Launcelot that lay in great peril.

HOW THE MAIDEN ELAINE DID ATTENDANCE UNTO SIR LAUNCELOT, AND OF HER LAMENTATION THAT HE SHOULD DEPART, AND HOW SHE DIED FOR HIS LOVE, AND HOW HER BODY WAS BROUGHT TO THE COURT AND OF HER BURYING. So as fair Elaine came to Winchester she sought there all about, and by fortune Sir Lavaine was ridden to play him, to enchafe his horse. And anon as Elaine saw him she knew him, and then she cried aloud unto him. And when he heard her anon he came to her, and then she asked her brother how did my lord, Sir Launcelot. Who told you, sister, that my lord's name was Sir Launcelot? Then she told him how Sir Gawaine by his shield knew him. So they rode together till that they came to the hermitage, and anon she alighted.

So Sir Lavaine brought her in to Sir Launcelot; and when she saw him lie so sick and pale in his bed she might not speak, but suddenly she fell to the earth down suddenly in a swoon, and there she lay a great while. And when she was relieved, she shrieked and said: My lord, Sir Launcelot, alas why be ye in this plight? and then she swooned again. And then Sir Launcelot prayed Sir Lavaine to take her up: And bring her to me. And when she came to herself Sir Launcelot kissed her, and said: Fair maiden, why fare ye thus? ye put me to pain; wherefore make ye no more such cheer, for an ye be come to comfort me ye be right welcome; and of this little hurt that I have I shall be right hastily whole by the grace of God. But I marvel, said Sir Launcelot, who told you my name? Then the fair maiden told him all how Sir Gawaine was lodged with her father: And there by your shield he discovered your name. Alas, said Sir Launcelot, that me repenteth that my name is known, for I am sure it will turn unto anger. And then Sir Launcelot compassed in his mind that Sir Gawaine would tell Queen Guenever how he bare the red sleeve, and for whom; that he wist well would turn into great anger.

So this maiden Elaine never went from Sir Launcelot, but watched him day and night, and did such attendance to him, that the French book saith there was never woman did more kindlier for man than she. And so Sir Launcelot was big and strong again.

So then they made them ready to depart from the hermit. And so upon a morn they took their horses and Elaine le Blank with them; and when they came to Astolat there were they well lodged, and had great cheer of Sir Bernard, the old baron, and of Sir Tirre, his son. And so upon the morn when Sir Launcelot should depart, fair Elaine brought her father with her, and Sir Lavaine, and Sir Tirre, and thus she said:

My lord, Sir Launcelot, now I see ye will depart; now fair knight and courteous knight, have mercy upon me, and suffer me not to die for thy love. What would ye that I did? said Sir Launcelot. I would have you to my husband, said Elaine. Fair damosel, I thank you, said Sir Launcelot, but truly, said he, I cast me never to be wedded man. Then, fair knight, said she, will ye be my lover? Jesu defend me, said Sir Launcelot, for then I rewarded your father and your brother full evil for their great goodness. Alas, said she, then must I die for your love. Ye shall not so, said Sir Launcelot, for wit ye well, fair maiden, I might have been married an I had would, but I never applied me to be married yet; but because, fair damosel, that ye love me as ye say ye do, I will for your good will and kindness show you some goodness, and that is this, that wheresomever ye will beset your heart upon some good knight that will wed you, I shall give you together a thousand pound yearly to you and to your heirs; thus much will I give you, fair madam, for your kindness, and always while I live to be your own knight. Of all this, said the maiden, I will none, for but if ye will wed me, or else be my lover at the least, wit you well, Sir Launcelot, my good days are done. Fair damosel, said Sir Launcelot, of these two things ye must pardon me.

Then she shrieked shrilly, and fell down in a swoon; and then women bare her into her chamber, and there she made overmuch sorrow; and then Sir Launcelot would depart, and there he asked Sir Lavaine what he would do.

What should I do, said Sir Lavaine, but follow you, but if ye drive me from you, or command me to go from you. Then came Sir Bernard to Sir Launcelot and said to him: I cannot see but that my daughter Elaine will die for your sake. Father, said Sir Lavaine, she doth as I do, for sithen I first saw my lord Sir Launcelot, I could never depart from him, nor nought I will an I may follow him.

Then Sir Launcelot took his leave, and so they departed, and came unto Winchester. And when Arthur wist that Sir Launcelot was come whole and sound the king made great joy of him, and so did Sir Gawaine and all the knights of the Round Table except Sir Agravaine and Sir Mordred. Also Queen Guenever was wood wroth with Sir Launcelot, and would by no means speak with him, but estranged herself from him; and Sir Launcelot made all the means that he might for to speak with the queen, but it would not be.

Now speak we of the Fair Maiden of Astolat that made such sorrow day and night that she never slept, ate, nor drank, and ever she made her complaint unto Sir Launcelot. So when she had thus endured a ten days, that she feebled so that she must needs pass out of this world, then she shrived her clean, and received her Creator. And ever she complained still upon Sir Launcelot. Then her ghostly father bade her leave such thoughts. Then she said, why should I leave such thoughts? An I not an earthly woman? And all the while the breath is in my body I may complain me, for my belief is I do none offence though I love an earthly man; and I take God to my record I loved never none but Sir Launcelot du Lake, nor never shall, and a clean maiden I am for him and for all other; and sithen it is the sufferance of God that I shall die for the love of so noble a knight, I beseech the High Father of Heaven to have mercy upon my soul, and that mine innumerable pains that I suffered may be allegiance of part of my sins. For sweet Lord Jesu, said the fair maiden, I take thee to record, on thee I was never great offencer against thy laws; but that I loved this noble knight, Sir Launcelot, out of measure, and of myself, good Lord, I might not withstand the fervent love wherefore I have my death.

And then she called her father, Sir Bernard, and her brother, Sir Tirre, and heartily she prayed her father that her brother might write a letter like as she did indite it: and so her father granted her. And when the letter was written word by word like as she devised, then she prayed her father that she might be watched until she were dead. And while my body is hot let this letter be put in my right hand, and my hand bound fast with the letter until that I be cold; and let me be put in a fair bed with all the richest clothes that I have about me, and so let my bed and all my richest clothes be laid with me in a chariot unto the next place where Thames is; and there let me be put within a barget, and but one man with me, such as ye trust to steer me thither, and that my barget be covered with black samite over and over: thus father I beseech you let it be done. So her father granted it her faithfully, all things should be done like as she had devised. Then her father and her brother made great dole, for when this was done anon she died. And so the corpse and the bed were borne the next way unto Thames, and there a man, and the corpse, and all, were put into Thames; and so the man steered the barget unto Westminster, and there he rowed a great while to and fro ere any espied it.

So by fortune King Arthur and the Queen Guenever were speaking together at a window, and so as they looked into Thames they espied this black barget, and had marvel what it meant. Then the king called Sir Kay, and showed it him. Sir, said Sir Kay, wit you well there is some new tidings. Go thither, said the king to Sir Kay, and take with you Sir Brandiles and Agravaine, and bring me ready word what is there. Then these knights departed and came to the barget and went in; and there they found the fairest corpse lying in a rich bed, and a poor man sitting in the barget's end, and no word would he speak. So these knights returned unto the king again, and told him what they found. That fair corpse will I see, said the king. And so then the king took the queen by the hand, and went thither.

Then the king made the barget to be holden fast, and then the king and the queen entered with certain knights with them; and there he saw the fairest woman lie in a rich bed, covered unto her middle with many rich clothes, and all was of cloth of gold, and she lay as though she had smiled. Then the queen espied a letter in her right hand, and told it to the king. Then the king took it and said: Now am I sure this letter will tell what she was, and why she is come hither. So then the king and the queen went out of the barget, and so commanded a certain man to wait upon the barget.

And so when the the king was come within his chamber, he called many knights about him, and said that he would wit openly what was written within that letter. Then the king brake it, and made a clerk to read it, and this was the intent of the letter. Most noble knight, Sir Launcelot, now hath death made us two at debate for your love. I was your lover, that men called the Fair Maiden of Astolat; therefore unto all ladies I make my moan; yet pray for my soul and bury me at least, and offer ye my mass-penny: this is my last request. And a clean maiden I died, I take God to witness: pray for my soul, Sir Launcelot, as thou art peerless. This was all the substance in the letter. And when it was read, the king, the queen, and all the knights wept for pity of the doleful complaints. Then was Sir Launcelot sent for; and when he was come King Arthur made the letter to be read to him.

And when Sir Launcelot heard it word by word, he said: My lord Arthur, wit ye well I am right heavy of the death of this fair damosel: God knoweth I was never causer of her death by my willing, and that will I report me to her own brother: here he is, Sir Lavaine. I will not say nay, said Sir Launcelot, but that she was both fair and good, and much I was beholden unto her, but she loved me out of measure. Ye might have shewed her, said the queen, some bounty and gentleness that might have preserved her life. Madam, said Sir Launcelot, she would none other ways be answered but that she would be my wife, or else my love; and of these two I would not grant her, but I proffered her, for her good love that she shewed me, a thousand pound yearly to her, and to her heirs, and to wed any manner knight that she could find best to love in her heart. For madam, said Sir Launcelot, I love not to be constrained to love; for love must arise of the heart, and not by no constraint. That is truth, said the king and many knights: love is free in himself, and never will be bounden, for where he is bounden he looseth himself.

Then said the king unto Sir Launcelot: It will be your

worship that ye oversee that she be interred worshipfully. Sir, said Sir Launcelot, that shall be done as I can best devise. And so many knights went thither to behold that fair maiden. And so upon the morn she was interred richly, and Sir Launcelot offered her mass-penny; and all the knights of the Table Round that were there at that time offered with Sir Launcelot. And then the poor man went again with the barget. Then the queen sent for Sir Launcelot, and prayed him of mercy, for why that she had been wroth with him causeless. This is not the first time, said Sir Launcelot, that ye have been displeased with me causeless; but, madam, ever I must suffer you, but what sorrow I endure I take no force. So thus passed on all that winter, with all manner of hunting and hawking; and jousts and tourneys were many betwixt many great lords, and ever in all places Sir Lavaine gat great worship.

HOW SIR LAUNCELOT WENT TO REPOSE HIM AT A HERMITAGE, AND HOW HE WAS HURT OF A GENTLEWOMAN, AND OF A GREAT TOURNEY ORDAINED BY KING ARTHUR. Thus it passed on till Christmas, and then every day there was jousts made for a diamond, who that jousted best should have a diamond. But Sir Launcelot would not joust but if it were at a great jousts cried. But Sir Lavaine jousted there all that Christmas passingly well, and best was praised, for there were but few that did so well. Wherefore all manner of knights deemed that Sir Lavaine should be made knight of the Table Round at the next feast of Pentecost. So at-after Christmas King Arthur let call unto him many knights, and there they advised together to make a party and a great tournament and jousts, beside Westminster upon Candlemas Day.

Then Queen Guenever sent for Sir Launcelot, and said thus: I warn you that ye ride no more in no jousts nor tournaments but that your kinsmen may know you. And at these jousts that shall be ye shall have of me a sleeve of gold; and I pray you for my sake enforce yourself there, that men may speak of you worship; but I charge you as ye will have my love, that ye warn your kinsmen that ye will bear that day the sleeve of gold upon your helmet. Madam, said Sir Launcelot, it shall be done. And so either made great joy of other. And when Sir Launcelot saw his time he told Sir Bors that he would depart, and have no more with him but Sir Lavaine, unto the good hermit that dwelt in that forest of Windsor; his name was Sir Brasias; and there he thought to repose him, and take all the rest that he might, because he would be fresh at that day of jousts.

So Sir Launcelot and Sir Lavaine departed, that no creature wist where he was become, but the noble men of his blood. And when he was come to the hermitage, wit ye well he had good cheer. And so daily Sir Launcelot would go to a well fast by the hermitage, and there he would lie down, and see the well spring and burble, and sometime he slept there. So at that time there was a lady dwelt in that forest, and she was a great huntress, and daily she used to hunt, and ever she bare her bow with her; and no men went never with her, but always women, and they were shooters, and could well kill a deer, both at the stalk and at the trest; and they daily bare bows and arrows, horns and wood-knives, and many good dogs they had, both for the string and for a bate. So it happed this lady the huntress had abated her dog for the bow at a barren hind, and so this barren hind took the flight over hedges and woods. And ever this lady and part of her women costed the hind, and checked it by the noise of the hounds, to have met with the hind at some water; and so it happed, the hind came to the well whereas Sir Launcelot was sleeping and slumbering. And so when the hind came to the well, for heat she went to soil, and there she lay a great while; and the dogs came after, and umbecast about, for they had lost the very perfect feute of the hind. Right so came that lady the huntress, that knew by the dog that she had, that the hind was at the soil in that well; and there she came stiffly and found the hind, and she put a broad arrow in her bow, and shot at the hind, and over-shot the hind; and so by misfortune the arrow smote Sir Launcelot in the thick of the thigh, over the barbs. When Sir Launcelot felt himself so hurt, he hurled up woodly, and saw the lady that had smitten him. And when he saw she was a woman, he said thus: Lady or damosel, what that thou be, in an evil time bear ye a bow; the devil made you a shooter.

Now mercy, fair sir, said the lady, I am a gentlewoman that useth here in this forest hunting, and God knoweth I saw ye not; but as here was a barren hind at the soil in this well, and I weened to have done well, but my hand swerved. Alas, said Sir Launcelot, ye have mischieved me. And so the lady departed, and Sir Launcelot, as he might, pulled out the arrow, and so he went weakly to the hermitage ever more bleeding as he went. And when Sir Lavaine and the hermit espied that Sir Launcelot was hurt, wit you well they were passing heavy. Then with great pain the hermit gat out the arrow's head out of Sir Launcelot's thigh, and much of his blood he shed; and the wound was passing sore, and unhappily smitten; for it was in such a place that he might not sit in no saddle. Now so heaven me help, said Sir Launcelot, I shall be in the field upon Candlemas Day at the jousts, whatsomever fall of it. So all that might be gotten to heal Sir Launcelot was had.

So when the day was come Sir Launcelot let devise that he was arrayed, and Sir Lavaine, and their horses, as though they had been Saracens. Then they blew to the field; and there the King of Northgalis encountered with the King of Scots, and there the King of Scots had a fall; and the King of Ireland smote down King Uriens; and the King of Northumberland smote down King Howel of Brittany; and Sir Galahad, the haut prince, smote down Chaleins of Clarance. And then King Arthur was wood wroth, and ran to the King with the Hundred Knights, and there King Arthur smote him down; and after with that same spear King Arthur smote down three other knights.

All this doing saw Sir Launcelot, and then he came into the field with Sir Lavaine as it had been thunder. And then anon Sir Bors and the knights of his blood espied Sir Launcelot, and said to them all: I warn you beware of him with the sleeve of gold upon his head, for he is himself Sir Launcelot du Lake; and for great goodness Sir Bors warned Sir Gareth. I am well apaid, said Sir Gareth, that I may know him. But who is he, said they all, that rideth with him in the same array? That is the good and gentle knight Sir Lavaine, said Sir Bors. So Sir Launcelot encountered with Sir Gawaine, and there by force Sir Launcelot smote down Sir Gawaine and his horse to the earth, and so he smote down Sir Agravaine and Sir Gaheris, and also he smote down Sir Mordred, and all this was with one spear. Then Sir Lavaine met with Sir Palomides, and either met other so hard and so fiercely that both their horses fell to the earth. And then were they horsed again, and then met Sir Launcelot with Sir Palomides, and there Sir Palomides had a fall; and so Sir Launcelot or ever he stint, as fast as he might get spears, he smote down thirty knights, and the most part of them were knights of the Table Round; and ever the knights of his blood withdrew them, and made them ado in other places where Sir Launcelot came not.

And then King Arthur was wroth when he saw Sir Launcelot do such deeds; and then the king called unto him Sir Gawaine, Sir Mordred, Sir Kay, Sir Griflet, Sir Lucan the Butler, Sir Bedevere, Sir Palomides, Sir Safere, his brother; and so the king with these nine knights made them ready to set upon Sir Launcelot, and upon Sir Lavaine. All this espied Sir Bors and Sir Gareth. Now I dread me sore, said Sir Bors, that my lord, Sir Launcelot, will be hard matched. By my head, said Sir Gareth, I will ride unto my lord Sir Launcelot, for to help him, fall of him what fall may, for he is the same man that made me knight. Ye shall not so, said Sir Bors, by my counsel, unless that ye were disguised. Ye shall see me disguised, said Sir Gareth; and therewithal he espied a Welsh knight where he was to repose him, and he was sore hurt afore by Sir Gawaine, and to him Sir Gareth rode, and prayed him of his knighthood to lend him his shield for his. I will well, said the Welsh knight. And when Sir Gareth had his shield, the book saith it was green, with a maiden that seemed in it.

Then Sir Gareth came driving to Sir Launcelot all that

he might and said: Knight, keep thyself, for yonder cometh King Arthur with nine noble knights with him to put you to a rebuke, and so I am come to bear you fellowship for old love ye have shewed me. Gramercy, said Sir Launcelot. Sir, said Sir Gareth, encounter ye with Sir Gawaine, and I shall encounter with Sir Palomides; and let Sir Lavaine match with the noble King Arthur. And when we have delivered them, let us three hold us sadly together. Then came King Arthur with his nine knights with him, and Sir Launcelot encountered with Sir Gawaine, and gave him such a buffet that the arson of his saddle brast, and Sir Gawaine fell to the earth. Then Sir Gareth encountered with the good knight Sir Palomides, and he gave him such a buffet that both his horse and he dashed to the earth. Then encountered King Arthur with Sir Lavaine, and there either of them smote other to the earth, horse and all, that they lay a great while. Then Sir Launcelot smote down Sir Agravaine, and Sir Gaheris, and Sir Mordred; and Sir Gareth smote down Sir Kay, and Sir Safere, and Sir Griflet. And then Sir Lavaine was horsed again, and he smote down Sir Lucan the Butler and Sir Bedevere; and then there began great throng of good knights.

So this tournament and this jousts dured long, till it was near night, for the knights of the Round Table relieved ever unto King Arthur; for the king was wroth out of measure that he and his knights might not prevail that day. Then Sir Gawaine said to the king: I marvel where all this day be Sir Bors de Ganis and his fellowship of Sir Launcelot's blood, I marvel all this day they be not about you: it is for some cause said Sir Gawaine. By my head, said Sir Kay, Sir Bors is yonder all this day upon the right hand of this field, and there he and his blood do more worshipfully than we do. It may well be, said Sir Gawaine, but I dread me ever of guile; for on pain of my life, said Sir Gawaine, this knight with the red sleeve of gold is himself Sir Launcelot, I see well by his riding and by his great strokes; and the other knight in the same colours is the good young knight, Sir Lavaine. Also that knight with the green shield is my brother, Sir Gareth, and yet he hath disguised himself, for no man shall never make him be against Sir Launcelot, because he made him knight. By my head, said Arthur, nephew, I believe you; therefore tell me now what is your best counsel. Sir, said Sir Gawaine, ye shall have my counsel: let blow unto lodging, for an he be Sir Launcelot du Lake, and my brother, Sir Gareth, with him, with the help of that good young knight, Sir Lavaine, trust me truly it will be no boot to strive with them but if we should fall ten or twelve upon one knight, and that were no worship, but shame. Ye say truth, said the king; and for to say sooth, said the king, it were shame to us so many as we be to set upon them any more; for wit ye well, said King Arthur, they be three good knights, and namely that knight with the sleeve of gold.

So then they blew into lodging; but forthwithal King Arthur let send unto the four kings, and to the mighty duke, and prayed them that the knight with the sleeve of gold depart not from them, but that the king may speak with him. Then forthwithal King Arthur alighted and unarmed him, and took a little hackney and rode after Sir Launcelot, for ever he had a spy upon him. And so he found him among the four kings and the duke; and there the king prayed them all unto supper, and they said they would with good will. And when they were unarmed then King Arthur knew Sir

Launcelot, Sir Lavaine, and Sir Gareth. Ah, Sir Launcelot, said King Arthur, this day ye have heated me and my knights.

So they went unto Arthur's lodging all together, and there was a great feast and great revel, and the prize was given unto Sir Launcelot; and by heralds they named him that he had smitten down fifty knights, and Sir Gareth five-and-thirty, and Sir Lavaine four-and-twenty knights. Then Arthur blamed Sir Gareth because he left his fellowship and held with Sir Launcelot. My lord, said Sir Gareth, he made me a knight, and when I saw him so hard bestead, methought it was my worship to help him, for I saw him do so much, and so many noble knights against him; and when I understood that he was Sir Launcelot du Lake, I shamed to see so many knights against him alone. Truly, said King Arthur unto Sir Gareth, ye say well, and worshipfully have ye done and to yourself great worship; and all the days of my life, said King Arthur unto Sir Gareth, wit you well I shall love you, and trust you the more better. For ever, said Arthur, it is a worshipful knight's deed to help another worshipful knight when he seeth him in a great danger; for ever a worshipful man will be loath to see a worshipful man shamed; and he that is of no worship, and fareth with cowardice, never shall he show gentleness, nor no manner of goodness where he seeth a man in any danger, for then ever will a coward show no mercy; and always a good man will do ever to another man as he would be done to himself. So then there were great feasts unto kings and dukes, and revel, game, and play, and all manner of noblesse was used; and he that was courteous, true, and faithful, to his friend was that time cherished.

OF THE MONTH OF MAY AND OF TRUE LOVERS, AND HOW QUEEN GUENEVER RODE A-MAYING WITH CERTAIN KNIGHTS OF THE ROUND TABLE, AND CLAD ALL IN GREEN, AND HOW SIR MELIAGRANCE TOOK THE QUEEN AND HER KNIGHTS. And thus it passed on from Candlemas until after Easter, that the month of May was come, when every lusty heart beginneth to blossom, and to bring forth fruit; for like as herbs and trees bring forth fruit and flourish in May, in like wise every lusty heart, that is in any manner a lover, springeth and flourisheth in lusty deeds. For it giveth unto all lovers courage, that lusty month of May, in something to constrain him to some manner of thing more in that month than in any other month, for divers causes. For then all herbs and trees renew a man and woman, and likewise lovers call again to their mind old gentleness and old service, and many kind deeds that were forgotten by negligence. For like as winter rasure doth alway arase and deface green summer, so fareth it by unstable love in man and woman. For in many persons there is no stability; for we may see all day, for a little blast of winter's rasure, anon we shall deface and lay apart true love for little or nought, that cost much thing; this is no wisdom nor stability, but it is feebleness of nature and great disworship, whosomever useth this. Therefore, like as May month flowereth and flourisheth in many gardens, so in like wise let every man of worship flourish his heart in this world, first unto God, and next unto the joy of them that he promised his faith unto; for there was never worshipful man or worshipful woman, but they loved one better than another; and worship in arms may never be foiled, but first reserve the honour to God, and secondly the quarrel must come of thy lady: and such love I call virtuous love.

But nowadays men can not love seven night but they must have all their desires: that love may not endure by reason; for where they be soon accorded and hasty heat, soon it cooleth. Right so fareth love nowadays, soon hot soon cold: this is no stability. But the old love was not so; men and women could love together seven years, and no wanton lusts were between them, and then was love truth and faithfulness: and lo, in like wise was used love in King Arthur's days. Wherefore I liken love nowadays unto summer and winter; for like as the one is hot and the other cold, so fareth love nowadays. Therefore all ye that be lovers call unto your remembrance the month of May, like as did Queen Guenever, for whom I make here a little mention, that while she lived she was a true lover, and therefore she had a good end.

So it befell in the month of May, Queen Guenever called unto her knights of the Table Round, and she gave them warning that early upon the morrow she would ride a-Maying into woods and fields beside Westminster. And I warn you that there be none of you but that he be well horsed, and that ye all be clothed in green, outher in silk outher in cloth; and I shall bring with me ten ladies, and every knight shall have a lady behind him, and every knight shall have a squire and two yeomen; and I will that ye all be well horsed. So they made them ready in the freshest manner. And these were the names of the knights: Sir Kay le Seneschal, Sir Agravaine, Sir Brandiles, Sir Sagramore le Desirous, Sir Dodinas le Savage, Sir Ozanna le Cure Hardy, Sir Ladinas of the Forest Savage, Sir Persant of Inde, Sir Ironside, that was called the Knight of the Red Launds, and Sir Pelleas, the lover; and these ten knights made them ready in the freshest manner to ride with the queen. And so upon the morn they took their horses with the queen, and rode a-Maying in woods and meadows as it pleased them, in great joy and delights; for the queen had cast to have been again with King Arthur at the furthest by ten of the clock, and so was that time her purpose.

Then there was a knight that hight Meliagrance, and he was son unto King Bagdemagus, and this knight had at that time a castle of the gift of King Arthur within seven mile of Westminster. And this knight, Sir Meliagrance, loved passing well Queen Guenever, and so had he done long and many years. And the book saith he had lain in await for to steal away the queen, but evermore he forbare for because of Sir Launcelot; for in no wise he would meddle with the queen an Sir Launcelot were in her company, or else an he were near-hand her. And that time was such a custom the queen rode never without a great fellowship of men of arms about her, and they were many good knights, and the most part were young men that would have worship; and they were called the Queen's Knights, and never in no battle, tournament, nor jousts, they bare none of them no manner of knowledging of their own arms, but plain white shields, and thereby they were called the Queen's Knights. And then when it happed any of them to be of great worship by his noble deeds, then at the next Feast of Pentecost, if there were any slain or dead, as there was none year that there failed but some were dead, then was there chosen in his stead that was dead the most men of worship, that were called the Queen's Knights.

And thus they came up all first, ere they were renowned men of worship, both Sir Launcelot and all the remnant of them.

But this knight, Sir Meliagrance, had espied the queen well and her purpose, and how Sir Launcelot was not with her, and how she had no men of arms with her but the ten noble knights all arrayed in green for Maying. Then he purveyed him a twenty men of arms and an hundred archers for to destroy the queen and her knights, for he thought that time was best season to take the queen.

So as the queen had mayed and all her knights, all were bedashed with herbs, mosses and flowers, in the best manner and freshest. Right so came out of a wood Sir Meliagrance with an eight score men well harnessed, as they should fight in a battle of arrest, and bade the queen and her knights abide, for maugre their heads they should abide. Traitor knight, said Queen Guenever, what cast thou for to do? Wilt thou shame thyself? Bethink thee how thou art a king's son, and knight of the Table Round, and thou to be about to dishonour the noble king that made thee knight; thou shamest all knighthood and thyself; and me, I let thee wit, shalt thou never shame, for I had liefer cut mine own throat in twain rather than thou shouldest dishonour me. As for all this language, said Sir Meliagrance, be it as it be may, for wit you well, madam, I have loved you many a year, and never or now could I get you at such an advantage as I do now, and therefore I will take you as I find you.

Then spake all the ten noble knights at once and said: Sir Meliagrance, wit thou well ye are about to jeopard your worship to dishonour, and also ye cast to jeopard our persons howbeit we be unarmed. Ye have us at a great avail, for it seemeth by you that ye have laid watch upon us; but rather than ye should put the queen to a shame and us all, we had as lief to depart from our lives, for an if we other ways did, we were shamed for ever. Then said Sir Meliagrance: Dress you as well ye can, and keep the queen. Then the ten knights of the Table Round drew their swords, and the other let run at them with their spears, and the ten knights manly abode them, and smote away their spears that no spear did them none harm. Then they lashed together with swords, and anon Sir Kay, Sir Sagramore, Sir Agravaine, Sir Dodinas, Sir Ladinas, and Sir Ozanna were smitten to the earth with grimly wounds. Then Sir Brandiles, and Sir Persant, Sir Ironside, Sir Pelleas fought long, and they were sore wounded; for these ten knights, or ever they were laid to the ground, slew forty men of the boldest and the best of them.

So when the queen saw her knights thus dolefully wounded, and needs must be slain at the last, then for pity and sorrow she cried Sir Meliagrance: Slay not my noble knights, and I will go with thee upon this covenant, that thou save them, and suffer them not to be more hurt, with this, that they be led with me wheresomever thou leadest me, for I will rather slay myself than I will go with thee, unless that these my noble knights may be in my presence. Madam, said Meliagrance, for your sake they shall be led with you into mine own castle, with that ye will be ruled and ride with me. Then the queen prayed the four knights to leave their fighting, and she and they would not depart. Madam, said Sir Pelleas, we will do as ye do, for as for me I take no force of my life nor death. For as the French book saith, Sir Pelleas gave such buffets there that none armour might hold him.

HOW SIR LAUNCELOT HAD WORD HOW THE QUEEN WAS TAKEN, AND HOW SIR MELIAGRANCE LAID A BUSHMENT FOR LAUNCELOT, SO THAT HIS HORSE WAS SLAIN, AND HE RODE IN A CART TO SAVE THE QUEEN.

Then by the queen's commandment they left battle, and dressed the wounded knights on horseback, some sitting, some overthwart their horses, that it was pity to behold them. And then Sir Meliagrance charged the queen and all her knights that none of all her fellowship should depart from her; for full sore he dread Sir Launcelot du Lake, lest he should have any knowledging. All this espied the queen, and privily she called unto her a child of her chamber that was swiftly horsed, to whom she said: Go thou, when thou seest thy time, and bear this ring unto Sir Launcelot du Lake, and pray him as he loveth me that he will see me and rescue me, if ever he will have joy of me; and spare not thy horse, said the queen, neither for water, neither for land. So the child espied his time, and lightly he took his horse with the spurs, and departed as fast as he might. And when Sir Meliagrance saw him so flee, he understood that it was by the queen's commandment for to warn Sir Launcelot. Then they that were best horsed chased him and shot at him, but from them all the child went suddenly. And then Sir Meliagrance said to the queen: Madam, ye are about to betray me, but I shall ordain for Sir Launcelot that he shall not come lightly at you. And then he rode with her, and they all, to his castle, in all the haste that they might. And by the way Sir Meliagrance laid in an embushment the best archers that he might get in his country, to the number of thirty, to await upon Sir Launcelot, charging them that if they saw such a manner of knight come by the way upon a white horse, that in any wise they slay his horse, but in no manner of wise have not ado with him bodily, for he is over-hardy to be overcome.

So this was done, and they were come to his castle, but in no wise the queen would never let none of the ten knights and her ladies out of her sight, but always they were in her presence; for the book saith, Sir Meliagrance durst make no masteries, for dread of Sir Launcelot, insomuch he deemed that he had warning. So when the child was departed from the fellowship of Sir Meliagrance, within a while he came to Westminster, and anon he found Sir Launcelot. And when he had told his message, and delivered him the queen's ring: Alas, said Sir Launcelot, now I am shamed for ever, unless that I may rescue that noble lady from dishonour. Then eagerly he asked his armour; and ever the child told Sir Launcelot how the ten knights fought marvellously, and how Sir Pelleas, and Sir Ironside, and Sir Brandiles, and Sir Persant of Inde, fought strongly, but namely Sir Pelleas, there might none withstand him; and how they all fought till at the last they were laid to the earth; and then the queen made appointment for to save their lives, and go with Sir Meliagrance.

Alas, said Sir Launcelot, that most noble lady, that she should be so destroyed; I had liefer, said Sir Launcelot, than all France, that I had been there well armed. So when Sir Launcelot was armed and upon his horse, he prayed the child of the queen's chamber to warn Sir Lavaine how suddenly he was departed, and for what cause. And pray him as he loveth me, that he will hie him after me, and that he stint not until he come to the castle where Sir Meliagrance abideth, or dwelleth; for there, said Sir Launcelot, he shall hear of me an I am a man living, and rescue the queen and the ten knights the which he traitorously hath taken, and that shall I prove upon his head, and all them that hold with him.

Then Sir Launcelot rode as fast as he might, and the book saith he took the water at Westminster Bridge, and made his horse to swim over Thames unto Lambeth. And then within a while he came to the same place thereas the ten noble knights fought with Sir Meliagrance. And then Sir Launcelot followed the track until that he came to a wood, and there was a strait way, and there the thirty archers bade Sir Launcelot turn again, and follow no longer that track. What commandment have ye thereto, said Sir Launcelot, to cause me that am a knight of the Round Table to leave my right way? This way shalt thou leave, other-else thou shalt go it on thy foot, for wit thou well thy horse shall be slain. That is little mastery, said Sir Launcelot, to slay mine horse; but as for myself, when my horse is slain, I give right nought for you, not an ye were five hundred more. So then they shot Sir Launcelot's horse, and smote him with many arrows; and then Sir Launcelot avoided his horse, and went on foot; but there were so many ditches and hedges betwixt them and him that he might not meddle with none of them. Alas for shame, said Launcelot, that ever one knight should betray another knight; but it is an old saw, A good man is never in danger but when he is in the danger of a coward. Then Sir Launcelot went a while, and then he was foul cumbered of his armour, his shield, and his spear, and all that longed unto him. Wit ye well he was full sore annoyed, and full loath he was for to leave anything that longed unto him, for he dread sore the treason of Sir Meliagrance.

Then by fortune there came by him a chariot that came thither for to fetch wood. Say me, carter, said Sir Launcelot, what shall I give thee to suffer me to leap into thy chariot, and that thou bring me unto a castle within this two mile? Thou shalt not come within my chariot, said the carter, for I am sent for to fetch wood for my lord, Sir Meliagrance. With him would I speak. Thou shalt not go with me, said the carter. Then Sir Launcelot leapt to him, and gave him such a buffet that he fell to the earth stark dead. Then the other carter, his fellow, was afeard, and weened to have gone the same way; and then he cried: Fair lord, save my life, and I shall bring you where ye will. Then I charge thee, said Sir Launcelot, that thou drive me and this chariot even unto Sir Meliagrance's gate. Leap up into the chariot, said the carter, and ye shall be there anon. So the carter drove on a great wallop, and Sir Launcelot's horse followed the chariot, with more than a forty arrows broad and rough in him.

And more than an hour and an half Dame Guenever was awaiting in a bay window with her ladies, and espied an armed knight standing in a chariot. See, madam, said a lady, where rideth in a chariot a goodly armed knight; I suppose he rideth unto hanging. Where? said the queen. Then she espied by his shield that he was there himself, Sir Launcelot du Lake. And then she was ware where came his horse ever after that chariot, with the forty arrows in him. Alas, said the queen, now I see well and prove, that well is him that hath a trusty friend. Ha, ha, most noble knight, said Queen Guenever, I see well thou art hard bestead when thou ridest in a chariot. Then she rebuked that lady that likened Sir Launcelot to ride in a chariot to hanging.

It was foul mouthed, said the queen, and evil likened, so for to liken the most noble knight of the world unto such a shameful death. O Jesu defend him and keep him, said the queen, from all mischievous end. By this was Sir Launcelot come to the gates of that castle, and there he descended down, and cried, that all the castle rang of it: Where art thou, false traitor, Sir Meliagrance, and knight of the Table Round? now come forth here, thou traitor knight, thou and thy fellowship with thee; for here I am, Sir Launcelot du Lake, that shall fight with you. And therewithal he bare the gate wide open upon the porter, and smote him under his ear with his gauntlet, that his neck brast a-sunder.

HOW SIR MELIAGRANCE REQUIRED FORGIVENESS OF THE QUEEN, AND HOW SHE APPEASED SIR LAUNCELOT, AND HOW SIR LAUNCELOT CAME IN THE NIGHT TO THE QUEEN, AND HOW SIR MELIAGRANCE APPEACHED HER OF TREASON. When Sir Meliagrance heard that Sir Launcelot was there he ran unto Queen Guenever, and fell upon his knee, and said: Mercy, madam, now I put me wholly into your grace. What aileth you now? said Queen Guenever; forsooth I might well wit some good knight would revenge me, though my lord Arthur wist not of this your work. Madam, said Sir Meliagrance, all this that is amiss on my part shall be amended right as yourself will devise, and wholly I put me in your grace. What would ye that I did? said the queen. I would no more, said Meliagrance, but that ye would take all in your own hands, and that ye will rule my lord Sir Launcelot; and such cheer as may be made him in this poor castle ye and he shall have until to-morn, and then may ye and all they return unto Westminster; and my body and all that I have I shall put in your rule. Ye say well, said the queen, and better is peace than ever war, and the less noise the more is my worship.

Then the queen and her ladies went down unto the knight, Sir Launcelot, that stood wroth out of measure in the inner court, to abide battle; and ever he bade: Thou traitor knight come forth. Then the queen came to him and said: Sir Launcelot, why be ye so moved? Ha, madam, said Sir Launcelot, why ask ye me that question? Meseemeth, said Sir Launcelot, ye ought to be more wroth than I am, for ye have the hurt and the dishonour, for wit ye well, madam, my hurt is but little for the killing of a mare's son, but the despite grieveth me much more than all my hurt. Truly, said the queen, ye say truth; but heartily I thank you, said the queen, but ye must come in with me peaceably, for all thing is put in my hand, and all that is evil shall be for the best, for the knight full sore repenteth him of the misadventure that is befallen him. Madam, said Sir Launcelot, sith it is so that ye been accorded with him, as for me I may not be again it, howbeit Sir Meliagrance hath done full shamefully to me, and cowardly. Ah madam, said Sir Launcelot, an I had wist ye would have been so soon accorded with him, I would not have made such haste unto you. Why say ye so, said the queen, do ye forthink yourself of your good deeds? Wit you well, said the queen, I accorded never unto him for favour nor love that I had unto him, but for to lay down every shameful noise. Madam, said Sir Launcelot, ye understand full well I was never willing nor glad of shameful slander nor noise; and there is neither king, queen, nor knight, that beareth the life, except my lord King Arthur, and you, madam, should let me, but I should make Sir Meliagrance's heart full cold or ever I departed from hence. That wot I well, said the queen, but what will ye more? Ye shall have all thing ruled as ye list to have it. Madam, said Sir Launcelot, so ye be pleased I care not, as for my part ye shall soon please.

Right so the queen took Sir Launcelot by the bare hand, for he had put off his gauntlet, and so she went with him till her chamber; and then she commanded him to be unarmed. And then Sir Launcelot asked where were the ten knights that were wounded sore; so she showed them unto Sir Launcelot, and there they made great joy of the coming of him, and Sir Launcelot made great dole of their hurts, and bewailed them greatly. And there Sir Launcelot told them how cowardly and traitorly Meliagrance set archers to slay his horse, and how he was fain to put himself in a chariot. Thus they complained everych to other; and full fain they would have been revenged, but they peaced themselves because of the queen. Then, as the French book saith, Sir Launcelot was called many a day after le Chevaler du Chariot, and did many deeds, and great adventures he had. And so leave we of this tale le Chevaler du Chariot, and turn we to this tale.

So Sir Launcelot had great cheer with the queen, and then Sir Launcelot made a promise with the queen that the same night Sir Launcelot should come to a window outward toward a garden; and that window was y-barred with iron, and there Sir Launcelot promised to meet her when all folks were asleep. So then came Sir Lavaine driving to the gates, crying: Where is my lord, Sir Launcelot du Lake? Then was he sent for, and when Sir Lavaine saw Sir Launcelot, he said: My lord, I found well how ye were hard bestead, for I have found your horse that was slain with arrows. As for that, said Sir Launcelot, I pray you, Sir Lavaine, speak ye of other matters, and let ye this pass, and we shall right it another time when we best may.

Then the knights that were hurt were searched, and soft salves were laid to their wounds; and so it passed on till supper time, and all the cheer that might be made them there was done unto the queen and all her knights. Then when season was, they went unto their chambers, but in no wise the queen would not suffer the wounded knights to be from her, but that they were laid within draughts by her chamber, upon beds and pillows, that she herself might see to them, that they wanted nothing.

So when Sir Launcelot was in his chamber that was assigned unto him, he called unto him Sir Lavaine, and told him that night he must go speak with his lady, Dame Guenever. Sir, said Sir Lavaine, let me go with you an it please you, for I dread me sore of the treason of Sir Meliagrance. Nay, said Sir Launcelot, I thank you, but I will have nobody with me. Then Sir Launcelot took his sword in his hand, and privily went to a place where he had espied a ladder to-forehand, and that he took under his arm, and bare it through the garden, and set it up to the window, and there anon the queen was ready to meet him. And then they made either to other their complaints of many divers things, and then Sir Launcelot wished that he might have come in to her. Wit ye well, said the queen, I would as fain as ye, that ye might come in to me. Would ye, madam, said Sir Launcelot, with your heart that I were with you? Yea, truly, said the queen. Now shall I prove my might, said Sir Launcelot, for your love; and then he set his hands upon the bars of iron, and he pulled at them with such a might that he brast them clean out of the stone walls, and therewithal one of the bars of iron cut the brawn of his hand throughout to the bone; and then he leapt into the chamber to the queen. Make ye no noise, said the queen, for my wounded knights lie here fast by me. And when he saw his time that he might tarry no longer he took his leave and departed at the window, and put it together as well as he might again, and so departed unto his own chamber; and there he told Sir Lavaine how he was hurt. Then Sir Lavaine dressed his hand and staunched it, and put upon it a glove, that it should not be espied; and so the queen lay long in her bed until it was nine of the clock.

Then Sir Meliagrance went to the queen's chamber, and found her ladies there ready clothed. What aileth you, madam, said Sir Meliagrance, that ye sleep thus long? And right therewithal he opened the curtain for to behold her; and then was he ware of the blood of Sir Launcelot's hurt hand. When Sir Meliagrance espied that blood, then he deemed in himself that she was false to the king, and that it was the blood of some of the wounded knights. Ah, madam, said Sir Meliagrance, now I have found you a false traitress unto my lord Arthur; for now I prove well it was not for nought that ye laid these wounded knights within the bounds of your chamber; therefore I will call you of treason before my lord, King Arthur. And now I have proved you, madam, with a shameful deed; and that they be all false, or some of them, I will make good, for a wounded knight hath been here. That is false, said the queen, and that I will report me unto them all. Then when the ten knights heard Sir Meliagrance's words, they spake all in one voice and said to Sir Meliagrance: Thou sayest falsely, and wrongfully puttest upon us such a deed, and that we will make good any of us; choose which thou list of us when we are whole of our wounds. Ye shall not, said Sir Meliagrance, away with your proud language, for here ye may all see, that a wounded knight hath been here. Then were they all ashamed when they saw that blood; and wit you well Sir Meliagrance was passing glad that he had the queen at such an advantage, for he deemed by that to hide his treason. So with this rumour came in Sir Launcelot, and found them all at a great array.

HOW SIR LAUNCELOT ANSWERED FOR THE QUEEN, TO WAGE BATTLE AGAINST SIR MELIAGRANCE; AND HOW SIR LAUNCELOT WAS TAKEN IN A TRAP, BUT WAS DELIVERED OF A LADY, AND HOW HE FOUGHT WITH SIR MELIAGRANCE, HALF UNARMED, AND SLEW HIM. What array is this? said Sir Launcelot. Then Sir Meliagrance told him what he had found, and showed him the blood, And well I am sure, said Sir Meliagrance, here hath been one of her wounded knights, and therefore I will prove with my hands that she is a traitress unto my lord Arthur. Beware what ye do, said Launcelot, for an ye say so, an ye will prove it, it will be taken at your hands.

My lord, Sir Launcelot, said Sir Meliagrance, I rede you beware what ye do; for though ye are never so good a knight, as ye wot well ye are renowned the best knight of the world, yet should ye be advised to do battle in a wrong quarrel, for God will have a stroke in every battle. As for that, said Sir Launcelot, God is to be dread; but as to that

I say nay plainly, that this night none of these ten wounded knights was here with my lady Queen Guenever, and that will I prove with my hands, that ye say untruly in that now. Hold, said Sir Meliagrance, here is my glove that she is traitress unto my lord, King Arthur, and that this night one of the wounded knights was here. And I receive your glove, said Sir Launcelot. And so they were sealed with their signets, and delivered unto the ten knights. At what day shall we do battle together? said Sir Launcelot. This day eight days, said Sir Meliagrance, in the field beside Westminster. I am agreed, said Sir Launcelot. But now, said Sir Meliagrance, sithen it is so that we must fight together, I pray you, as ye be a noble knight, await me with no treason, nor none villainy the meanwhile, nor none for you. So God me help, said Sir Launcelot, ye shall right well wit I was never of no such conditions, for I report me to all knights that ever have known me, I fared never with no treason, nor I loved never the fellowship of no man that fared with treason. Then let us go to dinner, said Meliagrance, and after dinner ye and the queen and ye may ride all to Westminster. I will well, said Sir Launcelot.

Then Sir Meliagrance said to Sir Launcelot: Pleaseth it you to see the eftures of this castle? With a good will, said Sir Launcelot. And then they went together from chamber to chamber, for Sir Launcelot dread no perils; for ever a man of worship and of prowess dreadeth least always perils, for they ween every man be as they be; but ever he that fareth with treason putteth oft a man in great danger. So it befell upon Sir Launcelot that no peril dread, as he went with Sir Meliagrance he trod on a trap and the board rolled, and there Sir Launcelot fell down more than ten fathom into a cave full of straw; and then Sir Meliagrance departed and made no fare, as that he nist where he was.

And when Sir Launcelot was thus missed they marvelled where he was become; and then the queen and many of them deemed that he was departed as he was wont to do, suddenly. For Sir Meliagrance made suddenly to put away aside Sir Lavaine's horse, that they might all understand that Sir Launcelot was departed suddenly. So it passed on till after dinner; and then Sir Lavaine would not stint until that he ordained litters for the wounded knights, that they might be laid in them; and so with the queen and them all, both ladies and gentlewomen and other, went unto Westminster; and there the knights told King Arthur how Meliagrance had appealed the queen of high treason, and how Sir Launcelot had received the glove of him: And this day eight days they shall do battle afore you. By my head, said King Arthur, I am afeard Sir Meliagrance hath taken upon him a great charge; but where is Sir Launcelot? said the king. Sir, said they all, we wot not where he is, but we deem he is ridden to some adventures, as he is ofttimes wont to do, for he hath Sir Lavaine's horse. Let him be, said the king, he will be founden, but if he be trapped with some treason.

So leave we Sir Launcelot lying within that cave in great pain; and every day there came a lady and brought him his meat and his drink, and wooed him to love her; and ever the noble knight, Sir Launcelot, said her nay. Sir Launcelot, said she, ye are not wise, for ye may never out of this prison, but if ye have my help; and also your lady, Queen Guenever, shall be brent in your default, unless that ye be there at the day of battle. God defend, said Sir Launcelot, that she should be brent in my default; and if it be so, said Sir Launcelot, that I may not be there, it shall be well understanded, both at the king and at the queen, and with all men of worship, that I am dead, sick, or in prison. For all men that know me will say for me that I am in some evil case an I be not there that day; and well I wot there is some good knight either of my blood, or some other that loveth me, that will take my quarrel in hand; and therefore, said Sir Launcelot, wit ye well ye shall not fear me; and if there were no more women in all this land but ye, I would not say you otherwise. Then art thou shamed, said the lady, and destroyed for ever. As for world's shame, Jesu defend me; and as for my distress, it is welcome whatsoever it be that God sendeth me.

So she came to him the same day that the battle should be, and said: Sir Launcelot, methinketh ye are too hard-hearted, but wouldst thou but kiss me once I should deliver thee, and thine armour, and the best horse that is within Sir Meliagrance's stable. As for to kiss you, said Sir Launcelot, I may do that and lose no worship; and wit ye well an I understood there were any disworship for to kiss you I would not do it. Then he kissed her, and then she gat him, and brought him to his armour. And when he was armed, she brought him to a stable, where stood twelve good coursers, and bade him choose the best. Then Sir Launcelot looked upon a white courser the which liked him best; and anon he commanded the keepers fast to saddle him with the best saddle of war that there was; and so it was done as he bade. Then gat he his spear in his hand, and his sword by his side, and commended the lady unto God, and said: Lady, for this good deed I shall do you service if ever it be in my power.

Now leave we Sir Launcelot wallop all that he might, and speak we of Queen Guenever that was brought to a fire to be brent; for Sir Meliagrance was sure, him thought, that Sir Launcelot should not be at that battle; therefore he ever cried upon King Arthur to do him justice, or else bring forth Sir Launcelot du Lake. Then was the king and all the court full sore abashed and shamed that the queen should be brent in the default of Sir Launcelot. My lord Arthur, said Sir Lavaine, ye may understand that it is not well with my lord Sir Launcelot, for an he were alive, so he be not sick or in prison, wit ye well he would be here; for never heard ye that ever he failed his part for whom he should do battle for. And therefore, said Sir Lavaine, my lord, King Arthur, I beseech you give me license to do battle here this day for my lord and master, and for to save my lady, the queen. Gramercy, gentle Sir Lavaine, said King Arthur, for I dare say all that Sir Meliagrance putteth upon my lady the queen is wrong, for I have spoken with all the ten wounded knights, and there is not one of them, an he were whole and able to do battle, but he would prove upon Sir Meliagrance's body that it is false that he putteth upon my queen. So shall I, said Sir Lavaine, in the defence of my lord, Sir Launcelot, an ye will give me leave. Now I give you leave, said King Arthur, and do your best, for I dare well say there is some treason done to Sir Launcelot.

Then was Sir Lavaine armed and horsed, and suddenly at the lists' end he rode to perform this battle; and right as the heralds should cry: Lesses les aler, right so came in Sir Launcelot driving with all the force of his horse. And then Arthur cried: Ho! and Abide! Then was Sir Launcelot called on horseback to-fore King Arthur, and there he told openly to-fore the king and all, how Sir Meliagrance had served him first and last. And when the king, and the queen, and all the lords, knew of the treason of Sir Meliagrance they were all ashamed on his behalf. Then was Queen Guenever sent for, and set by the king in great trust of her champion. And then there was no more else to say, but Sir Launcelot and Sir Meliagrance dressed them unto battle, and took their spears; and so they came together as thunder, and there Sir Launcelot bare him down quite over his horse's croup. And then Sir Launcelot alighted and dressed his shield on his shoulder, with his sword in his hand, and Sir Meliagrance in the same wise dressed him unto him, and there they smote many great strokes together; and at the last Sir Launcelot smote him such a buffet upon the helmet that he fell on the one side to the earth. And then he cried upon him aloud: Most noble knight, Sir Launcelot du Lake, save my life, for I yield me unto you, and I require you, as ye be a knight and fellow of the Table Round, slay me not, for I yield me as overcome; and whether I shall live or die I put me in the king's hands and yours.

Then Sir Launcelot wist not what to do, for he had had liefer than all the good of the world he might have been revenged upon Sir Meliagrance; and Sir Launcelot looked up to the Queen Guenever, if he might espy by any sign or countenance what she would have done. And then the queen wagged her head upon Sir Launcelot, as though she would say: Slay him. Full well knew Sir Launcelot by the wagging of her head that she would have him dead; then Sir Launcelot bade him rise for shame and perform that battle to the utterance. Nay, said Sir Meliagrance, I will never arise until ye take me as yolden and recreant.

I shall proffer you large proffers, said Sir Launcelot, that is for to say, I shall unarm my head and my left quarter of my body, all that may be unarmed, and let bind my left hand behind me, so that it shall not help me, and right so I shall do battle with you. Then Sir Meliagrance started up upon his legs, and said on high: My lord Arthur, take heed to this proffer, for I will take it, and let him be disarmed and bounden according to his proffer. What say ye, said King Arthur unto Sir Launcelot, will ye abide by your proffer? Yea, my lord, said Sir Launcelot, I will never go from that I have once said.

Then the knights parters of the field disarmed Sir Launcelot, first his head, and sithen his left arm, and his left side, and they bound his left arm behind his back, without shield or anything, and then they were put together. Wit you well there was many a lady and knight marvelled that Sir Launcelot would jeopardy himself in such wise. Then Sir Meliagrance came with his sword all on high, and Sir Launcelot showed him openly his bare head and the bare left side; and when he weened to have smitten him upon the bare head, then lightly he avoided the left leg and the left side, and put his right hand and his sword to that stroke, and so put it on side with great sleight; and then with great force Sir Launcelot smote him on the helmet such a buffet that the stroke carved the head in two parts. Then there was no more to do, but he was drawn out of the field. And at the great instance of the knights of the Table Round, the king suffered him to be interred, and the mention made upon him, who slew him, and for what cause he was slain; and then the king and the queen made more of Sir Launcelot du Lake, and more he was cherished, than ever he was aforehand.

HOW SIR URRE CAME INTO ARTHUR'S COURT FOR TO BE HEALED OF HIS WOUNDS BY THE BEST KNIGHT OF THE WORLD, AND HOW HE WAS HEALED BY SIR LAUNCELOT. Then as the French book maketh mention, there was a good knight in the land of Hungary, his name was Sir Urre, and he was an adventurous knight, and in all places where he might hear of any deeds of worship there would he be. So it happened in Spain there was an earl's son, his name was Alphegus, and at a great tournament in Spain this Sir Urre, knight of Hungary, and Sir Alphegus of Spain encountered together for very envy; and so either undertook other to the utterance. And by fortune Sir Urre slew Sir Alphegus, the earl's son of Spain; but this knight that was slain had given Sir Urre, or ever he was slain, seven great wounds, three on the head, and four on his body and upon his left hand. And this Sir Alphegus had a mother, the which was a great sorceress; and she, for the despite of her son's death, wrought by her subtle crafts that Sir Urre should never be whole, but ever his wounds should one time fester and another time bleed, so that he should never be whole until the best knight of the world had searched his wounds; and thus she made her avaunt, wherethrough it was known that Sir Urre should never be whole.

Then his mother let make an horse litter, and put him therein under two palfreys; and then she took Sir Urre's sister with him, a full fair damosel, whose name was Felelolie; and then she took a page with him to keep their horses, and so they led Sir Urre through many countries. For as the French book saith, she led him so seven year through all lands christened, and never she could find no knight that might ease her son. So she came into Scotland and into the lands of England, and by fortune she came nigh the feast of Pentecost until King Arthur's court, that at that time was holden at Carlisle. And when she came there, then she made it openly to be known how that she was come into that land for to heal her son.

Then King Arthur let call that lady, and asked her the cause why she brought that hurt knight into that land. My most noble king, said that lady, wit you well I brought him hither for to be healed of his wounds, that of all this seven year he might not be whole. And then she told the king where he was wounded, and of whom; and how his mother had made known in her pride how she had wrought that by enchantment, so that he should never be whole until the best knight of the world had searched his wounds. And so I have passed through all the lands christened to have him healed, except this land. And if I fail to heal him here in this land, I will never take more pain upon me, and that is pity, for he was a good knight, and of great nobleness. What is his name? said Arthur. My good and gracious lord, she said, his name is Sir Urre of the Mount. In good time, said the king, and sith ye are come into this land, ye are right welcome; and wit you well here shall your son be healed, an ever any Christian man may heal him. And for to give all other men of worship courage, I myself will assay to handle your son, and so shall all the kings, dukes, and earls that be here present with me at this time; thereto will I command them, and well I wot they shall obey and do after my commandment. And wit you well, said King Arthur unto Urre's sister, I shall begin to handle him, and search unto my power, not presuming upon me that I am so worthy to heal your son by my deeds, but I will courage other men of worship to do as I will do. And then the king commanded all the kings, dukes, and earls, and all noble knights of the Round Table that were there that time present, to come into the meadow of Carlisle. And so at that time there were but an hundred and ten of the Round Table, for forty knights were that time away. All these hundred knights and ten searched Sir Urre's wounds by the commandment of King Arthur.

Mercy, said King Arthur, where is Sir Launcelot du Lake that he is not here at this time? Thus, as they stood and spake of many things, there was espied Sir Launcelot that came riding toward them, and told the king. Peace, said the king, let no manner thing be said until he be come to us. So when Sir Launcelot espied King Arthur, he descended from his horse and came to the king, and saluted him and them all. Anon as the maid, Sir Urre's sister, saw Sir Launcelot, she ran to her brother thereas he lay in his litter, and said: Brother, here is come a knight that my heart giveth greatly unto. Fair sister, said Sir Urre, so doth my heart light against him, and certainly I hope now to be healed, for my heart giveth unto him more than to all these that have searched me.

Then said Arthur unto Sir Launcelot: Ye must do as we have done; and told Sir Launcelot what they had done, and showed him them all, that had searched him. Jesu defend me, said Sir Launcelot, when so many kings and knights have assayed and failed, that I should presume upon me to enchieve that all ye, my lords, might not enchieve. Ye shall not choose, said King Arthur, for I will command you for to do as we all have done. My most renowned lord, said Sir Launcelot, ye know well I dare not nor may not disobey your commandment, but an I might or durst, wit you well I would not take upon me to touch that wounded knight in that intent that I should pass all other knights; Jesu defend me from that shame. Ye take it wrong, said King Arthur, ye shall not do it for no presumption, but for to bear us fellowship, insomuch ye be a fellow of the Table Round; and wit you well, said King Arthur, an ye prevail not and heal him, I dare say there is no knight in this land may heal him, and therefore I pray you, do as we have done.

And then all the kings and knights for the most part prayed Sir Launcelot to search him; and then the wounded knight, Sir Urre, set him up weakly, and prayed Sir Launcelot heartily, saying: Courteous knight, I require thee for God's sake heal my wounds, for methinketh ever sithen ye came here my wounds grieve me not. Ah, my fair lord, said Sir Launcelot, Jesu would that I might help you; I shame me sore that I should be thus rebuked, for never was I able in worthiness to do so high a thing. Then Sir Launcelot kneeled down by the wounded knight saying: My lord Arthur, I must do your commandment, the which is sore against my heart. And then he held up his hands, and looked into the east, saying secretly unto himself: Thou blessed Father, Son, and Holy Ghost, I beseech thee of thy mercy, that my simple worship and honesty be saved, and thou blessed Trinity, thou mayst give power to heal this sick knight by thy great virtue and grace of thee, but, Good Lord, never of myself. And then Sir Launcelot prayed Sir Urre to let him see his head; and then devoutly kneeling he ransacked the three wounds, that they bled a little, and forthwith all the wounds fair healed, and seemed as they had been whole a seven year. And in likewise he searched his body of other three wounds, and they healed in likewise; and then the last of all he searched that which was in his hand, and anon it healed fair.

Then King Arthur and all the kings and knights kneeled down and gave thankings and lovings unto God and to His Blessed Mother. And ever Sir Launcelot wept as he had been a child that had been beaten. Then King Arthur let array priests and clerks in the most devoutest manner, to bring in Sir Urre within Carlisle, with singing and loving to God. And when this was done, the king let clothe him in the richest manner that could be thought; and then were there but few better made knights in all the court, for he was passingly well made and bigly; and Arthur asked Sir Urre how he felt himself. My good lord, he said, I felt myself never so lusty. Will ye joust and do deeds of arms? said King Arthur. Sir, said Urre, and I had all that longed unto jousts I would be soon ready.

Then Arthur made a party of hundred knights to be against an hundred knights. And so upon the morn they jousted for a diamond, but there jousted none of the dangerous knights; and so for to shorten this tale, Sir Urre and Sir Lavaine jousted best that day, for there was none of them but he overthrew and pulled down thirty knights; and then by the assent of all the kings and lords, Sir Urre and Sir Lavaine were made knights of the Table Round. And Sir Lavaine cast his love unto Dame Felelolie, Sir Urre's sister, and then they were wedded together with great joy, and King Arthur gave to everych of them a barony of lands. And this Sir Urre would never go from Sir Launcelot, but he and Sir Lavaine awaited evermore upon him; and they were in all the court accounted for good knights, and full desirous in arms; and many noble deeds they did, for they would have no rest, but ever sought adventures.

HOW SIR AGRAVAINE AND SIR MORDRED WERE BUSY UPON SIR GAWAINE FOR TO DISCLOSE THE LOVE BETWEEN SIR LAUNCELOT AND QUEEN GUENEVER.

In May when every lusty heart flourisheth and bourgeoneth — for as the season is lusty to behold and comfortable, so man and woman rejoice and gladden of summer coming with his fresh flowers: for winter with his rough winds and blasts causeth a lusty man and woman to cower, and sit fast by the fire — so in this season, as in the month of May, befell a great anger and unhap that stinted not till the flower of chivalry of all the world was destroyed and slain; and all was long upon two unhappy knights, the which were named Agravaine and Sir Mordred, that were brethren unto Sir Gawaine. For this Sir Agravaine and Sir Mordred had ever a privy hate unto the queen Dame Guenever and to Sir Launcelot, and daily and nightly they ever watched upon Sir Launcelot.

So it mishapped, Sir Gawaine and all his brethren were in King Arthur's chamber; and then Sir Agravaine said thus openly, and not in no counsel, that many knights might hear it: I marvel that we all be not ashamed both to see and to know how Sir Launcelot goeth with the queen, and all we know it so; and it is shamefully suffered of us all, that we all should suffer so noble a king as King Arthur is so to be shamed.

Then spake Sir Gawaine, and said: Brother Sir Agravaine, I pray you and charge you move no such matters no more afore me; for wit you well, said Sir Gawaine, I will not be of your counsel. So God me help, said Sir Gaheris and Sir Gareth, we will not be knowing, brother Agravaine, of your deeds. Then will I, said Sir Mordred. I lieve well that, said Sir Gawaine, for ever unto all unhappiness, brother Sir Mordred, thereto will ye grant; and I would that ye left all this, and made you not so busy, for I know, said Sir Gawaine, what will fall of it. Fall of it what fall may, said Sir Agravaine, I will disclose it to the king. Not by my counsel, said Sir Gawaine, for an there rise war and wrack betwixt Sir Launcelot and us, wit you well brother, there will many kings and great lords hold with Sir Launcelot. Also, brother Sir Agravaine, said Sir Gawaine, ye must remember how ofttimes Sir Launcelot hath rescued the king and the queen; and the best of us all had been full cold at the heart-root had not Sir Launcelot been better than we, and that hath he proved himself full oft. And as for my part, said Sir Gawaine, I will never be against Sir Launcelot for one day's deed, when he rescued me from King Carados of the Dolorous Tower, and slew him, and saved my life. Also, brother Sir Agravaine and Sir Mordred, in like wise Sir Launcelot rescued you both, and threescore and two, from Sir Turquin. Methinketh brother, such kind deeds and kindness should be remembered. Do as ye list, said Sir Agravaine, for I will hide it no longer. With these words came to them King Arthur. Now, brother, stint your noise, said Sir Gawaine. We will not, said Sir Agravaine and Sir Mordred. Will ye so? said Sir Gawaine; then God speed you, for I will not hear your tales ne be of your counsel. No more will I, said Sir Gareth and Sir Gaheris, for we will never say evil by that man; for because, said Sir Gareth, Sir Launcelot made me knight, by no manner owe I to say ill of him. And therewithal they three departed, making great dole. Alas, said Sir Gawaine and Sir Gareth, now is this realm wholly mischieved, and the noble fellowship of the Round Table shall be disparpled: so they departed.

And then Sir Arthur asked them what noise they made. My lord, said Agravaine, I shall tell you that I may keep no longer. Here is I, and my brother Sir Mordred, brake unto my brothers Sir Gawaine, Sir Gaheris, and to Sir Gareth, how this we know all, that Sir Launcelot holdeth your queen, and hath done long; and we be your sister's sons, and we may suffer it no longer, and all we wot that ye should be above Sir Launcelot; and ye are the king that made him knight, and therefore we will prove it, that he is a traitor to your person.

If it be so, said Sir Arthur, wit you well he is none other, but I would be loath to begin such a thing but I might have proofs upon it; for Sir Launcelot is an hardy knight, and all ye know he is the best knight among us all; and but if he be taken with the deed, he will fight with him that bringeth up the noise, and I know no knight that is able to match him. Therefore an it be sooth as ye say, I would he were taken with the deed. For as the French book saith, the king was full loath thereto, that any noise should be upon Sir Launcelot and his queen; for the king had a deeming, but he would not hear of it, for Sir Launcelot had done so much for him and the queen so many times, that wit ye well the king loved him passingly well. My lord, said Sir Agravaine, ye shall ride to-morn a-hunting, and doubt ye not Sir Launcelot will not go with you. Then when it draweth toward night, ye may send the queen word that ye will lie out all that night, and so may ye send for your cooks, and then upon pain of death we shall take him that night with the queen, and outher we shall bring him to you dead or quick. I will well, said the king; then I counsel you, said the king, take with you sure fellowship. Sir, said Agravaine, my brother, Sir Mordred, and I, will take with us twelve knights of the Round Table. Beware, said King Arthur, for I warn you ye shall find him wight. Let us deal, said Sir Agravaine and Sir Mordred.

So on the morn King Arthur rode a-hunting, and sent word to the queen that he would be out all that night. Then Sir Agravaine and Sir Mordred gat to them twelve knights, and hid themself in a chamber in the Castle of Carlisle, and these were their names: Sir Colgrevance, Sir Mador de la Porte, Sir Gingaline, Sir Meliot de Logris, Sir Petipase of Winchelsea, Sir Galleron of Galway, Sir Melion of the Mountain, Sir Astamore, Sir Gromore Somir Joure, Sir Curselaine, Sir Florence, Sir Lovel. So these twelve knights were with Sir Mordred and Sir Agravaine, and all they were of Scotland, outher of Sir Gawaine's kin, either well-willers to his brethren.

So when the night came, Sir Launcelot told Sir Bors how he would go that night and speak with the queen. Sir, said Sir Bors, ye shall not go this night by my counsel. Why? said Sir Launcelot. Sir, said Sir Bors, I dread me ever of Sir Agravaine, that waiteth you daily to do you shame and us all; and never gave my heart against no going, that ever ye went to the queen, so much as now; for I mistrust that the king is out this night from the queen because peradventure he hath lain some watch for you and the queen, and therefore I dread me sore of treason. Have ye no dread, said Sir Launcelot, for I shall go and come again, and make no tarrying. Sir, said Sir Bors, that me repenteth, for I dread me sore that your going out this night shall wrath us all. Fair nephew, said Sir Launcelot, I marvel much why ye say thus, sithen the queen hath sent for me; and wit ye well I will not be so much a coward, but she shall understand I will see her good grace. God speed you well, said Sir Bors, and send you sound and safe again.

HOW SIR LAUNCELOT WAS ESPIED IN THE QUEEN'S CHAMBER, AND HOW SIR AGRAVAINE AND SIR MORDRED CAME WITH TWELVE KNIGHTS TO SLAY HIM. So Sir Launcelot departed, and took his sword under his arm, and so in his mantle that noble knight put himself in great jeopardy; and so he passed till he came to the queen's chamber. And then, as the French book saith, there came Sir Agravaine and Sir Mordred, with twelve knights with them of the Round Table, and they said with crying voice: Traitor-knight, Sir Launcelot du Lake, now art thou taken. And thus they cried with a loud voice, that all the court might hear it; and they all fourteen were armed at all points as they should fight in a battle. Alas, said Queen Guenever, now are we mischieved both. Madam, said Sir Launcelot, is there here any armour within your chamber, that I might cover my poor body withal? An if there be any give it me, and I shall soon stint their malice, by the grace of God. Truly, said the queen, I have none armour, shield, sword, nor spear; wherefore I dread me sore our long love is come to a mischievous end, for I hear by their noise there be many noble knights, and well I wot they be surely armed; against them ye may make no resistance. Wherefore ye are likely to be slain, and then shall I be brent. For an ye might escape them, said the queen, I would not doubt but that ye would rescue me in what danger that ever I stood in. Alas, said Sir Launcelot, in all my life thus was I never bestead, that I should be thus shamefully slain for lack of mine armour.

But ever in one Sir Agravaine and Sir Mordred cried: Traitor-knight, come out of the queen's chamber, for wit thou well thou art so beset that thou shalt not escape. O Jesu mercy, said Sir Launcelot, this shameful cry and noise I may not suffer, for better were death at once than thus to endure this pain. Then he took the queen in his arms, and kissed her, and said: Most noble Christian queen, I beseech you as ye have been ever my special good lady, and I at all times your true poor knight unto my power, and as I never failed you in right nor in wrong sithen the first day King Arthur made me knight, that ye will pray for my soul if that I here be slain; for well I am assured that Sir Bors, my nephew, and all the remnant of my kin, with Sir Lavaine and Sir Urre, that they will not fail you to rescue you from the fire; and therefore, mine own lady, recomfort yourself, whatsomever come of me, that ye go with Sir Bors, my nephew, and Sir Urre, and they all will do you all the pleasure that they can or may, that ye shall live like a queen upon my lands. Nay, Launcelot, said the queen, wit thou well I will never live after thy days, but an thou be slain I will take my death as meekly for Jesu Christ's sake as ever did any Christian queen. Well, madam, said Launcelot, sith it is so that the day is come that our love must depart, wit you well I shall sell my life as dear as I may; and a thousandfold, said Sir Launcelot, I am more heavier for you than for myself. And now I had liefer than to be lord of all Christendom, that I had sure armour upon me, that men might speak of my deeds or ever I were slain. Truly, said the queen, I would an it might please God that they would take me and slay me, and suffer you to escape. That shall never be, said Sir Launcelot, God defend me from such a shame, but Jesu be Thou my shield and mine armour!

And therewith Sir Launcelot wrapped his mantle about his arm well and surely; and by then they had gotten a great form out of the hall, and therewithal they rashed at the door. Fair lords, said Sir Launcelot, leave your noise and your rashing, and I shall set open this door, and then may ye do with me what it liketh you. Come off then, said they all, and do it, for it availeth thee not to strive against us all; and therefore let us into this chamber, and we shall save thy life until thou come to King Arthur. Then Launcelot unbarred the door, and with his left hand he held it open a little, so that but one man might come in at once; and so there came striding a good knight, a much man and large, and his name was Colgrevance of Gore, and he with a sword struck at Sir Launcelot mightily; and he put aside the stroke, and gave him such a buffet upon the helmet, that he fell grovelling dead within the chamber door. And then Sir Launcelot with great might drew that dead knight within the chamber door; and Sir Launcelot with help of the queen and her ladies was lightly armed in Sir Colgrevance's armour.

And ever stood Sir Agravaine and Sir Mordred crying: Traitor-knight, come out of the queen's chamber. Leave your noise, said Sir Launcelot unto Sir Agravaine, for wit you well, Sir Agravaine, ye shall not prison me this night; and therefore an ye do by my counsel, go ye all from this chamber door, and make not such crying and such manner of slander as ye do; for I promise you by my knighthood, an ye will depart and make no more noise, I shall as to-morn appear afore you all before the king, and then let it be seen which of you all, outher else ye all, that will accuse me of treason; and there I shall answer you as a knight should, that hither I came to the queen for no manner of mal engin, and that will I prove and make it good upon you with my hands. Fie on thee, traitor, said Sir Agravaine and Sir Mordred, we will have thee maugre thy head, and slay thee if we list; for we let thee wit we have the choice of King Arthur, to save thee or to slay thee. Ah sirs, said Sir Launcelot, is there none other grace with you? then keep yourselves.

So then Sir Launcelot set all open the chamber door, and mightily and knightly he strode in amongst them; and anon at the first buffet he slew Sir Agravaine. And twelve of his fellows, within a little while after, he laid them cold to the earth, for there was none of the twelve that might stand Sir Launcelot one buffet. Also Sir Launcelot wounded Sir Mordred, and he fled with all his might. And then Sir Launcelot returned again unto the queen, and said: Madam, now wit you well all our true love is brought to an end, for now will King Arthur ever be my foe; and therefore, madam, an it like you that I may have you with me, I shall save you from all manner adventures dangerous. That is not best, said the queen; meseemeth now ye have done so much harm, it will be best ye hold you still with this. And if ye see that as to-morn they will put me unto the death, then may ye rescue me as ye think best. I will well, said Sir Launcelot, for have ye no doubt, while I am living I shall rescue you. And then he kissed her, and either gave other a ring; and so there he left the queen, and went until his lodging.

OF THE COUNSEL AND ADVICE THAT WAS TAKEN BY SIR LAUNCELOT AND HIS FRIENDS FOR TO SAVE THE QUEEN. When Sir Bors saw Sir Launcelot he was never so glad of his home-coming as he was then. Mercy, said Sir Launcelot, why be ye all armed: what meaneth this? Sir, said Sir Bors, after ye were departed from us, we all that be of your blood and your well-willers were so dretched that some of us leapt out of our beds naked, and some in their dreams caught naked swords in their hands; therefore, said Sir Bors, we deem there is some great strife at hand; and then we all deemed that ye were betrapped with some treason, and therefore we made us thus ready, what need that ever ye were in.

My fair nephew, said Sir Launcelot unto Sir Bors, now shall ye wit all, that this night I was more harder bestead than ever I was in my life, and yet I escaped. And so he told them all how and in what manner, as ye have heard to-fore. And therefore, my fellows, said Sir Launcelot, I pray you all that ye will be of good heart in what need somever I stand, for now is war come to us all. Sir, said Bors, all is welcome that God sendeth us, and we have had much weal with you and much worship, and therefore we will take the woe with you as we have taken the weal. And therefore, they said all (there were many good knights), look ye take no discomfort, for there nis no bands of knights under heaven but we shall be able to grieve them as much as they may us. And therefore discomfort not yourself by no manner, and we shall gather together that we love, and that loveth us, and what that ye will have done shall be done. And therefore, Sir Launcelot, said they, we will take the woe with the weal. Gramercy, said Sir Launcelot, of your good comfort, for in my great distress, my fair nephew, ye comfort me greatly, and much I am beholding unto you. But this, my fair nephew, I would that ye did in all haste that ye may, or it be forth-days, that ye will look in their lodging that be lodged here nigh about the king, which will hold with me, and which will not, for now I would know which were my friends from my foes. Sir, said Sir Bors, I shall do my pain, and or it be seven of the clock I shall wit of such as ye have said before, who will hold with you.

Then Sir Bors called unto him Sir Lionel, Sir Ector de Maris, Sir Blamore de Ganis, Sir Bleoberis de Ganis, Sir Gahalantine, Sir Galihodin, Sir Galihud, Sir Menadeuke, Sir Villiers the Valiant, Sir Hebes le Renoumes, Sir Lavaine, Sir Urre of Hungary, Sir Nerounes, Sir Plenorius. These two knights Sir Launcelot made, and the one he won upon a bridge, and therefore they would never be against him. And Harry le Fise du Lake, and Sir Selises of the Dolorous Tower, and Sir Melias de Lile, and Sir Bellangere le Beuse, that was Sir Alisander's son Le Orphelin, because his mother Alice le Beale Pellerin was kin unto Sir Launcelot, he held with him. So there came Sir Palomides and Sir Safere, his brother, to hold with Sir Launcelot, and Sir Clegis of Sadok, and Sir Dinas, Sir Clarius of Cleremont. So these two-and-twenty knights drew them together, and by then they were armed on horseback, and promised Sir Launcelot to do what he would. Then there fell to them, what of North Wales and of Cornwall, for Sir Lamorak's sake and for Sir Tristram's sake, to the number of a fourscore knights.

My lords, said Sir Launcelot, wit you well, I have been ever since I came into this country well willed unto my lord, King Arthur, and unto my lady, Queen Guenever, unto my power; and this night because my lady the queen sent for me to speak with her, I suppose it was made by treason, howbeit I dare largely excuse her person, notwithstanding I was there by a forecast near slain, but as Jesu provided me I escaped all their malice and treason. And then that noble knight Sir Launcelot told them all how he was hard bestead in the queen's chamber, and how and in what manner he escaped from them. And therefore, said Sir Launcelot, wit you well, my fair lords, I am sure there nis but war unto me and mine. And for because I have slain this night these knights, I wot well as is Sir Agravaine Sir Gawaine's brother, and at the least twelve of his fellows, for this cause now I am sure of mortal war, for these knights were sent and ordained by King Arthur to betray me. And therefore the king will in his heat and malice judge the queen to the fire, and that may I not suffer, that she should be brent for my sake; for an I may be heard and suffered and so taken, I will fight for the queen, that she is a true lady unto her lord; but the king in his heat, I dread me, will not take me as I ought to be taken.

My lord, Sir Launcelot, said Sir Bors, by mine advice ye shall take the woe with the weal, and take it in patience, and thank God of it. And sithen it is fallen as it is, I counsel you keep yourself, for an ye will yourself, there is no fellowship of knights christened that shall do you wrong. Also I will counsel you my lord, Sir Launcelot, than an my lady, Queen Guenever, be in distress, insomuch as she is in pain for your sake, that ye knightly rescue her; an ye did otherwise, all the world will speak of you shame to the world's end. Insomuch as ye were taken with her, whether ye did right or wrong, it is now your part to hold with the queen, that she be not slain and put to a mischievous death; for an she so die the shame shall be yours. Jesu defend me from shame, said Sir Launcelot, and keep and save my lady the queen from villainy and shameful death, and that she never be destroyed in my default; wherefore my fair lords, my kin, and my friends, said Sir Launcelot, what will ye do? Then they said all: We will do as ye will do. I put this to you, said Sir Launcelot, that if my lord Arthur by evil counsel will to-morn in his heat put my lady the queen to the fire there to be brent, now I pray you counsel me what is best to do. Then they said all at once with one voice: Sir, us thinketh best that ye knightly rescue the queen; insomuch as she shall be brent it is for your sake, and it is to suppose, and ye might be handled, ye should have the same death, or a more shamefuller death. And sir, we say all, that ye have many times rescued her from death for other men's quarrels, us seemeth it is more your worship that ye rescue the queen from this peril, insomuch she hath it for your sake.

Then Sir Launcelot stood still, and said: My fair lords, wit you well I would be loath to do that thing that should dishonour you or my blood, and wit you well I would be loath that my lady, the queen, should die a shameful death; but an it be so that ye will counsel me to rescue her, I must do much harm ere I rescue her; and peradventure I shall there destroy some of my best friends, that should much repent me; and peradventure there be some, an they could well bring it about, or disobey my lord King Arthur, they would soon come to me, the which I were loath to hurt. And if so be that I rescue her, where shall I keep her? That shall be the least care of us all, said Sir Bors. How did the noble knight Sir Tristram, by your good will? kept not he with him La Beale Isoud near three year in Joyous Gard? and that same place is your own; and in like wise may ye do an ye list, and take the queen lightly away, if it so be the king will judge her to be brent; and in Joyous Gard ye may keep her long enough until the heat of the king be past. And then shall ye bring again the queen to the king with great worship; and then peradventure ye shall have thank for her bringing home, and love and thank where other shall have maugre.

That is hard to do, said Sir Launcelot, for by Sir Tristram I may have a warning; for when by means of treaties, Sir Tristram brought again La Beale Isoud unto King Mark from Joyous Gard, look what befell on the end, how shamefully that false traitor King Mark slew him as he sat harping afore his lady La Beale Isoud, with a grounden glaive he thrust him in behind to the heart. It grieveth me, said Sir Launcelot, to speak of his death, for all the world may not find such a knight. All this is truth, said Sir Bors, but there is one thing shall courage you and us all, ye know well King Arthur and King Mark were never like of conditions, for there was never yet man could prove King Arthur untrue of his promise.

So to make short tale, they were all consented that for better or for worse, if so were that the queen were on that morn brought to the fire, shortly they all would rescue her.

And so by the advice of Sir Launcelot, they put them all in an embushment in a wood, as nigh Carlisle as they might, and there they abode still, to wit what the king would do.

HOW SIR LAUNCELOT AND HIS KINSMEN RESCUED THE QUEEN FROM THE FIRE, AND HOW HE SLEW MANY KNIGHTS, AND OF THE SORROW OF KING ARTHUR.

Now turn we again unto Sir Mordred, that when he was escaped from the noble knight, Sir Launcelot, he anon gat his horse and mounted upon him, and rode unto King Arthur, sore wounded and smitten, and all forbled; and there he told the king all how it was, and how they were all slain save himself all only. Jesu mercy, how may this be? said the king; took ye him in the queen's chamber? Yea, so God me help, said Sir Mordred, there we found him unarmed, and there he slew Colgrevance, and armed him in his armour; and all this he told the king from the beginning to the ending. Jesu mercy, said the king, he is a marvellous knight of prowess. Alas, me sore repenteth, said the king, that ever Sir Launcelot should be against me. Now I am sure the noble fellowship of the Round Table is broken for ever, for with him will many a noble knight hold; and now it is fallen so, said the king, that I may not with my worship, but the queen must suffer the death. So then there was made great ordinance in this heat, that the queen must be judged to the death. And the law was such in those days that whatsomever they were, of what estate or degree, if they were found guilty of treason, there should be none other remedy but death; and outher the men or the taking with the deed should be causer of their hasty judgment. And right so was it ordained for Queen Guenever, because Sir Mordred was escaped sore wounded, and the death of thirteen knights of the Round Table. These proofs and experiences caused King Arthur to command the queen to the fire there to be brent.

Then spake Sir Gawaine, and said: My lord Arthur, I would counsel you not to be over-hasty, but that ye would put it in respite, this judgment of my lady the queen, for many causes. One it is, though it were so that Sir Launcelot were found in the queen's chamber, yet it might be so that he came thither for none evil; for ye know my lord, said Sir Gawaine, that the queen is much beholden unto Sir Launcelot, more than unto any other knight, for ofttimes he hath saved her life, and done battle for her when all the court refused the queen; and peradventure she sent for him for goodness and for none evil, to reward him for his good deeds that he had done to her in times past. And peradventure my lady, the queen, sent for him to that intent that Sir Launcelot should come to her good grace privily and secretly, weening to her that it was best so to do, in eschewing and dreading of slander; for ofttimes we do many things that we ween it be for the best, and yet peradventure it turneth to the worst. For I dare say, said Sir Gawaine, my lady, your queen, is to you both good and true; and as for Sir Launcelot, said Sir Gawaine, I dare say he will make it good upon any knight living that will put upon himself villainy or shame, and in like wise he will make good for my lady, Dame Guenever.

That I believe well, said King Arthur, but I will not that way with Sir Launcelot, for he trusteth so much upon his hands and his might that he doubteth no man; and therefore for my queen he shall never fight more, for she shall have the law. And if I may get Sir Launcelot, wit you well he shall have a shameful death. Jesu defend, said Sir Gawaine, that I may never see it. Why say ye so? said King Arthur; forsooth ye have no cause to love Sir Launcelot, for this night last past he slew your brother, Sir Agravaine, a full good knight, and almost he had slain your other brother, Sir Mordred, and also there he slew thirteen noble knights; and also, Sir Gawaine, remember ye he slew two sons of yours, Sir Florence and Sir Lovel. My lord, said Sir Gawaine, of all this I have knowledge, of whose deaths I repent me sore; but insomuch I gave them warning, and told my brethren and my sons aforehand what would fall in the end, insomuch they would not do by my counsel, I will not meddle me thereof, nor revenge me nothing of their deaths; for I told them it was no bote to strive with Sir Launcelot. Howbeit I am sorry of the death of my brethren and of my sons, for they are the causers of their own death; for ofttimes I warned my brother Sir Agravaine, and I told him the perils the which be now fallen.

Then said the noble King Arthur to Sir Gawaine: Dear nephew, I pray you make you ready in your best armour, with your brethren, Sir Gaheris and Sir Gareth, to bring my queen to the fire, there to have her judgment and receive the death. Nay, my most noble lord, said Sir Gawaine, that will I never do; for wit you well I will never be in that place where so noble a queen as is my lady, Dame Guenever, shall take a shameful end. For wit you well, said Sir Gawaine, my heart will never serve me to see her die; and it shall never be said that ever I was of your counsel of her death.

Then said the king to Sir Gawaine: Suffer your brothers

Sir Gaheris and Sir Gareth to be there. My lord, said Sir Gawaine, wit you well they will be loath to be there present, because of many adventures the which be like there to fall, but they are young and full unable to say you nay. Then spake Sir Gaheris, and the good knight Sir Gareth, unto Sir Arthur: Sir, ye may well command us to be there, but wit you well it shall be sore against our will; but an we be there by your strait commandment ye shall plainly hold us there excused: we will be there in peaceable wise, and bear none harness of war upon us. In the name of God, said the king, then make you ready, for she shall soon have her judgment anon. Alas, said Sir Gawaine, that ever I should endure to see this woful day. So Sir Gawaine turned him and wept heartily, and so he went into his chamber; and then the queen was led forth without Carlisle, and there she was despoiled into her smock. And so then her ghostly father was brought to her, to be shriven of her misdeeds. Then was there weeping, and wailing, and wringing of hands, of many lords and ladies, but there were but few in comparison that would bear any armour for to strength the death of the queen.

Then was there one that Sir Launcelot had sent unto that place for to espy what time the queen should go unto her death; and anon as he saw the queen despoiled into her smock, and so shriven, then he gave Sir Launcelot warning. Then was there but spurring and plucking up of horses, and right so they came to the fire. And who that stood against them, there were they slain; there might none withstand Sir Launcelot, so all that bare arms and withstood them, there were they slain, full many a noble knight. For there was slain Sir Belliance le Orgulous, Sir Segwarides,

Sir Griflet, Sir Brandiles, Sir Aglovale, Sir Tor; Sir Gauter, Sir Gillimer, Sir Reynolds' three brethren; Sir Damas, Sir Priamus, Sir Kay the Stranger, Sir Driant, Sir Lambegus, Sir Herminde; Sir Pertilope, Sir Perimones, two brethren that were called the Green Knight and the Red Knight. And so in this rashing and hurling, as Sir Launcelot thrang here and there, it mishapped him to slay Gaheris and Sir Gareth, the noble knight, for they were unarmed and unware. For as the French book saith, Sir Launcelot smote Sir Gareth and Sir Gaheris upon the brain-pans, where-through they were slain in the field; howbeit in very truth Sir Launcelot saw them not, and so were they found dead among the thickest of the press.

Then when Sir Launcelot had thus done, and slain and put to flight all that would withstand him, then he rode straight unto Dame Guenever, and made a kirtle and a gown to be cast upon her; and then he made her to be set behind him, and prayed her to be of good cheer. Wit you well the queen was glad that she was escaped from the death; and then she thanked God and Sir Launcelot. And so he rode his way with the queen, as the French book saith, unto Joyous Gard, and there he kept her as a noble knight should do; and many great lords and some kings sent Sir Launcelot many good knights, and many noble knights drew unto Sir Launcelot. When this was known openly, that King Arthur and Sir Launcelot were at debate, many knights were glad of their debate, and many were full heavy of their debate.

HOW KING ARTHUR AT THE REQUEST OF SIR GAWAINE CONCLUDED TO MAKE WAR AGAINST SIR LAUNCELOT, AND LAID SIEGE TO HIS CASTLE CALLED JOYOUS GARD.

So turn we again unto King Arthur, that when it was told him how and in what manner of wise the queen was taken away from the fire, and when he heard of the death of his noble knights, and in especial of Sir Gaheris and Sir Gareth's death, then the king swooned for pure sorrow. And when he awoke of his swoon, then he said: Alas, that ever I bare crown upon my head! for now have I lost the fairest fellowship of noble knights that ever Christian king held together. Alas, my good knights be slain away from me: now within these two days I have lost forty knights, and also the noble fellowship of Sir Launcelot and his blood, for now I may never hold them together no more with my worship. Alas that ever this war began. Now fair fellows, said the king; I charge you that no man tell Sir Gawaine of the death of his two brethren; for I am sure, said the king, when Sir Gawaine heareth tell that Sir Gareth is dead he will go nigh out of his mind. Mercy Jesu, said the king, why slew he Sir Gareth and Sir Gaheris, for I dare say as for Sir Gareth he loved Sir Launcelot above all men earthly. That is truth, said some knights, but they were slain in the hurtling as Sir Launcelot thrang in the thick of the press; and as they were unarmed he smote them and wist not whom that he smote, and so unhappily they were slain. The death of them, said Arthur, will cause the greatest mortal war that ever was; I am sure, wist Sir Gawaine that Sir Gareth were slain, I should never have rest of him till I had destroyed

Sir Launcelot's kin and himself both, or else he to destroy me. And therefore, said the king, wit you well my heart was never so heavy as it is now, and much more I am sorrier for my good knights' loss than for the loss of my fair queen; for queens I might have enow, but such a fellowship of good knights shall never be together in no company. And now I dare say, said King Arthur, there was never Christian king held such a fellowship together; and alas that ever Sir Launcelot and I should be at debate. Ah Agravaine, Agravaine, said the king, Jesu forgive it thy soul, for thine evil will, that thou, and thy brother Sir Mordred, hadst unto Sir Launcelot, hath caused all this sorrow: and ever among these complaints the king wept and swooned.

Then there came one unto Sir Gawaine, and told him how the queen was led away with Sir Launcelot, and nigh a twenty-four knights slain. O Jesu defend my brethren, said Sir Gawaine, for full well wist I that Sir Launcelot would rescue her, outher else he would die in that field; and to say the truth he had not been a man of worship had he not rescued the queen that day, insomuch she should have been brent for his sake. And as in that, said Sir Gawaine, he hath done but knightly, and as I would have done myself an I had stood in like case. But where are my brethren? said Sir Gawaine, I marvel I hear not of them. Truly, said that man, Sir Gareth and Sir Gaheris be slain. Jesu defend, said Sir Gawaine, for all the world I would not that they were slain, and in especial my good brother, Sir Gareth. Sir, said the man, he is slain, and that is great pity. Who slew him? said Sir Gawaine. Sir, said the man, Launcelot slew them both. That may I not believe, said Sir Gawaine, that ever he slew my brother, Sir Gareth; for I dare say my brother Gareth loved him better than me, and all his brethren, and the king both. Also I dare say, an Sir Launcelot had desired my brother, Sir Gareth, with him he would have been with him against the king and us all, and therefore I may never believe that Sir Launcelot slew my brother. Sir, said this man, it is noised that he slew him.

Alas, said Sir Gawaine, now is my joy gone. And then he fell down and swooned, and long he lay there as he had been dead. And then, when he arose of his swoon, he cried out sorrowfully, and said: Alas! And right so Sir Gawaine ran to the king, crying and weeping: O King Arthur, mine uncle, my good brother Sir Gareth is slain, and so is my brother Sir Gaheris, the which were two noble knights. Then the king wept, and he both; and so they fell a-swooning. And when they were revived then spake Sir Gawaine: Sir, I will go see my brother, Sir Gareth. Ye may not see him, said the king, for I caused him to be interred, and Sir Gaheris both; for I well understood that ye would make over-much sorrow, and the sight of Sir Gareth should have caused your double sorrow. Alas, my lord, said Sir Gawaine, how slew he my brother, Sir Gareth? Mine own good lord I pray you tell me. Truly, said the king, I shall tell you how it is told me, Sir Launcelot slew him and Sir Gaheris both. Alas, said Sir Gawaine, they bare none arms against him, neither of them both. I wot not how it was, said the king, but as it is said, Sir Launcelot slew them both in the thickest of the press and knew them not; and therefore let us shape a remedy for to revenge their deaths.

My king, my lord, and mine uncle, said Sir Gawaine, wit you well now I shall make you a promise that I shall hold by my knighthood, that from this day I shall never fail Sir Launcelot, until the one of us have slain the other. And therefore I require you, my lord and king, dress you to the war, for wit you well I will be revenged upon Sir Launcelot; and therefore, as ye will have my service and my love, now haste you thereto, and assay your friends. For I promise unto God, said Sir Gawaine, for the death of my brother, Sir Gareth, I shall seek Sir Launcelot throughout seven kings' realms, but I shall slay him or else he shall slay me. Ye shall not need to seek him so far, said the king, for as I hear say, Sir Launcelot will abide me and you in the Joyous Gard; and much people draweth unto him, as I hear say. That may I believe, said Sir Gawaine; but my lord, he said, assay your friends, and I will assay mine. It shall be done, said the king, and as I suppose I shall be big enough to draw him out of the biggest tower of his castle.

So then the king sent letters and waits throughout all England, both in the length and the breadth, for to assummon all his knights. Thereof heard Sir Launcelot, and purveyed him of many good knights, for with him held many knights, and some for his own sake, and some for the queen's sake. Then came King Arthur with Sir Gawaine with an huge host, and laid a siege all about Joyous Gard, both at the town and at the castle, and there they made strong war on both parties. But in no wise Sir Launcelot would ride out, nor go out of his castle, of long time; neither he would none of his good knights to issue out, neither none of the town nor of the castle, until fifteen weeks were past.

Then it befell upon a day in harvest time, Sir Launcelot looked over the walls, and spake on high unto King Arthur and Sir Gawaine: My lords both, wit ye well all is in vain that ye make at this siege, for here win ye no worship but maugre and dishonour; for an it list me to come myself out and my good knights, I should full soon make an end of this war. Come forth, said Arthur unto Launcelot, an thou durst, and I promise thee I shall meet thee in midst of the field. God defend me, said Sir Launcelot, that ever I should encounter with the most noble king that made me knight. Fie upon thy fair language, said the king, for wit you well and trust it, I am thy mortal foe, and ever will to my death day; for thou hast slain my good knights, and full noble men of my blood, that I shall never recover again. Also thou hast dishonoured my queen, and holden her many winters, and sithen like a traitor taken her from me by force.

My most noble lord and king, said Sir Launcelot, ye may say what ye will, for ye wot well with yourself will I not strive; but thereas ye say I have slain your good knights, I wot well that I have done so, and that me sore repenteth; but I was enforced to do battle with them in saving of my life, or else I must have suffered them to have slain me. And as for my lady, Queen Guenever, except your person of your highness, and my lord Sir Gawaine, there is no knight under heaven that dare make it good upon me, that ever I was a traitor unto your person. And where it please you to say that I have holden my lady your queen many winters, unto that I shall ever make a large answer, and prove it upon any knight that beareth the life, except your person and Sir Gawaine, that my lady, Queen Guenever, is a true lady unto your person as any is living unto her lord, and that will I make good with my hands. Howbeit it hath like her good grace to have me in chierté, and to cherish me more than any other knight; and unto my power I again have deserved her love, for ofttimes, my lord, ye have consented that she should be brent and destroyed, in your heat, and then it fortuned me to do battle for her, and ere I departed from her adversary they confessed their untruth, and she full worshipfully excused. And at such times, my lord Arthur, said Sir Launcelot, ye loved me, and thanked me when I saved your queen from the fire; and then ye promised me for ever to be my good lord; and now methinketh ye reward me full ill for my good service. And my good lord, meseemeth I had lost a great part of my worship in my knighthood an I had suffered my lady, your queen, to have been brent, and insomuch she should have been brent for my sake. For sithen I have done battles for your queen in other quarrels than in mine own, meseemeth now I had more right to do battle for her in right quarrel. And therefore my good and gracious lord, said Sir Launcelot, take your queen unto your good grace, for she is both fair, true, and good.

Fie on thee, false recreant knight, said Sir Gawaine; I let thee wit my lord, mine uncle, King Arthur, shall have his queen and thee, maugre thy visage, and slay you both whether it please him. It may well be, said Sir Launcelot, but wit you well, my lord Sir Gawaine, an me list to come out of this castle ye should win me and the queen more harder than ever ye won a strong battle. Fie on thy proud words, said Sir Gawaine; as for my lady, the queen, I will never say of her shame. But thou, false and recreant knight, said Sir Gawaine, what cause hadst thou to slay my good brother Sir Gareth, that loved thee more than all my kin? Alas, thou madest him knight thine own hands; why slew thou him that loved thee so well? For to excuse me, said Sir Launcelot, it helpeth me not, but by the faith that I owe to the high order of knighthood, I should with as good will have slain my nephew, Sir Bors de Ganis, at that time. But alas that ever I was so unhappy, said Launcelot, that I had not seen Sir Gareth and Sir Gaheris.

Thou liest, recreant knight, said Sir Gawaine, thou slewest him in despite of me; and therefore, wit thou well I shall make war to thee, and all the while that I may live. And then Sir Gawaine made many men to blow upon Sir Launcelot; and all at once they called him false recreant knight.

Then when Sir Bors de Ganis, Sir Ector de Maris, and Sir Lionel heard this outcry, they called to them Sir Palomides, Sir Safere's brother, and Sir Lavaine, with many more of their blood, and all they went unto Sir Launcelot, and said thus: My lord Sir Launcelot, wit ye well we have great scorn of the great rebukes that we heard Gawaine say to you; wherefore we pray you, and charge you as ye will have our service, keep us no longer within these walls; for wit you well plainly, we will ride into the field and do battle with them; for ye fare as a man that were afeard, and for all your fair speech it will not avail you. For wit you well Sir Gawaine will not suffer you to be accorded with King Arthur, and therefore fight for your life and your right, an ye dare.

Then either party made them ready on the morn for to do battle, and great purveyance was made on both sides; and Sir Gawaine let purvey many knights for to wait upon Sir Launcelot, for to overset him and to slay him. And on the morn at underne Sir Arthur was ready in the field with three great hosts. And then Sir Launcelot's fellowship came out at three gates, in a full good array; and Sir Lionel came in the foremost battle, and Sir Launcelot came in the middle, and Sir Bors came out at the third gate. Thus they came in order and rule, as full noble knights; and always Sir Launcelot charged all his knights in any wise to save King Arthur and Sir Gawaine.

Then came forth Sir Gawaine from the king's host, and he came before and proffered to joust. And Sir Lionel was a fierce knight, and lightly he encountered with Sir Gawaine; and there Sir Gawaine smote Sir Lionel throughout the body, that he dashed to the earth like as he had been dead; and then Sir Ector de Maris and other more bare him into the castle. Then there began a great stour, and much people was slain; and ever King Arthur was nigh about Sir Launcelot to have slain him, and Sir Launcelot suffered him, and would not strike again. So Sir Bors encountered with King Arthur, and there with a spear Sir Bors smote him down; and so he alighted and drew his sword, and said to Sir Launcelot: Shall I make an end of this war? and that he meant to have slain King Arthur. Not so hardy, said Sir Launcelot, upon pain of thy head, that thou touch him no more, for I will never see that most noble king that made me knight neither slain ne shamed. And therewithal Sir Launcelot alighted off his horse and took up the king and horsed him again, and said thus: My lord Arthur, for God's love stint this strife, for ye get here no worship, an I would do mine utterance; but always I forbear you, and ye nor none of yours forbeareth me. My lord, remember what I have done in many places, and now I am evil rewarded.

Then when King Arthur was on horseback, he looked upon Sir Launcelot, and then the tears brast out of his eyen, thinking on the great courtesy that was in Sir Launcelot more than in any other man; and therewith the king rode his way, and might no longer behold him, and said: Alas, that ever this war began. And then either parties of the battles withdrew them to repose them, and buried the dead, and to the wounded men they laid soft salves; and thus they endured that night till on the morn. And on the morn by underne they made them ready to do battle. And then Sir Bors led the forward.

So upon the morn there came Sir Gawaine as brim as any boar, with a great spear in his hand. And when Sir Bors saw him he thought to revenge his brother Sir Lionel of the despite that Sir Gawaine did him the other day. And so they, that knew either other, feutred their spears, and with all their mights of their horses and themselves, they met together so felonously that either bare other through, and so they fell both to the earth; and then the battles joined, and there was much slaughter on both parties.

So when Sir Gawaine was hurt, they on King Arthur's party were not so orgulous as they were toforehand to do battle. Of this war was noised through all Christendom, and at the last it was noised afore the Pope; and he considering the great goodness of King Arthur, and of Sir Launcelot, that was called the most noblest knights of the world, wherefore the Pope called unto him a noble clerk that at that time was there present — the French book saith, it was the Bishop of Rochester — and the Pope gave him bulls under lead unto King Arthur of England, charging him upon pain of interdicting of all England, that he take his queen Dame Guenever unto him again, and accord with Sir Launcelot.

HOW THE POPE SENT DOWN HIS BULLS TO MAKE PEACE, AND HOW SIR LAUNCELOT BROUGHT THE QUEEN TO KING ARTHUR. So when this Bishop was come to Carlisle he shewed the king these bulls. And when the king understood these bulls he nist what to do: full fain he would have been accorded with Sir Launcelot, but Sir Gawaine would not suffer him; but as for to have the queen, thereto he agreed. And then the Bishop had of the king his great seal, and his assurance as he was a true anointed king that Sir Launcelot should come safe, and go safe, and that the queen should not be spoken unto of the king, nor of none other, for no thing done afore time past; and of all these appointments the Bishop brought with him sure assurance and writing, to shew Sir Launcelot.

So when the Bishop was come to Joyous Gard, there he shewed Sir Launcelot how the Pope had written to Arthur and unto him, and there he told him the perils if he withheld the queen from the king. It was never in my thought, said Launcelot, to withhold the queen from my lord Arthur; but, insomuch she should have been dead for my sake, meseemeth it was my part to save her life, and put her from that danger, till better recover might come. And now I thank God, said Sir Launcelot, that the Pope hath made her peace; for God knoweth, said Sir Launcelot, I will be a thousandfold more gladder to bring her again, than ever I was of her taking away; with this, I may be sure to come safe and go safe, and that the queen shall have her liberty as she had before; and never for no thing that hath been surmised afore this time, she never from this day stand in no peril.

So the Bishop departed and came to the king at Carlisle, and told him all how Sir Launcelot answered him; and then the tears brast out of the king's eyen. Then Sir Launcelot purveyed him an hundred knights, and all were clothed in green velvet, and their horses trapped to their heels; and every knight held a branch of olive in his hand, in tokening of peace. And the queen had four-and-twenty gentlewomen following her in the same wise; and Sir Launcelot had twelve coursers following him, and on every courser sat a young gentleman, and all they were arrayed in green velvet, with sarps of gold about their quarters, and the horse trapped in the same wise down to the heels, with many ouches, y-set with stones and pearls in gold, to the number of a thousand. And she and Sir Launcelot were clothed in white cloth of gold tissue; and right so as ye have heard, as the French book maketh mention, he rode with the queen from Joyous Gard to Carlisle. And so Sir Launcelot rode throughout Carlisle, and so in the castle, that all men might behold; and wit you well there was many a weeping eye. And then Sir Launcelot himself alighted and avoided his horse, and took the queen, and so led her where King Arthur was in his seat: and Sir Gawaine sat afore him, and many other great lords. So when Sir Launcelot saw the king and Sir Gawaine, then he led the queen by the arm, and then he kneeled down, and the queen both. Wit you well then was there many bold knights there with King Arthur that wept as tenderly as though they had seen all their kin afore them. So the king sat still, and said no word. And when Sir Launcelot saw his countenance, he arose and pulled up the queen with him, and thus he spake full knightly.

My most redoubted king, ye shall understand, by the Pope's commandment and yours, I have brought to you my lady the queen, as right requireth; and if there be any knight, of whatsomever degree that he be, except your person, that will say, or dare say, but that she is true and clean to you, I here myself, Sir Launcelot du Lake, will make it good upon his body, that she is a true lady unto you; but liars ye have listened, and that hath caused debate betwixt you and me. For time hath been, my lord Arthur, that ye have been greatly pleased with me when I did battle for my lady, your queen; and full well ye know, my most noble king, that she hath been put to great wrong ere this time; and sithen it pleased you at many times that I should fight for her, meseemeth, my good lord, I had more cause to rescue her from the fire, insomuch she should have been brent for my sake. For they that told you those tales were liars, and so it fell upon them; for by likelihood had not the might of God been with me, I might never have endured fourteen knights, and they armed and afore purposed, and I unarmed and not purposed. And as Jesu be my help, said Sir Launcelot, I slew never Sir Gareth nor Sir Gaheris by my will; but alas that ever they were unarmed that unhappy day. But thus much I shall offer me, said Sir Launcelot, if it may please the king's good grace, and you, my lord Sir Gawaine, I shall first begin at Sandwich, and there I shall go in my shirt, barefoot; and at every ten miles' end I will found and gar make an house of religion, of what order that ye will assign me, with an whole convent, to sing and read, day and night, in especial for Sir Gareth's sake and Sir Gaheris. And this shall I perform from Sandwich unto Carlisle; and every house shall have sufficient livelihood. And this shall I perform while I have any livelihood in Christendom; and there nis none of all these religious places, but they shall be performed, furnished and garnished in all things as an holy place ought to be, I promise you faithfully. And this, Sir Gawaine, methinketh were more fairer, holier, and more better to their souls, than ye, my most noble king, and you, Sir Gawaine, to war upon me, for thereby shall ye get none avail.

Then all knights and ladies that were there wept as they were mad, and the tears fell on King Arthur's cheeks. Sir Launcelot, said Sir Gawaine, I have right well heard thy speech, and thy great proffers, but wit thou well, let the king do as it pleaseth him, I will never forgive my brothers' death, and in especial the death of my brother, Sir Gareth. And if mine uncle, King Arthur, will accord with thee, he shall lose my service; for wit thou well thou art both false to the king and to me. Sir, said Launcelot, he beareth not the life that may make that good; and if ye, Sir Gawaine, will charge me with so high a thing, ye must pardon me, for then needs must I answer you. Nay, said Sir Gawaine, we are past that at this time, and that caused the Pope, for he hath charged mine uncle, the king, that he shall take his queen again, and to accord with thee, Sir Launcelot, as for this season, and therefore thou shalt go safe as thou camest. But in this land thou shalt not abide past fifteen days, such summons I give thee: so the king and we were consented and accorded ere thou camest. And else, said Sir Gawaine, wit thou well thou shouldst not have come here, but if it were maugre thy head. And if it were not for the Pope's commandment, said Sir Gawaine, I should do battle with mine own body against thy body, and prove it upon thee, that thou hast been both false unto mine uncle King Arthur, and to me both; and that shall I prove upon thy body, when thou art departed from hence, wheresomever I find thee.

HOW SIR LAUNCELOT DEPARTED FROM THE KING AND FROM JOYOUS GARD OVER SEAWARD, AND HOW KING ARTHUR AND SIR GAWAINE WITH A GREAT HOST MADE WAR ON SIR LAUNCELOT. Then Sir Launcelot sighed, and therewith the tears fell on his cheeks, and then he said thus: Alas, most noble Christian realm, whom I have loved above all other realms, and in thee I have gotten a great part of my worship, and now I shall depart in this wise. Make thou no more language, said Sir Gawaine, but deliver the queen from thee, and pike thee lightly out of this court. Well, said Sir Launcelot, an I had wist of this short coming, I would have advised me twice or that I had come hither; for an the queen had been so dear to me as ye noise her, I durst have kept her from a fellowship of the best knights under heaven.

And then Sir Launcelot said unto Guenever, in hearing of the king and them all: Madam, now I must depart from you and this noble fellowship for ever; and sithen it is so, I beseech you to pray for me, and say me well; and if ye be hard bestead by any false tongues, lightly, my lady, let send me word, and if any knight's hands may deliver you by battle, I shall deliver you. And therewithal Sir Launcelot kissed the queen; and then he said all openly: Now let see what he be in this place that dare say the queen is not true unto my lord Arthur, let see who will speak an he dare speak. And therewith he brought the queen to the king, and then Sir Launcelot took his leave and departed; and there was neither king, duke, nor earl, baron nor knight, lady nor gentlewoman, but all they wept as people out of their mind, except Sir Gawaine. And when the noble Sir Launcelot took his horse to ride out of Carlisle, there was sobbing and weeping for pure dole of his departing; and so he took his way unto Joyous Gard. And then ever after he called it the Dolorous Gard. And thus departed Sir Launcelot from the court for ever.

And so when he came to Joyous Gard he called his fellowship unto him, and asked them what they would do. Then they answered all wholly together with one voice, they would as he would do. My fair fellows, said Sir Launcelot, I must depart out of this most noble realm, and now I shall depart it grieveth me sore, for I shall depart with no worship; for a banished man departed never out of no realm with worship, and that is my heaviness, for ever I fear after my days that men shall chronicle upon me that I was banished out of this land; and else, my fair lords, be ye sure, an I had not dread shame, my lady, Queen Guenever, and I should never have departed.

Then spake many noble knights, as Sir Palomides, Sir Safere his brother, and Sir Bellangere le Beuse, and Sir Urre, with Sir Lavaine, with many others: Sir, an ye be so disposed to abide in this land we will never fail you; and if ye list not to abide in this land there nis none of the good knights that here be will fail you.

Truly, said Sir Launcelot, I thank you all of your good saying. So they were accorded to go with Sir Launcelot to his lands; and to make short tale, they trussed, and paid all that would ask them; and wholly an hundred knights departed with Sir Launcelot at once, and made their avows they would never leave him for weal nor for woe.

And so they shipped at Cardiff, and sailed unto Benwick: some men call it Bayonne, and some men call it Beaume, where the wine of Beaume is. And then Sir Launcelot stuffed and furnished and garnished all his noble towns and castles.

Then King Arthur and Sir Gawaine made a great host ready, to the number of threescore thousand; and all thing was made ready for their shipping to pass over the sea, and so they shipped at Cardiff. And there King Arthur made Sir Mordred chief ruler of all England, and also he put Queen Guenever under his governance; because Sir Mordred was King Arthur's son, he gave him the rule of his land and of his wife; and so the king passed the sea and landed upon Sir Launcelot's lands, and there he brent and wasted, through the vengeance of Sir Gawaine, all that they might overrun.

And upon the morn early, in the dawning of the day, as Sir Launcelot's knights looked out, they saw the city of Benwick besieged round about; and fast they began to set up ladders, and then they defied them out of the town, and beat them from the walls wightly. Then came forth Sir Gawaine well armed upon a stiff steed, and he came before the chief gate, with his spear in his hand, crying: Sir Launcelot, where art thou? is there none of you proud knights dare break a spear with me? Then Sir Bors made him ready, and came forth out of the town, and there Sir Gawaine encountered with Sir Bors. And at that time he smote Sir Bors down from his horse, and almost he had slain him; and so Sir Bors was rescued and borne into the town. Then came forth Sir Lionel, brother to Sir Bors, and thought to revenge him; and either feutred their spears, and ran together; and there they met spitefully, but Sir Gawaine had such grace that he smote Sir Lionel down, and wounded him there passing sore; and then Sir Lionel was rescued and borne into the town. And thus Sir Gawaine came every day, and he failed not but that he smote down one knight or other.

So thus they endured half a year, and much slaughter was of people on both parties. Then it befell upon a day, Sir Gawaine came afore the gates armed at all pieces on a noble horse, with a great spear in his hand; and then he cried with a loud voice: Where art thou now, thou false traitor, Sir Launcelot? Why hidest thou thyself within holes and walls like a coward? Look out now, thou false traitor knight, and here I shall revenge upon thy body the death of my three brethren.

Then Sir Launcelot bade saddle his strongest horse, and bade let fetch his arms, and bring all unto the gate of the tower; and then Sir Launcelot spake on high unto King Arthur, and said: My lord Arthur, and noble king that made me knight, wit you well I am right heavy for your sake, that ye thus sue upon me; and always I forbear you, for an I would have been vengeable, I might have met you in midst of the field, and there to have made your boldest knights full tame. And now I have forborne half a year, and suffered you and Sir Gawaine to do what ye would do; and now may I endure it no longer, for now must I needs defend myself, insomuch Sir Gawaine hath appealed me of treason; the which is greatly against my will that ever I should fight against any of your blood, but now I may not forsake it; I am driven thereto as a beast to bay.

Then Sir Gawaine and Sir Launcelot departed a great way asunder, and then they came together with all their horses' might as they might run, and either smote other in midst of their shields; but the knights were so strong, and their spears so big, that their horses might not endure their buffets, and so their horses fell to the earth; and then they avoided their horses, and dressed their shields afore them. Then they stood together and gave many sad strokes on divers places of their bodies, that the blood brast out on many sides and places. Then had Sir Gawaine such a grace and gift that an holy man had given to him, that every day in the year, from underne till high noon, his might increased those three hours as much as thrice his strength, and that caused Sir Gawaine to win great honour. And for his sake King Arthur made an ordinance, that all manner of battles for any quarrels that should be done afore King Arthur should begin at underne; and all was done for Sir Gawaine's love, that by likelihood, if Sir Gawaine were on the one part, he should have the better in battle while his strength endureth three hours; but there were but few knights that time living that knew this advantage that Sir Gawaine had, but King Arthur all only.

Thus Sir Launcelot fought with Sir Gawaine, and when Sir Launcelot felt his might evermore increase, Sir Launcelot wondered and dread him sore to be shamed. For as the French book saith, Sir Launcelot weened, when he felt Sir Gawaine double his strength, that he had been a fiend and none earthly man; wherefore Sir Launcelot traced and traversed, and covered himself with his shield, and kept his might and his braid during three hours; and that while Sir Gawaine gave him many sad brunts, and many sad strokes, that all the knights that beheld Sir Launcelot marvelled how that he might endure him; but full little understood they that travail that Sir Launcelot had for to endure him. And then when it was past noon Sir Gawaine had no more but his own might. When Sir Launcelot felt him so come down, then he stretched him up and stood near Sir Gawaine, and said thus: My lord Sir Gawaine, now I feel ye have done; now my lord Sir Gawaine, I must do my part, for many great and grievous strokes I have endured you this day with great pain.

Then Sir Launcelot doubled his strokes and gave Sir Gawaine such a buffet on the helmet that he fell down on his side, and Sir Launcelot withdrew him from him. Why withdrawest thou thee? said Sir Gawaine; now turn again, false traitor knight, and slay me, for an thou leave me thus, when I am whole I shall do battle with thee again. I shall endure you, Sir, by God's grace, but wit thou well, Sir Gawaine, I will never smite a felled knight.

And then he turned him and went his way toward the city. And Sir Gawaine evermore calling him traitor knight, and said: Wit thou well Sir Launcelot, when I am whole I shall do battle with thee again, for I shall never leave thee till that one of us be slain. Thus as this siege endured, and as Sir Gawaine lay sick near a month, and when he was well recovered and ready within three days to do battle again with Sir Launcelot, right so came tidings unto Arthur from England that made King Arthur and all his host to remove.

HOW SIR MORDRED TOOK ON HIM TO BE KING OF ENGLAND, AND HOW KING ARTHUR RETURNED TO DOVER, AND OF THE BATTLE THERE, AND HOW SIR GAWAINE WAS SLAIN. As Sir Mordred was ruler of all England, he

SIR·MORDRED·WENT·AND·LAID·A·MIGHTY·SIEGE·ABOUT·THE·TOWER·OF·LONDON·AND·SHOT·GREAT·GUNS·

did do make letters as though that they came from beyond the sea, and the letters specified that King Arthur was slain in battle with Sir Launcelot. Wherefore Sir Mordred made a parliament, and called the lords together, and there he made them to choose him king; and so was he crowned at Canterbury, and held a feast there fifteen days; and afterward he drew him unto Winchester, and there he took the Queen Guenever, and said plainly that he would wed her which was his uncle's wife and his father's wife. And so he made ready for the feast, and a day prefixed that they should be wedded; wherefore Queen Guenever was passing heavy. But she durst not discover her heart, but spake fair, and agreed to Sir Mordred's will. Then she desired of Sir Mordred for to go to London, to buy all manner of things that longed unto the wedding. And because of her fair speech Sir Mordred trusted her well enough, and gave her leave to go. And so when she came to London she took the Tower of London, and suddenly in all haste possible she stuffed it with all manner of victual, and well garnished it with men, and so kept it.

Then when Sir Mordred wist and understood how he was beguiled, he was passing wroth out of measure. And a short tale for to make, he went and laid a mighty siege about the Tower of London, and made many great assaults thereat, and threw many great engines unto them, and shot great guns. But all might not prevail Sir Mordred, for Queen Guenever, for fair speech nor for foul, would never trust to come in his hands again.

Then came the Bishop of Canterbury, the which was a noble clerk and an holy man, and thus he said to Sir Mordred: Sir, what will ye do? will ye first displease God and sithen shame yourself, and all knighthood? Sir, said the noble clerk, leave this opinion or else I shall curse you with book and bell and candle. Do thou thy worst, said Sir Mordred, wit thou well I shall defy thee. So the Bishop departed and did the cursing in the most orgulist wise that might be done. And then Sir Mordred sought the Bishop of Canterbury, for to have slain him. Then the Bishop fled, and took part of his goods with him, and went nigh unto Glastonbury; and there he was as priest hermit in a chapel, and lived in poverty and in holy prayers, for well he understood that mischievous war was at hand.

Then came word to Sir Mordred that King Arthur had araised the siege for Sir Launcelot, and he was coming homeward with a great host, to be avenged upon Sir Mordred; wherefore Sir Mordred made write writs to all the barony of this land, and much people drew to him. For then was the common voice among them that with Arthur was none other life but war and strife, and with Sir Mordred was great joy and bliss. Thus was Sir Arthur depraved, and evil said of. Lo ye all Englishmen, see ye not what a mischief here was! for he that was the most king and knight of the world, and most loved the fellowship of noble knights, and by him they were all upholden, now might not these Englishmen hold them content with him. Lo thus was the old custom and usage of this land; and also men say that we of this land have not yet lost nor forgotten that custom and usage. Alas, this is a great default of us Englishmen, for there may no thing please us no term. And so fared the people at that time. And so Sir Mordred drew with a great host to Dover, for there he heard say that Sir Arthur would arrive.

So upon Trinity Sunday at night, King Arthur dreamed that Sir Gawaine had warned him that if he fought on the morn he should be slain. Then the king commanded Sir Lucan the Butler, and his brother Sir Bedivere, with two bishops with them, and charged them in any wise, an they might, Take a treaty for a month day with Sir Mordred, and spare not, proffer him lands and goods as much as ye think best. So then they departed, and came to Sir Mordred, where he had a grim host of an hundred thousand men. And there they entreated Sir Mordred long time; and at the last Sir Mordred was agreed for to have Cornwall and Kent, by Arthur's days: after, all England, after the days of King Arthur.

Then were they condescended that King Arthur and Sir Mordred should meet betwixt both their hosts, and everych of them should bring fourteen persons; and they came with this word unto Arthur. Then said he: I am glad that this is done: and so he went into the field. And when Arthur should depart, he warned all his host that an they see any sword drawn: Look ye come on fiercely, and slay that traitor, Sir Mordred, for I in no wise trust him. In like wise Sir Mordred warned his host. And so they met as their appointment was, and so they were agreed and accorded thoroughly; and wine was fetched, and they drank. Right soon came an adder out of a little heath bush, and it stung a knight on the foot. And when the knight felt him stung, he looked down and saw the adder, and then he drew his sword to slay the adder, and thought of none other harm. And when the host on both parties saw that sword drawn, then they blew beams, trumpets, and horns, and shouted grimly. And so both hosts dressed them together. And thus they fought all the long day, and never stinted till the noble knights were laid to the cold earth; and ever they fought still till it was near night, and by that time was there an hundred thousand laid dead upon the down. Then was Arthur wood wroth out of measure, when he saw his people so slain from him.

Then the king looked about him, and then was he ware, of all his host and of all his good knights, were left no more alive but two knights; that was Sir Lucan the Butler, and his brother Sir Bedivere, and they were full sore wounded. Jesu mercy, said the king, where are all my noble knights become? Then was King Arthur ware where Sir Mordred leaned upon his sword among a great heap of dead men. Now give me my spear, said Arthur unto Sir Lucan, for yonder I have espied the traitor that all this woe hath wrought. Sir, let him be, said Sir Lucan, for he is unhappy; and if ye pass this unhappy day, ye shall be right well revenged upon him. Good lord, remember ye of your night's dream, and what the spirit of Sir Gawaine told you this night; yet God of his great goodness hath preserved you hitherto. Therefore, for God's sake, my lord, leave off by this, for blessed be God ye have won the field, for here we be three alive, and with Sir Mordred is none alive; and if ye leave off now this wicked day of destiny is past. Tide me death, betide me life, saith the king, now I see him yonder alone he shall never escape mine hands, for at a better avail shall I never have him. God speed you well, said Sir Bedivere.

Then the king gat his spear in both his hands, and ran toward Sir Mordred, crying: Traitor, now is thy death-day come. And when Sir Mordred heard Sir Arthur, he ran until him with his sword drawn in his hand. And there

King Arthur smote Sir Mordred under the shield, with a foin of his spear, throughout the body, more than a fathom. And when Sir Mordred felt that he had his death wound he thrust himself with the might that he had up to the bur of King Arthur's spear. And right so he smote his father Arthur, with his sword holden in both his hands, on the side of the head, that the sword pierced the helmet and the brain-pan, and therewithal Sir Mordred fell stark dead to the earth; and the noble Arthur fell in a swoon to the earth, and there he swooned ofttimes. And Sir Lucan the Butler and Sir Bedivere ofttimes heaved him up. And so weakly they led him betwixt them both, to a little chapel not far from the sea-side. And when the king was there he thought him well eased.

Then Sir Lucan saw by the moonlight, how that pillers and robbers were come into the field, and who that were not dead all out, there they slew them for their harness and their riches. When Sir Lucan understood this work, he came to the king as soon as he might, and told him all what he had heard and seen. Therefore by my rede, said Sir Lucan, it is best that we bring you to some town. I would it were so, said the king. But I may not stand, mine head works so. Ah Sir Launcelot, said King Arthur, this day have I sore missed thee: alas, that ever I was against thee, for now have I my death, whereof Sir Gawaine me warned in my dream.

HOW KING ARTHUR COMMANDED TO CAST HIS SWORD EXCALIBUR INTO THE WATER, AND HOW HE WAS DELIVERED TO LADIES IN A BARGE, AND AS TO THE DEATH OF KING ARTHUR, AND HOW QUEEN

GUENEVER MADE HER A NUN. Then Sir Lucan took up the king the one part, and Sir Bedivere the other part, and in the lifting Sir Lucan fell in a swoon, and therewith the noble knight's heart brast. Alas, said the king, this is to me a full heavy sight, to see this noble duke so die for my sake, for he would have holpen me, that had more need of help than I. Alas, he would not complain him, his heart was so set to help me: now Jesu have mercy upon his soul! Then Sir Bedivere wept for the death of his brother. Leave this mourning and weeping, said the king, for all this will not avail me; for wit thou well an I might live myself, the death of Sir Lucan would grieve me evermore; but my time hieth fast, said the king. Therefore, said Arthur unto Sir Bedivere, take thou Excalibur, my good sword, and go with it to yonder water side, and when thou comest there I charge thee throw my sword in that water, and come again and tell me what thou there seest.

So Sir Bedivere departed, and by the way he beheld that noble sword, that the pommel and the haft was all of precious stones; and then he said to himself: If I throw this rich sword in the water, thereof shall never come good, but harm and loss. And then Sir Bedivere hid Excalibur under a tree. And so, as soon as he might, he came again unto the king, and said he had been at the water, and had thrown the sword in the water. What saw thou there? said the king. Sir, he said, I saw nothing but waves and winds. That is untruly said of thee, said the king, therefore go thou lightly again, and do my commandment; as thou art to me lief and dear, spare not, but throw it in. Then Sir Bedivere returned again, and took the sword in his hand; and then him thought sin and shame to throw away that noble sword, and so eft he hid the sword, and returned again, and told to the king that he had been at the water, and done his commandment. What saw thou there? said the king. Sir, he said, I saw nothing but the waters wap and waves wan. Ah, traitor untrue, said King Arthur, now hast thou betrayed me twice. Who would have weened that thou, that hast been to me so lief and dear, and thou art named a noble knight, would betray me for the richness of the sword? But now go again lightly, for thy long tarrying putteth me in great jeopardy of my life, for I have taken cold. And but if thou do now as I bid thee, if ever I may see thee, I shall slay thee with mine own hands; for thou wouldst for my rich sword see me dead.

Then Sir Bedivere departed, and went to the sword, and lightly took it up, and went to the water side; and there he bound the girdle about the hilts, and then he threw the sword as far into the water as he might; and there came an arm and an hand above the water and met it, and caught it, and so shook it thrice and brandished, and then vanished away the hand with the sword in the water. So Sir Bedivere came again to the king, and told him what he saw. Alas, said the king, help me hence, for I dread me I have tarried over long. Then Sir Bedivere took the king upon his back, and so went with him to that water side. And when they were at the water side, even fast by the bank hoved a little barge with many fair ladies in it, and among them all was a queen, and all they had black hoods, and all they wept and shrieked when they saw King Arthur. Now put me into the barge, said the king. And so he did softly; and there received him three queens with great mourning; and so they set them down, and in one of their laps King Arthur laid his head. And then that queen said: Ah, dear brother, why have ye tarried so long from me? alas, this wound on your head hath caught over-much cold. And so then they rowed from the land, and Sir Bedivere beheld all those ladies go from him. Then Sir Bedivere cried: Ah my lord Arthur, what shall become of me, now ye go from me and leave me here alone among mine enemies? Comfort thyself, said the king, and do as well as thou mayst, for in me is no trust for to trust in; for I will into the vale of Avilion to heal me of my grievous wound: and if thou hear never more of me, pray for my soul. But ever the queens and ladies wept and shrieked, that it was pity to hear. And as soon as Sir Bedivere had lost the sight of the barge, he wept and wailed, and so took the forest; and so he went all that night, and in the morning he was ware betwixt two holts hoar, of a chapel and an hermitage.

Then was Sir Bedivere glad, and thither he went; and when he came into the chapel, he saw where lay an hermit grovelling on all four, there fast by a tomb was new graven. When the hermit saw Sir Bedivere he knew him well, for he was but little to-fore Bishop of Canterbury, that Sir Mordred banished. Sir, said Bedivere, what man is there interred that ye pray so fast for? Fair son, said the hermit, I wot not verily, but by deeming. But this night, at midnight, here came a number of ladies, and brought hither a dead corpse, and prayed me to bury him; and here they offered an hundred tapers, and they gave me an hundred besants. Alas, said Sir Bedivere, that was my lord King Arthur, that here lieth buried in this chapel. Then Sir Bedivere swooned; and when he awoke he prayed the hermit he might abide with him still there, to live with fasting and prayers. For from hence will I never go, said Sir Bedivere, by my will, but all the days of my life here to pray for my lord Arthur. So there bode Sir Bedivere with the hermit that was to-fore Bishop of Canterbury, and there Sir Bedivere put upon him poor clothes, and served the hermit full lowly in fasting and in prayers.

Thus of Arthur I find never more written in books that be authorised, nor more of the very certainty of his death heard I never read, but thus was he led away in a ship wherein were three queens; that one was King Arthur's sister, Queen Morgan le Fay; the other was the Queen of North-galis; the third was the Queen of the Waste Lands. Also there was Nimue, the chief lady of the lake, that had done much for King Arthur. More of the death of King Arthur could I never find, but that ladies brought him to his burials; and such one was buried there, that the hermit bare witness that sometime was Bishop of Canterbury, but yet the hermit knew not in certain that he was verily the body of King Arthur: for this tale Sir Bedivere, knight of the Table Round, made it to be written.

Yet some men say in many parts of England that King Arthur is not dead, but had by the will of our Lord Jesu into another place; and men say that he shall come again, and he shall win the holy cross. I will not say it shall be so, but rather I will say: here in this world he changed his life. But many men say that there is written upon his tomb this verse: **Hic iacet Arthurus, Rex quondam, Rexque futurus**. Thus leave I here Sir Bedivere with the hermit, that dwelled that time in a chapel beside Glastonbury, and there was his hermitage. And so they lived in their prayers, and fastings, and great abstinence. And when

Queen Guenever understood that King Arthur was slain, and all the noble knights, Sir Mordred and all the remnant, then the queen stole away, and five ladies with her, and so she went to Almesbury; and there she let make herself a nun, and ware white clothes and black, and great penance she took, as ever did sinful lady in this land, and never creature could make her merry; but lived in fasting, prayers, and alms-deeds, that all manner of people marvelled how virtuously she was changed.

HOW WHEN SIR LAUNCELOT HEARD OF THE DEATH OF KING ARTHUR, HE CAME TO ENGLAND, AND FOUND QUEEN GUENEVER AT ALMESBURY, AND HOW SIR LAUNCELOT TOOK THE HABIT ON HIM AS A HERMIT.

Now leave we Queen Guenever in Almesbury, a nun in white clothes and black, and there she was Abbess and ruler as reason would; and turn we from her, and speak we of Sir Launcelot du Lake, that when he heard in his country that Sir Mordred was crowned king in England, and made war against King Arthur, his own father, and would let him to land in his own land; also how that Sir Mordred had laid siege about the Tower of London, because the queen would not wed him; then was he wroth out of measure, and said to his kinsmen: Alas, that double traitor Sir Mordred, now me repenteth that ever he escaped my hands, for much shame hath he done unto my lord Arthur. Alas, said Sir Launcelot, that ever I should live to hear that most noble king that made me knight thus to be overset with his subject in his own realm.

Then they made them ready in all the haste that might be, with ships and galleys, for Sir Launcelot and his host to pass into England. And so he passed over the sea till he came to Dover, and there he landed with seven kings, and the number was hideous to behold. Then Sir Launcelot enquired of men of Dover where was King Arthur become. Then the people told him how that he was slain, and Sir Mordred and an hundred thousand died on a day; and how Sir Mordred gave King Arthur there the first battle at his landing, and there was good Sir Gawaine slain; and on the morn Sir Mordred fought with the king upon Barham Down, and there the king put Sir Mordred to the worse. Alas, said Sir Launcelot, this is the heaviest tidings that ever came to me. Now, fair sirs, said Sir Launcelot, shew me the tomb of Sir Gawaine. And then certain people of the town brought him into the castle of Dover, and shewed him the tomb. Then Sir Launcelot kneeled down and wept, and prayed heartily for his soul. And that night he made a dole, and all they that would come had as much flesh, fish, wine and ale, and every man and woman had twelve pence, come who would. Thus with his own hand dealt he this money, in a mourning gown; and ever he wept, and prayed them to pray for the soul of Sir Gawaine.

And on the morn all the priests and clerks that might be gotten in the country were there, and sang mass of Requiem; and there offered first Sir Launcelot, and he offered an hundred pound; and then the seven kings offered forty pound apiece; and also there was a thousand knights, and each of them offered a pound; and the offering dured from morn till night, and Sir Launcelot lay two nights on his tomb in prayers and weeping.

Then on the third day Sir Launcelot called the kings, dukes, earls, barons, and knights, and said thus: My fair lords, I thank you all of your coming into this country with me, but we came too late, and that shall repent me while I live, but against death may no man rebel. But sithen it is so, said Sir Launcelot, I will myself ride and seek my lady, Queen Guenever, for as I hear say she hath had great pain and much disease; and I heard say that she is fled into the west. Therefore ye all shall abide me here, and but if I come again within fifteen days, then take your ships and your fellowship, and depart into your country, for I will do as I say to you.

So he departed and rode westerly, and there he sought a seven or eight days; and at the last he came to a nunnery, and then was Queen Guenever ware of Sir Launcelot as he walked in the cloister. And when she saw him there she swooned thrice, that all the ladies and gentlewomen had work enough to hold the queen up. So when she might speak, she called ladies and gentlewomen to her, and said: Ye marvel, fair ladies, why I make this fare. Truly, she said, it is for the sight of yonder knight that yonder standeth; wherefore I pray you all call him to me.

When Sir Launcelot was brought to her, then she said to all the ladies: Through this man and me hath all this war been wrought, and the death of the most noblest knights of the world; for through our love that we have loved together is my most noble lord slain. Therefore, Sir Launcelot, wit thou well I am set in such a plight to get my soul-heal; and yet I trust through God's grace after my death to have a sight of the blessed face of Christ, and at domesday to sit on his right side, for as sinful as ever I was are saints in heaven. Therefore, Sir Launcelot, I require thee and beseech thee heartily, for all the love that ever was betwixt us, that thou never see me more in the visage; for as well as I have loved thee, mine heart will not serve me to see thee, for through thee and me is the flower of kings and knights destroyed; therefore, Sir Launcelot, go to thy realm, and there take thee a wife, and live with her with joy and bliss; and I pray thee heartily, pray for me to our Lord that I may amend my misliving. Now, sweet madam, said Sir Launcelot, would ye that I should now return again unto my country, and there to wed a lady? Nay, madam, wit you well that shall I never do, for I shall never be so false to you of that I have promised; but the same destiny that ye have taken you to, I will take me unto, for to please Jesu, and ever for you I cast me specially to pray. For sithen ye have taken you to perfection, I must needs take me to perfection, of right. For I take record of God, in you I have had mine earthly joy; and if I had found you now so disposed, I had cast me to have had you into mine own realm.

But sithen I find you thus disposed, I ensure you faithfully, I will ever take me to penance, and pray while my life lasteth, if I may find any hermit, either gray or white, that will receive me. Wherefore, madam, I pray you kiss me and never no more. Nay, said the queen, that shall I never do, but abstain you from such works. And they departed. But there was never so hard an hearted man but he would have wept to see the dolour that they made; for there was lamentation as they had been stung with spears; and many times they swooned, and the ladies bare the queen to her chamber.

And Sir Launcelot awoke, and went and took his horse,

and rode all that day and all night in a forest, weeping. And at the last he was ware of an hermitage and a chapel stood betwixt two cliffs; and then he heard a little bell ring to mass, and thither he rode and alighted, and tied his horse to the gate, and heard mass. And he that sang mass was the Bishop of Canterbury. Both the Bishop and Sir Bedivere knew Sir Launcelot, and they spake together after mass. But when Sir Bedivere had told his tale all whole, Sir Launcelot's heart almost brast for sorrow, and Sir Launcelot threw his arms abroad, and said: Alas, who may trust this world! And then he kneeled down on his knee, and prayed the Bishop to shrive him and assoil him. And then he besought the Bishop that he might be his brother. Then the Bishop said: I will gladly; and there he put an habit upon Sir Launcelot, and there he served God day and night with prayers and fastings.

Thus the great host abode at Dover. And then Sir Lionel took fifteen lords with him, and rode to London to seek Sir Launcelot; and there Sir Lionel was slain and many of his lords. Then Sir Bors de Ganis made the great host for to go home again; and Sir Bors, Sir Ector de Maris, Sir Blamore, Sir Bleoberis, with more other of Sir Launcelot's kin, took on them to ride all England overthwart and endlong, to seek Sir Launcelot. So Sir Bors by fortune rode so long till he came to the same chapel where Sir Launcelot was; and so Sir Bors heard a little bell knell, that rang to mass; and there he alighted and heard mass. And when mass was done, the Bishop, Sir Launcelot, and Sir Bedivere, came to Sir Bors. And when Sir Bors saw Sir Launcelot in that manner clothing, then he prayed the Bishop that he might be in the same suit. And so there was an habit put upon him, and there he lived in prayers and fasting. And within half a year, there was come Sir Galihud, Sir Galihodin, Sir Blamore, Sir Bleoberis, Sir Villiars, Sir Clarras, and Sir Gahalantine. So all these seven noble knights there abode still. And when they saw Sir Launcelot had taken him to such perfection, they had no lust to depart, but took such an habit as he had.

Thus they endured in great penance six year; and then Sir Launcelot took the habit of priesthood of the Bishop, and a twelvemonth he sang mass. And there was none of these other knights but they read in books, and holp for to sing mass, and rang bells, and did bodily all manner of service. And so their horses went where they would, for they took no regard of no worldly riches. For when they saw Sir Launcelot endure such penance, in prayers, and fastings, they took no force what pain they endured, for to see the noblest knight of the world take such abstinence that he waxed full lean.

And thus upon a night, there came a vision to Sir Launcelot, and charged him, in remission of his sins, to haste him unto Almesbury: And by then thou come there, thou shalt find Queen Guenever dead. And therefore take thy fellows with thee, and purvey them of an horse bier, and fetch thou the corpse of her, and bury her by her husband, the noble King Arthur. So this avision came to Sir Launcelot thrice in one night.

HOW SIR LAUNCELOT WENT WITH HIS EIGHT FELLOWS TO ALMESBURY, AND FOUND THERE QUEEN GUENEVER DEAD, WHOM THEY BROUGHT TO GLASTONBURY, AND HOW SIR LAUNCELOT SICKENED AND

DIED, AND WAS BORNE TO JOYOUS GARD FOR TO BE BURIED, AND HOW CONSTANTINE REIGNED NEXT AFTER ARTHUR, AND OF THE END OF THIS BOOK. Then Sir Launcelot rose up or day, and told the hermit. It were well done, said the hermit, that ye made you ready, and that you disobey not the avision. Then Sir Launcelot took his eight fellows with him, and on foot they yede from Glastonbury to Almesbury, the which is little more than thirty mile. And thither they came within two days, for they were weak and feeble to go. And when Sir Launcelot was come to Almesbury within the nunnery, Queen Guenever died but half an hour afore. And the ladies told Sir Launcelot that Queen Guenever told them all or she passed, that Sir Launcelot had been priest near a twelvemonth, And hither he cometh as fast as he may to fetch my corpse; and beside my lord, King Arthur, he shall bury me. Wherefore, the queen said in hearing of them all, I beseech Almighty God that I may never have power to see Sir Launcelot with my worldly eyen; and thus, said all the ladies, was ever her prayer these two days, till she was dead. Then Sir Launcelot saw her visage, but he wept not greatly, but sighed. And so he did all the observance of the service himself, both the dirige, and on the morn he sang mass. And there was ordained an horse bier, with an hundred torches ever brenning about the corpse of the queen, and ever Sir Launcelot with his eight fellows went about the horse bier, singing and reading many an holy orison, and frankincense upon the corpse incensed. Thus Sir Launcelot and his eight fellows went on foot from Almesbury unto Glastonbury.

And when they were come to the chapel and the hermitage, there she had a dirige, with great devotion. And on the morn the hermit that sometime was Bishop of Canterbury sang the mass of Requiem with great devotion. And Sir Launcelot was the first that offered, and then also his eight fellows. And then she was wrapped in cered cloth of Raines, from the top to the toe, in thirtyfold; and after she was put in a web of lead, and then in a coffin of marble. And when she was put in the earth Sir Launcelot swooned, and lay long still, while the hermit came and awaked him, and said: Ye be to blame, for ye displease God with such manner of sorrow-making. Truly, said Sir Launcelot, I trust I do not displease God, for He knoweth mine intent. For my sorrow was not, nor is not, for any rejoicing of sin, but my sorrow may never have end. For when I remember of her beauty, and of her noblesse, that was both with her king and with her, so when I saw his corpse and her corpse so lie together, truly mine heart would not serve to sustain my careful body. Also when I remember me how by my default, mine orgule and my pride, that they were both laid full low, that were peerless that ever was living of Christian people, wit you well, said Sir Launcelot, this remembered, of their kindness and mine unkindness, sank so to mine heart, that I might not sustain myself. So the French book maketh mention.

Then Sir Launcelot never after ate but little meat, ne drank, till he was dead. For then he sickened more and more, and dried, and dwined away. For evermore, day and night, he prayed, but sometime he slumbered a broken sleep; ever he was lying grovelling on the tomb of King Arthur and Queen Guenever. So within six weeks after, Sir Launcelot fell sick, and lay in his bed; and then he sent for the Bishop that there was hermit, and all his true fellows. Then Sir Launcelot said with dreary voice: Sir Bishop, I pray you give to me all my rights that longeth to a Christian man. It shall not need you, said the hermit and all his fellows, it is but heaviness of your blood, ye shall be well mended by the grace of God to-morn. My fair lords, said Sir Launcelot, wit you well my careful body will into the earth, I have warning more than now I will say; therefore give me my rights. So when he was houseled and anealed, and had all that a Christian man ought to have, he prayed the Bishop that his fellows might bear his body to Joyous Gard. Some men say it was Alnwick, and some men say it was Bamborough. Howbeit, said Sir Launcelot, me repenteth sore, but I made mine avow sometime, that in Joyous Gard I would be buried. And because of breaking of mine avow, I pray you all, lead me thither. Then there was weeping and wringing of hands among his fellows.

So at a season of the night they all went to their beds, for they all lay in one chamber. And so after midnight, against day, the Bishop that then was hermit, as he lay in his bed asleep, he fell upon a great laughter. And therewith all the fellowship awoke, and came to the Bishop, and asked him what he ailed. Ah Jesu mercy, said the Bishop, why did ye awake me? I was never in all my life so merry and so well at ease. Wherefore? said Sir Bors. Truly, said the Bishop, here was Sir Launcelot with me with mo angels than ever I saw men in one day. And I saw the angels heave up Sir Launcelot unto heaven, and the gates of heaven opened against him. It is but dretching of dreams, said Sir Bors, for I doubt not Sir Launcelot aileth nothing but good. It may well be, said the Bishop; go ye to his bed, and then shall ye prove the sooth. So when Sir Bors and his fellows came to his bed they found him stark dead, and he lay as he had smiled, and the sweetest savour about him that ever they felt.

Then was there weeping and wringing of hands, and the greatest dole they made that ever made men. And on the morn the Bishop did his mass of Requiem; and after, the Bishop and all the nine knights put Sir Launcelot in the same horse bier that Queen Genever was laid in to-fore that she was buried. And so the Bishop and they all together went with the body of Sir Launcelot daily, till they came to Joyous Gard; and ever they had an hundred torches brenning about him. And so within fifteen days they came to Joyous Gard. And there they laid his corpse in the body of the quire, and sang and read many psalters and prayers over him and about him. And ever his visage was laid open and naked, that all folks might behold him. For such was the custom in those days, that all men of worship should so lie with open visage till that they were buried. And right thus as they were at their service, there came Sir Ector de Maris, that had seven years sought all England, Scotland, and Wales, seeking his brother, Sir Launcelot.

And when Sir Ector heard such noise and light in the quire of Joyous Gard, he alighted and put his horse from him, and came into the quire, and there he saw men sing and weep. And all they knew Sir Ector, but he knew not them. Then went Sir Bors unto Sir Ector, and told him how there lay his brother, Sir Launcelot, dead; and then Sir Ector threw his shield, sword, and helm from him. And when he beheld Sir Launcelot's visage, he fell down in a swoon. And when he waked it were hard any tongue to tell the doleful complaints that he made for his brother. Ah Launcelot, he said, thou were head of all Christian knights, and now I dare say, said

Sir Ector, thou Sir Launcelot, there thou liest, that thou were never matched of earthly knight's hand. And thou were the courteoust knight that ever bare shield. And thou were the truest friend to thy lover that ever bestrad horse. And thou were the truest lover of a sinful man that ever loved woman. And thou were the kindest man that ever struck with sword. And thou were the goodliest person that ever came among press of knights. And thou was the meekest man and the gentlest that ever ate in hall among ladies. And thou were the sternest knight to thy mortal foe that ever put spear in the rest. Then there was weeping and dolour out of measure.

Thus they kept Sir Launcelot's corpse aloft fifteen days, and then they buried it with great devotion. And then at leisure they went all with the Bishop of Canterbury to his hermitage, and there they were together more than a month. Then Sir Constantine, that was Sir Cador's son of Cornwall, was chosen king of England. And he was a full noble knight, and worshipfully he ruled this realm. And then this King Constantine sent for the Bishop of Canterbury, for he heard say where he was. And so he was restored unto his Bishopric, and left that hermitage. And Sir Bedivere was there ever still hermit to his life's end, but Sir Bors, Sir Ector, Sir Blamore, and Sir Bleoberis, went into the Holy Land thereas Jesu Christ was quick and dead. For the book saith, so Sir Launcelot commanded them for to do, or ever he passed out of this world. And these four knights did many battles upon the miscreants or Turks. And there they died upon a Good Friday for God's sake.

Here is the end of the book of King Arthur, and of his noble knights of the Round Table, that when they were whole together there was ever an hundred and fifty. And here is the end of the death of Arthur. I pray you all, gentlemen and gentlewomen that readeth this book of Arthur and his knights, from the beginning to the ending, pray for me while I am alive, that God send me good deliverance, and when I am dead, I pray you all pray for my soul. For this book was ended the ninth year of the reign of King Edward the Fourth, by Sir Thomas Maleore, knight, as Jesu help him for his great might, as he is the servant of Jesu both day and night.

GLOSSARY

GLOSSARY

Abate, depress, calm.
Abought, paid for.
Accompt, account.
Accorded, agreed.
Ado, business.
Adoubted, afraid.
Again, against, in the presence of.
Againsay, retract.
Aligement, alleviation.
Allegeance, alleviation.
Allow, approve.
Almeries, chests.
Alther, *gen. pl.*, of all.
Amounted, mounted.
An, if.
An-angered, made the object of anger.
Anealed, anointed.
Apair, weaken.
Appeach, impeach.
Appealed, challenged, accused.
Araged, enraged, confused.
Araised, raised.
Arase, obliterate.
Areared, reared.
Array, plight, state of affairs.
Arson, saddle-bow.
Assoil, absolve.
Assotted, infatuated.
At, of, by.
At-after, after.
Aumbries, chests.
Avail (at), at an advantage.
Avision, vision.
Avoid, quit, get clear of.
Avow, vow.
Await, watch for.

Bachelors, probationers for knighthood.
Barbican, gate-tower.
Battle, division of an army.
Bawdy, dirty.
Beale, beautiful.
Beams, trumpets.
Be-closed, enclosed.
Become, *pp.*, befallen, gone to.
Bedashed, splashed.
Behests, promises.
Behight, promised.
Beholden (beholding) to, obliged to.
Behote, promised.
Beseen, appointed, arrayed.
Bestead, beset, placed.
Betake, entrust.
Betaught, entrusted, recommended.
Betid, happened.
Betook, committed, entrusted.
Blank, white.
Bobaunce, boasting, pride.
Borrows, pledges.
Bote, remedy.
Bound, ready.
Bourder, jester.
Braced, embraced.
Brachet, little hound.
Braid, quick movement.
Brake, communicated.
Brast, burst, break.
Breaths, breathing holes.
Brief, shorten.
Brim, fierce, furious.
Brised, broke.
Bur, hand-guard of a spear.
Burble, bubble.
Burbling, bubbling.
Burgenetts, buds, blossoms.
Bushment, ambush.
By and by, immediately.

Cankered, malignant.
Cantel, slice, strip.
Careful, sorrowful, full of troubles.
Cast (of bread), batch.
Cere, wax over, embalm.
Certes, certainly.

Chafe, heat.
Charged, burdened.
Chariot, cart.
Cheer, countenance, entertainment.
Chierte, dearness.
Cognisance, badge, mark of distinction.
Coif, head-piece.
Comfort, strengthen, help.
Complished, complete.
Condescended, agreed.
Conserve, preserve.
Cost, side.
Costed, kept up with.
Courage, disposition.
Courage, *v.*, encourage.
Courtelage, courtyard.
Covin, deceit.
Croup, crupper.

Daffish, foolish.
Danger (in), in the power of.
Dawed, *v. tr.*, revived; *intr.*, dawned.
Deadly, mortal, human.
Deal, part, whit.
Debate, quarrel, strife.
Deceivable, deceitful.
Defend, forbid.
Defoiled, trodden down, deflowered.
Degree (win or yield the), rank, superiority.
Deliverly, adroitly.
Departed, divided, parted.
Departition, departure, sundering.
Descrive, describe.
Did off, doffed.
Dight, prepared.
Disadventure, misfortune.
Discover, reveal.
Diseased, unwell.
Disherited, disinherited.
Disparpled, scattered.
Dissever, distinguish.
Distained, sullied, dishonoured.
Disworship, shame.
Do, cause.
Dole, gift of alms.
Dole, sorrow.
Dolour, grief.
Don, gift.
Doted, foolish.
Draughts, recesses.
Drenched, drowned.
Dress, make ready.
Dressed up, raised.
Dretching, being troubled in sleep.
Driving, riding fast.
Dure, endure, last.
Duresse, bondage, hardship.
Dwine, dwindle.

Eased, entertained.
Eft, after, again.
Eftures, passages.
Embushed, concealed in the woods.
Em, uncle.
Empoison, poison.
Enchafe, heat.
Enchieve, achieve.
Endlong, alongside of, along.
Enforce, constrain.
Engine, device.
Enow, enough.
Ensured, assured.
Entermete, meddle.
Errant, wandering.
Estates, ranks.
Evenlong, along.
Everych, each, every one.

Fain, gladly.
Fare, *sb.*, ado, commotion
Faren, *pp.*, treated.
Faute, *v.*, lack.
Fealty, oath of fidelity.
Fear, frighten.
Feute, trace, track.
Feuter, set in rest, couch.
Fiaunce, affiance, promise.
Flang, flung, rushed.
Flatling, prostrate.
Fleet, float.
Flemed, put to flight.
Foiled, defeated, shamed.
Foin, thrust.
Foot-hot, hastily.
For-bled, spent with bleeding.
Force (no), no concern.
Fordo, destroy.
Forecast, preconcerted plot.
For-fared, worsted.
Forfend, forbid.
Forfoughten, weary with fightng.
Forhewn, hewn to pieces.
Forjousted, tired with jousting, worsted.
Forthdays, far advanced in the day.
Forthink, repent.
Fortuned, happened.
Forward, vanguard.
Forwhy, because.

Free, noble.
Freshed, refreshed.

Gar, cause.
Germane, closely allied.
Gest, deed, story.
Glaive, sword.
Glasting, barking.
Glatisant, barking, yelping.
Gree, degree, superiority.
Greed, *pp.*, pleased, content.
Grimly, ugly.
Grovelling, lying face downwards.

Hair, a hair-shirt.
Hale and how, a sailor's cry, heave-ho.
Halp, stumbled.
Halse, embrace.
Harbingers, messengers sent to prepare lodgings.
Harness, armour.
Haut, high, noble.
Hauteyn, haughty.
Heavy, sad.
Hete, command.
Hied, hurried.
High (on), aloud.
Hight, called.
Hilled, covered, concealed.
Holp, helped.
Holts, woods.
Hough-bone, back part of knee-joint.
Houselled, given the Eucharist.
Hove, hover, wait about.
Hurled, dashed, staggered.

Intermeddled, mixed.

Japer, joker.
Japes, jests.
Jesseraunt, a short cuirass.
Journey, day of battle.

Keep, *v.*, care, reck.
Kemps, champions.
Kind, nature.
Kindly, natural.
Knights parters, marshals.
Knowledging, acknowledgment, confession.

Lain, conceal.
Langering, sauntering.
Large, generous.
Largess, liberality.
Laund, waste, plain.
Lazar-cot, leper-house.
Lead, *sb.*, leaden seal.
Learn, teach.
Lears, cheeks.
Leaved, leafy.
Leech, physician.
Let, caused to.
Let, hinder.
Lief, dear.
Lieve, believe.
List, desire, pleasure.
Lith, joint.
Livelihood, income, estate.
Long unto, belong to, fit.
Long on (upon), because of.
Loos, praise.
Loveday, day for settling disputes.
Loving, praising.
Lusk, lubber.
Lusts, inclination, pleasure.

Makeless, matchless.
Makers, authors, poets.
Mal engine, evil intent.
Mal-fortune, ill-luck, mishap.
Marches, borders.
Mass-penny, offering at mass for the dead.
Masteries, feats.
Matchecold, machicolated, with holes for defence.
Maugre, *sb.*, despite.
Measle, disease.
Meddle, engage in battle.
Mickle, much.
Minever, ermine.
Mischieved, hurt.
Mischievous, painful.
Miscreature, unbeliever.
Mo, more.
More and less, rich and poor.
Mote, may.
Motes, notes on a horn.
Mountenance, amount of, extent.
Moved, suggested.
Much, great.

Naked, unarmed.
Namely, especially.
Ne, nor.
Near-hand, near, nearly.
Nesh, soft, tender.
Nill, will not.
Nis, ne is, is not.
Nist, ne wist, knew not.
Noblesse, nobleness.
Nobley, nobility, splendour.

Noised, reported.
Nold, would not.
Not for then, nevertheless.

Obeissance, obedience.
Or, before.
Orgule, haughtiness.
Orgulist, haughtiest.
Orgulité, pride, arrogance.
Orgulous, proud.
Orison, prayer.
Other, or.
Ouches, jewels.
Ought, owned.
Outcept, except.
Outher, or.
Out-take, except.
Overthwart, *adj.*, cross.
Overthwart, *sb.*, mischance.
Overthwart and endlong, by the breadth and length.

Painture, painting.
Pair of beads, rosary.
Paitrelles, breastplate of a horse.
Parage, dignity.
Parclos, partition.
Pareil, like.
Passing, surpassingly.
Pavilion, tent.
Peaced, quieted,
Perdy, par Dieu.
Perish, destroy.
Peron, tombstone.
Pight, pitched.
Pike, steal away.
Pill, plunder.
Pillers, plunderers.
Pleasaunce, pleasure.
Plenour, complete.
Pointling, aiming.
Pont, bridge.
Posseded, possessed.
Press, throng, crowd.
Prime, 6.0 A.M.
Prise, capture.
Puissance, power.
Purvey, provide.
Purveyance, provision.

Quarrels, arrowheads.
Questing, barking.
Quick, alive.

Raced (rased), tore.
Raines, Rennes.
Ransacked, searched.
Rash, rush.
Rasing, rushing.
Rasure, cuttingness.
Raught, reached, fetched.
Rechate, bugle-note of recall.
Recover, rescue.
Rede, *sb.*, counsel, *v.* advise.
Rejoice, enjoy.
Religion, religious order.
Reneye, deny.
Report, refer.
Retrayed, drew back.
Rightwise, rightly.

Sacring, consecrating.
Sad, serious.
Sadly, heartily, earnestly.
Samite, silk stuff with gold or silver threads.
Sangreal, Holy Grail.
Sarps, girdles.
Saw, proverb.
Scripture, writing.
Search, probe wounds.
Semblant, semblance, appearance.
Sewe, follow.
Sewer, officer who served and tasted dishes.
Sheef, thrust.
Sheer-Thursday, Thursday in Holy Week.
Shend, harm.
Shenship, disgrace.
Shent, undone, disgraced, blamed.
Shrew, sturdy knave.
Shrewd, knavish.
Sib, akin to.
Sideling, sideways.
Siege, seat.
Siker, sure.
Sith, since.
Slade, valley.
Soil (to go to), hunting term for taking to water.
Sort, company.
Sperd, bolted.
Spere, ask, inquire.
Sperhawk, sparrowhawk.
Spiritualites, sacred places.
Stead, place.
Stert, started, rose quickly.
Steven, voice.
Stigh, path.
Stilly, silently.
Stint, *sb.*, fixed revenue.
Stint, *v.* stop.
Stonied, astonished, became confused.

Stour, battle.
Strait, narrow.
Strake, blow a horn.
Sue, pursue.
Surcingles, saddle girths.
Sweven, dream.

Tatches, qualities.
Term, period of time.
Tho, then.
Thrang, pushed.
Till, to.
To-brast, burst.
To-drive, be carried away.
To-fore, before.
To-hew, hewed.
Took, gave.
To-shivered, broken to pieces.
Traced, advanced and retreated.
Trasing, pressing forward.
Traverse, move sideways.
Trenchant, cutting, sharp.
Trest, hunting term.
Truage, tribute.
Trussed, packed.

Ubblie, sacred wafer, Host.
Umbecast, cast about.
Umbre, shade.
Unavised, thoughtlessly.
Underne, 9–12 A.M.
Ungoodly, rudely.
Unhappy, unlucky.
Unhilled, uncovered.
Unnethe, scarcely.
Unsiker, unstable.
Unwarly, at unawares.
Unwrast, untwisted, unbound.
Up-so-down, upside down.
Usurped, encroached.
Utterance, uttermost.

Venery, hunting.
Villain, man of low birth.
Visors, the perforated parts of helmets.
Void, empty.

Wagging, shaking.
Waits, watches.
Wake, watch.
Wallop, gallop.
Wan, ebb.
Wap, ripple.
Ware, aware.
Warison, reward.
Warn, forbid, refuse.
Weeds, garments.
Weltered, rolled about.
Where, whereas.
Wield, possess, have power over.
Wight, brave, strong.
Wite, *v.*, blame.
Withsay, oppose.
Witting, knowledge.
Wold or nold, would or would not.
Wonder, *adj.*, wondrous.
Wonder, *adv.*, wondrously.
Wonderly, wonderfully.
Wood, mad.
Woodness, madness.
Wood shaw, thicket of the wood.
Worship, honour.
Worship, *v.*, cause to be honoured.
Worth, befall (woe worth, woe befall).
Wot, know.
Wrack, destruction.
Writhe, twist.
Wrothe, twisted.

Yede, ran, went.
Yelden, yielded.
Yolden, yielded.
Y-wis, certainly.

THE END